The Concert Hall Killer

The
Concert
Hall
Killer

JONATHAN WHITELAW

Harper
North

HarperNorth
Windmill Green
24 Mount Street
Manchester M2 3NX

A division of
HarperCollins*Publishers*
1 London Bridge Street
London SE1 9GF

www.harpercollins.co.uk

HarperCollins*Publishers*
Macken House
39/40 Mayor Street Upper
Dublin 1
D01 C9W8

First published by HarperNorth in 2024

1 3 5 7 9 10 8 6 4 2

A catalogue record for this book
is available from the British Library

PB ISBN: 978-0-00-862641-9
TPB ISBN: 978-0-00-862642-6

Printed and bound in the UK using 100%
renewable electricity at CPI Group (UK) Ltd, Croydon

This book contains FSC™ certified paper and other controlled
sources to ensure responsible forest management.

For more information visit: www.harpercollins.co.uk/green

For the three of you. To days to come

Chapter 1

LOCUS ISTE

Janice ran as fast as she could, only looking back when she had time to catch a breath. She could feel her lungs burning, her legs turning to jelly. The lactic acid was coursing through her muscles, driving her on and tormenting her at the same time. She knew that if she slowed down, even just a little, he would be on her. And then it would be over.

Her feet slapped on the wet pavement. She splashed through the puddles as the rain came down in waves from the bruised and broken sky. The streetlights wobbled as the wind blew hard, a cold Cumbrian night that carried more than a chill for her. She was terrified, scared of slipping, scared of tripping over her own feet. If she did that, she would be down. She couldn't let that happen. She knew too much. She had to escape, had to be rid of him. If she didn't, other people would die. She couldn't let that happen either.

Penrith's streets were deserted. She was alone. The shops and businesses on either side of the street were dark and cold. It was the middle of the night, nobody with any sense was out at this time. They knew better. Janice knew better. Yet here she was – running for her life down an empty high street hoping and praying she'd see another dawn.

1

Her feet were aching, her legs now cramping. She had to keep going, just a little further. She'd reach the station soon enough, then she'd be safe. She could make the call and this would be over forever. Only Janice knew that wasn't the case. Everything she'd seen, everything she'd done, it would haunt her for the rest of her life.

It was a badge of dishonour. And it was seared onto her chest forever. So why was she running? Why did she still care? Why not slow down, why not stop? Why not *let* him catch her?

Her body seemed to respond to those thoughts. The pain had grown too much. She was slowing. The long strides became little trots and eventually she stopped. She bent over double, feeling the rain lashing against her sodden shirt, her breath smoking in front of her in great chugs and plumes, like a steam engine battling uphill. She laughed now, laughed at how ridiculous this had all been. She knew that she could never outrun him, there was no chance of that. Who had she been kidding all of this time? She had *wanted* to be caught.

Before she could consider it all, a big, coarse hand grabbed her from behind. It pulled her upright quick and sharp. She was forced up against the wall, face pressed against the cold, damp stone. She could feel his breath against the back of her neck. It stank of whisky, hot and heavy. He leaned in close to her, close enough she could feel his lips almost kissing her ear, and...

He let out a huge sneeze, so loud that the whole street shook a little.

'Cut!' Simon Nakamba came stomping forward from behind the cameras. The rest of the crew held its collective breath. They'd been here a thousand times before with the temperamental director. Most of them knew what to expect. And it wasn't pretty.

'What the hell was *that* all about?' Nakamba screamed.

'Sorry Simon, I just, I just had to sneeze, that's all,' said Derek, the lead actor.

He wiped his nose on the sleeve of his sodden jacket.

'It's all this bloody rain, it's given me a chill, darling. I know I look twenty-one in some of my headshots, but I'd like to see my forty-first birthday, if you don't mind. Why couldn't we film in the Bahamas or something?'

'The Bahamas?' Nakamba asked. 'Are you serious? You want us to film *The Locus,* about a Cumbrian murderer, in the *Bahamas*? Did I hear you right?'

'I'm just saying,' he said. 'It's not like Penrith in the dark and cold is an inviting place, is it? I mean look at poor Pip down there, she's facehugging a wall with her feet in a puddle.'

'Hey, keep me out of this, Derek!' said Pip. 'I'm not the one who ruined the shot. I was waiting patiently for you to murder me.'

The leading lady stood up as a runner came and wrapped her in a huge, insulated coat. A cigarette was in her mouth and lit before anyone could blink. The whole set was being stripped and readied for another take, the street awash with people now. Huge spotlights were being repositioned as crew and cameras moved back up the road for first positions. Derek was about to go too when Nakamba stopped him.

'You're on your last chance, your final warning, are you listening to me, Del Boy?' he asked, his voice low.

'Hey, back off Simon,' Derek said. 'Remember' whose name is at the top of this script.'

'You've actually read the script then?' the director fired back.

'I'm warning *you*,' said the actor. 'Lay off me.' He prodded Nakamba in the chest. 'I've heard all about this bad-boy attitude you've been trying to get away with,' he said. 'How you like to throw tantrums, like to smash the set up and go off sulking. Well that doesn't cut any mustard with me, pal, got that? I've been nominated for a Bafta.'

'Yeah, a Scottish Bafta,' Pip sniggered.

'The most exclusive kind, I'd say. Anyway, a Bafta is a Bafta,' Derek scolded her. 'And it's more than you've ever had.'

'Is that right?'

'Yeah, it is.'

'Both of you, just shut up!' Nakamba's voice really did make the street tremble. All movement on the late-night set came to an instant stop. Nobody dared move a muscle or look away.

'Last warning, both of you,' said the director. 'This production is three weeks behind and has gone over budget more times than I can count. I have the network asking me constantly where this block of filming is. I've got the local tourist board hustling me for more cash that we don't have. And I have a headache so bad and so constant that it would make a black hole think twice about swallowing me. I've got a reputation, yes I admit that. It's a reputation for making quality film and television drama, and it's something I've worked my whole adult life to achieve. So if you think I'm going to let some has-been entertainer waiting out the panto off-season like you, Derek, ruin that, you've got another thing coming.'

Pip sniggered again, taking a long draw from her cigarette.

'And as for you,' Nakamba snapped his head around to his leading lady. 'If you call all of the last ten minutes acting then I'd like to meet the moronic sod who said you could make it in this industry. Have you ever heard of choreography? No, I don't suppose they teach that for soap operas. Ham acting maybe, chewing the scenery definitely. But not acting. Sort it or you'll be opening with Prince Charming here at Brighton Palladium faster than you can say "tastefully shot calendar".'

The two actors stood still like the rest of the crew, their heads bowed. Nakamba gave them both long, hard stares before turning back towards the set. Everyone sprung into action, clearing a ten-metre radius away from the furious director. He liked it that way. It made him feel important and powerful. Why else would he be freezing and wet at two in the morning in Penrith? The money, maybe. The art, definitely not. Simon Nakamba was in it for the power.

He knew that got him places, got him what he wanted. And right now he felt as powerful as ever.

Chapter 2

THE STARS WILL SHINE TONIGHT

There was an excited energy about the Penrith bingo club tonight. Everyone was talking about the same thing. It was hard luck if you had any other news or gossip. No matter how juicy the rumour, how salacious the whisper or hearsay, there was no room for it. Not tonight. Tonight was all about *The Locus*.

The enigmatic and hugely successful TV show was in town for filming. It was a firm favourite with the bingo club, and it would have been hard to find someone who wasn't excited about the cast and crew descending on Penrith. Not that you could have missed them of course. A fleet of lorries and vans had setup in the middle of the town, blocking off great swathes of streets, alleyways and pavements.

Traffic was chaos in the mornings and afternoons and the local posties were going spare about their deliveries. Not that anyone else really minded. The chance to see Penrith on screen was too good an opportunity to be really mad at. A sense of civic pride had gripped the whole town. And the high water-mark of that pride was most definitely the bingo club.

Amita Khatri had to wonder, though, where all of this emotion had suddenly come from. In all the years she had been a staple member of the group, she couldn't ever recall seeing them get so jittery or giddy over something like this. And that included a murder and murderer in their midst. And the day they'd run out of biscuits.

What was normally a relatively staid and sensible group of pensioners, some in their nineties, was now buzzing around the church hall like a gang of excited schoolchildren. Amita's heart went out to poor Father Ford who had to herd them all into some sensible shape for the game. He was already ten minutes late starting, his face like a sweaty rhubarb, fussing by the door and furrowing his brow. Amita was about to get up and go help him when she felt a familiar hand clap her shoulder.

'What have you heard then?' asked Georgie Littlejohn.

'Heard about what?' she asked.

'You know, the filming, *The Locus*. Everyone is so caught up in it all. I've never seen them like this before. The club, the whole town even, is whipped into a froth.'

'Frothing at the mouth more like,' said Amita under her breath.

Georgie shot her an unconvinced look. The self-crowned Queen of the Penrith Bingo Club had hearing that would rival a Mexican bat. Not to mention her hawk-like attention to minutiae and detail. Amita bit her tongue. She shouldn't have been so glib.

'Well?' asked Georgie expectantly.

'Well what?' asked Amita back.

'What do you know about the filming?'

Georgie had spent the last half hour hoovering up all the gossip and rumour she could from the club members. She had dashed from one side of the hall to the other and back again, assimilating anything and everything she could about *The Locus*. Amita knew she would only now be bothering her if the rest had been drained of their intel.

'Nothing really,' she said, deliberately disappointing her friend.

'Oh,' said Georgie, wrinkling her nose. 'That's not what I heard.'

'No?' Amita didn't like the sound of that.

'No, it's not. I heard that you had taken a little wander down to where those big film cameras and lights were spotted on the high street and saw something... interesting.'

Amita felt her cheeks flushing. It had all been perfectly innocent. She had been out for a walk earlier that day, nothing wrong with that. In fact, she always liked to go for a walk on a Wednesday to stretch her legs as she knew she'd be cooped up all evening in the bingo hall.

Her natural path from the house had led her into town and, yes, she'd maybe taken a slight detour to see what all the fuss was about. She'd watched the other series of *The Locus* as keenly as everyone else. She was allowed to be there, wasn't she? But still, she didn't like to include herself in the feeding frenzy of excitement her fellow members had whipped up. After all, in recent years she'd been busy with real crime-solving rather than the fictional kind on TV.

'I don't know what you mean, Georgie,' she said, fussing with her bingo marker.

'I heard, from a very reliable source, that you took some pictures,' said Georgie. 'Some interesting pictures of, say, members of the cast.'

Amita felt a tingle run up her arms and down her spine. The excitement of being close to the set, of seeing the huge lighting rigs, the runners, the monitors and, yes, what she thought was a critical scene, came flooding back. It had been exhilarating. She'd never seen any proper celebs before, let alone on her own doorstep. And when she'd snapped a surreptitious picture or two, even she couldn't have anticipated catching a crucial moment.

'I couldn't possibly comment,' she said with a wry smile.

'Amita!' Georgie clapped her hands on her thighs. 'You *must* tell me what you saw. We're all desperate to know *something* of what they're filming here!'

Amita revelled in the attention for a moment. Some of the other regulars from her table were looking and listening now. Judy Moskowitz, the usually level-headed and straight-talking banker's wife, gave her a glare.

'You *know* something, don't you?' she said.

'She knows, she knows,' cackled Ethel down the end of the table.

'I wish you lot would leave her alone,' groaned Sandy. 'You're worse than the Spanish Inquisition with this silly telly programme.'

'It is *not* silly, Sandy,' snapped Georgie. 'We're enthusiasts, we're fans, and if one of us knows what's going on then we have a right to know. Isn't that right, Amita?'

Amita gave a gentle smile. She nodded over to Sandy who was huffing, his tobacco-stained moustache twitching over his top lip.

'It's alright, Sandy,' she said. 'They're only having a bit of fun.'

He made an inaudible grunt as she fished out her phone. That nervous energy seemed to spread out from Georgie, Judy, Ethel and the rest of the table, reaching the far corners of the church hall fast. Suddenly everyone was meandering over to see what the fuss was about.

'Eh... ladies and gentlemen?' Father Ford bleated, but his pleas fell on deaf ears.

Nobody was interested in bingo right now, nor the pastor's protestations. All they wanted to know was what Amita Khatri had for them.

The crowd huddled in close around Amita and Georgie. She looked about, dozens of eager faces all staring down at her, whispering and talking, speculating about what she might have for them.

'This is ridiculous,' said Sandy, being nudged in the back of the head by a stray elbow.

'The circus has come to town!' laughed Ethel, bobbing about in her wheelchair.

'Come on then, out with it,' said someone.

'What's she got?' asked another.

'Is it to do with the filming?'

'Your public awaits you, Amita,' said Georgie, always the master of ceremonies.

Amita suddenly felt quite nervous. She hadn't expected this kind of reaction from the bingo club. And she certainly wasn't used to holding court; she liked to think she was usually more subtle than this.

'I'm not sure it's *that* interesting,' she said, trying to temper expectations.

She unlocked her phone. Another excited intake of breath went around the geriatrics. She scrolled through her pictures until she found what she had taken at the set earlier today.

'Now, it's a little blurry, I was a little nervous,' she said, selecting one image and making it bigger for those with bad eyesight. 'But I think, I *think* I could make out Pip Potter.'

The crowd all leaned in as one huge collective. There was some jostling for a better view and Sandy let out another groan as his foot was stomped on.

'But if you look closely,' said Amita, her breath catching in her throat. 'I think you can make out that she is covered in... blood.'

Amita had never been much for public speaking or performances. When she was a little girl she'd hated being on stage at school for recitals and orchestra. But even she let herself enjoy the moment when the bingo club erupted in a huge cheer of disbelief, celebration and intrigue. One of the leading lights of *The Locus*, potentially dead and out of the series? There had been a moment's silence as Amita's audience registered what she was implying, then came the clapping, hollering and endless pats on her back. She wasn't quite sure she had done anything, she'd only been in the right place at the right time. But it seemed she had struck a chord with the gossip-hungry Penrith bingo club desperate not just to know what was going on with their favourite show – but to know it *first*.

'Ladies and gentlemen, please,' said Father Ford, trying to restore some semblance of order. 'We really should get started, Mr Jones the janitor won't be happy if we linger on past our allotted closing time. He has to tidy this place up for the young mothers' club coming in tomorrow morning.'

The crowd began to disperse. A few more congratulations were given to Amita as the pensioners all took up their seats. Sandy was still huffing, deliberately stretching his arms and rolling his shoulders as the others cleared off. Ethel was still laughing and Judy gave a knowing smile across the table.

'You were holding out on us, you old devil,' she said. 'Hadn't seen anything, my backside.'

Amita laughed. As everyone got ready for the evening's bingo activities, Georgie leaned in close and whispered.

'We have to get down there, tomorrow,' she said. 'Material like this, people will pay good money for these kinds of things.'

'I don't know about that, Georgie,' she said. 'I just happened to be there when the actors and extras were filming and took a quick photo. It's hardly trading in state secrets.'

'Spoilers, Amita, spoilers – that's what you've got there. My niece, Eugenie, you remember her, she was the equestrian champion for the whole of Cumbria.'

'Yes, I remember.' Amita did her best not to roll her eyes at the millionth mention of Georgie's super-talented family.

'She tells me that snippets like this are big business on the internet, you know, online. All of the newspapers and websites love these kinds of things. We should organise a little party to go down there tomorrow morning, see what else we can snap. There might be some serious money to be made.'

Amita didn't like the sound of that idea. In fact, she loathed it. It had been one thing to wander past solo and take a serendipitous snap, but it was quite another to set out on some kind of septuagenarian raiding party. She was about to voice her dislike when the first numbers were called by Father Ford. Georgie readjusted herself and started marking her card. She nodded at Amita and winked. That was that then, she thought – from unassuming OAP to paparazzi in one fell swoop.

Chapter 3

WE USED TO BE FRIENDS

'Good grief,' said Jason.

It had barely taken Amita thirty seconds to tell him of Georgie's plan. As always, he was parked a little down the road, waiting for his mother-in-law to finish bingo and get a lift home. Amita had climbed in, plugged in her seatbelt and proceeded to reveal all about the plan to go snooping around *The Locus* set in the morning.

'You know there are rules for that sort of thing,' he said, pulling the car away in a hurry. 'You can't just go about taking pictures of things. Yes, you were on a public road, and no, they probably don't mind one little old lady having a gander at the set, but a flock of you descending is going to be hard to ignore. And there are what they call "reasonable expectations of privacy" in workplaces and all of that to think about.'

'I know that, Jason, I'm all too aware of that fact,' she said. 'And less of the "little old lady"' lark, please. We are third-agers. It's Georgie, all of this celebrity and excitement has gone to her head. She should watch her blood pressure, it's not the best as it is. Too much stimulation and she'll drop dead."

'And wouldn't that be a shame.'

'Jason!' Amita shouted.

She batted him on the arm, which actually hurt. Amita's new Senior Boxercise class at the leisure centre was clearly paying off. He winced, steadying the wheel.

'I was only joking!' he protested.

'You should be ashamed,' she scolded him again. 'Imagine saying something like that. How would you feel if her son-in-law said that about me?'

Jason didn't answer.

'Nothing will come of it anyway,' she continued. 'I told her that before we left tonight. I said that all of the big name celebrities – Pip Potter, Derek Veland and all of those people, they're probably all away by now. Packed up and headed back to Manchester or London or wherever. They won't be hanging around set any longer than the bare minimum. But you know what she's like when she has an idea in that buffoon head of hers.'

'Especially if it involves gossip,' he said. 'What did she think of those snaps you took earlier? I bet she was fuming with jealousy.'

Amita cracked a smile. She remembered the attention, the glory. The whole bingo club at her command, hanging on her every word. It had been intoxicating. And all while Georgie played second fiddle beside her.

'I must admit, it did feel rather good,' she said.

'I *knew* it!' Jason laughed and slapped the wheel. 'I knew all along you took your rivalry with Georgie Littlejohn more seriously than you admitted.'

'Nonsense,' she said, coming back down to Earth with a bump.

'Oh, come off it, Amita. You've sat in that very seat for years telling me how the bingo club is just a jolly night out for local pensioners and *not* the intricate social experiment and vipers nest it *actually* is.'

'I have absolutely no idea what you're talking about, Jason,' she said, tilting her nose into the air. 'I merely said that I enjoyed the enthusiasm from my fellow bingo club patrons for my little picture of Pip Potter. That's not a crime, is it?'

'No, it's not,' he continued to smile. 'But becoming the Pied Piper of Penrith and leading a battalion of your chums down there isn't all that cool.'

Amita knew he was right. She let out a long sigh.

Jason seemed to pick up on her disappointment. He wasn't inclined to upset his mother-in-law at the best of times. Tonight, however, he was trying extra hard to stay in her good books. A very late dinner reservation for two was at stake. It was rare he and his wife managed a cup of tea, let alone a meal out, with no kids or Amita.

'Look, I was only pulling your leg, you know,' he said. 'It's obviously a good thing that you're so popular and your skills are appreciated. You know I've come to value your nose for a story over the last few years – it's only fair your bingo compatriots appreciate your talents too.'

'I don't really care about the glory,' said Amita. 'It's just Georgie. She's like a dog with a bone when she gets an idea. And there's nothing any of us can do to talk her out of it. I should have kept my big mouth shut tonight and not mentioned I'd been down to the set at all. It's easier to tell a little white lie in those kinds of situations. Instead, I let it go to my head. Now we're all traipsing down there at the crack of dawn to do goodness knows what.'

Jason felt an uncomfortable knot forming in his stomach. He knew all too well how much the bingo club meant to his mother-in-law. It had become something of a staple of his life too over the last few years – for good and bad reasons. He also knew how difficult it could be to put them off the scent when they got the whiff of scandal or intrigue, but also how welcoming and comforting it could be for Amita. It was a community of very different people, all drawn together over a common interest. And to be fair, they had done a pretty good job of spotting the kind of details other folk overlooked, of paying attention to people often ignored. They weren't a bad bunch and surely they couldn't cause that much trouble just showing up on the edge of a TV shoot. Maybe he shouldn't have been so harsh on her.

'What's the harm in having a wander down to the set anyway?' he said, trying to comfort her. 'It's not like you're going to see a great deal. You got the best of it the other day, I bet. You'll all traipse down there in the morning rain, get soaking wet, see a couple of parked-up lorries and totter back up the road for tea and biscuits.'

Amita raised her eyebrow at the use of 'totter' – after all, she was probably in better physical shape than her son-in-law, but nevertheless she nodded. Jason wasn't sure if he had done enough to put her at ease. She had a tendency to internalise these sorts of things, put up a brick wall around her worries that even he found difficult to break down. At least he had tried.

They pulled up outside the house. Amita let out another sigh as she gathered up her things, not forgetting her handbag, her most trusted companion. They got out and headed up the garden path.

'You don't *have* to go tomorrow, you know,' he said, fetching his door keys. 'You could just tell Georgie that you're feeling sick.'

'I can't do that!' Amita's face went slack. 'You can't tell "Dr" Littlejohn that you're ill. She's had every disease, condition and syndrome under the sun. And what's more, she considers herself to be a leading armchair-expert when it comes to remedies. She'd be round here with a set of diagnostic questions and half the contents of a pharmacy. Honestly Jason, I hope she donates her body to medical science when she passes on. How she's survived this long with all of her alleged ailments is nothing short of a miracle.'

'Now who's being morbid?' he said, opening the front door.

Radha was standing at the bottom of the stairs. She looked wonderful. Jason never quite knew how his wife could maintain such beauty while peeling a kid's plaster off her good frock. Whenever he was in charge, he felt like he looked like a scarecrow who'd been pecked at and pulled apart by the birds he was supposed to be frightening.

'You look wonderful. Hot date or something?' He winked at her as he came in.

'Stop it,' she said, lifting her bag. 'This is a school night. I can't remember the last time that happened.'

'I can't remember what I had for breakfast, Radha,' he said, swapping his anorak for something a little more formal.

'Are you still alright to look after the kids, Mum?' she asked.

Amita hesitated, lost in her own little world. When she realised she had to answer, she snapped back into reality.

'Of course, you two have a good time,' she said.

'It's all too fancy for my liking,' said Radha, fetching her own coat. 'I don't know why we can't just go grab a burger.'

'Because it's our tenth wedding anniversary,' said Jason.

'It *was* our tenth wedding anniversary, nine months ago.'

'Honestly, you try to do something nice once in a while, a candlelit dinner at a posh restaurant with a waiting list as long as your arm, and all you get is aggro,' he smiled. 'You should have raised a better child, Amita, I blame you.'

Again Amita didn't say anything. Radha nudged Jason in the ribs and nodded at her mother. He shook his head.

'I'll go out to the car then,' she said. 'Don't be long. They'll probably give the table away to younger, keener, more Instagram-able punters if we're any later.'

She headed out the door. Jason buttoned up his shirt and tried to skirt around what was bothering Amita.

'Maybe I can tell Georgie I had to stay up late babysitting and I can't go on her jaunt tomorrow. As if I have time to be skulking about film sets with her.'

'Your schedule is *that* busy, is it?' Jason said, attempting to flatten a clump of his unruly hair.

She pursed her lips.

'I'll have you know, Jason Brazel, that there's a very important W.I. coffee morning coming up and nobody, including Georgie, has lifted a finger to organise anything yet. Then there's the Scouts' autumn fundraiser at Askling Manor that needs to be properly prepared for.'

'Askling Manor? For a Scouts fundraiser?' he scoffed. 'That's a luxury hotel, Amita. A bit upmarket for Rice Krispie squares and "beat the goalie" is it not?'

'In your day, Jason, perhaps,' she said, taking off her trainers. 'But these days fundraising activities attract the great and the good from across the county.'

He shrugged. Clearly there was lots he didn't understand, not just about Amita's social schedule but the modern world in general. He preferred it that way.

'No, no, I'll just have to keep the peace and go with the loyal fanbase to the set tomorrow morning,' she said, resigned to her fate.

'I don't know what all the fuss is about anyway,' said Jason. 'That show is all a load of cobblers if you ask me.'

'Jason,' she said. 'How could you?'

'Come off it, Amita, you *know* it's codswallop. Everyone does,' he said. 'It's all so serious, so po-faced. Nobody ever cracks a smile, let alone a joke. And there are car chases every two minutes. I highly doubt any respectable police officer would *ever* behave the way that Pip Potter pal of yours would.'

'It's won a bucketload of awards, Jason,' she said.

'It's overblown hocum.'

'It's been hailed as one of the most realistic police programmes of all time!'

'It's up its own backside.'

'There are millions of people around the world who tune into it on a Sunday night when it's on.'

'Cobblers.'

She threw her hands up in the air. He let out a laugh.

'And that's another thing,' said Jason. 'God forbid you don't like it – you're rounded on by a fanbase that's like rabid dogs who've been left to starve for a week.'

'We're not rabid, Jason,' she said succinctly. 'We just have an appreciation for the way it builds a puzzle – and god knows, don't we all need to know that, whatever happens in the real world, in *The Locus*, the bad guys will get caught, victims get recognition and there's justice served? That's all.'

He let out an unconvinced groan. Even as a local reporter, he'd seen enough real crimes committed and didn't need to add more murder and mayhem to his life.

'You should come with us tomorrow,' she said. 'To see just how much we enjoy it. I think you'll be surprised. And you never know, you might get a story out of it. I understand spoilers and the like get good traction in the newspapers these days.'

'And who told you that?' he asked.

Amita pulled on her slippers and started up the stairs to check on her grandchildren. She didn't answer him but he knew.

'Of course,' he said, shaking his head. 'Georgie Littlejohn.'

Chapter 4

THE LONELY MAN

Jason usually hated fancy restaurants. If it wasn't the general pretention of places like this, it was the severe lack of actual food that tended to appear on the plate in front of him. He was yet to go to so-called 'fine dining' and 'haute cuisine' without longing for a kebab on the way home.

Tonight was proving to be no exception to the rule, despite all the hype about this place. The room was hot and stuffy, the armpits of his shirt were stuck to him and his stomach was grumbling. Anniversary or not, he was struggling to remind himself why this had been a good idea in the first place.

'Everyone else seems to be getting fed before us,' he said, tugging at his collar. 'We could have eaten and been home by now if we'd gone to *Naan'maste* or the *Eastside Kitchen*.'

'Jason, we're supposed to be out for a romantic date night for our anniversary,' said Radha. 'Not getting home as fast as we can with a takeaway before *Match of the Day*. Behave yourself. And this was *your* idea, remember?'

Jason looked about the restaurant. Everyone seemed painfully young and hip in here. As a man who had felt middle-aged since he was a teenager, he didn't need to be reminded of his own mortality. What was worse, the other diners all seemed to be enjoying themselves immeasurably more than him.

The Herdwick Hogget was the hottest ticket in town, and beyond. It had taken considerable begging on Jason's part to get a table considering the length of the waiting list. Not to mention the glowing review he had promised. Nine months on from the actual anniversary was relatively speedy for a place of this repute. He knew he should have been more grateful. He just felt so uncomfortable.

He felt Radha staring at him. A decade of marriage meant he had developed a sixth sense for *that* look. He knew it long before he could see it, an icy glare that made the top of his head go cold.

'I'm sorry,' he said. 'I shouldn't be moaning. We don't get out without the kids very often. I shouldn't be sitting here like Victor Meldrew complaining about every little thing. This place has put Cumbrian food on the map and we're here to find out why. '

'Well put, Brazel,' said Radha. 'Anyone would think you were a journalist.'

'Ha,' he laughed. 'Pull the other one. The way things are at the moment I couldn't write and get published if *I* paid *them*.'

'You'll be fine. Work will pick up.'

'So everybody keeps saying,' he sighed. 'And yet I don't feel any more reassured.'

Jason slumped his shoulders. Radha watched her husband for a moment. She'd seen him like this plenty of times before. And every time she knew that he would eventually come around. Being married to Jason Brazel was as much about man-management as it was about for better, for worse, for richer, for poorer, in sickness and in health. She placed her wine glass down and leaned a little closer to him.

'You have, by far and away, the worst memory of anyone I've ever met, Jason,' she said.

'What?' He looked up.

'How many times have we sat around a table and talked about your career and what you perceive to be the end of the world as we know it? A hundred maybe? No, a thousand. We've been together for what feels like centuries, Jason, and I'm yet to see one of those years go past where you *don't* have a crisis of faith over your ability.'

'Crisis of faith is one thing, Radha. Not being able to pay the bills and keep the heating on is something altogether more worrying!'

'Have we ever not paid a bill yet?' she asked. 'Have we ever been turfed out of our house by burly men called Sid and Lenny? Have your children ever gone without a thing? I've seen you survive the internet changing the face of news, the so-called death of the local paper and now this whole "fake news" malarkey. And you're still here, trying to write stories about what really matters for most people. Life and death, and, ok, maybe pot-holes and parking, too.'

Jason shook his head. He knew what she was doing and he loved her for it.

'Well...' he said sheepishly.

'Come on,' said Radha. 'Sure, the work has dried up a bit. But that won't stop you. You're a journalist, a good one at that. You've got a better nose for a story than anyone I've ever known. And, what's more, you can actually write – and that's because you care about the people you write about. I know it's been tough the last month, but it won't last forever. We've gone longer with you out of work, remember?'

'I try not to,' he said glumly.

'You've just got to pick yourself up, dust yourself off and keep plugging away. If for nothing else but that I can't put up with Moping Jason skulking around the house.'

She reached across the table and took his hand. He watched her then slid his fingers between hers.

'Thank you,' he said, voice cracking a little.

'What for?' she smiled back.

'You know what for,' he said. 'For not throwing me out on my backside with the rest of the rubbish. And going and getting somebody with a proper job instead of this old hack.'

'Ah, that,' Radha laughed. 'Put it this way, I've not had a better offer in a long time. So you're probably safe for now, Brazel.'

'Ouch.' He feigned a jab. 'Now what does *that* say about both of us?'

They held hands for a moment longer, sitting in silence looking at each other. Jason felt relieved just to be in that moment. The past while had been a little challenging, he readily admitted. Not since he had been made redundant by the local paper had work been regular. A series of big scoops had made up for the general drought but it was far from a steady income. He was snarky and irritated all of the time and he hated being that way.

Just knowing that Radha had his back was enough to lift his mood. Even here in this trendy restaurant with people having a much better time than him.

Right on cue, a waiter appeared at the table. He offered a weak smile as he placed their plates down in front of them. He vanished before Jason could make his well-prepared remark.

'Where's the rest of it?' he said, staring down at the fashionable portion sizes. 'I mean just look at that, the rabbit would send it back hungry.'

'What did I just tell you?' she said. 'We're here to have a lovely, romantic evening just the two of us. So tuck into your celery, try a spoonful of whatever that black goo is on top of it, give me a nice big smile and no more complaining. Okay?'

'Yes, m'lud,' he said, flapping his napkin.

He poked about the plate a little, deciding which small mound of dinner to tuck into first. He reckoned he'd be lucky if there were five mouthfuls to be had. Radha, however, seemed to be having a good time. So he decided the best course of action would be to draw those morsels out as long as possible.

Scooping up the nearest pile, the fork was halfway to his mouth when Radha stopped him.

'Look over there,' she said, nodding over behind his shoulder. 'Isn't that one of the folk from *The Locus*?'

The name of the show was enough to draw a groan from him.

'Radha, please,' he said. 'I had an absolute earful from your mother on the drive home tonight. That bloody programme has a lot to answer for. It's like the whole town has gone absolutely potty. And for what? A bunch of overpaid primadonnas pretending to play detective. Please, they should try the real thing once in a while, it might help them do their jobs better.'

'You would know,' she said. 'You and my mother love playing detective.'

'We don't play,' he said, scooping up his fork again, ready for another try.

'Seriously, though.' She was whispering now. 'I think that's one of the crew over there, close to the kitchens. What's his name again, the director? Simon Nakamba. He's a big shot. He's done loads of things. Look, over there.'

Jason rolled his eyes. He turned in his chair but Radha stopped him.

'No, don't look!' she said, stifling a shout.

'What? You just told me to look!'

'No, that's not what I meant. You can't just *look*.'

'What?'

'I mean you've got to be subtle,' said Radha. 'You can't just turn around and ogle the man. He's trying to have his dinner like the rest of us.'

'Then what am I supposed to do? Use that handy third eye I have on the back of my head?'

'Try to be a bit less obvious. You're the journalist, aren't you?'

Jason frowned. He picked up his as yet unused knife, made a show of dropping it onto the floor and then looked shocked.

'Oh dear,' he said. 'I appear to have dropped my knife. Better get down and pick it up before I lose it, hadn't I?'

Radha's eyes closed briefly to avoid having to watch her husband's pantomime. Jason smiled at his own brilliance. He stood up slowly, adjusted his cuffs and collar and turned around to pick up the fallen knife. As he did so, he scanned the room for a face that he would vaguely recognise from the media frenzy around the series.

It didn't take long for Jason to spot the celebrity director in their presence. Simon Nakamba was on his feet now, swigging straight from a ludicrously expensive bottle of wine. The whole room had suddenly fallen silent and everyone was watching him. He drained the bottle and slammed it down hard on the table beside him. Every patron except Jason flinched at the sound.

Nakamba let out a belch. He smiled, leered at the rest of his dinner party and swayed slightly, uneasy on his feet.

'Do *any* of you know what I've had to go through to get to where I am today?' he shouted, the words drunkenly spilling out of his mouth. 'Do you have *any* idea what it's been like for me to get to this stage? This platform? Do you? Of course you don't. You're all from lovely, rich households where mummy and daddy could pay for your little filmmaking hobby. Me? I had to work for it, for every moment of film, for every audition, for every rejected screenplay and slant and slight on who I was, who I *am*.'

He stumbled a little and corrected himself against a chair. His eyes were bloodshot and glassy. He stared down his embarrassed dinner guests one by one, thrusting an angry finger at each of them around the table. 'And you lot just sit there and pretend you're my friends,' he said vindictively. 'You smile and you nod and you blow smoke up my rear end, all until something new and better comes along. Well, I'm sick of it.'

'Simon, please, sit down,' said one of the others at his table.

She reached up and tried to take his hand. He pulled it away and wobbled backwards. Everyone in the room was staring at him and he sensed it. He snorted loudly, half-smiling, half-scowling at his audience.

'No, no, I've had enough of being told what to do,' he slurred. 'I've been in this industry twenty-three years. I've been at the top, then the bottom and now, because I'm helming this silly little detective show, I'm back at the summit. I don't need you or anybody else playing my nursemaid. Not anymore.'

He staggered away from the table, his knees buckling a little. He slumped forward and the whole restaurant held its collective breath. Before he could fall flat on his face, he managed to stop himself. Nakamba didn't seem to care. He looked about and spied a glass of wine on a nearby table. Snatching it up, he drained it in one gulp before anyone could stop him. He threw the glass down and stumbled on.

'Simon!' called someone from his table.

The silence was starting to recede. In its place were shocked gasps and whispers of disapproval. This was not what the fine diners of *The Herdwick Hogget* expected when they came to feast on the hand-picked menu. Although this kind of celebrity meltdown was something money couldn't buy.

Simon Nakamba stopped. He turned, slowly, with a theatrical glint in his glassy eyes, and raised his middle finger. He blew a loud raspberry back towards his table and started to laugh. Another collective gasp of outrage rippled through the restaurant. Weaving his way through the tables, he edged closer and closer to Jason. When he reached him, he straightened up, eyes struggling to focus.

'What are *you* looking at?' he asked.

Nakamba was so close Jason could feel the warmth of his breath on his face. He blinked, taking a step back and giving the director enough of a berth to pass by. Nakamba muttered something as he snaked past and lumbered out of the door. Jason, along with everyone else, watched him vanish into the night before starting up their conversations again. Although there was only one topic on their lips.

He turned back to face Radha. She looked shellshocked, her mouth hanging open. He cleared his throat and sat back down, replacing his knife on the table and clasping his hands.

'So,' he said, as Radha shook away her disbelief. 'Do you think that was him then?'

Chapter 5

BAD THINGS

'Does everyone have a buddy?'

Georgie's voice echoed about the car park and disturbed a few birds from their nests. If they weren't up before, they certainly were now. Amita stifled a yawn as she huddled close to Jason and the others. There was a damp coolness to the air that was making her bones hurt.

She was no stranger to an early start; in fact, she prided herself on being up before the rest of the family. However, a five-in-the-morning jaunt with Georgie Littlejohn was a much harder pill to swallow than getting up to enjoy the private peace of the pre-dawn. Especially when the self-anointed doyenne of the Penrith Bingo Club was on imperious form.

'We'll be leaving for the set shortly so make sure you've got everything. Bottles of water, your cameras, all of that,' said Georgie. 'Has everyone been to the bathroom?'

That one made Amita laugh. She normally asked the same of the grandchildren before a long bus journey. Rightly or wrongly, she had assumed a group of a dozen pensioners had the wit and foresight to know when and for how long they could hold it in. Now Georgie was brandishing a furled umbrella aloft like she was a strange mix between bossy tour guide and charging knight at a joust.

'Is she always so chirpy this early in the morning?' asked Jason.

'I'm glad to say I don't usually see Georgie at 5am so I wouldn't know,' she answered.

'How can one woman be so absolutely complete and thorough in how intolerable she is? It must be a record or something.'

'I'm sure it is,' she said, trying to keep from yawning again. 'But speaking of intolerable, what's all this about Simon Nakamba last night?'

Jason had started telling Amita about his run-in with the director, in the car that morning, but he'd become distracted when he almost ran over the gathered faithful of the bingo club, all tottering around close to the entrance of the car park when they arrived.

'He made a complete ass of himself, Amita,' he whispered. 'Everyone was looking at him. He was drunk as a skunk, and that's putting it mildly. He flipped a finger and shouted at everyone and–'

'Morning, morning, morning,' said Georgie, interrupting him.

Jason quickly shut his mouth. In the powder-keg world of Penrith pensioner politics, he knew he couldn't give anything away for free.

Amita was glad she had him well trained.

'Lovely to see you, Jason,' said Georgie. 'I had no idea you'd be joining our little expedition to the set.'

'Strictly professional, Georgie,' he said with a forced smile. 'That and I can't keep myself away from you lovely lot for more than five minutes, otherwise I'll wilt and die.'

'Oh you,' said Georgie, laughing and patting his arm. 'You could charm the birds from the trees, Jason Brazel.'

'Good grief,' said Amita under her breath.

'I assume you'll be each other's travel buddy then,' Georgie said. 'It's only a short jaunt up the high street to the set but I want everyone to stay together and be safe. Not that I need to tell you two why, of course. You've got a knack for finding trouble.'

Amita winced at that little comment. Was it a barb or just distasteful? She couldn't tell.

'I'm looking for a chum,' came a familiar voice from behind them.

Amita looked around and saw Sandy towering over her. Georgie clapped her hands.

'What luck,' she said, a broad smile stretching across her made-up, wrinkly face. 'Sandy, you can buddy up with Amita, in that case, and I'll take Jason.'

'What?' Jason almost choked.

'That's settled then, come along young Mr Brazel.'

Before he could react, she had slipped her arm into the crook of his elbow and led them off. Jason peered back over his shoulder at his mother-in-law and Sandy, eyes bulging as he silently pleaded for help. Amita could only give him a cheeky little wave as Georgie marched him to the front of the group.

'He's in trouble now,' chuckled Sandy.

'And he doesn't know the half of it.' She turned to him. 'I'm surprised to see you here though, Sandy. I didn't think this was your kind of thing.'

'It's not,' he sniffed, scratching his forehead beneath his flat cap. 'But old Ethel wanted to come along and I usually do the heavy lifting and push her about on things like this.'

'Where is she?' Amita looked about for the oldest member of the club.

'She's not feeling very well, it turns out,' he said sadly. 'The nurses were in with her late last night and she wasn't up for the early start.'

'Oh blimey,' she said. 'I hope she's alright.'

'She'll be fine,' Sandy said. 'She's tough as old boots, that one. I've always said that Ethel will bury the rest of us and I wasn't kidding.'

'Very true,' Amita agreed. 'That still doesn't explain why you're here though. You could have had a lie-in instead of skulking about with the rest of us at the film set. Didn't you say it was just a silly TV show? My son-in-law Jason has already said he's not in *The Locus* fan group.'

Sandy tilted his head a little to the side. He looked about the gathered group and came to a stop on Georgie showing Jason off like a new handbag to the others.

'Yeah, well, maybe I was being a bit harsh,' he said. 'When you get to our age, Amita, you shouldn't be so much of a stick-in-the-mud that you end up missing out. That's not what life is all about. When else will I get an up-close look at a TV shoot? I'm reminding myself to say yes to new things.'

'Very well put.' She smiled warmly at him. 'It's good to see you, as always, Sandy. And yes, I'd love you to chum me. Otherwise I'd be on my own, seeing as my partner-in-crime son-in-law over there has been poached by Ms Littlejohn, tour guide and battalion leader extraordinaire.'

They both laughed at that. Georgie and Jason had made it to the head of the group. She held up her umbrella again, the bright pink material a neon beacon in the chill gloom of the morning.

'Off we go then,' she shouted to the group. 'Come along, Jason.'

The pensioners all followed her dutifully. Despite the very early start, everyone seemed in good spirits. They were eager to visit the set and perhaps see *The Locus* production in full swing.

'So,' said Sandy. 'Your friend Irvine not with you this morning?'

Amita felt her eyebrows draw down automatically. The subject of her on-again, off-again companion always made her a little uncomfortable.

'No, not this morning,' she said, as diplomatically as possible. 'He's actually down in Wales this week visiting his daughter and grandchildren.'

'How nice,' said Sandy.

Amita looked up at the big man. She spotted a wry smirk tugging at his mouth beneath his moustache.

'What?' she asked.

'Pardon?' He raised his eyebrows, his cap lifting a little.

'You're smiling.'

'Am I?' he laughed. 'I didn't realize.'

'Sandy.' She drew out his name. 'Are you laughing at me?'

'Certainly not,' he said. 'I wouldn't dare do something like that with you, Amita.'

'Then what is it?'

'Nothing,' he continued to smile. 'Nothing at all.'

'We're just... friends. That's all.'

'Oh I'm sure you are,' he said.

'We are.'

'Of course.'

'Nothing else to it.'

'Naturally.'

'We're simply two old pensioners who enjoy each other's company once in a while,' she said. 'There's no crime in that, is there?'

'Not that I'm aware of, Amita, no,' he said.

'Good.'

'Good indeed.'

'Fine.'

'Fine,' he said.

They walked on two more paces before she stopped.

'And even if there *was* something in it, it's not to say I can't go anywhere without him,' she protested.

Sandy stopped a little ahead. He turned to face her, hands in the pockets of his huge overcoat, sharp eyes glistening beneath the rim of his cap.

'Absolutely,' he smiled at her.

'I mean, it's not like we're engaged or anything,' she went on. 'This is the twenty-first century and I'm a fully grown woman, a grandmother no less. I can make my own decisions and not feel guilty about them. Yes?'

Sandy shrugged. 'I couldn't agree more,' he said. 'I'm glad I asked.'

She started up again and they walked to join the rest of the group. Amita felt something strange tugging in her chest. She couldn't quite work out what it was. Only that she didn't like the feeling one bit. She shook her head and tried to think of something else. Sandy said nothing as he walked beside her. Having him close felt good, reassuring, she had to admit that to herself. He was an old friend and they'd been through a lot together. She could always rely on Sandy for anything. And she hoped he felt the same way about her. She didn't want her friendship with Irvine to change anything between them.

Much to her frustration, and a little relief, Georgie's umbrella shot up once more into the air ahead of them. The group came to a shuffling halt just shy of a crossroads in the centre of Penrith.

'Listen up everyone, can I have your attention?' said Georgie, her voice echoing off the silent buildings surrounding them. Jason was still stuck to her hip, wincing as she shouted at the others. 'We're about to head around to the main filming location. Now, my nephew's girlfriend's third cousin is an actor and says that we should all be very quiet, especially if it's what's called a hot set.'

'What's a hot set?' asked Sandy, leaning down to Amita.

'No idea,' she replied, straining to see Georgie through the huddled mass of shoulders and heads.

'So we should try to keep our chit-chat to a minimum,' she went on. 'If we act like the well-mannered, good house-guests I know we can be, I'm sure the staff won't mind us having a proper look around the place.'

Quiet murmurs of agreement went around the ramshackle tour group.

'I should warn you though.' Georgie was suddenly quite serious. 'We could quite literally see *anything* when we look around here, even at this hour. There will no doubt be *lots* of famous faces, in front of and behind the camera. For the sake of our reputation as a club and as a town, try to keep your excitement to manageable levels. We don't want these big television people thinking we're nothing but squawking yokels, do we? *Some* of you may have already been snapping away,' Georgie shot a look at Amita. 'But let's not all go in looking for selfies and signatures. We are the elder statesmen of Penrith and we should behave accordingly, remember.'

'She always knows how to give us a good time, doesn't she?' whispered Sandy.

Amita playfully slapped his arm and urged him to be quiet.

When she was happy that her pep talk and instructions had been taken on board by the group, Georgie tugged on Jason's jacket and led the group on towards the set.

'You know something, Amita,' said Sandy. 'I don't know why you carry on listening to all the others.'

'What do you mean?' she asked.

'Georgie and everyone else. You're a smart woman, clever and funny, sharper than the lot of us put together. You aren't afraid to look at things differently and you're not easily fobbed off. I won't say I don't worry about you sometimes, getting caught up in these investigations of yours, asking questions of dangerous people, but you're your own woman, Amita. I was only joshing you about Irvine back there, you know. A bit of a lark. You shouldn't have to worry about what you do or what people think, any of that game. You should just be who you are, that's all that matters... to me anyway.'

Amita felt a lump burning in her throat. She stopped and looked up at Sandy. The big man stared down at her. He pulled a hand free from his pocket and reached out for Amita's. She was about to thank him when a blood-curdling scream cut through the morning air.

Before she really knew what she was doing, she'd raced off down the street, leaving Sandy standing on his own. It was instinct now to run towards trouble rather than away. She hurtled around the corner, sequinned trainers clapping against the damp paving stones and sending up spray behind her. The gathered group of the Penrith Bingo Club was stopped a little way up the street. Beyond them, the unmistakable blue flashing lights of police cars gave everything an eerie hue. It was only then that Amita stopped and felt faintly ridiculous. She'd come to watch a crime drama being filmed and then got spooked when she heard a scream and some sirens? She hoped no one had seen her panicked response – clearly the events of the last couple of years had made her radar for trouble a little too sensitive. Still, no point missing out on the action now she was here.

Amita barged her way through the group to reach the front, Georgie Littlejohn stood shaking, a hand clasped to her mouth. Jason was beside her, face pale in the blue light. Maybe she had been right – Georgie might have got wrapped up in the drama, but Jason wasn't a fan – why would he look so spooked if it was just another scene?

'What's happening?' asked Amita. 'Jason? What's going on?'

Neither he nor Georgie answered her. They were standing gawping at the street ahead. Three police cars were blocking off the entrance to the set of *The Locus*. Officers were hurrying around all over the place, trying to clear the scene. They certainly looked like the real deal rather than actors. Amita peered through the chaos at two large spotlights that were pointing towards the entrance of one of the buildings beyond the line. She recognised the focus of their beams right away: the Alhambra, the local concert hall.

The lights were focused, beaming down at the doors. And there was something else, something breaking the pool of brilliant, bright light.

There, sat slumped against the door of the theatre, was a figure. Amita peered – hoping it was a repeat of yesterday and they'd caught another star filming a gruesome scene. But as she got a clear look, there was no mistaking what she saw. This was no actor. No stunt double. There, under the lights, lay Simon Nakamba – dead.

'Oh my god!' Georgie sobbed, grabbing Amita by both shoulders and spinning her away from the grisly sight. 'What's going to happen to the show now?'

Before Amita could chide Georgie for her ghoulish response, the police came to move the club away from the crime scene. The officers herded the pensioners back down the street, Amita and Jason shuffling backwards, both trying to make sense of the tableau on the concert hall steps. Amita grabbed his hand and turned, trying to get away from what she had seen, what they had all seen, as quickly as possible.

She spotted Sandy standing at the rear of the crowd, a sad look pulling his square jaw downwards. Amita knew immediately it was going to be one of those days. She could feel the questions burning in her mind already. She wondered if Jason could see the curiosity in her expression as she turned to him.

'Well,' said Jason, sucking in the morning air. 'At least you got me away from Georgie.'

Chapter 6

DANSE MACABRE

Amita sat staring at the tea in its polystyrene cup. She was pretty sure she shouldn't have been given a cup like that. It seemed soddly outdated. Strange, she thought, how the mind works during a time of extreme stress.

She took a deep breath. She felt like she had been doing a lot of that recently, especially this morning. Quitting her secret smoking habit was proving difficult. The temptation was always to get away from it all in the attic with one of her illicit roll-ups. Only the deep breaths had been catching in her chest recently and she was faced with the reality of what her habit was doing.

Going cold turkey came with its challenges though. And she was finding the whole thing much harder and more annoying than she would have liked. Now, clasping her cup and feeling the heat, she had never longed for a cigarette more. Seeing a world-famous director lying dead in front of a theatre could do that to a woman.

It was another body, another police crime scene. Amita wasn't the superstitious type, regardless of what Jason tried to tell her. She didn't go in for bad luck or losing streaks. There was always a logical explanation to be had somewhere down the line. You just had to look hard enough and pay attention to detail.

And yet here she was – another awful death she had witnessed. The bodies were beginning to pile up. Sandy was right – she had a gift for getting into trouble.

The church hall was busy. Mr Jones had very kindly opened up early to let the club members who had visited the set get in from the cold. Once the police had ushered them quickly from the scene, everyone had felt at a loss as to what to do. They needed somewhere to go and process what they'd just seen. Where better, then, than club headquarters? Georgie, in typical fashion, had organised a tea rota and made sure everyone was watered. Amita was grateful. She was so busy already trying to run scenarios about what she'd seen that she reckoned she would have struggled to flip the immersion heater on, let alone rally the troops.

Everyone had settled into their usual seats now. Nobody was really talking, save for the odd whisper or comment about how awful the morning had been. Amita took another deep breath.

Jason sat down beside her, breaking the monotony.

'I couldn't find any biscuits,' he said. 'Father Ford must keep them under lock and key. Georgie was feigning ignorance but I reckon she knows where the Jaffa Cakes and Hobnobs are kept.'

'They're in the vestry,' said Amita. 'Nobody ever thinks to look in there.'

'Makes sense,' he said.

She didn't look up from her tea. Jason sensed something was wrong.

'You alright?' he asked.

'Yes,' she said.

'You don't look it.'

'No, I don't imagine I do,' she said. 'Discovering a corpse isn't part of my beauty regime, Jason.'

'Alright, keep your hair on,' he said, offended. 'I saw it too, you know. We all did.'

'Him,' said Amita.

'What?'

'Him, you saw *him* – Simon Nakamba. Not it, him, he was a person, Jason, a man, living and breathing. He wasn't an object or a thing. He was a human being.'

Jason scratched at the stubble on his chin.

'Yes, I know that,' he said. 'What's gotten into you, eh? Why are you having a pop at me?'

Amita was going to rebuke him, but she didn't have the energy. She started picking at the rim of her polystyrene cup.

'Sorry,' she said. 'It's just…'

She trailed off. The torn and ragged edge of the cup was getting closer and closer to her tea. One false move and the whole table would be covered.

'It's just what?' he asked.

Amita looked about the table. Sandy was down in his regular chair, close to the end where Ethel would normally have been. He was dozing, collar of his coat turned up around his ears, cap pulled down over his eyes. His head was bobbing up and down and a little snore would come from him every few seconds. Georgie was nowhere to be seen, probably off barking out instructions at the nearest hapless soul conscripted into her tea-making mission. They were effectively alone at the table, everyone else a safe distance away.

'Why does this keep happening to us?' asked Amita, keeping her voice low.

'What do you mean?' asked Jason.

'Death, murder, killers on the loose, why us?' she asked.

'Hang on a minute,' he said. 'Who says Nakamba was murdered?'

'You saw the police there; it looked like a crime scene to me.'

'Yes, of course, but it was a body found in a public space. It's standard police procedure, Amita. It was just unfortunate timing that we all showed up before they could properly cover up the body, or remove it. I mean, you'd have to be some sort of clairvoyant to think a dozen pensioners would appear before the crack of dawn, wouldn't you?'

Amita had a gnawing in her gut. It was slowly crawling up her spine, making her shiver.

'I know a murder when I see one, Jason. We *both* do.'

'Just relax,' he said, looking about too. 'We can't jump to conclusions, Amita. That's gotten us into trouble before. This could all be perfectly innocent.'

'Simon Nakamba, an eminent TV director, household name, turns up dead outside a theatre. Come on Jason, you're a bit slow at times but you're not *that* slow.'

'Oi!' he yelped.

A few of the others looked over – Barbara McLemore from the village hall mob darting a suspicious look at them both. Jason smiled politely then returned to the conspiracy.

'I told you earlier,' he said. 'The state Nakamba was in at the restaurant last night, he could very easily have done himself some damage, *permanent* damage. He was in no shape to be doing anything and nobody went with him when he left.'

'Why didn't you go check on him?' she asked.

'Me?' he snorted. 'Why would I go and check on him? He was out with three other people and none of them seemed that bothered. He alienated a whole room of diners before staggering about, stealing a glass of wine, and breaking it by the way, before shoving past me in about as rude a manner as anyone can. He clearly wasn't a people person, Amita.'

'Why do you say that?' she asked, suspicious.

'Well, just as I said,' he scratched his chin again. 'You get an idea of someone pretty instantly. What's the old phrase? You can only make a first impression once.'

'Very true,' she nodded.

'And he was coming across as a complete buffoon, a selfish and arrogant one at that,' he went on. 'He was lording it over his companions, spouting off about how he'd made it all on his own and had to put up with all sorts. It was pretty awkward, I won't lie. And when he went, everyone in the place seemed a bit happier.'

Amita was still nodding. Jason could see her mind working. He could practically hear the cogs and wheels whirring around inside her head.

'Hold on,' he said. 'Hold on just a second here. Don't do what I think you're doing, Amita.'

'That sentence doesn't make any sense,' she said sharply. 'You're supposed to be a journalist.'

'Don't change the subject either!' He wagged a finger at her. 'I know you're going down that fatal route where you convince yourself there's something sinister going on before the powers that be have even left the scene.'

'Can you blame me?' Amita blurted.

It was Jason's turn to sigh. He pinched the bridge of his nose.

'No, I don't,' he groaned. 'It's just… well, we can't always fear the worst. People die, it happens. We don't *always* have to be chasing bad guys.'

'And bad women,' she interjected.

'And bad women. That's what the police are for. We don't even know if there is any bad guy or gal to chase in this case. He might have simply had an accident, bumped his head, succumbed to the frankly appalling amount of alcohol he'd had at dinner last night. Anything. Or, maybe, just maybe, it was his time.'

Amita considered all of this. She had been considering it since they arrived back at the church hall. She wanted to believe it, she really did. But that gut instinct, that little voice that reared its ugly head time and time again was whispering in her ear.

'Do you believe that?' she asked her son-in-law.

Jason blinked. 'What?' he asked, trying to buy time.

'Do you believe all of that, what you just said, about him having an accident or it simply being his time?' she asked him. 'Do you think Simon Nakamba's death was straightforward and innocent?'

'Well…' he puffed out his cheeks. 'I don't know. I really don't, Amita.'

'Exactly!' she shouted. 'And this is my point, Jason. We don't know. We can't say for certain either way whether this was an accident, fate or something sinister. We just can't say.'

'That's what I'm trying to tell you,' he said. 'There's no point going down a murderous rabbit-hole when it might be perfectly innocent, Amita. I would have thought we would know all of that by now.'

Amita nodded. She knew she had a tendency to let her imagination run away from her. Although it had steered them well in the past. She had to stay focused, stay calm and relax. There might be nothing in any of this, as Jason was explaining. Simon Nakamba may have just died in the street. A tragedy, of course, but nothing more. Only, there was something wrong, something she just couldn't shake.

'You saw him, sitting there, didn't you?' she asked him, her voice low.

'I did,' he said.

'You saw how he was sitting, propped up against the doors of the concert hall. He was just sitting there, lifeless.'

'He was dead, Amita, that's one of the defining features of corpses.'

'And the lights.' She was staring past him now. 'Those lights from the set. They were pointing down at him, looking at him, like they had been put there deliberately. That's not right, Jason. That's not right at all.'

His cheeks drained a little of colour. He started to try and explain it all away but stopped before he could get any words out.

'Somebody put him there, Jason, I know it,' she said, her face pulled in with worry. 'This was no accident, no twist of fate. Simon Nakamba was murdered. And the killer *wanted* him to be found like that.'

Jason swallowed. The stale taste of the bingo club tea made him feel a little ill. Although he knew there was more to it than that. He sat back in his chair and puffed out his cheeks.

'Blimey,' he said.

'Blimey indeed,' said Amita.

'I'm sure the police are way ahead of us on this,' he said. 'They're professional detectives, Amita. They don't need us doing anything.'

'You could ask them,' she said.

'Ask them what? If they need any help?'

'You could ask them if they're treating it as murder,' she said. 'It would be a good story for you, maybe get you some national attention again. Simon Nakamba was a public figure with a huge profile. Think about that as an exclusive.'

Jason felt a little pang of excitement. Awful as it was, the word exclusive had a stimulating effect on him.

'Again, I see what you're trying to do,' he said. 'You want me to call up DI Arendonk and put her in a compromising position, just so you know your theory is right and you can go off on another murder hunt.'

'And what's wrong with that?' she asked bluntly.

'Well… it's…'

He had no good answer for her. Amita gave him a knowing smile, but it quickly faded.

'If there's another killer on the loose, I'd like to know about it,' she said. 'We've got a duty, you and I. You might very well scoff and call me the Sheriff of Penrith, Jason, but there's been nobody over the past few years who has looked out for this town more than we have. And if another murderer is running around, then we should do all we can to bring them in. No?'

'Not tonight, lads!' Sandy woke with a startle. He sniffed and snorted, blinking his brain back into the world of the living. Jason and Amita concluded their conflab and tried not to look guilty.

'Sorry,' Sandy apologised. 'Early start and all that. I must have dozed off. What's going on?'

'That's quite alright, Sandy,' said Amita.

'You've missed being recruited by Georgie Littlejohn on her mission to feed the five thousand.'

Sandy laughed at that. He rubbed his eyes and took off his cap. He looked over at Jason and Amita, his brow wrinkling.

'What's the matter with you two?' he said. 'You look like you've just seen a ghost.'

Chapter 7

AN ORDINARY COPPER

Detective Inspector Sally Arendonk had a headache. She always had a headache these days. She wondered if it was just part of the job. A senior detective in a provincial Cumbrian town. On paper, at least, it sounded quite quaint, peaceful even. One of the main reasons she had transferred from Merseyside Police was for a quieter life. Moving from the hustle and bustle of a city like Liverpool to the bucolic tranquillity of Penrith and Cumbria had seemed like the ideal career move. That was until she arrived.

In her short time as the new DI, she'd been landed with murder and mayhem. From local businessmen savagely cut down in the prime of their lives to little old ladies with dangerous pasts, the Lake District had not been what she'd expected. This was supposed to be a quiet patch, where sheep-rustling and petty theft were the order of the day. Not a wild frontier straight out of a Western.

Thursday mornings were supposed to be her quiet time. The CID offices were normally empty until nine. The other detectives would eventually shamble in with half-eaten breakfasts down their fronts, all a little groggy from the pub the previous evening. Arendonk liked to come in a little earlier, before the phones started ringing off the hook and the smell of stale booze clogged up the air conditioning.

This was when she could do her paperwork. This was when she could answer all of those emails that had been building and building in her inbox. This was when she could do all of those other things that didn't involve catching bad guys. This Thursday morning, however, was a bit different.

She knew right away that she shouldn't have answered her phone. The vibrating on the desk had made her tea ripple – like a T-Rex was stomping its way towards the police station. She had glanced up at the big clock near the door and noted it was before seven. Too early, she had thought, far too early for something serious to have happened. But of course, she should have known better.

In her experience as a detective, she had learned a few things about policework. Firstly, it never really stopped, even after your shift ended. And secondly, any phone call before a decent hour of the day was *always* bad news. Tentatively she had picked up her phone.

'Simon Nakamba is dead,' had been the curt, simple message from an officer down at the film set.

Four words. That's all it had taken to ruin her day, week, possibly year. The filming in the centre of Penrith had been a constant thorn in the side of the local police. From traffic disruption to wrangling and negotiating with the tourist board and politicians who all considered it to be the best thing since sliced bread. Then there was the production crew and cast to deal with. Some stars had demanded extra protection. Others wanted to shadow real officers to get their parts down to a fine art.

Thankfully Arendonk hadn't had to deal with the day-to-day issues. But a sour mood had hung over the station since the filming had begun. Every copper in town was sick of it and couldn't wait to see the back of those huge trailers and lorries that had allegedly brought some razzle dazzle to Penrith but in fact had brought a whole lot of paperwork and extra shifts.

If Arendonk had hoped to avoid it all, those aspirations had been dashed in the space of one sentence. Thankfully her police instincts had kicked in and she had gone into autopilot, instructing the officers on the scene to lock everything down and get ready for a full inspection. Otherwise she'd still be sitting there, staring into space, working out the implications of what she'd just heard.

The suspicious death of a high-profile celebrity. On her patch. Before she'd had her first sip of tea. This was going to be a rough one, she knew it.

The headache had started somewhere just after nine. How she'd managed to get two hours without it was nothing short of a minor miracle. But it was here now and was driving her mad. In fairness to the headache, it wasn't only its fault. The CID office was now frothing with excitement and jittery nerves over this strange case that had landed in their laps. Some officers seemed glad of the chance to prove themselves on a national stage. They almost *hoped* it was sinister. Then there were others that were dreading the scrutiny.

The phones were buzzing and ringing non-stop. If it wasn't Cumbria Police high command demanding updates mere seconds after their last call, it was the media office scrambling around trying to create a strategy. Arendonk was at the centre of the maelstrom. Years of experience had taught her that, while speed was of the essence, it didn't make up for proper fact-finding and analysis – two things that were harder to come by in the glare of a media circus. But famous or anonymous, everyone was equal to Sally when their case number hit her desk and, as a police officer, she felt her duty to the dead was as acute as her duty to the living.

Her stomach grumbled. Her tea sat untouched, alongside it the cinnamon roll she'd treated herself to from the twenty-four-hour bakery up the road. She reached out to pick up the pastry but stopped herself. She seemed to have developed a sixth sense for impending doom. Not necessarily a bad trait for a police detective, she granted. However, this newfound spiritual awareness played absolute havoc with her eating patterns. And usually meant she went hungry.

She stared down at the phone perched beside her cinnamon roll. She willed it to react, to light up with a message or an incoming call, something. She couldn't explain the sensation, it was like a tingling all over her body. To the rest of the squad room she must have looked ridiculous, sitting there staring down at the pastry and her phone. Arendonk didn't care though. She knew something was wrong, something was coming and she didn't want to get caught with a mouthful of crumbs.

Then the thought struck her. In the time that she had spent anticipating something ruining her breakfast, she could have eaten the thing by now.

'This is ridiculous,' she said quietly.

Sally Arendonk was a professional, a good detective, a good cop and a good person. If she wanted to eat her cinnamon roll, she could, anytime she wanted. Without fear of reprisal or interruption.

With that fresh motivation in mind, she picked up the pastry and went to take a bite. On cue, her phone began to buzz.

'Oh for crying out loud!' she shouted, slamming the snack down on the desk and scooping up her phone in one motion.

'This better be good!' she said.

'Sally?' came a familiar voice.

'Jason Brazel, are you spying on me?' she asked.

'What?' he blurted with a cough.

'You, along with everybody else, seem to know *exactly* when I'm trying to have thirty seconds to myself. It's uncanny, so uncanny in fact that I'm starting to suspect that my flat is bugged, my phone is hacked and you're probably sitting watching me through the webcam on my computer as we speak.'

She waved flippantly at her monitor. Nothing happened.

'I'm not sure what I'm being accused of here,' said Jason. 'It all sounds very serious and very slanderous though. Should I get my lawyers involved?'

'You've got a lawyer?' Arendonk said.

'Oh yes, a very good one,' he laughed. 'She's so good, she's also my wife.'

'Your wife's a lawyer?' She could hardly believe what she was hearing. 'And yet you and your mother-in-law get entangled in all kinds of highly illegal shenanigans on an all too regular basis?'

'Regular is a bit strong. Be fair, Sally.'

'DI Arendonk to you, Brazel,' she said.

'Yes, sorry.'

Arendonk rubbed her forehead. She suddenly felt guilty for snapping at Jason.

'It's been one of those mornings,' she said.

'I'll bet,' he agreed. 'Celebrity murdered and left in public, that's hardly going to be good for the old grey matter, am I right?'

'You could say something like that. However, I don't think you were calling up to state the bleeding obvious. And besides, who says it's murder?'

'Damn,' he said.

'You have to be up pretty early in the morning to catch me out, Brazel,' she smiled. 'And besides, you're a better journalist than that.'

'That's very kind of you, Detective Inspector,' she could hear him smiling down the line. 'But as it happens, I *was* up pretty early this morning and so no, this isn't a social call.'

'What do you want?'

'Well, actually, it's not what I want, but what I can give you.'

Arendonk sat up. 'Go on, you have my attention.'

Jason cleared his throat. It was loud and she pulled the phone away from her ear.

'I was out for dinner last night with Radha, that's my wife, the lawyer,' he said.

'Ok,' she replied.

'And Mr Nakamba was sitting at another table, just behind us in fact.'

'That's not a crime.'

'No, but his behaviour was... strange to say the least.'

'Strange in what way?' asked Arendonk.

'Strange in that he was making an absolute spectacle of himself in front of some quite horrified diners, myself included.'

'You? Horrified? I don't believe that for a second, Jason. You're a hard-nosed hack who wades through the strange corners of society. Or at least that's what your LinkedIn profile says.'

'I have a LinkedIn profile?' he said.

'Oh yes.'

'News to me. I must have succumbed to some digital peer pressure...'

'What was Nakamba doing then?'

'He was drunk, that much was clear. He was shouting, yelling his head off at the others he was with.'

'Did you see who they were?'

'No, I didn't recognise them,' said Jason. 'We just assumed they were from the production crew. He seemed to know them well enough, although he accused them of not knowing him at all, not knowing what he'd gone through.'

'What time was this?' she asked, tearing a scrap of paper from a pad and finding her pen.

'It must have been almost ten. We had a late-sitting table at *The Herdwick Hogget* for our anniversary,' he said. 'He left after the spectacle, straight out of the door. He bumped a few tables on the way right enough, but whatever happened to him must have occurred after he left the place.'

'And you said he was drunk, yeah?' she asked, scribbling down notes.

'As a skunk,' replied Jason. 'He was in no fit shape to do anything, much less defend himself if he was attacked, which I assume he was.'

'I thought journalists were forbidden to assume,' she said, replacing her pen in her pocket.

'You really don't know us well, do you, Detective?'

Arendonk laughed. She leaned back in her chair, staring down at the scrap of paper. She was thinking, trying to piece together Nakamba's movements, who he had been with, who might have had cause to harm him. All of the good detective work she'd learned and had total faith in. Then an alarming thought interrupted her flow.

'Hold on,' she said. 'Why are you telling me this?'

Jason didn't reply.

'What are you after, Brazel? You and Amita aren't thinking of doing anything stupid now, are you?'

'Absolutely not!' he shouted. 'Believe me, when you've had a couple of unexpected run-ins with murder victims, as I have, you get keen to avoid stumbling across any more of them.'

'Not a luxury I can afford, I'm afraid,' she said wryly. 'Go on then, spit it out,' she continued. 'Despite what you think of my general knowledge of journalism, I know *you* a little better. And more importantly I suspect that you're in the market for a trade-off.'

'Perhaps,' he said.

'What do you want?'

'Nothing, not really,' he said. 'Just a little exclusive heads-up on when you're going to announce this is a murder investigation, that's all.'

'That's all, is it?' she said.

'Come on, Sally... DI Arendonk. It's been a bit desperate on the bylines front for me recently. I'm only looking to make some scratch so I can, you know, pay a mortgage and put food in my children's tummies, that sort of thing.'

Arendonk sighed. She liked Jason Brazel, and his mother-in-law Amita for that matter. And she couldn't deny the wonderful help they had turned out to be with her first major case in Penrith. She didn't like doing deals with journalists though. It was just a little too seedy for her liking, a little too close to bending the rules.

She was, by her own reckoning and her colleagues's, as straight an arrow as they came. That said, she was also a human being and liked to think some of that humanity filtered into making her a better officer of the law.

She looked about to see who was watching her. The other CID detectives were all busy, or trying to look it. She bent over a little, pretending to be picking something up from beneath her desk.

'I couldn't possibly comment,' she said, her voice hushed. 'However, if you were to report that a murder investigation had been launched after some suspicious marks were found on the deceased's arms, then I wouldn't need to correct you. And *before* midday when the official word will be released, it might be of some use to you. If you catch my drift.'

'I think I hear you loud and clear,' he said.

'Well, that will be that then,' she said.

'I guess it will. Lovely to talk to you again, as always.'

'Oh stop it, Brazel, please,' she said. 'Before I need a bucket.'

'Very good.'

She was about to hang up when a thought shot through her mind like a bolt of lightning.

'Jason!' she shouted, loud enough the whole squad room could hear.

'What?'

'Do *not* start your own investigation into this, do you understand me?' she said sternly. 'I appreciate everything you did before. But this is *not*, I repeat, *not* the kind of case you want to get mixed up in. Not with Nakamba's level of profile. Hell, even *I* don't want to be involved. Is that understood?'

'Absolutely it is,' he said. 'You have my word, Sally.'

'DI Arendonk.'

'Yes, sorry, DI Arendonk. Thanks again.'

The line went dead. She cleared the screen and placed her phone face down on her desk. The scrap of paper with the timings Jason had provided lay beside her cinnamon roll. She went to pick up the snack and finally tuck in.

'Sally!' came a shout from across the squad room. 'It's MP Sheila Mulberry's office on the phone. They want to know what they can say about Simon Nakamba.'

Right on time, her appetite was gone.

Chapter 8

NEWS SCOOP

Jason sat back and wriggled his toes. The warmth of the electric fire felt very welcome on the soles of his feet. The holes in the bottoms of his socks letting the heat in helped with that.

That warmth wasn't just from the fire of course. Jason was feeling pretty relieved. In no small part thanks to Sally Arendonk. Her heads-up that Simon Nakamba had been murdered had given Jason the lifeline he needed after a lean few months. A quick rattle of two hundred words emailed to a couple of news-hungry editors and his breaking news was all over the internet – with thirty minutes to spare before the official announcement.

To celebrate as the London bean-counters worked out his fee, he had decided to take the afternoon off from looking for any more breaking news. If someone found a crisp in the shape of Ullswater or a pothole caused a tailback at the station during rush hour, the scoop would have to wait until tomorrow now. He was now back downstairs in front of the fire enjoying the peace and quiet of his living room, content in the belief he had got over his reporter's block.

He had waited long enough to have this sensation. Indeed, there had been times in the past few months where he had wondered if he would ever feel it again. Now it was here, he was going to savour every sweet, electrically furnaced moment.

The front door clicked open. A gust of razor-sharp, early winter's air came shuddering in and almost knocked him sideways on the sofa.

'Yes, just in here, thank you,' came Amita's voice from the hall.

She had the tone of a headmistress, no, a drill sergeant, barking out instructions and orders that *must* be obeyed. More fool the man or woman who didn't do exactly as she said. That spelled trouble of course. Jason got up, his tranquillity ruined.

He tentatively put his head around the living room door. The cold air was like a slap in the face.

'Amita,' he said.

'Hold on, Jason, just a moment,' she said. 'Let these gentlemen drop this off first.'

'Amita.'

Two grunting, surly-faced men came marching up the driveway. Between them was a huge, portable blackboard, squiggling and squeaking on ancient casters. It rattled loudly as it hit the front step and one of the men let out an unhappy curse.

'Where's this going, love?' he asked, sniffing loudly through his enormous nostrils.

'Just in the living room,' she said.

'Amita...' said Jason, warily.

'Pop it in front of the fireplace for now, thank you.'

'Amita!'

''Scuse us, mate,' said Nostrils.

He barged past Jason, almost knocking him on his back. The delivery man and his colleague proceeded to twist, angle and fiddle the giant chalkboard through the front door and into the living room.

'Amita, what are you doing? Have you lost your mind?' he asked his mother-in-law.

'Don't be silly, Jason,' she tutted. 'This is for work.'

'Work? It's a bloomin' blackboard. I haven't seen one of those things since I was at school.'

'So you went to school then?' she smirked.

There was a loud thump. The delivery men cursed again and Jason hurried into the living room. He couldn't see any damage, just the giant chalkboard that now took up most of the far wall and even a little corner of the television. They grunted as they walked past him and back out of the front door.

'I don't get it Amita, why the heck would you give house-room to this? I mean, don't get me wrong, it's very kind of you to take an interest in my work, and yes, I'm getting my journalistic mojo back, you'll be glad to hear. But I'm a reporter, not a Victorian schoolteacher, so I'm not sure this is exactly the kind of cutting-edge tech that's going to get me a front page splash on the nationals. Plus, that wonky wheel and splintering side suggest it's even more decrepit than me. Dare I say it, it's... junk.'

'It's not junk, Jason, it's essential to our plans. And not for your work but for our work,' she said.

'Our plans? Our work?' Jason's eyes widened.

'How many times when we've been investigating have I asked you to do something, to speak to someone, to come up with some insight or idea as to who a murderer is or note down one of my hunches? And how many times have you completely forgotten to follow it up?'

'Isn't that because I'm usually busy suggesting we keep our noses out of police business?' he said.

'This is true, very true in fact.' She patted her hand across the rubbery, stained surface of the blackboard. 'And you know I only ever say we should get involved if I think our friends down at the station have overlooked some small detail or two. That's why I managed to snaffle this dear old thing. It can be a place for all of our ideas, all of our leads, everything we come across on the day-to-day investigations.'

Before Jason could shut down Amita's notions of them as the caped crusaders of Cumbria, a loud bang made him jump. He spun around. Nostrils was back, glaring at him.

'Chalk,' he growled.

He pointed down at a metal bucket filled to the brim with multicoloured sticks of chalk. A little cloud of dust was slowly rising from the collection, like the aftershock of a bomb.

Nostrils coughed loudly, wiped his forehead on his sleeve and then took his leave again.

'Thank you for your help,' shouted Amita. 'Tell your manager I have the money for him.'

'You *paid* for this monstrosity?' Jason yelped.

Nostrils grunted something and both delivery men headed out the front door.

'I'm not explaining this one to Radha,' Jason said, folding his arms. 'This is entirely your doing Amita. You can take the rap.'

'She'll be fine,' she said, taking off her coat. 'I think it's marvellous, don't you? Can you believe that lovely little primary school in Yanwath are throwing all these lovely old blackboards away. They're upgrading to "interactive boards" apparently. It's just not the same.'

'You know me, I can't handle anything more high-tech than my old brick of a phone, but kids today find this stuff second-nature. It's progress, Amita. And who are we to stand in its way?'

Amita didn't get the chance to answer. The doorbell rang twice and someone called from the hall.

'Knock, knock.'

A scruffy-looking man poked his head around the living room door. He flashed a smile that reminded Jason of a crocodile eyeing up its next meal. He was short, with a pot belly poking out over his creased suit trousers. His jacket was crumpled, a tie slung loosely around his neck.

'Ah, Mr Brunger,' said Amita. 'How much do I owe you for the blackboard?'

'This is what I like about you, Mrs K, you're always on time with the wonga,' he said, rubbing his hands together, still smiling.

He shuffled into the living room, eyeing the place up and down.

'Nice place you've got here, Mrs K, lovely little drum away from all the noise. I could get you a decent price for it on the open market.'

'It's not hers and it's not for sale,' said Jason, cocking an eyebrow. 'And you are?'

'Jason, don't be so rude,' she scolded him, searching for her purse.

'That's alright, Mrs K, don't worry about it,' said Brunger. 'You must be Jason. I don't think we've been formally introduced, have we? Although I've heard all about you from Mrs K here. She speaks very highly of you, sir.'

He offered his hand. Jason looked at it, noting his filthy fingernails.

'Malcolm Brunger,' he said, flashing a smile so wide Jason could see a gold tooth where a molar used to be.

'And how do you know my mother-in-law exactly?' he asked suspiciously. 'You don't look old enough to run the numbers at the bingo club. And you're certainly not W.I. material.'

'Jason,' Amita hissed, rummaging around in her handbag.

'I like him, Mrs K. I bloody like him,' Brunger cackled. 'He's a card. Just like you said.'

'A card?' Jason wrinkled his nose.

'I do a little business with your mum-in-law and her pals down the church hall now and then,' said Brunger. 'The lovely old dears down there will give me a list of the things they're after and I get it for them, cheap, like.'

'Aren't there supermarkets for that sort of thing?' asked Jason.

'Yeah, sure, if you want to get ripped off,' he laughed. 'Have you seen how expensive razorblades are these days? And don't get me started on eggs, we'll be here until half past eight tonight if I get going on eggs. Through the roof they are.'

'Mr Brunger here helps us all out,' said Amita, waving her purse about. 'He'll drop by the church hall every couple of days with his van and takes orders. He has a lot of friends in the commodities market, don't you?'

'Absolutely.' He gave a little bow. 'You see, Jace, these lovely old ladies and gents have only got their pensions to live on. And that wouldn't feed the cat these days. So I help them out wherever I can.'

'With a tidy profit, of course, I imagine' said Jason.

Brunger bowed his head a little. He was still smiling though, his expression hadn't changed.

'We've all got to eat, right, Jace?'

'That's right, we do,' said Amita, darting Jason a severe look of disapproval. 'And Mr Brunger has been very kind with his time and his efforts to the whole bingo club and beyond. He got me this beautiful old blackboard and I'm sure we'll put it to good use.'

She handed over a fistful of notes. Brunger stuffed them into the inside pocket of his suit jacket without counting. He winked at Amita and tipped Jason a little half-hearted salute.

'Pleasure doing business with you as always, Mrs K.' He blew her a kiss. 'And lovely to meet you after all this time, Jace. You've a lovely home here.'

He skipped out of the living room with a whistle. The front door closed with a slam.

'Jace?' Jason said with a sneer. 'Jace? I've never been called Jace in my life. Just who the hell is this Brunger character anyway, Amita?'

'He's a very kind young man who helps me and the others out,' she said succinctly, picking up some chalk from the bucket. 'Which is more than can be said for you.'

'He seems dodgy,' he said. 'Did you see how he was looking at everything in this room. He was probably casing the joint. I'll wedge a chair under the front door handle tonight just to be sure.'

'Don't be ridiculous,' she said, starting to write on the blackboard. 'Yes, he's perhaps a little... unconventional in his sales techniques. But he's been a lifesaver for lots of the other OAPs in the club. And for that we're grateful.'

Jason couldn't really argue with that. He wandered over to the window to make sure Brunger had gone. There was no sign of him out in the garden or the street. Reluctantly he retreated.

'What are you writing?' he asked.

'I'm putting together a little diagram, to get some of my thoughts into order,' she said. 'At the centre is Simon Nakamba and from there we'll work out.'

Jason sat back down on the sofa. The blackboard was conveniently blocking all the warmth from the fire. He tutted quietly.

'Typical,' he said.

'What's that?' she asked.

'Nothing.'

Amita was busy creating her masterpiece. He watched her, watched how she moved, furiously writing away on her new toy. She was worse than the kids. Although he had to admit it was nice to see her so energised. He felt slightly guilty now for his earlier sojourn on the sofa. He could do with some of his mother-in-law's get-up-and-go.

'If I'm not mistaken,' he said, leaning back. 'This looks like the beginnings of a murder investigation.'

Amita didn't answer. She was too busy.

'I said,' he got up. 'This looks like the beginnings of a murder investigation. This wouldn't be what you had in mind when you kept talking about 'our work' and 'our plans' before, was it? I was hoping you were drafting me in to sort out a new tea rota for the bingo club, not drag me into another one of your investigations. I'm busy, I've got a day job to do.'

He wandered over to the blackboard. Amita was scribbling away, bubbles branching off from the central name of Nakamba.

'Amita, are you listening to me?' he asked.

'I am,' she said. 'And I'm ignoring you. And you didn't look very busy when I came in, so I don't see what harm it'll do if you answer a question or two for me.'

She had drawn several question marks about the blackboard with words like 'motives' and 'suspects' underlined. Pip Potter and Derek Veland, the two leads of the show were also circled, along with other various phrases, times and places.

'You told Arendonk that you saw the victim last night?' she asked again.

'That's right.'

'Well, what did she say?'

There was an eagerness to Amita now. She could feel her curiosity taking over, her sense that justice should be done, no matter what. Jason could almost smell that enthusiasm.

'She thanked me for the information,' he said. 'Then I said I'd appreciate any heads-up on if it was being treated as a murder investigation. She said it was. I called an editor I know, wrote the story and I'm getting a cheque. That's all, Amita, that's all that's happened between me seeing you this morning and us standing right here.'

'I see,' she said solemnly.

'And that really is it, Amita. I gave Arendonk my word that we wouldn't interfere.'

Amita didn't answer him. She didn't have to. He already knew the answer and probably didn't have to ask it.

'You say that every time, Jason,' she said.

'I know I do,' he replied. 'And I *mean it* every time. This is a high-profile case. Nakamba was a household name, apparently. We run the risk of becoming embroiled in it all and having our own lives poked and prodded if we stick our noses in where they aren't wanted. The press will be crawling all over this place tomorrow, from far and wide. Especially now that the word is out it is a murder.'

'Thanks to you,' she said.

'That's my job,' he said defensively. 'You know that. I don't mind you playing detective here, in the confines of the living room with your new blackboard. But it has to stop there and go no further.'

'Don't you want to know what happened?' she tried weakly.

'I'll find out when Arendonk and the plod get the answers, that's enough for me.'

'You know that's not true,' she said.

'It is.' He folded his arms, the first hint of a shakiness in his convictions. 'I'm perfectly happy to sit back, let the skilled detectives of His Majesty's Constabulary do their jobs, and read about it like everyone else does.'

'Cobblers!' It was Amita's turn to shout. 'I've never known you to just "sit back and read about it like everyone else does"– it's not your style, Jason Brazel. You're a liar, and, quite frankly, far too good a journalist to be coming out with rubbish like that.'

'That's the second time today I've heard that. Maybe I'm not as good a journalist as you and everyone else think I am, Amita.'

There was a moment's pause between them. Amita was drawing him an unconvinced, disapproving glare. Jason eventually buckled.

'No, you're right, I *am* curious,' he conceded, sitting back down. 'But that still doesn't mean I think you and I should take our speculation any further than these four walls.'

He ran his hands through his hair for the umpteenth time. He knew he should stop doing it; Radha was telling him he was going bald on one side of his head. He didn't want to end up looking like his father. He dropped his hands and laid them flat on his thighs, determined not to move them again.

'You're putting me in a hell of a position here Amita,' he said. 'I gave my word to Sally. She's a good woman, a great cop. She threw me a lifeline earlier. I've got a byline in tomorrow's papers because of her. She made me promise not to do anything on the side and I really, really want to keep my word.'

Amita bowed her head. She knew the quandary he faced. It couldn't be easy for him. She had seen the turmoil and stress he'd been put through these past few weeks *not* being in work. As much as Jason Brazel liked to show a little bravado at times, Amita knew that he was desperately fragile when it came to his career. Now, having done good work, he was getting back on his feet.

'I can't do it alone,' she said, her mouth dry. 'You know I can't, Jason. And I don't much want to, either.'

'Then don't do it at all,' he said. 'Seriously, you don't have any skin in this game, Amita. It's not like it's not going to get investigated – he's a name, there'll be all the top brass making sure all possibilities are followed up. Let the police do what they do. It's their jobs. Catching murderers is a dangerous business, we both know that. Let somebody else take the risk.'

'I know,' she said with a sad sigh, shaking her head. 'I know how dangerous it is. I know the risks we've run. But it's not about the danger and it's not about us, unbelievably. It's about making sure justice is done and, as the last couple of years have shown, sometimes the police miss things. Unusual crimes require unusual perspectives. Nakamba wasn't killed without forethought – he was posed at the concert hall, a maestro mown down. You know this, Jason. We can't let this sort of thing go unchecked on our doorstep. We have a duty.'

'The police do, not us Amita,' he said, looking to the ceiling for inspiration. 'It's their jobs. We have our own lives to live. I'm a journalist and you… you play bingo.'

Amita's bottom lip trembled a little. Jason could see she was fighting back the tears. She turned to face the blackboard, away from him. Jason's stomach dropped.

'Amita,' he called after her. 'Amita, I'm sorry. I didn't mean… I didn't mean it like that. You keep the whole family together! In fact, it's because we need you so much that I don't want you up to all this risky business. I'm just trying to look out for us, both of us, the whole family. That's all.'

She tried to smile but her mouth wouldn't respond. Jason felt awful. He went to his mother-in-law, reaching out and hugging her warmly.

'I'm sorry,' he said. 'I've been a terrible grump recently, I know. It's just work, it drags me down.'

'I know, I know that, Jason,' she sniffed, pulling away and looking at him. 'You're right, I know I shouldn't go about poking my nose in where it doesn't belong. And I know that I shouldn't ever, ever jeopardise your relationship with Sally Arendonk or any of your sources. I know I'm just a silly old fuddy-duddy with too much time on her hands.'

'Oh come on now Amita,' he said, smiling warmly. 'You're not that old.' He attempted a weak laugh. 'And as for fuddy-duddy? Would a fuddy-duddy have the best sequinned leisurewear north of the Blackpool ballroom?'

That made them both feel better. Amita produced a convenient handkerchief from the sleeve of her cardigan. She blew her nose and sighed.

'You're right, we should let the police get on with their jobs. It does sound like they are taking it seriously this time.'

Jason nodded. He had made a promise to Arendonk not to get involved. And that was what he intended. It might not have been what he wanted. But he was grateful to the detective inspector for all of her help and he knew the case was in good hands.

Still, though, the curiosity was there. Amita had been right about that part. He knew he shouldn't be listening to it, or to his mother-in-law. Maybe then he wouldn't make the dubious decisions he had a nasty habit of making.

'So we're agreed?' he hesitated. 'That blackboard will be used purely for theoretical investigations. We will keep our noses firmly out of police business and, only as and when they release information, you will plot it here and stay firmly out of any danger.'

Amita stayed schtum and Jason clearly took her silence for agreement. 'In that case, it won't hurt to go through what we know, will it? Since we're just – you know – shadowing...'

'What are you talking about?' Amita asked, dabbing her tears.

'Nakamba was found outside the concert hall in town,' he said. 'No signs of injury: throat cut, broken neck, that sort of thing.'

'Not that any of us could see,' said Amita, clearly sensing the intrigue in Jason's voice and keen not to stop his train of thought. 'He looked like a man but there was something amiss, something unhuman about him. It was dreadful.'

'Yeah, I know,' he said.

Amita stared at her son-in-law. He was thinking, the tendons in his temples flexing and tightening, over and over again.

'What's the matter?' she asked.

'Nothing,' he said.

'You're thinking about something.'

'What? No, nothing, it's nothing.'

'You were thinking about doing something stupid, weren't you, Jason?'

His face flushed a little.

'A look,' he said. 'One look, at the crime scene, tomorrow, after Radha gets back and everyone has gone home for the night. I don't see how that would cause any great consternation with our friend, the right honourable DI Sally Arendonk. And then after that, it's definitely just back to the blackboard. Strictly theory only. After tomorrow.'

'It could just be by chance that we happen to pass the concert hall, after all,' said Amita, casually.

'Exactly,' Jason agreed. 'It's a free country after all, people can go wandering wherever they like, can't they?'

'They can, the last I checked,' she said.

'Right then,' he said. 'It's a date, with my mother-in-law, in the middle of winter, to go see where a man was robbed of his life. Wonderful stuff.'

Chapter 9

LIGHT AND TUNEFUL

A bitterly cold wind had kicked up that afternoon. The weak sun was growing ever dimmer as it sank in the winter sky. The Penrith streets were already starting to darken and Amita pulled her coat about her a little bit tighter. She never really liked this time of the day during the winter. The council could never get the timing of the streetlights down. There was always an hour or so that probably could be lit better, but it wasn't quite full-on darkness either. The purgatory always made her a little uneasy. And she kept looking back over her shoulder to make sure they weren't being followed.

The set loomed up ahead, just as it had earlier. The huge production trucks and lorries stood like silent, intimidating giants. All of the large lights and lamps were dark now and it appeared the place was deserted. Only the flapping police tape that clapped as the wind caught it showed any sign that this was a murder scene. Nobody was standing on guard.

'By 'eck it's cold,' said Jason, at her side.

He tucked his chin into his scarf, brow wrinkling as he pressed on into the wind. Amita dug in the pocket of her coat and produced a spare pair of gloves.

'Here,' she said. 'You should always carry your own.'

'I can't wear these,' he said, looking down at them.

'Why not?'

'Look at them!'

Jason snatched the gloves with his ice-cold hands. He waved them in Amita's face.

'They're bright pink with polka-dots! I can't wear these! I'm an investigative reporter, not a children's TV host.'

'And you'd rather get frostbite would you? Grow up, Jason,' she said.

He snorted and tried to blow some heat into his cupped hands. It wasn't working. He gave another unintelligible grunt and pulled on the bright pink woollen gloves. He didn't say it aloud but there was instant relief.

'There aren't many people about here this afternoon,' said Amita, nodding up the street towards the set.

'The pubs are open, the crew are all probably drowning their sorrows,' replied Jason.

'I suppose I wouldn't blame them. It must have come as quite a shock.'

'The only thing more shocking was his behaviour last night in the restaurant,' he said. 'I imagine if our Mr Nakamba wasn't the one who was murdered, he'd be propping up the bar as we speak.'

'Was he really that bad?' asked Amita as they neared the police tape and the edge of the set.

'Absolutely legless, he was,' Jason whistled. 'Now I've seen kaylied, lord I've been there myself a good few times, before you say anything.'

'My lips are sealed.'

'But Nakamba was at the dangerous sweet spot – inebriated enough to speak his mind unfiltered, but not so sloshed as to be unintelligible and get away with it. Oh no, he commanded quite an audience, staggering about, shouting and swearing at the other folk he was with. It was awkward. Or at least it would have been if I wasn't feeling so spooked by it all.'

'Spooked?' asked Amita, sniffing.

Jason shrugged.

'I don't know what it was,' he said. 'I couldn't put my finger on it at the time. I think I was just so shocked. But there was something really intimidating about Nakamba. I mean, he wasn't the biggest bloke you're ever going to see. But his voice, it was like a foghorn. And the way he carried himself, even drunk as a skunk. I wouldn't have liked to be on his wrong side, like the folk he was with. He was giving them an earful, hammering on about how he'd been through the ringer, constantly fighting for his place in the industry. I can't imagine what they must have said to him to spark that temper.'

Amita let it all sink in as they approached the edge of the set. The entrance to the concert hall was heavily cordoned off, police tape wrapped around the handles of the doors, stretching out to lampposts like macabre maypole ribbons. Amita slowed as they drew closer. Jason could sense she was uneasy.

'You alright?' he asked her, squeezing her elbow.

'Yes, fine,' she lied. 'Tell me about who Nakamba was with. Did you recognise any of them?

'No,' he said. 'I don't think Radha did either. It was her who spotted Nakamba in the first place. I reckon she would have said something if she knew any of the others.'

'I agree, we'll ask her later,' said Amita. 'And how many were there?'

'Another three, or maybe four actually. I don't know, I was watching Nakamba all of the time. It was sort of hard to take your eyes away from him, to be perfectly honest. He was making such a scene.'

Jason nodded over towards the concert hall steps.

'Here we are then, returned to the scene of the crime. It doesn't get any easier, does it?'

Amita nodded. She swallowed, her throat and mouth dry and an awful taste making her a little queasy. This was proving harder than she had thought. She was glad Jason was there with her.

'Should we take a closer look?' she asked.

'Steady on, Amita,' he said, looking about the place. 'I know we said we were only going for a walk and all of that. It's a bit harder to explain when we've meandered beneath rolls and rolls of police incident tape, don't you think?'

But Amita's insatiable curiosity had kicked in. She opened her bag, took out a tin of travel sweets and let them fall. They bowled right across the paving stones and under the cordon. Amita focused on the crime scene ahead and steeled herself. Lifting up the tape, she quickly ducked under and hurried towards the theatre and concert hall.

'Hang on,' said Jason 'I don't think rescuing some rogue Murray Mints is reason enough to contaminate a crime scene, Amita.' But she was halfway to the steps already, and he wasn't letting her go alone so, with a glance over his shoulder, he followed.

They jogged slowly across the street, winding their way through the huge lorries and equipment that had been scattered about the set. It was strange how different the whole street seemed now on this side of the tape. Amita and Jason must have walked along this stretch of the road a million times. Yet now, because it was going to be on TV, it all seemed new, almost fake, as if with a gust of wind the facades might blow over and reveal everything was just pretend.

As they approached, Jason began to get a little nervy. He was always the same in deserted streets like this. He was never sure if somebody was going to leap out and shout surprise at any moment. Jason hated surprises. Especially if they were from the police.

'A quick shifty and then let's go,' he said, clapping his hands and stamping his feet for warmth. 'I don't want to push our luck.'

Amita stopped on the pavement a few yards from the doors of the concert hall, one hand clutching her rescued bonbons. The police tape was flapping louder here, entangling itself like streamers. The clapping of the plastic was almost like an applause welcoming them to the scene. It gave Amita shivers as she tried to focus.

'This was some sort of message, from the killer, I mean,' she said to Jason.

'What do you mean?' he asked, constantly looking up and down the street to make sure they weren't being watched.

'It can't be a coincidence that Nakamba was found here, outside a centre for the arts – someone wanted to bring the curtain down on him deliberately. The lights were trained on him too, you saw that.'

Jason nodded grimly.

'That means it was deliberate,' she went on. 'We don't know if he was killed here or murdered somewhere else and dumped here. It almost doesn't matter. Whoever did this *wanted* him to be discovered outside the concert hall. It's a message, Jason, I'm certain of it.'

'A message to who?' he asked. 'Or do I not want to find out?'

'I don't know,' she said.

'Why Nakamba? Why not somebody local or one of the actors? Then there's the crew, there must be dozens of them. What was so special about him?'

'I don't know that either,' said Amita. 'It's such a popular show, a big deal. Surely there would have been more obvious targets to make a bigger splash if it was publicity the murderer was after? He was the director, a household name. But I bet fans and viewers couldn't pick him out of a lineup. Not like the actors.'

'You mean like Pip Potter?'

'I thought you didn't watch it' asked Amita with a wry smile.

Jason blushed a little.

'How often do we get glamorous actresses just kicking around in this town, Amita? Give a guy a break, would you?'

Amita laughed a little.

'I won't tell Radha if you don't.'

'That would be kind,' he said.

Jason turned his attention quickly to the crime scene before his mother-in-law changed her mind.

'Well, I'm not sure about you, but I don't know what I'm looking for here,' he said. 'It's just an empty doorway covered in police tape. The police will have gone over this place with a fine-tooth comb and removed anything of interest.'

'Yes, I suppose you're right,' she said.

A loud clank echoed through the empty set and made them both jump.

'What was that?' asked Jason, breathless.

'I'm not sure,' said Amita, scanning the street.

Everything was still and quiet now. The sun had vanished behind the tall buildings of the street and everything was covered in gloom. The street lights hadn't flickered on yet, long, heavy shadows creeping out from every shop door, window and alcove.

'Maybe it was nothing,' said Jason.

'Yes, maybe,' she replied. 'Or the wind.'

They remained perfectly still, somehow hoping that by not moving they'd blend in with the rest of the dormant set and equipment. Then a bright, white flash blinded both of them. They yelped, scrambling to cover their eyes. Jason stumbled backwards. His legs got tangled up in the police tape and he lost his footing. Amita pawed blindly to stop him falling over and was pulled down too. They landed in a heap at the entrance of the concert hall.

'What... what's going on?' Amita shouted.

'Your knee is pressing on my bladder!' Jason squealed.

In a flash, the light was gone. They both blinked, trying to adjust their eyes as they untangled themselves. Footsteps clicked towards them as Amita managed to get to her feet.

When her vision returned to normal, she peered through the gloom. A small figure in an oversized puffer jacket and thick fur hood came into view through the darkness.

'Who... who are you?' gasped Amita.

'East 17, by the looks of it.' Jason blinked, still blinded by the light.

'I was about to ask you two the same question,' said the figure in the big coat.

Amita helped Jason up and they shuffled away from the concert hall.

'Sorry, we were just...' she trailed off.

'Yeah, we were just...' said Jason, rubbing his eyes.

The figure pulled down the hood of the puffer jacket to reveal a fresh-faced young woman. Her emerald eyes were wide and bright, even in the gloom. She stared at Jason and Amita for a moment, as if working something out. Then she clapped her hands together.

'Oh my god,' she said. 'You're Amita Khatri.'

Amita was about to fire back the excuse she'd finally came up with but was halted in her steps.

'I...' she stammered.

'It's you, isn't it? You're Amita. Which would make *you* Jason Brazel, her son-in-law.'

Jason wasn't quite so polite with his shock.

'Who the hell are *you* and how do you know who we are?'

The young woman clapped her hands again. Her friendly smile stretched from ear to ear.

'I can't believe it's you two. You're both like proper local legends. This is insane, absolutely insane. Wait until I tell some of my friends. Well, my only friends actually. They're a bit weird like me. They love all the true crime stuff. I can't wait to see their faces when I tell them I've met a pair of actual, real-life sleuths. This is amazing, I'm so, so lucky. Can I get a selfie with you?'

She pulled out her phone. It was taking all of Amita's energy just to keep up with her. Jason was too far behind. He waved his hands in the air.

'Hold on, hold on, time out, please,' he said. 'Go back to the start because I seem to have missed the opening hour of this farce. How do you know who we are? Have we met?'

She clicked her tongue.

'That is *such* a Jason thing to say,' she smiled.

He didn't smile back. Amita stifled a laugh as the young woman stepped forward. She hunkered down between them and took a picture on her phone. Checking it, she held it to her heart.

'Thank you so much for this,' she said. 'It means the world. I'm absolutely delighted, overwhelmed actually to have met you. I've followed everything you've done, the Frobisher case, that business with the painting, all of it. You two are *so* good. You should have your own TV show or something.'

'Right, that does it!' Jason shouted. 'You need to tell us right now who you are and how you know so much about us!'

Amita placed a hand on his shoulder, trying to calm him down. The young woman seemed undeterred but she thought a less aggressive tack might prove more valuable.

'We're very flattered, dear,' she said. 'And you'll have to excuse my son-in-law. He can get a bit too excited when he's stressed.'

'Stressed?' Jason gulped. 'She knows our life story, Amita! We've never seen her before in our lives and she knows about what we do.'

'If you could give us a little background, dear,' she ignored him. 'Just so we're on the same wavelength.'

The young woman nodded.

'Yeah, sure, of course,' she said, forcing her face to be more serious. 'I should have said, you're right. My name is Lisa. I'm one of the runners here on set. I like to do my research before they send me to wherever it is they'll be filming next. I'm not long in this job but I love to know the ins and outs of places. I've always been like that, drove my mum crazy when I was younger.'

'Oh you're still young, dear,' smiled Amita.

'You're *so* lovely, Amita,' she said. 'I love true crime, comes with working on a police show like *The Locus* I guess. I came across a blog online that talked about two locals who solved crimes on the side – a journalist and his mother-in-law.'

'Blog?' Jason asked.

'Website,' said Amita. 'Do you have it there?'

Lisa nodded. She brought the site up on her phone. Amita immediately recognised it.

'Barry,' she said.

'Barry?' Jason coughed. 'You mean that conspiracy theorist you found online? He's writing about us?'

'He's very good,' said Lisa. 'He champions you, says you're both the last bastion of good in a world gone mad.'

'That's Barry alright,' said Amita. 'He was very kind to help with something we worked on before. He's a lovely man but he needs to get out more, I think.'

'Probably, but who doesn't, right?' Lisa laughed. 'Like I said, this is such a thrill for me. Barry does such a great job with the details, I feel like I know you both already...'

She trailed off. She looked about the street then down at the entrance of the concert hall. Some of the police tape was still stuck to Jason's shoe. She leaned down and peeled it off, holding it in both her hands.

'Wait a minute,' she said, her face slack. 'Are you... are you two looking into Simon's murder?'

Before either Jason or Amita could answer, Lisa was hopping up and down, screaming with excitement. They tried to hush her down, her cheers echoing about the silent set.

'I can't believe this!' she said. 'I actually stumbled into one of your investigations. This is unreal!'

'Please, Lisa, calm down,' Amita said. 'We're not supposed to be here. You know that if you're part of the crew.'

'This is amazing,' she said. 'I'm... I'm speechless.'

'Could have fooled me,' murmured Jason.

'So what have you found out?' she asked.

Amita was a little reluctant to spill the details.

'We can't really tell you, Lisa,' she said. 'You might lose your job.'

'Oh don't worry about that, this is more important,' she waved her away. 'Have you spoken to Pip Potter yet?'

'Pip Potter!'

Jason's voice reached a new height he hadn't been capable of for almost thirty years. Amita tutted.

'Try to contain your excitement, for all of our sakes, Jason,' she said.

'Pip Potter, yes,' Lisa laughed. 'I'm just heading to collect her now. We have a production meeting and she's the star of the show. Or at least she likes to think she is. You can chum me if you like. I'll even see if she'll give you an autograph, if that's more of your thing.'

'I'm not sure–'

'Absolutely!' said Jason, cutting his mother-in-law off. 'That would be delightful.'

'Good,' Lisa smiled. 'Follow me then. I can't believe this. Meeting *the* Jason and Amita. This is the best day of my life!'

She started off up the street. Jason was about to follow when Amita tugged on his arm.

'Are you sure this is a good idea?' she whispered.

'We're only going to say hello,' he said. 'And you never know, this Pip Potter might have some insight into our dead friend Simon Nakamba. She worked with him closely, after all. You don't get if you don't ask, an old journalism mantra.'

'You've changed your tune pretty quickly,' Amita cocked an eyebrow. 'Just so you know, I'll be beside you every second while we're in Ms Potter's company.'

'Yes, yes, yes,' Jason batted her away.

He started up the street after Lisa. Amita had to take a moment to recompose herself. Learning she had a fan hadn't quite been in the schedule for today. It hadn't ever occurred to her that she would *ever* have a fan for *anything*. Throw a grisly murder into the mix and an appointment with a bonafide celebrity and it had all the makings of a day to remember. She'd had plenty of those recently. And not all of them went to plan.

Chapter 10

SILKS AND SATINS

'And then my agent phones me up and says that some comic book nerds in Hollywood want me to play an alien with tentacles for arms, can you believe that?'

The massage therapist rolled her eyes. She had made sure Pip Potter couldn't see her. The young actress was lying face down on the table, her shoulders being worked on furiously.

It wasn't the first time she'd rolled her eyes. And she doubted it would be the last before the end of the session.

'I said to him, Tony, if you think I'm going to spend six months shooting a film where I'm in makeup for ten hours every day, you've got another thing coming,' Pip droned on. 'And that's how I ended up here, in Penrith, in the middle of the winter, up to my neck in puddle water. What a life, I tell you.'

The actress rolled over. The therapist wasn't done but she'd given up trying to talk to the TV star. Instead she made her way down to Pip's feet and began rubbing them. The actress was a little suspicious, staring down at her through her face-mask.

'Are you getting on alright down there?' she asked.

'Yes, very well Ms Potter, very well,' replied the therapist.

'You're not saying very much.'

'Just concentrating on your feet,' she said. 'You carry quite a lot of tension there. I want to try and relieve some of that.'

'The only thing that will relieve my tension is a fast train out of Penrith.' Pip reached over to a little table beside the bed. She delicately plucked two slices of cucumber and placed them on her eyes. 'They've had me running about five miles a day, up and down that bloody high street out there – in the rain of course. And it's always raining around here. You'd carry a lot of tension in your feet if you had to do that too.'

'Yes, I probably would,' the massage therapist laughed nervously, working out a knot in Pip's arch.

'Honestly, the things I do for this job. Maybe I should have gone with the tentacles instead.'

The gentle cooing of whale song and soft light from the scented candles dotted around the therapy room maintained a semblance of calm. The therapist was just happy for the silence.

That silence didn't last very long. A heavy knock at the door made her knuckles slip. Pip let out a squeal as she sat bolt upright in her recliner.

'Bloody hell!' she shouted.

'Sorry, Ms Potter,' said the therapist. 'I'll go see who that is at the door. They shouldn't be disturbing us.'

'See they don't,' said the actress. 'The production company is paying good money for me to be treated and I'm expected to come out relaxed, not like a chewed string. Get the door, will you.'

The massage therapist stifled her frustration. She got up, cursed her aching knees, and opened the door. A wave of cool air passed over her, washing away the scented warmth of the treatment room and for a moment she feared she'd unthinkingly let the paparazzi in. The relief was only short-lived as three very odd people stood on the other side, all of them smiling at her.

'Can I help you?' she asked them.

'We're here to see Pip Potter,' said Lisa. 'It's a matter of urgency.'

'But... she's having her massage therapy.'

'Yeah, I know, but like I said, it's all a bit urgent.'

'But... but...'

The therapist tripped over her words. Before she could put up any further resistance, Lisa had pushed her way into the therapy room. Amita and Jason stuck closely behind her, making their own apologies as they entered.

Pip sat upright with her arms folded across her chest. The fluffy robe and charcoal facemask caught Jason a little by surprise. He hadn't quite been expecting to see one of the foremost stars of TV in such a relaxed state. A rush of blood to his head made him suddenly very nervous and he dropped his gaze to the floor.

'Oh, terribly sorry,' he stuttered, 'I should, we should, come back later.'

'You've ruined my massage already,' sniped Pip. 'You might as well come in and make yourselves at home, whoever you are.' Far from seeming awkward, she seemed entirely unbothered to be barely clad in company.

'We're big fans,' said Amita, offering a hand, seeming equally unflustered about meeting one of her heroes wrapped in only a dressing gown. 'Well, I am anyway. I've followed you on *The Locus* from the very first episode. You make the screen come alive when you're in shot.'

Pip basked in the praise, then held up her hands and wriggled her fingers.

'I'm covered in oil, you'll have to forgive me,' she said. 'I wasn't expecting fans, or indeed, the crew, this afternoon. You're crew, aren't you? I'm sure I know your face. I'm meant to be resting and healing my trauma.'

She darted an unimpressed look towards Lisa. The facemask gave her an edge of menace. Although, from the few seconds he had been in her company, Jason reckoned Pip Potter didn't need any added dread about her.

'Yeah, that's kind of my fault,' said Lisa. 'I've been sent to fetch you. The producers are holding an emergency meeting at six.'

'What for?' sighed Pip.

Lisa didn't answer. She looked at Amita and then to Jason who was still staring at the floor. Even the message therapist seemed a little bewildered at the actress' question.

'Mr Nakamba,' said Lisa slowly.

'Still dead, is he?' she sneered, theatrically.

The room may have been hot and stuffy, but the atmosphere was now icily cold. Jason closed his eyes. This was beyond awkward. His own fairly low tolerance for cringeworthy scenarios was notorious. He had never wanted the ground to swallow him up quite so badly. Or quickly.

Pip Potter seemed to detect the shift. Her comment had created a morgue-esque atmosphere. She cleared her throat.

'Yes, well, he was always very demanding,' she said, kicking her feet off the side of the table. 'If it wasn't one thing it was another. He was a complicated man in life and I suppose he'll prove the same in death. What is it about then – our lines for the press? "Terrible tragedy, sad loss to the profession etc etc"?'

Lisa shoved her hands into the pockets of her huge, padded parka. They were so deep that her arms were swallowed almost all the way up to her elbows. She clicked her tongue.

'Yeah, I guess,' she said, pretending to kick something with the toe of her shoe. 'All I know is the producers are hosting an emergency meeting at Askling Manor around six this evening. They sent me to fetch you. It's a three-line whip. Those were my instructions.'

'If I must,' said Pip. 'I'll need to get changed. I can't very well turn up looking like the Bride of Frankenstein, can I?'

She forced a chirpy laugh. Nobody joined her. Jason could feel his cheeks getting hotter and hotter.

'It's been a very stressful few days,' said Pip, trying to salvage at least some goodwill. 'Simon Nakamba was everything to me in many ways. He was difficult to work with at times, but aren't all geniuses? His death came as a terrible shock when I found out yesterday.'

There was a falseness about her words that jarred with Jason. He wondered if her grief was going to be just as much of a performance as her screen work was. Amita had obviously picked up on it too. She stepped forward, questions at the ready.

'Amita Khatri,' she said. 'And this is my son-in-law Jason.'

'You're police?' asked the actress.

'No, not police,' she replied.

'I didn't think so,' said Pip. 'You're both too short for starters.'

Jason caught a fleeting glimpse of Pip's bare shins as she walked around the therapy table. His blushing grew worse and he kept his eyes glued to the floor.

'My brothers are bobbies in Manchester,' she said. 'And I don't think you two meet the height requirements somehow.'

'Very good, yes,' Amita feigned a laugh. 'No, we're not with the police. We're just a couple of concerned citizens, that's all. We have a look into these sorts of things from time to time. Don't we, Jason?'

'What?'

He looked up instinctively. Pip, Amita, Lisa the runner and the disgruntled massage therapist were all staring at him. Jason was no stranger to conflict, it came with the territory, being a journalist. And if the last few years of his life had been anything to go by, he should be completely used to these sorts of situations.

Only this time it was different. Angry farmers with shotguns, crazed murderers swinging shovels. Even maniacal pensioners couldn't hold a candle to four expectant women all looking at him to say something.

'Blimey,' he managed. 'Is it hot in here or just me? It's hot in here, right? I'm not just imagining things, am I?'

None of them answered. Amita merely gave a sad shake of the head.

'Forgive him, Ms Potter, he's not usually like this,' she said. 'Stringing a sentence together is normally one of his more commendable abilities, especially given he's a journalist by trade.'

'I see,' said the actress. 'Well, be that as it may, you're hardly here on a social call, are you?'

'No, we're not,' said Amita. 'As I said, we're doing our own investigation alongside the official one. And we wondered if you might have any insight into Mr Nakamba's goings-on.'

Pip slowly peeled the charcoal-infused sheet-mask down from her face. She looked completely different underneath, natural and clean. Jason knew actors had many faces, but this was a bit literal, even for him. He couldn't help but stare as he lingered close to the door, half-expecting another layer under the last one Pip had pulled away.

'Insight into Simon Nakamba?' said Pip. 'Now there is a question I'm sure hundreds of psychiatrists have tried to answer.'

'Pardon me?'

'He was intense,' said the actress, throwing the facemask over to the bin, which it missed and lay awkwardly on the floor next to it like a shroud. 'Absolutely bonkers.'

'But I thought you said he was everything to you?' asked Amita.

'He was. On set, I mean. The creative heart of this series,' she said. 'He was a genius, of course. He turned what was a little cop show into the most watched programme in Europe, maybe even the world, if ratings keep rising like they have been. His vision, his ability to create magic on the screen, that was all him. But he'd lose his temper at the least little thing. He'd bring whole productions to a standstill if it wasn't just as he had instructed. I've even heard that he'd not bother showing up for work if the weather wasn't what he wanted. An absolute tyrant and maniac. But a very talented one too. I don't think anything was ever good enough for Simon Nakamba. No one was ever as perfect as he wanted them to be – no one else prepared to sacrifice as much for their art as he was.'

'He was award-winning, isn't that right?' asked Amita.

'You're right,' said Lisa, stepping forward a little. 'He had a number of awards for his work, over the last few years in particular.'

'Including *The Locus*,' said Pip. 'We won a BAFTA last year for best drama. God, I can still see us all now at the table, waiting for the announcement. I was so nervous. Simon was supremely unbothered though, twirling his fingers like he was waiting to collect a takeaway. What you thought would bother him didn't even raise as much as an eyebrow. Then something tiny, something insignificant would cause him to fly off the handle and storm off a set.'

'And did *you* ever cause him to go mad?' asked Amita.

'How long have you got?' Pip laughed. 'Actors weren't Simon's favourite people in the world. And that's a shame when you're a flipping director. You kind of need us to put the whole thing on, do you know what I mean?'

'Quite,' said Amita. 'Do you think there was anyone who might want to harm Mr Nakamba? Anyone in particular on this shoot, for example?'

'Again, how long do you have?' Pip nodded over at Lisa. 'I was used to him, I've worked on this show for years. But the newer runners, this season's crew, a lot of them have never seen his outbursts before. I don't imagine they took very kindly to it at all.'

Amita looked at Lisa. The young runner remained silent.

'What about the night before he died?' she asked. 'Were you with him? We understand he went for a late dinner in town.'

'I don't really know what Simon did when he left the set at night,' said Pip. 'He was fiercely private in some ways. He could be into all sorts and I wouldn't know. He is, was, a hard man to get on with, not someone to open his heart readily. You'll forgive me if I'm not entirely surprised that he's wound up murdered.'

The comment seemed to linger. Pip leaned on the therapy table. A curl of red hair had dropped from beneath the towel wrapped about her head. She blew it away from her eyes, cool and collected. There was an imperiousness to her. She held herself tall and dignified while everyone else crammed into the tiny room.

'Now if you'll excuse me, folks, I think I've been more than accommodating,' she said.

'Yes, of course,' said Amita. 'Thank you very much for your time and information.'

'I assume I'll be getting briefed on what's happening here?' she asked Lisa. 'I've already spent the day doing nothing. I'd like to get home if we're closing things up here.'

'I'm not sure, Ms Potter,' said Lisa. 'My instructions were just to come and collect you for the meeting at the hotel. The rest of the cast are already there, I believe, along with the producers.'

'Rest of the cast? Don't make me laugh,' said Pip. 'Good luck getting Derek Veland to do something during sunlight hours. Derek will still be sozzled from last night, knowing him.'

She guided Amita, Jason and Lisa to the door. The massage therapist opened it and ushered them all out.

'Thank you again, Ms Potter,' said Amita, bowing a little. 'I'm such a big fan of the show and this was a real treat to meet you, albeit in rather ghastly circumstances.'

'Yes, well, good luck,' said Pip.

She closed the door. The lock clicked shut.

'Nice to see you!' Jason called, finally finding his voice again.

He immediately felt a great relief to be out of the room and away from Pip Potter's semi-clad company. He doused himself in the hand sanitiser at the door to try and banish the awkwardness he'd felt. Amita and Lisa both gave him a perplexed look.

'What?' he asked, slowly realising it was air freshener he'd just liberally applied.

'Honestly,' said Amita, rolling her eyes and shaking her head at Lisa. 'You just can't take him anywhere.'

The women walked off down the corridor, Jason trailing behind. He didn't know how he was going to explain this one away to Radha, especially as he'd be arriving home in a noxious cloud of something rather inauspiciously called 'Lakeside Romance'.

Chapter 11

I COULD BE SO GOOD FOR YOU

'I told you this thing would come in handy,' said Amita.

She was drawing big circles and lines on the blackboard that now dominated the living room. Jason was trying to peer around her to catch the last of the news and sport on the television. Every time he thought he had an angle, his mother-in-law would obstruct the important detail. He'd long given up on trying to hear what was being said. At least he could admire the pictures and colours.

'I can't believe you're alright with this,' he said to Radha, sat beside him on the sofa. 'I had been looking forward to you reading your mum the riot act for having this *monstrosity* in the front room.'

'It's easier to go with the flow,' she said, sighing. 'When you're out at work all day and then have two wild animals to feed and entertain when you come home, you learn to just breathe and take it easy.'

'Clara and Josh aren't all that bad,' he said.

'I wasn't talking about the bairns.'

Jason took that one to heart. He knew when he'd been beaten. He crossed his arms and tried to look around Amita again to catch the midweek scores.

'I don't know how we managed without this wonderful old blackboard, Jason. I really don't,' she said.

'No, nor do I,' he groaned.

Amita took a step back to survey her work. The TV was now completely obscured. Jason bit his tongue and tried to take a leaf out of his wife's book. He counted to ten, hoping it would help. It didn't.

'I've put Pip Potter in the suspects column, as you can see here,' she said, circling her in red chalk. 'I think that little outburst we saw earlier is enough to at least put some suspicion in our minds. Don't you agree?'

He didn't. He looked at the spider diagrams that now filled the blackboard. It was hurting his head trying to unjumble the web of lines, circles, arrows, names and words.

'What makes you think she killed Nakamba?' he asked. 'She didn't speak very highly of him. And given I was in the man's company for all of five minutes, I can't really blame her.'

'I didn't say I thought she killed Nakamba. I said I was putting her in the list of suspects – she could have killed him. And she gave us a motive in her dislike of him. Though, yes, I grant you she said that was a common theme.' Amita fiddled with the chalk. 'She said that other crew and cast members might not appreciate his behaviour on set. So she could have motive,' she said. 'She was fairly forthright in telling us that Simon Nakamba had a temper. What if he had been abusive to her in the past? That's the kind of thing that festers in people's imaginations.'

'It's pretty thin, Amita,' he said. 'Pip Potter didn't strike me as the type to let a few bad words and diva-like behaviour get under her skin. She's as big a star as he is, maybe even bigger. She's onscreen, isn't she, he's behind the camera. She would have more to lose by doing something like that. I'm not buying it.'

'Perhaps,' she said. 'There was something about the way she spoke about him though. Like she'd prepared the speech already.'

'That is what actors do though,' said Jason. 'And I hope actors are more open these days to revealing the horrors that used to happen on casting couches.'

'What?' asked Radha. 'Was he one of these creeps you read about in the papers?'

Amita wrinkled her nose. Jason shuddered.

'We don't know, no suggestion of anything like that so far,' he said. 'But Pip Potter seemed adamant that he was capable of flying off the handle over the least little thing. I don't imagine that makes for a very conducive work environment.'

'Being a bad colleague – or even a bad drunk – may not be pleasant,' said Amita. 'But it's hardly grounds for murder. There's a killer somewhere who must know more about Nakamba than we've uncovered so far. We need to speak to more people that knew him.'

'Fat chance of that. They're probably sat with all the other top brass at Askling Manor as we speak,' said Jason.

'Is that where they're staying?' asked Radha.

Jason nodded. Amita drew a few lines under the hotel and resort's name on the board.

Jason looked at the rest of the writing on the blackboard. At the centre was Simon Nakamba's name. Much like the production of *The Locus*, he was there, in the eye of the storm. Now he was dead. Somewhere amongst all of that noise was an answer.

'Did you say Askling Manor?' asked Radha.

Jason and Amita turned to face her.

'That's where Pip Potter was going tonight?'

'Yes, for an emergency production meeting,' said Amita. 'That lovely young girl, what was her name again, the runner?'

'Lisa,' said Jason.

'Yes, Lisa. She was taking her there when we… stumbled across her.'

'That sounds painful,' said Radha.

'Not as painful as being recognised,' said Jason.

'You were recognised?' A little smirk made the corner of his wife's mouth curl upwards.

'Don't get us started,' Amita waved her away. 'Just a complete coincidence, that's all. I'm not even entertaining the notion of fame. Not when there's a murderer on the loose.'

Radha looked at Jason. He shrugged his shoulders, pretending to be suave.

'What can I say, you have a famous husband,' he said.

'Infamous maybe,' said Radha. 'That Askling Manor, it's a pretty fancy place.'

'They're pretty fancy people,' he said. 'Actors and crew and the like. Can't say I'm surprised, it's the perfect place to hole up. Out of the way, in the middle of the country, loads of facilities and high-end restaurants. Makes sense.'

'I wonder if Sarah still runs it,' she said, fetching her phone.

'Sarah?' asked Jason.

Amita hesitated a moment. He could feel her tensing up.

'Who's Sarah?' he asked.

'Sarah Paris,' said Amita. 'Radha and her used to be friends at school.'

There was a disapproving tone in the way she spoke. Even saying the woman's name seemed to be bitter and painful for her. Jason was intrigued.

'Thanks for that, Mum,' snorted Radha. '"Friends at school"? We were inseparable. For years, we were like family.'

'Don't I know it,' Amita said under her breath.

'Inseparable? How come I've never heard of her then?'

He could cut the tension between the two of them with a knife. The living room had suddenly become a battlefield. And he was in No Man's Land.

'Do you want to tell him, Mum? Or will I?' said Radha, still scrolling through her phone, deliberately avoiding eye contact.

'That's not fair, Radha,' said Amita. 'It was a long time ago. You're grown up now. You both are.'

'Does someone want to tell me what's going on here? What have I missed?'

There was no answer forthcoming. Radha stared down at her phone. Amita stared down at her slippers.

'This is ridiculous,' he said, throwing his arms up in the air. 'What could possibly be so bad that the two of you are literally speechless? Did this Sarah woman murder somebody? Did she steal from your piggy bank? What?'

Radha looked up. She held her phone up to Jason, the website of Askling Manor on the screen.

'She's the owner and chief operating officer,' she said. 'Her bio on the website says she inherited the resort from her parents when they died. Looks like she made something of herself after all, eh Mum?'

Amita didn't respond. She was still staring down at her feet, a piece of chalk being turned over and over in her hands.

'I said what I said and I did what I did, Radha,' she said, her voice low. 'Nothing can change that now. I thought I was doing the right thing, for you, for the family. You can't hold a grudge over something that happened a long time ago.'

'Actually, that's the definition of a grudge,' said Jason.

That drew scalding looks from both of them. He swallowed a dry gulp.

'I'm just saying, that's all,' he held up his hands. 'Don't shoot the messenger, especially when he doesn't have a clue as to what's going on.'

Radha dropped her death stare. She stood up and shoved her phone in her pocket.

'I'm going to bed,' she said. 'I've got to get up early in the morning, see the kids off, that kind of thing. If your investigations take you to Askling Manor then say hello to Sarah for me, would you? I'm sure she'll be *delighted* to see you again, Mum. After all these years.'

She stomped out of the living room, slamming the door behind her. Jason had learned to get used to doors banging in the house. The kids put on an exhibition tantrum from time to time and he had to admit he was just as guilty of doing it when he wanted to punctuate a point too. Even Amita, when she was really riled, could give a door a good slam. A proper hinge rattler.

When the loud bang had stopped ringing in Jason's ears, he turned to his mother-in-law. Her face was pulled tight, lips pursed, eyes focused now on the blackboard.

'Well?' he asked. 'Do you want to tell me what's suddenly sent my wife to bed at seven in the evening? I'd like to know before I go up to the lion's den.'

'It's nothing,' she said curtly. 'Just a disagreement that happened a very long time ago. It's not worth reopening old wounds.'

'That's not how it looks from where I'm standing,' he said. 'The wound looks well and truly gaping from here.'

Amita looked hard at the blackboard. He could tell she was miles away, deep in thought, going over what had just happened and how they had got there. She always flexed the tendons in her temples when she was thinking hard. It was a little tell that Jason had picked up on over the years. Right now those tendons were tighter than piano strings.

'We should probably try to speak with some of the others from the production,' said Amita. 'Build up a better picture of what Simon Nakamba was like on set. We can't just rely on one person's testimony, even if that is the star of the show. It wouldn't be fair or thorough.'

So much for this being a purely theoretical exercise. Their impromptu chat with Pip Potter seemed to have upgraded this into full-scale investigation. Jason winced when he thought about how he'd explain this one to Sally. But at the same time he wasn't trying to persuade Amita out of it. She knew he had the bit between his teeth too.

'A trip to Askling Manor then?' he asked. 'Should I pack my swimming trunks?'

Amita didn't reply. A part of her mind was clearly still brooding over her conversation with her daughter. Jason knew he should leave the subject well alone.

Then again, he was a journalist. And that made him a nosey parker by nature.

Chapter 12

WHERE YOU LEAD

Askling Manor looked indomitable on the horizon. The stately, medieval country house was squat and sturdy. It had weathered centuries of Cumbrian snow, sleet, rain and sunshine. Not that you could tell. The whole building was stout and proud, defiant almost, against the rolling countryside a few miles south of Penrith.

Jason always liked driving this way. He believed that the splendour of Cumbria was at its finest round here. He wasn't quite sure where the notion had come from, only that he'd believed it to be true since he was a little boy. Askling Manor only helped his theory. The grand main building was now considered one of the best hotels in the area, and it was famous for its equally well-known guests and their entourages.

'We should be very careful in here,' said Amita.

She hadn't spoken very much on the journey. Breakfast had been a curt affair. Radha had remained pretty much silent, deliberately avoiding her mother's gaze and dashing off to work early. Amita, in turn, hadn't tried to build any bridges or share words. The kids had, thankfully, remained ignorant as he bustled them off to school. But Jason felt like he was stuck in the middle of the two superpowers of his household.

He knew better, however, than to go prodding. If they didn't want to talk about Sarah Paris then that was fine. For now.

'The truth will out,' he said to himself.

'What's that?' asked Amita.

Jason panicked for a moment. He had been lost in his own thoughts, replaying the argument from the night before and at breakfast. He hadn't realised he had spoken aloud.

'Nothing,' he said, panicking a little.

The road curved around. The distinctive silhouette of Askling Manor vanished behind the tops of the trees. Everything felt a little more claustrophobic here, although Jason suspected it was the elephant in the room making him feel a little close. The road weaved around through the wood until a splendid entrance came into view. They pulled in and followed the long driveway, lined by imperious pine trees that all stood to attention as they passed.

The main entrance of the estate opened up before them. The car park was filled with sports cars and SUVs that flaunted their expense. Jason felt broke just for taking a look. He pulled up at a quiet corner of the forecourt outside the resort and they climbed out.

'What's the plan then?' he asked, feet crunching on the sandy gravel.

'I was sort of hoping you might have an idea,' said Amita. 'I don't imagine they'll simply let us stroll in and start fraternising with the cast and crew, do you?'

'No, I shouldn't have thought so,' he said. 'Especially when their director has just been murdered. Which reminds me.'

He stopped and peered about the car park. His mouth curled and he let out a grunt.

'What is it?' she asked.

'I don't see any police around here,' he said. 'That's a bit strange, don't you think? The main man at the helm of this whole production was savagely killed just a few nights ago, everyone who is anyone is holed up in this luxury hotel and there isn't a single bobby on the beat.'

Amita frowned. She hadn't noticed the lack of a police presence on the way in. Her mind was a million miles away. Now that Jason said it, it was glaringly obvious. She cursed herself for not noticing.

'It does seem odd,' she said. 'Perhaps they've done all they can with witnesses and the like.'

'Yeah, but you would think they would be protecting the rest of the production,' said Jason. 'I mean, what if we were the killers? We could just stroll up like this, walk in the front door and pick off anyone we liked.'

'That's quite enough of that sort of talk, Jason,' Amita tutted. 'I know I'm in spry shape but I don't think I'd easily get mistaken for an assassin.'

'I don't know,' he said, looking down at her feet. 'Those sequined trainers scream "international hitwoman-for-hire" chic.'

They walked through the main doors and into the lobby of the resort. It was grand yet welcoming at the same time, immaculately modern inside, despite the ancient exterior. Guests and staff were busy whizzing around in front of them and nobody seemed to notice their arrival. It was for the best, thought Jason, he was doing an awful lot of staring. He'd never been to this place but had heard plenty of chatter. Lavish luxury in the heart of Cumbria, that sort of thing. Now he was here it was clear the public relations people had been spot on.

'Can I help you?' came a friendly, if slightly firm, voice from behind.

Jason and Amita turned around in unison. A short man in a hotel uniform of tie, waistcoat and smart jacket was glaring at them from behind the main reception desk. His delicate features remained prim and proper, although his eyes were burrowing into both of them.

'Bugger,' Amita whispered. 'We've been rumbled already and we're only just in the door.'

'Hang on,' said Jason, suddenly hit with inspiration.

He strode purposely over to the reception desk. The staff member watched his every move, measuring him up as he approached.

'Good morning, my man,' said Jason, affecting a plummy Received Pronunciation.

Anita managed to swallow at least some of her surprise. She kept her mouth firmly shut, despite wanting it to dangle open at her son-in-law's sudden change of accent.

'Jeffrey Brazel-Smythe,' he went on. 'I'm a reporter for *About Town* magazine, you've heard of us, I'm sure.'

The man behind the desk cocked an eyebrow. Jason didn't give him a chance to answer.

'Seems like the johnnies on the newsdesk got the times all mixed up for my interview with Derek Veland,' he went on. 'I was supposed to be here two nights ago but I've only just got off the train you see – rescheduled after all that nasty business with the director chappy. Any chance you could point me in Derek's direction? Much appreciated.'

Jason tried to remain calm. He wasn't quite sure where any of this was coming from. But, like most things in his journalism career, he just went with it. He was even warming to his performance as he continued. He wished he'd put on a cravat that morning. Although, of course, he'd have to actually own a cravat before being able to wear one, he supposed.

'And who is... this?' asked the man, looking over at Amita.

'Keep up, old chap,' Jason snorted. 'This is my photographer. You couldn't expect me to take the snaps, lord no. I don't know my way around the camera at all. That's why I've got Dulcie here as my right-hand woman. Isn't that right, Dulcie?'

Amita nodded silently, left an awkward pause then mimed taking a photo, as if she was in a rather slow game of charades.

'So there you are,' Jason turned back to the receptionist. 'I don't want to rush you, old bean, but we're hoping to catch the train back down to London this afternoon. A quick in and out and we'll be out of your hair.'

The man behind the desk considered all of this. Jason continued to stare at him. He knew he was pushing his luck here. He was hardly dressed like a society writer for some upmarket lifestyle magazine. The dirty anorak and ill-fitting stonewashed jeans were a bit of a giveaway. But he'd remained confident, imperviously so and he just hoped it was enough to get them through the door. The posher you were, the scruffier you were, someone had once told him. If that really was the case, then he might be mistaken for being very, very posh – or so he hoped.

'Very well,' sighed the receptionist. 'The sooner these television people are out of my hair the better, if you ask me.'

'And why's that?' asked Amita, finally finding her voice.

'Demand, demand, demand, that's all it is,' he said bitterly. 'We usually cater to a certain type of guest here at Askling Manor. Not the riff raff that's meandered through the doors at all hours with *these* particular guests.'

'That's a little snobbish, don't you think?' asked Amita, her hackles rising.

The man sneered horribly at her. He was about to say something when Jason intervened.

'Oh don't listen to Dulcie,' he laughed. 'She's a world class photographer but her politics are a little questionable at times. She'd have us all sharing a bath plug if she could. Wouldn't you, deary?'

That drew a haughty laugh from the receptionist. Jason chortled too. Amita's face was like a slab of concrete.

'Very good,' he said, wiping away a tear from his mousy little eyes. 'Mr Veland is in the Ruskin Suite, on the top level. I can phone him and let him know you're on your way.'

'No, no,' said Jason, batting him away with a flouncy hand. 'I'd rather surprise him. We were both dry bobs at Eton together. The blighter used to copy my homework ahead of class and the beaks never knew any different. Can you believe that?'

He tugged Amita away from the desk and walked quickly towards the staircase at the far side of the lobby. When they were safely out of earshot, she turned to him.

'Dry bob? Beaks? Eton, what was *that* all about, Jason?' she asked. 'How do you know where Derek Veland went to school?'

'I don't have the foggiest notion, Amita,' he said, climbing the stairs. 'But you know these thespian types, they're all the same, all old public school boys. We were in a bit of a bind and I had to think fast, didn't I? I thought I'd chance my arm and use some of the old Brazel razzamatazz on that oaf at the front desk to get us in. And it worked, didn't it?'

Amita smiled wryly. It *had* worked. They climbed the stairs and made their way through the hotel until they reached the top floor. There was nobody about, the corridors silent and empty. Passing by the doors, they came to the end of the hallway. A small, brass plaque that read *Ruskin Suite* was positioned above the electronic lock.

'Mr Veland likes his champagne, I see,' said Amita, noting the empty bottles, dirty plates and cutlery left on a tray beside the door.

'An insatiable appetite for life,' Jason agreed.

He knocked on the door once. There was no response. He tried again. Still nothing. He looked at Amita.

'Maybe he's not up yet,' he said.

Amita checked her watch.

'It's gone nine thirty,' she said disapprovingly. 'A man of his standing should be up and about, seizing the day.'

'Steady on, Amita,' said Jason. 'He's an actor, and a lush, by the looks of things.'

He nudged one of the empty bottles with his toe.

'We don't all have kids to take to school and mothers-in-law who like to chase down savage killers.'

'You know what I mean, Jason,' she said.

She knocked on the door of the suite. Once again there was no answer from the other side.

'Maybe he's gone out?' said Jason. 'Or he hasn't come home yet.'

'Or maybe something more sinister has happened to him.'

Jason didn't like the sound of that. There was an ominous note to his mother-in-law's tone. The lack of police around the hotel had seemed like a minor quirk only a few moments ago. Now, with no answer at Derek Veland's door, it all seemed a little darker.

'Surely not,' he said. 'I mean... There's probably a dozen reasons as to why he's not answering his door.'

'Like?' she asked.

'Like...'

Jason didn't have the luxury of getting to think. Heavy footsteps were thumping up the corridor. He peered over Amita's shoulder and saw the snippy receptionist doing his best not to break into a run. He was accompanied by two other men, both dressed in the same uniform although they looked much burlier and brutish.

'Damn,' said Jason.

'What? What is it?' asked Amita, looking around.

'You!' shouted the receptionist. 'Stop right there! This is a private hotel and you're trespassing!'

'Quick!' Amita grabbed Jason hand.

She pulled him across the corridor away from the Ruskin Suite. Shouldering a door open, they spilled into a drafty stairwell.

'I thought it would have taken longer for them to realize I'm a fraud!' Jason shouted after Amita, chasing her down the stairs. 'I mean, I thought I was pretty convincing!'

'Just keep running!' she said.

The receptionist and his goons were close behind. Jason could hear them clanking down the stairs behind them. This was a nightmare. All he could think about was what would be put on the police report. He imagined the look of disappointment DI Arendonk would give him as she read out the rap sheet. A journalist caught impersonating a journalist and fleeing from posh hotel staff. Hardly his finest hour.

As bad as all of that was, it was nothing compared to the stakes Amita was playing with. She would be able to weather the embarrassment, Jason figured, even being the hot topic of gossip in Penrith would be bearable. But how would she fare in the face of outright exile from the bingo club if she was caught? Her fellow members might have loved one of their own saving the day or playing Miss Marple and piecing the clues together – but only if it was all strictly above board. The Penrith Bingo Club did not tolerate rule breaking – whether that came in the form of using the wrong kind of dabber or fraudulently gaining entry to a luxury hotel.

They reached the bottom of the stairs and another door. This time Jason was the first one through. A narrow, dank corridor was waiting for them on the other side. The place reeked of damp and the strip lights were flickering.

'Not so nice here,' he said.

'Hurry up,' Amita shoved him along the corridor, footsteps echoing after them.

She spotted a door ajar a little further up the hallway. Thinking fast, she bundled Jason inside. Before he could protest, she clamped a hand over his mouth. Hiding in the dark, they peered through the tiny gap. The receptionist and goons hurried past them. They didn't stop. Their footsteps and grunting slowly faded and both Jason and Amita breathed in relief.

'Bloody hell,' she said. 'That was close. I'm never letting you take the lead again, Jason. You get us into all kinds of trouble.'

'Me!' he yelped, freeing his mouth. 'I've lost count the amount of times you've rubbed people up the wrong way!'

'Yes, but you should know better.'

'I should know better? You're meant to be the elder stateswoman of this relationship.'

'I beg your pardon!'

'I'm just the lackey, here to do the heavy lifting. You're the one who always says you're the intellect and brains of the operation. In fact, you're the one who talked me into accompanying you here today.'

'Oh don't be ridiculous. You were keen as mustard – any whiff of a reason to keep digging around and you were here like a shot.'

'Would you two shut up?'

This third voice in the conversation gave them both a startle. The lights blinked on above them, revealing a small, cramped cupboard filled with towels and linen. Near the back wall was a large bin piled high with dirty laundry. The heap began to move and stir until a face emerged from the bedsheets, pillowcases and other assorted dirties.

'Some of us have a hangover worthy of Zeus himself,' groaned Derek Veland, emerging erratically from the sheets, more pound-shop Poseidon than Zeus.

The actor pulled himself free of the laundry and rubbed his face. He sucked in a huge gulp of the close air of the cupboard and let out a filthy burp before flashing a devilish grin at Jason and Amita.

'How do you do?' he said, voice like a sputtering tank, loud and dramatic. 'I'm Derek Veland.' He gave an exaggerated bow, nearly stumbling into the stockpiles of bleach and tiny shower gels as he did so. When it became clear no gasp or round of applause was forthcoming from his meagre audience, he continued. 'Star of stage and screen. But you probably know that. Are you here with my room service?'

Jason and Amita had seen lots to shock them over the years. The sight of a renowned stage and screen star emerging from a mountain of hotel laundry and looking ready to either pass out or deliver a monologue to a shelf unit full of travel kettles was a possible contender for strangest of the lot.

Chapter 13

COLLEGE BOY

The deepening smell of stale alcohol, body odour and the kind of eye-watering cheap cologne she thought they'd stopped making in the 1980s almost brought a tear to Amita's eyes. Derek Veland was unsteady on his feet and about as dishevelled as a human being could possibly get. His long overcoat was stained and soaking wet, his shirt practically unbuttoned to the navel, his shoes squelching with every haphazard step.

He lumbered over from the laundry bin, patting his chest. Cursing quietly to himself, he eventually found a crooked cigarette perched behind his ear.

'Ah, there we are,' he said, placing it with remarkable finesse between his puckered, cracked lips. 'You wouldn't happen to have a light between you?'

'I don't smoke,' said Jason, entranced by the actor.

'Good man,' he said, winking slowly. 'It's incredibly bad for your chest and ruins the throat. Can you believe that they used to tell you it was good for you? Can you believe that?'

'I can,' said Jason. 'And, if you know it's bad for you, why are you still doing it?'

Veland puffed out his chest. He tried to ogle Jason but his lack of balance was defeating him. He stood sideways, as if about to start a duel, dropped a shoulder, a bulging eye lolling around and settling on him.

'Because I'm a bloody idiot, that's why,' he slurred. 'And idiocy does what idiocy wants.'

'You're not supposed to smoke inside anyway,' said Amita, more to cover the fact that she too would have done anything for a cigarette right now.

Veland rounded on her. His slightly glum aggression twisted immediately. He pushed his hair from his eyes and sniffed loudly.

Amita prepared for a tirade about his right to smoke wherever he wanted. Veland seemed like a man rather used to getting his own way.

'Madame, you are, quite honestly, the most beautiful woman I have ever seen in my life,' he said, head held high.

'Pardon me?' Amita blurted, unable to keep the smile from her face.

'It's true,' the actor went on. 'I've performed in every theatre, every club, every dive and den from Keswick to Kolkata, London to Little Rock, Shenyang to Santiago de los Caballeros, and *you* are by far the most gorgeous creature I have ever had the distinguished pleasure of resting my eyes on. You know, I've always liked an older woman – life experience, it makes things, shall we say – interesting?'

'Oh stop it,' said Amita, waving a hand at him. 'You're quite clearly still drunk, Mr Veland.'

'Nonsense,' he said, smiling at her, arms outstretched. 'I'm never drunk during daylight hours. But, if you're offering to top me up, as the Bard once wrote, good friends, go in and taste some wine with me.'

He pointed a quivering finger towards the door and marched past them. Pulling it open, Jason and Amita could do nothing but follow him. They checked that the coast was clear, no sign of the receptionist and staff.

'Mr Veland, I think we should get you back to your suite,' said Jason. 'And perhaps you'd be so kind as to answer a couple of questions we'd like to ask you.'

'You can't be serious, Jason,' Amita whispered to him. 'The man is drunker than a barrel full of monkeys!'

'Don't *you* start quoting lyrics now too,' he snapped.

'What lyrics?'

Jason shook his head. He gently tapped on Veland's shoulder and guided him back down the hallway towards the fire escape.

'Why don't we head back to your room, eh? Have a nice little chat.'

'You're a saucy one,' Veland scoffed. 'I'll have you know that I'm not that sort of chap, Mr...?'

'Jeffrey Brazel-Smythe,' he said, affecting his accent again. 'I'm a reporter for *About Town* magazine and this is–'

'Oh Jason, give over,' said Amita with a weary sigh. 'Let's not go over all of that again. I don't think I could stand it.'

Veland gave them both a puzzled look. Jason reluctantly nodded. He wasn't sure he could keep up the charade much longer anyway. Not that Veland was in any fit shape to know who they were. He wasn't wholly convinced the actor even knew *where* he was.

'Yes, sorry,' he said. 'I'm Jason and this is Amita, my mother-in-law.'

'Ah, Amita, endless truth and friendship,' he smiled. 'Of course it is. I can't think of a better moniker for a woman of untamed attraction.'

He flung open his arms as if expecting Amita to swoon into them. She pulled away, helping Jason to guide him up the first few steps towards the third floor. They jostled the star back and forth, taking each step one at a time. Veland occasionally protested, rubbing his head and complaining about the pain, but they eventually made it. The third level of the hotel was still deserted as they stumbled to the door of his suite.

'Do you have a key, Mr Veland?' asked Amita, out of breath.

'Check his pockets,' said Jason.

He rummaged around in Veland's coat and found a keycard. Swiping it, the door of the suite unlocked and they were in. The room inside would have been lavish if it wasn't a complete wreck. The bed was unmade, the curtain rail hanging off the wall, a table and chairs upturned on the floor. There was a lingering odour of staleness that was making her feel quite ill.

They dumped Veland down on the edge of the bed and he flopped backwards, laughing at something. Amita immediately went over to the windows and opened them, fresh air gusting in for what she presumed was the first time in days, if not weeks. On the other side of the room, two large patio doors led to a small balcony and she threw those open too. Through the billowing drapes she could see the countryside rolling off into the horizon. A lovely view, if only she had time to enjoy it.

'I don't think this is a good idea,' she said, turning back to Jason. 'He's in no fit shape to answer our questions, Jason. Just look at him.'

'*Now* you think it's not a good idea? Not when you set up a blackboard and home incident room to rival GCHQ? Or when we walked in on Pip Potter wearing only cucumber and towelling? Suddenly you get some scruples? Well, we're in too deep now, I say. Tell me my brief turn as an old Etonian and the hundred yard dash we did to escape the staff wasn't for nothing, Amita. We might not get another shot at this,' he replied. 'I mean, yes, he's not exactly at his best, but it's better than nothing.'

'I don't know,' she said.

Veland was lying on the bed, arms spread wide. Some gentle snoring was making his nose whistle, his face set in a beatific, knowing smile. Amita raised her eyebrows.

'I'm not sure this is exactly ethical, Jason.'

'You might have considered that before you ducked under the crime scene tape yesterday – or, for that matter, when we got into that spot of bother with Mrs Mulberry last year. But what did you tell me then? Fine principles and lofty ideals are lovely things to have – but when there's a killer on the loose, there's not always time to play by the book.'

'Alright,' she nodded. 'Let's just be quick about it.'

Jason nodded too, as if he needed convincing himself. 'Most people might not have the highest opinion of journalists, but I have my own code of honour and I wouldn't tarnish it if I didn't think we might be doing some good. As well as the little matter of an exclusive, I admit.' He leaned over Veland.

'Derek,' he said, softly. 'Derek, wakey wakey. We want to ask you a couple of questions, if that's alright?'

The actor continued to snore. Jason looked at Amita and shrugged his shoulders.

'Mr Veland!' she suddenly shouted.

It was enough to jolt the TV star wide awake and almost send Jason crashing to the floor in fright.

'Bloody hell!' he gasped. 'That's everyone from here to Helvellyn wide awake.'

Amita ignored the jibe. She sat down beside Veland on the edge of the bed and gently rubbed his back.

'Are you feeling any better, Mr Veland?' she asked.

Veland seemed a little more together now. He was blinking and licking his lips.

'Water?' he croaked. 'I must have water.'

Jason headed for the ravaged mini bar and found an unopened bottle. He handed it to the actor who glugged down half in one gulp. Wiping his mouth on his sleeve, he puffed out his cheeks and looked about him.

'Rough night,' he said. 'Wait, didn't I have a cigarette?'

'And I told you, you aren't allowed to smoke inside,' said Amita.

He let out a sigh.

'Yes, of course,' he said. 'I still think you're beautiful though.'

'Oh brother,' Jason rolled his eyes.

'Mr Veland, we're here to ask you about Simon Nakamba, if you don't mind.'

'Simon?' the actor seemed suddenly deflated. 'Bloody awful what happened to him. Bloody awful. Came as a great shock to me.'

'I'll bet,' said Jason, unconvinced.

'Did you know him well?' asked Amita. 'I mean, aside from working on *The Locus*.'

'No, not really,' he sniffed. 'The man was a bit of an imbecile actually. A total prima donna. You always knew you were working on a Simon Nakamba set because he liked to remind you every ten seconds of how brilliant he was.'

'He was difficult to work with then?'

'Difficult?' Veland laughed and then spluttered into a coughing fit. 'He was impossible. Every day there was something new, some little irritation that he wouldn't let go. Don't get me wrong, he had cause enough to complain a lot of the time. You should see the state of some of the crew on this shoot. Honestly, you'd think we were putting on a school play, not shooting an award-winning crime drama. But anything could set him off. Short fuse, you know.'

He drained the bottle of water and set it down between his feet.

'We've heard from some of your colleagues that Nakamba was a perfectionist,' said Jason. 'Do you think that's what got him killed?'

'Colleagues?' Veland sneered. 'I'm an actor, not an accountant. I don't have *colleagues*. I have co-stars. Although I prefer to think of them as supporting cast. And even that's generous on this show. More accurate to say I've got people who try their best to ruin the shots I'm in and moan constantly about the bad food and working conditions. She usually gets up around one in the afternoon if you're lucky.'

'Pip Potter?' Amita asked nervously.

'The very same. You've spoken to her, I take it?'

'We have,' said Jason, feeling relieved again that at least this interview was being held with everyone fully-dressed.

'Christ,' said Veland. 'We'll never hear the end of how *utterly* devastated she is now. She'll be dining out on losing "a close personal friend and inspiration" on breakfast telly for years to come no doubt. I can almost hear her now. She'll be flapping her gums about how it's been "deeply traumatic" and yet "truly transformative for her creative process". If she gets on to how "the nation has lost one of its leading lights", you owe me a tenner.'

'You two don't get along, then?' asked Amita.

'That would be an understatement,' said Veland.

'And how were you with Simon?' asked Jason.

He rubbed his face, scratching at his days' old stubble. Getting up, he wobbled a little before finally steadying himself. Sauntering over to one of the few chairs that hadn't been destroyed, he unfurled a set of trousers.

'I told you, the man was a complete fruitcake,' he said, digging in the pockets. 'He wouldn't know my talent if it came up and slapped him across the face. Which I did, a few times actually.'

'You fought with him?'

'All of the time.' He found a lighter and a packet of ciga-rettes. 'He thought he was this big, tough working-class hero. A real man's man, you know? So there were a couple of times

I told him to show me what he had, show me his metal. Got a black eye from him once, though the darlings in makeup managed to hide it very well. I think he was expecting me to flounce off the show, or report him. But he picked the wrong chap. He could throw a punch but I always had the upper hand. I used to box at boarding school. I can handle myself, if that little twit wanted some rough stuff, and give as good in return.'

He threw some imaginary punches that almost sent him flying to the floor. Out of breath, he lit a cigarette.

Amita cleared her throat and nodded at a small sign on the wall by the door. Veland gave it a quick glance, puffing away.

'Not even in one's own boudoir?' he asked, squinting. 'Honest to god, what next? You can't smoke anywhere these days. If I choose to shorten my life in a hundred pleasurable ways, what business is it of anyone else?'

'It's a rather lovely hotel suite in a 12th-century country house, Mr Veland,' said Amita politely. 'I don't think the staff or owners give a fig about your lungs, but I expect they do care about their hand-painted silk wallpaper and what looks like a rather flammable antique four-poster bed.'

Veland made some inaudible grunt and waved her away. He took three long, burning draws on his cigarette before crushing it out on the carpet.

Amita winced.

'Wait a minute,' he said, looking around. 'How the hell did I get back in here?'

'We brought you up the stairs,' said Jason. 'You were in a laundry cart in a cupboard.'

'Oh, that's right,' he rubbed his forehead. 'Like I said, rough night. Are you two with the hotel then?'

'No, we're not,' said Amita, standing up. 'We're looking into Mr Nakamba's death.'

'So you're the rozzers?'

'No, we're not cops,' said Jason.

'You're not police and you're not staff. Who the hell are you then, if you pardon my rather profane French, and why the devil should I answer any of your questions?'

Amita looked awkwardly at Jason.

'We're just a pair of concerned private citizens, Mr Veland, that's all,' she said. 'The police are conducting their own murder investigation but we find that sometimes our friends in CID are rather too busy to look at every angle, so we like to think we're helping out the good folk of Penrith by making sure nothing gets overlooked, by deploying our own methods.'

'Your *own* methods?' He didn't sound convinced. 'Forgive me, my dear, but you don't look like much of a private investigator.'

'Your forgiveness will have to wait, Mr Veland,' she said with a flash of anger. 'And if you don't mind me saying, you're hardly looking or acting like the much-respected thespian that the public has come to cherish over the years of your career.'

Jason couldn't hide his smile. He contained a laugh and just about stopped himself from punching the air in celebration of Amita's comeback. Veland seemed to sense this and let out a half grunt of approval.

'Very good,' he said, tilting his head at her. 'Like I said before, you're beautiful, but forgive an old fool if that briefly blinded me as to your intellect, fair lady.'

Jason had rarely seen a hammier display than this outside of the gammon fridge in Co-Op. But then he watched Veland briefly drop the luvvie act as his body language changed.

'Look, I've been on the lash for the better part of thirty-six hours. You're lucky I'm able to stand up with the amount of booze and chemicals I've shoved down my throat in that time. Will there be anything else I can help you out with?'

Veland was getting impatient. The longer he was awake, the more sober he was becoming. Amita could tell that their time was up.

'No thank you, Mr Veland,' she said. 'I think we've probably taken up enough of your time as it is. Thank you, though, for your insight.'

She headed for the door. Veland stood to one side, feet crunching on broken glass scattered about the floor. Jason joined his mother-in-law. The actor stopped him with a heavy hand, fingers digging into his shoulder.

'You know, it would be a really dreadful shame if any of this got out, into the public realm,' he said, his voice ominous and brooding.

'Any what?' asked Jason, genuinely perplexed, Amita too.

'This,' Veland waved about the room. 'How I'm living here, how I look, where you found me, that sort of thing. I've got a bit of a reputation you know, as hard as that is to believe, but I'm rather respected in acting circles. And, as you so roundly say, Ms Amita, with the public too. I was once considered for James Bond, did you know that?'

'You?' said Jason, before he realised it was out.

'Yes,' the actor licked his lips. 'I think fans of *The Locus* have been put through enough over the last few days. I wouldn't want them having to read about my minor hijinks and escapades, would you? You know what these bloody journalists are like, they'll print anything these days if it gives someone a giggle. Just because I've had one too many sherries, doesn't mean I should be in the gossip columns, just because some scribbler lacks the skill to dig up some proper news. Wastrels, they are, wastrels.'

Amita had known Jason a very long time. She knew his quirks, his habits, how far she, or anyone else, could push his patience. She also knew all too well what set him off – including a slight on his professional integrity. The air seemed to fizz above his head now as he stood staring at Derek Veland, pupils shrinking to tiny pinpricks. Admittedly, neither gent looked like they were in a position to inflict much damage on one another – but they both looked willing to try.

'Nobody will hear about any of this, Mr Veland,' she said, stepping between them. 'You can rely on our discretion, you have my word. Isn't that right, Jason?'

It took a moment for Jason to acknowledge her. His jaw was clamped firmly shut, tendons flexing. Only when he felt Amita's hand on his chest easing him away from Veland did he snap out of his seething fury.

'Yes,' he said, biting back his urge to yell that he thought the public might be slightly more bothered about finding a murderer than knowing that Derek Veland couldn't make his own bed.

'That would be super,' said Veland with an arrogant laugh. 'Here, this might help to remind you a bit of your word.'

He pulled out a wad of fifty pound notes from his pocket. He pushed them into Jason's hand and clapped them, winking.

'Buy yourselves something nice on the way home, eh? A nice bottle of Bolly or something. Always nice to meet some fans. Dare say it was watching the show that got you into all this investigating stuff. It's another unseen burden I bear – being an inspiration to ordinary people like, well, like you two.'

Now it was Amita's turn to be angry. She contained herself long enough to get to the door, guiding Jason by the elbow. She was about to close the door of the suite behind her when Veland shouted out.

'And if you see the cleaners, tell them to shake a leg, would you? I'm living in squalor here.'

The door clicked shut. Jason and Amita stood for a moment, both simmering with anger, staring across the hallway, neither of them speaking. It took a moment or two for either of them to break the spell. Jason looked down at the money in his hand, over three hundred pounds, from what he could see.

'Lovely chap,' he said sarcastically. 'National treasure.'

'Yes,' agreed Amita. 'Thoroughly nice bloke.'

Chapter 14

THANK YOU FOR BEING A FRIEND

Amita wished she could take solace in the bingo club. But she was finding it hard to concentrate on anything after her run-in with Derek Veland. The arrogant actor's words were still ringing in her ears and seemed to dominate her waking thoughts. Veland's behaviour had, of course, raised the inevitable question – was *he* Simon Nakamba's murderer? Amita couldn't be sure.

There was no question of capability. Veland was a big man, capable of handling himself, and clearly prone to erratic and destructive outbursts when under the influence. The way he had stopped Jason dead, his physical presence, everything about him proved that, should he turn angry, there could be no stopping him. And he certainly hadn't spoken very highly of Simon Nakamba in the short time she had been in his company. Whether it was enough to make him a genuine suspect or not was another matter. He hadn't seemed like he had anything to hide – apart from the gossip columnists.

Amita knew all too well that she couldn't let her own dislike of Veland get in the way of her investigation. Although it was very hard to put to one side. The man was a boorish snob, drunk on his own celebrity, not to mention other things.

But she had been led astray by her dislike of people before. It was a dangerous tack to take. She had to be as impartial and unbiased as possible. That's what a good investigator would do, she thought.

She made her way across the church hall. It was strangely quiet. There were a few regulars at their seats on other tables. She gave them polite nods as she made her way to her usual spot. Only one person was at her table – Pauline Saxon. She checked her watch to make sure she hadn't got the time wrong.

'Evening Pauline,' she said, placing her bag down. 'It's quiet tonight. Where is everyone?'

Pauline Saxon hadn't been coming to the Wednesday night gatherings for very long. And as such, Amita knew next to nothing about her. She'd migrated to her table quite naturally and any time she spoke to her she had been polite and friendly. From what Amita had heard, mostly from Georgie, naturally, Pauline was new to Penrith and freshly retired from a career in IT. She seemed like a free spirit, easy-going and relaxed and not bothered by what the rest of the world thought of her, or the Penrith gossip grapevine. The baggy blouses, flouncy skirts, unkempt frizzy hair and sandals didn't scream Silicon Valley to her. Quite the opposite, in fact.

Pauline's two sandalled feet were up on the table now and she was sitting back in her chair, dozing. She wore a satisfied, utterly relaxed smile on her tanned face. She slowly blinked her eyes open.

'Oh, hello Anita,' she said, still smiling. 'I didn't hear you come in.'

Amita was going to correct her over the mistaken name. She hated doing things like that, always worrying it made her sound petty or, worse still, vain. She was just about building the courage when Pauline started stretching. She rolled her shoulders around and around before pulling one leg back far enough she could put it behind her head. Amita immediately looked away, embarrassed.

'Are you alright, Anita?' asked Pauline.

'I... erm... yes...' she said. 'I've... I've just never seen anyone who was able to do that before.'

'Do what?' asked Pauline.

'*That*,' she answered, thoroughly awkwardly.

She waved a hand back behind her at Pauline. She didn't dare look around. The other pensioner just laughed a little.

'Oh, right,' she said. 'Yes, sorry, I didn't get a chance to do my yoga this evening. I was in a bit of a rush and had to rush out of the door. I have to stretch though, otherwise I become stiff as a board.'

'Yes, I'm sure you do,' said Amita, still looking away.

'And if you think this is odd, you should have seen me ten years ago,' Pauline went on. 'I was like a pipe cleaner.'

Amita tried to remove the image of Pauline Saxon bending and contorting from her mind. She realised she couldn't keep standing there, looking away. She took a deep breath and turned back around, sitting down and trying not to stare at Pauline's rainbow leggings doing a passable impression of a boa constrictor. It didn't work, however. Pauline was still stretching, now with *both* ankles behind her head. Amita couldn't look away now – Pauline not only appeared to be defying the laws of physics, she also appeared to be risking a rather nasty accident. She was rocking a little back and forward on the firm plastic seat. Amita busied herself with getting her blotter and glasses from her handbag and hoped she wouldn't be called on to remember the first aid course she'd attended last year. So far the only time anyone had needed that was when one of the Rotary Club had accidentally inhaled the garnish on a yule log and Sandy had deployed the Heimlich. But if Pauline didn't stop her stretching, Amita predicted she'd be having to deploy her sewing kit. She feared a seam splitting almost as much as she feared Pauline taking a tumble.

Eventually Pauline stopped. She removed her legs from behind her head and let out a satisfied sigh.

'That's better,' she said. 'You were saying something, my lovely?'

Amita had forgotten pretty much everything in the face of her neighbour's chair acrobatics. Relieved to not be looking at parts of Pauline Saxon she didn't want to acknowledge, she felt her mind whirring back into action.

'I was just remarking on how quiet it is in here tonight,' she said. 'Bingo kicks off in ten minutes and there's hardly a soul in here.'

'I'm still new to all of this, I'm afraid,' said Pauline. 'I'm still struggling to remember everyone's names, tell the truth, Anita.'

Amita said nothing.

'How are you finding it all?' she asked instead. 'Are you enjoying being here in Penrith?'

'Oh yes,' said Pauline. 'It's such a different pace of life here to where I've been for the past thirty years.'

'And where was that?'

'Here and there,' she said. 'London, New York, Los Angeles.'

'Blimey,' said Amita.

'Tokyo, Hong Kong, Tel Aviv, Cape Town, Buenos Aires,' she went on. 'Melbourne, Amsterdam, Zurich. I met the most handsome yogi you're ever likely to see when I lived in Bangalore. He taught me how to control my Chitta, and another few things I won't mention in polite company.'

She winked at Amita who tried her best to ignore her.

'You're from India, no?'

'I'm from Penrith,' she said, in a voice that only thinly veiled how tired she was of being asked questions like this. 'By way of Sheffield. My parents immigrated and brought the family to England.'

119

'Of course,' said Pauline. 'I think the stern woman told me that.'

'Stern woman?' asked Amita.

'You know, the one who's always bossing everyone around, what's her name?' she clicked her fingers, searching for the answer.

'Georgie,' said Amita.

'That's the one,' Pauline laughed. 'I told you, I'm no good with names. She was here just a moment ago too.'

Amita had never been more relieved to know that Georgie was close by.

'Where did she go?' she asked.

'Out the back door, I think,' said Pauline, pointing lazily towards the back of the hall. 'Her and a few of the others said they had to collect something. I don't know, Anita, I wasn't really paying attention.'

She didn't hang around. Amita moved quickly from her usual spot, not wanting to explain herself to Pauline. She hurried over to the back entrance of the church hall and opened the heavy fire escape door. It creaked loudly enough on its hinges that the gathered crowd of pensioners on the other side all spun around with guilty looks on their faces. Georgie was there, clutching two heavy looking plastic bags. Judy Moskowitz, Barbara McLemore, Albert Chamberlain, all of the regulars were beside her. And at the centre of the gathering was Malcolm Brunger, smiling his crocodile smile as always, a large wheelbarrow filled to the top, with more plastic bags by his side.

'Amita, darling, lovely to see you!' he shouted, voice echoing off the damp walls of the little courtyard behind the hall. 'I'm just taking fresh orders, are you in?'

'In for what?' she asked.

'Scotch,' said Albert Chamberlain. 'Mr Brunger here has a contact up in Edinburgh who can get us whisky at cost price. Bloody bargain it is, too.'

He held up his own plastic bag and clinked together the bottles inside.

'And then there's butter,' Barbara McLemore piped up. 'It cost me five pounds just last week in the supermarket for a pack of butter. Mr Brunger got me the industrial stuff they use in bakeries for half of that.'

'That's right,' Brunger laughed. 'Half the price and double the amount. Lovely stuff.'

The gathering all agreed, passing quiet murmurs of approval around each other. Amita felt like she had disturbed some secret meeting of a cult.

'What are you doing out here in the cold?' she asked nobody in particular. 'You'll catch your death.'

'Yeah, it's a bit of a long story, that one,' said Brunger, scratching his ear.

'It's that bloody Father Ford,' said Judy Moskowitz. 'He's only gone and had a hissy fit about us getting our bargains from Mr Brunger here on church property.'

'What?'

'Yeah,' said Brunger. 'Seems that he didn't take too kindly to me offering him a complimentary bottle of imported Latvian vodka if he turned a bit of a blind eye.'

'Oh,' said Amita.

Brunger shrugged.

'Still, I've done business in a lot worse places, Mrs K, believe me,' he laughed. 'Now, who was next?'

There was a sudden scramble among the customers. Amita had to laugh as she watched Georgie Littlejohn and the others all waving their little receipts at Brunger and his wheelbarrow. For the briefest of moments, she was able to stop thinking about suspects and whether a killer was walking among them. It was a relief, to be sure. Even if it was all too fleeting.

'Ahem,' came a disgruntled voice from behind her.

Father Ford had appeared at her shoulder. He was looking stern, or as stern as a mild-mannered rural vicar could. He folded his arms, trying to look intimidating. It wasn't working and he quickly let them drop by his side again, more uncomfortable in his own skin than usual. Amita could see the sweat on his trembling top lip.

'I was about to start this evening's bingo, ladies and gentlemen,' he said, voice cracking just a little bit. 'But I see you are all very busy out here with Mr Brunger, instead.'

The collected club members stopped their impulse-buying. They all looked down to the ground, heads hung low like toddlers told off for eating too many biscuits. Slowly they began to trudge back into the church hall. Their bags clinked as they walked past Father Ford who, despite his nerves, was holding fast with his disapproval. The crowd dissipated, Georgie Littlejohn the last to traipse inside. She didn't look at Amita as she passed, and kept her head down as the vicar threw her a disapproving glare.

With the flock safely back in the church hall, Father Ford turned to Brunger. The ever-so-slightly dodgy trader was still smiling, his wheelbarrow all but empty of plastic bags.

'Same time again next week, Father?' he asked flippantly. 'I'll have some of those nice black cardigans that you like coming in from Albania in the week. They're about forty quid if you went up town but I'll let you have them for a tenner each as you're a man of the cloth.'

Father Ford turned scarlet, although Amita wasn't sure if it was from anger or embarrassment. He said something under his breath and motioned to close the fire exit door. Amita smiled wryly at Brunger who winked in her direction.

'See you around, Mrs K,' he said, giving a little bow.

The door slammed with a heavy clank that made her ears ring. With Brunger locked outside, Father Ford seemed to breathe a little easier. He slumped against the wall, blinking as he mopped his brow.

'Good grief,' he said.

'Are you alright there, Father?' asked Amita.

'What? Yes, absolutely, thank you Amita,' he gasped. 'I'm just not used to such dreadful confrontation. Did you see the murderous look in that man's eyes? I thought he was going to lunge at me with a knife for putting a stop to his black-market racketeering.'

It took all of Amita's effort not to burst out laughing. Mr Brunger, for all his patter, was hardly some prohibition-era mobster. All she could do was clap the vicar on the shoulder to reassure him that he was quite safe. They walked back into the main hall as everyone took up their seats. Amita returned to her table. She was relieved to see Pauline's legs were now back under the table and the others were looking suitably chastened for their retail frenzy. Sandy had arrived with Ethel who looked to be back in tip-top health.

'What's wrong with you lot then?' asked the big man. 'You've got faces like burst sofas.'

Nobody answered. He looked across at Amita.

'Something I said?' he asked.

'Economical ambiguity, Sandy,' said Amita. 'Best not to get involved if you're not already.'

'Ah,' he said, tapping his nose. 'Malcolm Brunger has been around then, has he? He'd sell his own grandmother.'

'Only if there was a demand for it,' she replied. 'And I'm not sure any of our friends here have need for another pensioner in their pantry.'

'No, quite,' Sandy laughed warmly. 'Although, that said, do you know what I've been after for a long time? One of those old wireless sets, you know the ones, with proper buttons and a tuner and all that. Like we used to listen to when we were kids.'

'The old Bakelite ones, yes!' said Amita.

'That's the one,' he snapped his fingers. 'They gave a good click when you turned the knobs. It's all touch screen this and digital that. I can't work the damn things. But one of those old radios would be magic.'

'And the smell,' she said. 'Do you remember the smell of those old wireless sets?'

'Oh don't, Amita,' he said. 'You'll set me off.'

'Well I'm sure Mr Brunger will be able to help you out on that front, Sandy. As you can see, he has quite the reputation as a crowd pleaser.'

'Yeah,' Sandy chuckled to himself as the game got underway.

If Brunger's presence had been a nice distraction, Sandy had warmed Amita's heart. Having him close by seemed to make everything that little bit brighter. And at the moment, with everything going on, that's exactly what she needed.

Chapter 15

CHICKEN MAN

There was an awkward silence in the living room at Jason's house. Nobody wanted to tell the others to switch off *The Locus*. Nobody wanted to put their head above the parapet. Jason, least of all. He'd already been scolded one too many times for daring to suggest that he didn't like or watch the show. Now they were all stuck watching a repeated episode that had been put on in tribute to Simon Nakamba.

Then there was the cold war between Amita and Radha to contend with. Things were starting to thaw slightly. There had been a brief interaction after bingo, an acknowledgement and an offer to put the kettle on. Jason could still feel the tension between them though. There was bad blood there, all stemming back to this Sarah Paris woman. They hadn't stuck around at Askling Manor to find out more about her and he didn't have the courage to go probing at home. Not tonight anyway.

'I can't believe how young Pip Potter looks,' said Radha, curled up on the sofa beside him.

'She's actually quite fresh faced in real life,' he said.

The words were out before he had a chance to even think about not saying them. A chance to think better of it.

'Oh really?' said Radha, accusingly. 'Would this be from when you were left in a room with her and she was wearing nothing but a dressing gown and a smile?'

'Radha, come on, play fair,' he said. 'Not only was your mother there too, but so was her massage therapist and a runner. And I spent the majority of the time staring at the floor and feeling ridiculous. Amita, tell her!'

Amita didn't answer him. She was staring at the screen, biting her thumbnail. She was lost in the episode, watching the action unfolding for the tenth time since it was originally broadcast years ago.

'Mum's silence speaks volumes, Jason,' said Radha.

'I was mortified!' he yelped. 'I barely looked at her. We wouldn't have even been there if it hadn't been for your mother's insistence. Have a go at her!'

'You seemed to put your embarrassment to one side long enough to notice how young her complexion looks,' she said.

'She's a TV star!' he said. 'They're always rubbing unicorn's blood over their faces and all of that sort of thing in search of eternal youth. I was merely remarking that she was noticeably younger-looking in real life than she sometimes appears on screen.'

'So it's all about looks with you, is it Jason?' Radha continued. 'Do you have any idea how difficult it is for actors, especially female actors, to continue getting decent parts the older they get? And that's mostly down to people like you who have such an unhealthy focus on how they look and what their complexion is like.'

'But... but...'

Jason looked across at Amita again, hoping for at least something to help with his protests. His mother-in-law was still engrossed watching the TV. Jason turned back to Radha, ready for another plea. But he stopped before he could start. She was sat beside him, a devilish grin on her face.

'You bugger!' he shouted, throwing a cushion at her. 'You're winding me up, aren't you?'

'Of course I am!' she threw the cushion back at her husband. 'What do you take me for? A total numbskull? You get awkward if you see a glimpse of ankle or a smooch on the TV – I don't have you down for lascivious behaviour towards bona fide celebs!'

Jason let his head rest back on the sofa, wondering why he fell for Radha's wind-ups every time.

'You gave me quite a fright there,' he said. 'I thought I was in proper bother.'

'Oh come on Jason, behave yourself,' said Radha. 'Pip Potter would eat you alive, anyway.'

He frowned and turned to face her.

'Pardon me?' he asked. 'I was only looking away from her to shield her from my rugged machismo, I'll have you know.'

Radha laughed and nodded at the screen.

'Looks like our favourite actress is about to meet a gruesome end.'

The action was fast and blurry on the screen. Pip was speeding in a police car through the streets of London or Manchester, Jason couldn't tell which. She lost control and the motor went screeching off the road, smashing through a wall and flying through the air before landing in a canal with an almighty splash. The last scene was of Pip Potter struggling with the door as the squad car sank below the surface. Then the credits rolled.

'I bet she survives,' Jason snorted.

'Of course she does, there's another two series after this. And they're filming the new one now,' said Radha.

'If they carry on filming after all that's gone on,' said Amita.

'Oh you've decided to join us, have you?' asked Jason.

'What?'

'You were locked in a trance watching an episode you've probably seen a dozen times already,' he said. 'And you weren't very helpful when my wife, your daughter, was accusing me of having an affair with Pip Potter.'

'An affair?' Amita said. 'You? And Ms Potter? Come off it Jason, she's gorgeous.'

'And what is that supposed to mean?' Jason added with faux-indignance.

'I'm not so sure airing that was such a fitting tribute to Simon Nakamba,' said Amita, reclining in her armchair. 'There was an awful lot of violence in that one,' she shook her head. 'I just don't think it's appropriate given he was murdered. Crime feels a lot less cosy when it's on your street not on your screen.'

'True. More tea?' asked Radha.

Amita and Jason both said yes. Radha went off to the kitchen to put the kettle on. The pair sat in silence.

'What are you thinking?' he asked his mother-in-law.

'I'm not sure,' said Amita, still biting her nails. 'We've spoken to Pip Potter and Derek Veland now. Neither of them seemed to think very highly of their director.'

'True,' he sighed. 'Do we think Nakamba's temper and all of his antics are enough to warrant him being killed?'

'Nothing warrants anyone *ever* being killed, Jason. You know that.'

'You know what I mean,' he said. 'We've been down this road before and you know that motive is the key. Simon Nakamba might have had a temper on him and he sounds like a total nightmare to work with. But is that really enough to drive someone to murder? And if so, why now? Why here? He's had an illustrious career. What's so special about this shoot here in Penrith? What if it was just bad luck – he stumbled across a drug deal or yelled abuse at the wrong bloke outside a pub?'

'Forget it, Jason. That pose, that location – this is deliberate, remember. Penrith isn't short of dark snickets and corners, but they picked the concert hall. This is personal. But personal to who?' She steepled her fingers under her chin. 'I'm just not sure. People can do very strange things when they're pushed to their limits. We've seen that plenty of times. Potter and Veland are too obvious, too ready to tell strangers they didn't like their director. It's the quiet ones we need to find.'

'Ain't that the truth,' Jason rubbed at the back of his head.

Amita pored over everything in her head. She stood up and walked over to the blackboard still sitting in front of the fire. She blew out her cheeks.

'Nevertheless,' she said. 'There was something about Derek Veland that just didn't sit right with me. I don't think he's our killer but he's hiding something.'

'Is this the leading man?' asked Radha, bringing in the tea.

'Yes, we found him to be open enough, if a little unsteady on his feet.'

'Absolutely bladdered,' added Jason. 'And smelling like a brewery by all accounts.'

'He was definitely unstable,' said Amita. 'One minute he's sitting opening up about fisticuffs with Nakamba, the next he's throwing bank notes at Jason and I and insisting we don't go to the press.'

'Happens all the time,' said Jason. 'These big stars don't want the bad publicity coming out when it's not on their own schedule. They like to hide their vices until the very last minute. Then, when a newspaper gets a sniff, they'll do a big high profile sit-down interview with them and give them the exclusive story, on their terms, of course.'

'If he was drunk or high when you spoke to him, you can't reasonably take his behaviour as being reflective of who he is,' said Radha. 'He can always plead diminished responsibility due to his addictions. You can see the weepy, self-centred interviews already…'

Amita nodded. 'But I don't see Pip Potter being able to murder Simon Nakamba and then dump his body outside the theatre either.'

'How do you know he wasn't killed there?' asked Radha.

'We worked it out,' said Jason, pointing at a little chalk timeline along the bottom of the blackboard. 'If he left the restaurant before us, then he must have gone somewhere else. If he'd gone straight to the theatre steps and been killed there, somebody would have found him before the morning. There would still have been people knocking around the set until late last night.'

'So he's left dinner in a tizz, gone somewhere else, been murdered and then dumped at the concert hall,' said Radha.

'That's what we think,' said Amita.

'Your killer needs to be physically strong then,' she said. 'Not necessarily to overpower Nakamba, he was pretty kaylied when we saw him. But to move him, that's no mean feat. What about murder weapon or cause of death? Have the police released those details?'

'No,' said Jason. 'Just that there were marks on his arms when they found the body. I was thinking about asking DI Arendonk if she might have any other snippets I could share but, truth be told, I don't think I could look her in the eye right now. All it would take is one of her hard looks and I'd confess all about our jaunt to Askling Manor.'

The late-night news was on now. Radha turned the volume up as a story on Nakamba's murder started. A reporter was standing at the edge of the set, the theatre crime scene in the background.

'Simon Nakamba's body was found here, in the centre of Penrith, earlier this week,' said the journalist. 'The police confirmed that the death is being treated as suspicious and they have launched a murder investigation. The cause of death has not yet been released. An outpouring of grief has been felt from the entertainment industry where Simon Nakamba was a well-liked and respected figure. Pip Potter, star of *The Locus*, which is filming here in Penrith at the moment, had this to say about the late director.'

The screen cut to a video package showing Nakamba on various red carpets. He was smiling, waving to the cameras, suave and smart in a tuxedo that covered his barrel chest. Pip Potter appeared on screen, perfect makeup, eyes a little watery.

'I just can't believe that he's gone,' she said. 'He was bursting with life, so enthusiastic. He loved working on this show and thought that the new series was going to be the best yet. He was a kind, generous, giving man who had time for absolutely everyone on set. I'm going to miss him beyond words.'

Amita snorted a little.

'Mum?' asked Radha. 'Are you alright?'

'Nothing,' she said. 'It's just, well, Ms Potter has said everything that Derek Veland rather bitterly said she would. Almost word for word, like she was reading from a script. Rather convincing tears though – I wonder if she's hiding half an onion just out of shot.'

The broadcast played more highlights from Nakamba's career before cutting back to the reporter at the crime scene.

'There has been no official word from the production company whether filming will continue in light of Simon Nakamba's murder,' he said. 'Or what tributes are being planned for the director. Local police say that their investigations are continuing and that they hope to have a breakthrough soon. Back to the studio.'

Radha turned the volume down again.

'There we have it,' she said. 'Officially the police are no further forward.'

'It's a real brainteaser this one,' said Jason, draining his mug. 'A director that nobody likes, two stars who talk absolute rubbish in public and hated his guts behind the scenes. And nothing to go on but a body outside the concert hall. What about this imminent breakthrough – what have they got they're not telling people about?'

Amita chimed in too. 'Precisely. Where's the CCTV evidence, where's the public appeal for people seen around the time of death?'

'I suspect they're not releasing that information direct to the inner circle of the Penrith bingo club, Mum,' laughed Radha. It was the friendliest the pair had been in days.

'Perhaps,' said Amita. 'Or perhaps not.'

'You've got a plan?' asked Jason.

'I think we should do a little more digging into Derek Veland,' she said, tapping his name on the board. 'As always, it's not what people tell us that really matters – it's what they don't say that counts.'

'And what about Nakamba?' asked Jason. 'Don't you think we should stand up some of the things that are being said about him?'

'What do you mean?' asked Amita.

'Well, the guy can't defend himself, can he?' he said. 'We're taking at face value what Pip, Veland and Lisa the runner are saying about him. As we've just seen, Pip Potter is an outstanding actress who can turn on the tears when she wants to. Veland is a drunk and a lothario. And Lisa is just a runner on set with no experience to benchmark things against. Hardly top-quality character witnesses, are they?'

She thought about what he was saying for a moment. Then agreed.

'Good point,' she said. 'Why don't you take Nakamba's history and I'll look into Veland? We can cover more ground that way.'

'Fine,' said Jason. 'Just promise me you can defend yourself if he tries any funny business.'

Amita nodded at her handbag, never out of her reach. Jason wasn't sure if it was the most effective weapon but, then again, he would never dare look inside it to see what his mother-in-law was carrying. He yawned. Amita was hovering over him. He looked up at her.

'What?' he asked.

'What are you waiting for?'

'Pardon me?'

'Well?'

'It's almost eleven at night, Amita!'

'Don't put off until tomorrow what you can do today,' said Amita. 'My dear mother used to say that, didn't she Radha?'

'She did,' said Radha. 'She was also as mad as a box of frogs. So you'll forgive me if I don't take Granny Matangini's sage wisdom as something to live by.'

'That's your grandmother you're talking about,' said Amita.

'Fresh eyes in the morning I think, Amita' said Jason.

'Fine,' Amita huffed. 'If you're not going to make a start, then I will. Goodnight to you both.'

She stormed out of the living room, closing the door with a dramatic thump behind her. Jason looked at his wife and frowned.

'Now you've done it,' he said. 'You've questioned the sanity of Granny Matangini. I'll be dealing with the fall out of that remark for months.'

'It was true!' said Radha. 'The woman used to collect pictures of cakes and keep them in a scrapbook. And she was diabetic too.'

Family heritage aside, Jason was ready for bed. He stretched again and went to the door. He stopped just shy of the handle.

'What's wrong?' asked Radha.

'I'm going to have to do some work before bed, aren't I?' he asked her, wincing.

Radha smiled. She got up, collected the mugs and kissed him on the cheek.

'You're a good son-in-law,' she said.

Somehow that didn't make Jason feel any better as he thought of the prospect of the wee small hours illuminated only by the glow of his laptop screen.

Chapter 16

BRAND NEW DAY

The first watery light of dawn crept through the crack in the curtains of Amita's room. It was enough to wake her up, and in a bad mood. She sat up, her phone dropping from her chest and onto the floor with a thump. It took her a moment to realize where she was and what had happened. She must have dozed off sometime in the early hours. She was still in her tracksuit and slippers.

'Morning, sunshine!'

Amita almost jumped out of her skin. As her eyes adjusted to waking up, she'd completely missed the fact that Jason was sitting in the corner. A sudden embarrassment came over her and she scrambled about for her duvet.

'Jason!' she shouted. 'What are you doing in here!'

'Eh, it's my house, Amita,' he said.

'Yes, I know that, I'm all too aware of that fact. What I mean is, what are you doing *here* in my bedroom? You're never here! Were you watching me sleep?'

'What? No!' he shouted back. 'What kind of weirdo do you take me for?'

'I won't answer that question.'

'Actually, I was here to give you an early morning coffee and a hash brown,' he said, licking his fingers. 'But I got bored waiting for you to wake up so I ate it. Your coffee is here though.'

He got up and handed Amita a still-steaming mug. She gratefully took it, still clutching her duvet up around her chest.

'And I have some even better news to report,' he said.

'This had better be good,' she said. 'I'm not used to being woken up like this, with strange men watching me while I sleep. I'm a pensioner, I have rights you know.'

'The right to remain silent seems to have slipped your mind,' he said under his breath.

'What was that?'

'Nothing,' he said. 'Look, we're wasting valuable time here. I did some digging around last night, despite my hope that I might actually get to bed at a reasonable hour.'

'And?' she asked.

'Well,' he pulled out some folded printouts from his back pocket and sat down on the edge of Amita's bed. 'It would seem that both Pip Potter and Derek Veland were right.'

'About what?' she asked, the warm smell of coffee chasing away her sleepiness.

'It would seem that Mr Simon Nakamba was not what you would call the calmest of characters.'

'We knew that Jason – you and Radha saw him in full flow. What we need to establish is if there's a pattern of behaviour or just a recent turn of events.'

Jason began flipping through the pages. Amita took them one by one. Each was a news report he had printed out. There were various pictures of Nakamba throughout his career. Some showed him to be very young.

'He burst onto the scene in the late nineties,' Jason went on. 'Fresh out of RADA where he was top of his class in technical theatre and stage management. He bummed around for a couple of years working on little projects, small independent films that were nominated for awards. Nothing that made any money, that sort of thing. Then finally, about six years after he graduated, he gets a chance to direct something at The Globe in London for the Royal Shakespeare Company.'

'*Much Ado About Nothing*,' said Amita, finding a review.

'That's it. He's in with the bricks now, or so he thinks,' said Jason. 'The show is a bit of a flop; critics called it a bit too contemporary for Shakespeare. Which makes sense, I guess, when you have your characters all Gulf War veterans and that sort of thing. I prefer my Shakespeare to be ruffs and tights, personally.'

'And when was the last time you saw anything by Shakespeare?' she asked.

'Touché,' said Jason. 'Anyway, regardless, Nakamba's reputation as this hot-shot young director takes a bit of a battering. Until he heads to the States and falls in with the Hollywood crowd. He does some TV work over there and then, in 2012, he gets tapped up to direct a big comic-book blockbuster. It's the coup he's been waiting for, the golden ticket. Only…'

'Things don't go to plan,' said Amita, staring down at a news report from the time.

'No, they don't,' said Jason. 'Rumours of in-fighting, bullying, misogyny, the works, are swirling around him. The studio bosses have enough of this upstart troublemaker from England and sack him after about three months. It's a disgrace and he flies back home and seems to fall off the face of the earth. That is until a little cop show called *The Locus* shows up on late-night TV and becomes an immediate hit.'

'He's given a lifeline,' said Amita. 'A chance at redemption. The show is a massive success and he's back on the awards ceremony circuit, and now the nation mourns his loss.'

'Exactly,' said Jason.

He sat back and awaited the adulation for his night's work. Amita wasn't forthcoming with any.

'Anything about his background?' she asked. 'Where he grew up, the type of home he came from?'

'Seemed pretty normal from what I could gather from interviews he's given over the years,' said Jason. 'Mum and dad, semi in Streatham. They're both dead, I think. No other family mentioned anywhere. He was an only child.'

Jason sifted through his research.

'Certainly nothing hugely unusual in his background.'

'No,' said Amita, concerned. 'But those rumours of his behaviour on that film set, they were clearly substantiated enough for the studio to sack him. And it would make sense that he carried that resentment with him.'

'It's a lot easier to get rid of an unknown person behind the camera than somebody who has a mantlepiece full of awards and gongs,' he said. 'And, as much as it pains me to admit, *The Locus* is one of the biggest shows on TV. And a lot of that is down to Nakamba.'

Amita nodded. She stared down at the news reports and stories scattered all over her bed. The picture was clear – Simon Nakamba had his own demons to battle. Rightly or wrongly he had a reputation that seemed to follow him around But none of this brought them any nearer to figuring out a motive for his grisly demise.

'What about you?' asked Jason. 'Did you find any dirt on our drunk leading man?'

'Nothing we didn't already know,' said Amita with a yawn. 'I must have fallen asleep last night watching interviews he's given over the years. I suspect you were right, though, about secret vices. A little bit of booze probably fits with his exuberant character – but anything more wild than that, well, I don't imagine his reputation as a venerated titan of the stage would have a lot to gain with that coming out.'

'No,' said Jason. 'Normally it takes breaking point to reach that stage.'

'He sees himself as something of a charmer though,' said Amita, remembering what she had watched online. 'Every time there's a female interviewer, he's always, I don't know… oilier than with men. It's almost as if he thinks he's… he's…'

'God's gift to women?' Jason smiled wryly.

'Yes, something like that,' said Amita.

'And what about you, Amita? Are you beyond his charming, infectious smile and electric personality?'

'Jason, behave yourself,' she tutted. 'I'm old enough to be his mother. And besides, when you've been shouted at and can see the broken capillaries in the man's nose as he turns scarlet in front of you, there's no going back.'

'Fair enough,' said Jason.

He clapped his hands on his thighs and stood up. Gathering the papers, he waited for instruction.

'What's our next move, then?' he asked.

'I think we should probably try and speak to some of the rest of the crew.'

'Seems to make a lot of sense to me,' said Jason. 'Back to Askling Manor?'

'Only if they're still there,' she said.

'And how do we find that out?'

'Hang on a moment,' she said, reaching for her phone. 'It won't take me long to find out the stars' whereabouts.'

Jason rolled his eyes. The lightning fast network of Penrith's senior citizens was something that both amazed and bothered him in equal measure. A shiver went down his spine as he thought about what they might have on him. It didn't bear thinking about.

Chapter 17

PARK AVENUE BEAT

Jason caught sight of something through the spindly trees of the woodland that lined either side of the road. They were close to the resort, the entrance just around the corner.

'Hang on,' he said, slowing the car. 'What's all this about then?'

They pulled into the main driveway of the hotel. Amita peered up the road ahead. Blue flashing lights were dotted around the entranceway of the hotel. A number of police officers in hi-vis jackets were wandering around. A large incident response van was also on the scene, taking up room in the car park outside the front of Askling Manor.

'This all seems eerily familiar,' she said. 'Or hopefully they've just realised their lax security yesterday was leaving them open to trouble. Maybe we did them a favour by showing how easily the corridors could be breached.' The optimism in her voice sounded forced and fading as they both took in the scene.

As they drew nearer to the front of the historic building, a uniformed officer came walking towards them. He held up a gloved hand and wandered around to the driver's side. Jason rolled down the window.

'Good morning folks, guests are we?' he asked.

'Just visitors,' said Amita.

'No visitors this morning, I'm afraid, the whole place has been locked down.'

'What's happened?' asked Jason.

'I'm not at liberty to say, sir. If you'd like to turn around and head back up to the main road. I'm sure there will be news soon on when the hall will open again.'

There was a finality to the officer's instructions. He straightened himself up, puffing out his chest, enough to indicate he wouldn't be taking any further questions. Jason rolled up the window and began to turn the car around.

'I've got a dreadful feeling about all of this,' said Amita.

'Yeah, me too,' Jason agreed. 'I feel like a turkey who's just been chosen for Christmas dinner.'

'Please, Jason,' she said.

They drove back along the driveway and up to the main road. Jason flipped the indicator but Amita switched it off.

'What are you doing?' he asked.

'Pull into that layby over there, across the road,' she pointed at the small inlay opposite them.

'What for?'

'We need to find out what's going on in there,' she said. 'And the police will recognise the car if we go back up there now.'

'And how else are we going to get in?'

Amita produced her phone. She tapped away and then showed Jason some pictures.

'The hotel has a spa,' she said. 'There's a separate entrance. It takes up the whole back side of the building, looking out into the fields. A few of the WI have been there for swimming and pampering. It's not really my thing, as you know. Cardio all the way for me. I want to run and keep fit, not listen to panpipes while someone prods at me.'

'Indeed.'

'Georgie is never away from the place, though. Her ever-so generous son is forever giving her vouchers for these kinds of things. I think he just does it so he doesn't have to spend time with her.'

'Oh yeah, the famously generous son,' Jason rolled his eyes. 'Making the rest of us look bad for the last hundred years.' He felt guilty about the heated footwarmer he'd bought Amita for her last birthday. Then he remembered the tartan cummerbund and braces set she'd bought him. He didn't know who lived a cummerbund lifestyle – but it certainly wasn't him.

'It suits Georgie, of course,' Amita went on. 'It means she can try to cosy up with the owner, Sarah Paris.'

Jason felt a jolt. The mention of Sarah Paris was a surprise. The name had been like a dirty word the last day or so. To hear Amita speak so freely, he wasn't quite sure what to do.

'Yeah, about that,' he drummed his fingers on the steering wheel.

Amita wouldn't meet his eye. She was rubbing her hands over and over. It was a little tell Jason had picked up on over the years. She wasn't a fidgeter as a rule. She only behaved like that when she was worried about something.

'Look, you don't have to tell me anything, Amita,' he said. 'But you and Radha clearly have some beef with this woman. It's probably a lot easier if you just get it out in the open and I don't have to be in the dark anymore.'

To his surprise, she nodded.

'She was very friendly with Radha at school,' she said. 'She was a wild child, a free spirit, if I was putting it kindly. I didn't particularly like her, I won't make any bones about that, Jason. She was insubordinate to teachers, me, her parents, everyone. She was a bad influence. But Radha and her had a special bond. They were close, very close.'

'Blimey,' he said. 'So what happened?'

A look of deep shame tugged at Amita's brow.

'There was an incident,' she said. 'Just before Radha was about to sit her GCSEs. She was predicted straight As, she was capable of it, you know that. But Sarah wasn't interested in studying. She was out until all hours, smoking, drinking, all of that. Her parents owned and ran Askling Manor, it wasn't what it is today of course, but it was still successful. Sarah never seemed to care.'

'I see where this is going,' he said.

'I forbade Radha from seeing Sarah, from spending time with her,' said Amita. 'Just until after the exams. I hoped that it might break the cycle, maybe show Radha that she didn't need to be around someone like Sarah Paris. But you know what teenagers are like, Jason.'

'I do,' he said. 'I used to be one, as hard as you might find that to believe.'

'There was an unpleasantness at school, ten days before the GCSEs started. Some money had been stolen from the charity fund. The teachers were convinced it was Radha and Sarah. I said it couldn't possibly be my daughter, I would have tanned her hide if she did something like that. I threw Sarah Paris under the bus.'

'And was Radha innocent?' asked Jason.

Tears were forming in Amita's eyes. She shook her head.

'Bloody hell,' said Jason. 'What happened to Sarah?'

'Expelled,' said Amita, croaking. 'Radha confessed to me and told me I had to tell the school, but I didn't say anything. I didn't want her to jeopardise her future. I tried to make her understand, I only had her best interests at heart. Sarah was always going to go off the rails – I just didn't want her taking Radha with her. Eventually she moved past it, or forgave me, I don't know which.'

'I'm not so sure about that,' he said. 'She seemed clear enough about what happened and how she felt the other night there. What about Sarah, did she not dob Radha in? How did her parents react?'

'I don't know if they very much cared,' she said. 'They were a strange couple, very focused on their business, very driven. I think that's why she was the way she was. Always looking for attention, from them, from Radha, from everyone or anyone really. They died in a car crash about several years ago now. She didn't have siblings, just her. She inherited the estate all to herself. Although I did hear something on the grapevine about her having a child, I didn't see an engagement or wedding in the Herald, and you know I never usually miss the Births, Marriages and Deaths column.'

Don't I know it. Especially the deaths. 'Well, she's clearly had her hands full inheriting and running a hotel like that solo – and she's made a success of it – whether in their memory or despite their neglect,' said Jason. 'But I can see why Radha feels so upset about it all – guilt and anger combined is a terrible mix.'

'Ghastly business. I shouldn't have done it. Sarah was guilty, but so was Radha. She thought she'd owned up and then had to watch her friend get punished'.

Jason had seen remorse during his time as a reporter. When he wasn't out covering giant marrow competitions or apparitions in slices of toast, he had conducted some serious and hard-hitting interviews. Local politicians, business owners or just someone in the wrong place at the wrong time: he had learned to pick up on cues and body language, to be able to tell when somebody was lying. Amita, his mother-in-law, was as genuine as he knew she could be. She looked awful, guilty, shoulders slumped and defeated.

'It is what it is,' he said, not sounding very comforting.

'Yes, I'm afraid so,' she sniffed, trying to perk up. 'If we can get around the back, away from the police, we should be able to slip inside without anyone noticing. You can see why I wouldn't get a warm welcome from Sarah Paris if she saw me. But we've got to get in somehow.'

Jason wasn't convinced. He let out a groan to indicate so.

'It's either that or we don't find out what's happened in there and get to the bottom of this until more people get hurt,' she said. 'What would you rather happen?'

'I'd rather we weren't arrested for breaking into a crime scene.'

'We won't be,' said Amita, her turn to be less than convincing. 'We don't actually know there's been another crime. We might just be two people in urgent need of a spa day. There's nothing illegal about that.'

Amita turned in her seat. She peered out through the back window, the police cars far down the long driveway leading to the resort.

'Come on Jason, just a quick look,' she said. 'There's something going on here and we need to know. If it's nothing, fine, nothing ventured and nothing gained.'

'It never is nothing, though, is it Amita? We both know that by now.'

Chapter 18

FALLING

Climbing out of the car, Jason and Amita made their way down the service road that led to the back of Askling Manor. They were about halfway when she ducked off the tarmac.

'Come on,' she said.

'What? Come on where? Amita, that's a bloomin' forest,' he said, waving at the trees.

'Just follow me, ok?' she said.

They clambered over a small wire fence. The mud was wet, old leaves shed in the autumn squelching beneath trainers and boots. Weaving between the trees, they kept an eye on the flashing lights of the gathered police vehicles outside the front of the resort.

The ground gave way a little and Jason almost fell, the dirt rising all the way up to his knee. Amita stopped and helped him free and they pressed on, taking a wide arc away from the manor house and staying out of sight.

The woodland curved round the main building and the huge glass annex at the back came into view. The trees gave way and there was a stretch of open field between them and the spa building. Amita paused. She checked to make sure nobody had spotted them wandering through the woods.

'We'll have to make a run for it,' she said, breath smoking in front of her.

'Run? Amita, I don't run,' moaned Jason. 'I stopped running when I left school.'

'Well you're going to have to run now,' she tutted. 'Otherwise the police will see us and throw us in prison.'

'That's not what you said back in the car! What happened to us just being keen spa-goers?' Jason ventured.

'You're covered in mud up to your knees and you've got twigs in your hair – you don't exactly look like you're having a casual stroll before you hit the sauna, Jason. So that brings us back to my original plan: run!'

Amita dashed out into the open. She spryly raced across the field, footwork deftly gliding over the pitted grass and clumps of turf. Jason took a deep breath. His own sprint wasn't anywhere near as elegant or efficient. He wobbled and twisted, stifling a groan as he went over on his ankles and thudded across the field.

Mercifully the imposing walls of Askling Manor soon reared up in front of him. He collapsed onto the path that ran along the outer edge of the building, panting for breath.

'You should really do something about your fitness,' said Amita. 'You're not an old man, Jason. Someone of your age shouldn't find that distance challenging.'

'Not now, Amita,' he said, slowly getting to his feet. 'Just not now.'

He assessed himself. He was not just covered in mud, but a layer of sweat too. His nose was running and his lungs were burning. Even if they did get inside, he'd stand out like a sore thumb among the steamed and preened guests of the leisure complex.

'Let's try a door,' said Amita.

They made their way along the edge of the building, passing windows and little terraces with cast iron tables and chairs still out from the summer months. The huge glass annex was straight ahead. The windows were steamed up, blurry figures moving on the other side. When they reached the giant panoramic panes of glass, Amita stopped.

'There should be a fire exit or something around here,' she said.

'Here, what about this?'

Jason pushed down on a long bar. A door opened and a gust of warm air came wafting out. The smell of chlorine mingled with eucalyptus and made Jason's eyes water.

'Here goes nothing,' he said as they stepped inside.

The impressive glass structure housed a good-sized pool and a collection of smaller baths and hot tubs. A few guests were dotted around the edge, sprawled out on lounge chairs enjoying the atmosphere or an early morning swim. If there'd been a crime committed, there was no sign of it in this palace of pleasure.

'Let's go, quickly,' said Amita.

They slipped inside and made their way towards the main entrance of the spa. The only staff they saw were huddled together talking and no one seemed to notice them as they passed through quickly. They quick-marched up a corridor that was meant to lead to the main body of the hotel.

'Does any of this seem odd to you?'

'What?' she asked.

'Nobody seems to have seen us.'

'Maybe they've got bigger problems,' said Amita. 'There are police all over the place after all. Just not doing laps of the pool.'

'True,' Jason agreed.

The main lobby of the plush hotel opened up in front of them. While the corridors from the spa had been deserted, this place was a hive of activity. Staff, guests and police were all buzzing around the main desks and front entranceway. Nobody seemed to know where they were going but they had to get there quickly.

'Watch out,' said Jason.

He grabbed Amita by the shoulders and bundled her over towards the wall. They were shielded from the hubbub behind a huge, decorative monstera plant. Peering through the leaves, Amita wrestled herself free of Jason's grip.

'What's gotten into you?' she asked.

'Over there, look,' said Jason.

He pointed through the plant towards the open lobby. There, among the chaos and confusion, DI Sally Arendonk was standing briefing a small gaggle of plain-clothes officers.

'Oh no,' whispered Amita.

'Oh no is right,' Jason agreed. 'Do you think she saw us?'

Jason could feel the colour draining from his face. If it was just a stepping-up of security, Sally wouldn't have been here. He watched Arendonk from the safety of the plant. She looked concerned, focused. He really didn't want to let her down by getting caught sniffing around the hotel.

'I think we should go,' he whispered. 'We can't risk Arendonk seeing us. She's been too good to us for us to keep pushing her buttons.'

The sound of someone clearing their throat answered Jason before his mother-in-law could. Slowly, the pair turned around. An older gentleman wearing a similar morning coat with matching waistcoat to the receptionist from the other day was staring at them. He cocked a perfectly plucked eyebrow, pale blue eyes peering over a set of half-moon spectacles.

'Can I help you at all?' he asked. 'I'm happy to arrange for our plants to be transported to your rooms for your inspection. If, indeed, you are guests at the hotel.'

Jason and Amita slowly stood to their full heights. The well-presented staff member eyed them both up and down. He stopped at Jason's dirty leg and ruined boots and then gave another little sneer.

'That won't be necessary,' said Amita, trying to sound amicable. 'We were looking for the spa. We were just... taken aback a little by the sight of all these police.'

The sneer on the staff member's face tightened. He gave a quick glance around the lobby and cleared his throat again.

'Yes, an unfortunate business,' he said. 'We've been assured that the disruption to normal services will be kept to a minimum while they are here.'

'What unfortunate business exactly?' asked Jason.

'I'm not in a position to say, sir,' came the reply.

'Oh go on,' prodded Jason. 'A fancy place like this swarming with cops. And you as...' he paused while he looked at the badge on the man's lapel. 'You as head receptionist, you've got to be in the know, right?'

The man shifted a little uneasily on his feet, well-polished shoes squeaking. He looked around, making sure nobody was listening in.

'A guest has taken ill,' he said quietly. 'And now the police are involved. That's all I'm at liberty to say.'

'Ill?' asked Amita. 'How ill are we talking? Is it catching?'

'I absolutely cannot say any more,' said the man, cutting the air with his hands. 'Now, if you are residents here I would strongly urge you both to return to your rooms until the police have concluded their business. My staff are going around providing vouchers for our bistro, complimentary of Askling Manor, as a small token of our appreciation under the circumstances or, if you are looking for the day spa, where I believe they can provide you with some overshoes, I would–'

'Oi!'

Arendonk's voice seemed to boom over the rest of the lobby's hubbub. Jason and Amita instinctively snapped their heads around towards the detective. She was staring right at them, her gang of officers watching too.

'Oh no,' said Amita.

'We need a swift exit!' Jason hissed, pulling Amita through the door to the corridor. There was no handy laundry cupboard this time. He thought about pleading his case to

Arendonk but it was her junior officers who came crashing through the doors after them. They didn't look quite as understanding as the D.I.

'Leg it!' Jason shouted.

For the second time that morning he found himself running. Not only that, he was once again bolting through one of the nicest hotels in Cumbria. The splinters in his shins were still fresh enough to cause him great discomfort as he hobbled down the corridor, racing back towards the spa. Amita had no such problems, taking an early lead. They weaved between the other guests and staff until they reached the spa annex.

Jason knew he was going too fast to stop. It was an instinct, a long-buried memory of his lack of coordination that took him back to school sports days and the nightmares that went along with them. His foot slipped on something wet near the edge of the pool. It went out from underneath him but his momentum carried him forward. There was a still, almost peaceful moment where he must have been in the air, no part of him connected with the Earth. Then came the splash as he tumbled head first into the pool.

A flurry of bubbles and panic engulfed him as his mind tried to catch up with his body. He tried to shout but his mouth filled with water. He flapped around until the whole world came flooding back in a cacophony of noise and mayhem.

Someone grabbed him and pulled him up. He was deposited at the side of the pool, coughing and spluttering, soaked to the skin. Two feet appeared beside him, sensible boots beneath the edges of equally sensible suit trousers. Jason didn't need to look up to know who it was.

'Mr Brazel,' said Arendonk, squatting down beside him. 'Thought we'd go for a morning swim, did we?'

Chapter 19

STRAIGHT UP AND DOWN

'I'm getting a bit sick of turning up to police stations dressed in only a house coat,' said Jason.

His teeth were chattering as he pulled the fluffy collar of the Askling Manor robe tightly about him. His bare knees were bobbing up and down beneath the interview table, complimentary flip flops clapping with every tap.

'Serves you right for running around like a maniac,' said Amita, sat beside him. 'Have you never been told you shouldn't run along the sides of swimming pools?'

'I have,' he said. 'And I wouldn't have been running if you hadn't taken off when Arendonk spotted us.'

'Me?' Amita's voice went strangely high. 'It was you who said run.'

'No it wasn't,' said Jason. 'I hate running.'

'You did, Jason,' she insisted. 'Running away from police detectives, does that sound like something I would condone? I'm a respectable senior citizen.'

'It doesn't matter now,' he said. 'We're here, caught red-handed and I'm freezing my backside off having taken an unexpected dip. Once, just once, I would like to be sat in this police station fully clothed with absolutely nothing to feel guilty about. Is that really such a hard thing to ask for?'

'You reap what you sow,' said Amita.

'And what's that supposed to mean?'

She sniffed and sat up a little straighter.

'My mother used to say that,' she said. 'She was a great believer in the universe giving back to you what you put out into it. It's a very popular notion these days but she was always going on about it. She taught me and my brothers and sisters that you can make your own luck in this world and that your actions will always have consequences.'

'What do you mean?' asked Jason.

'Look at what we've been through these past few years. It's all about actions and consequences. Things never really change, do they? I mean, technology, fashion, the width of trouser legs might alter, but it's all still the same world, just dressed up a little differently. History always repeats itself.'

'Thank you for that,' Jason sighed. 'If I wasn't depressed before, I certainly am now.'

The door of the interview room swung open with a dramatic whoosh. Sally Arendonk came marching in, strides full of purpose and vigour. She rounded the table and didn't bother to sit down. She leaned over Jason and Amita, who both stiffened their shoulders like kids preparing for an audience with the headteacher.

'Right, you two,' said the DI. 'Before you start bombarding me with excuses, I want to know two things. One, what were you doing at Askling Manor? – and bear in mind I've seen the guest list so I know you weren't there for a jolly old weekend.'

'On my salary? You must be kidding,' scoffed Jason.

Arendonk gave him a long, hard glare. He was quiet after that.

'And two,' she went on. 'What part of don't get involved in a high-profile murder case do either of you not understand? Is it the high profile part? The murder? Or do I need to spell it out, word for word, what keeping your noses out actually involves?'

Silence. Jason looked over to his mother-in-law for some inspiration. There was nothing forthcoming as Amita turned to him for the same.

'Well...' she started.

'Hang on!' Arendonk raised a finger. 'Think very, very carefully about what you're about to say, Ms Khatri. It could be the difference between you both walking out of here of your own volition. Or me throwing the book at you and sending you to the holding cells for a very long time.'

'On what charge?' asked Jason.

'I don't know, I haven't made one up yet,' said the DI. 'But I'm sure I can think of something.'

'Police corruption manifest,' he said under his breath.

'What was that?'

'Nothing.'

Arendonk's daggers continued in Jason's direction. Amita leaned forward on the table.

'Detective Inspector, we know it was misguided but we truly meant no harm,' she said.

'Ok, not the start I was expecting,' Arendonk sat down opposite them, disarmed by the contrition. 'I was expecting you to tell me you were both practising a bit of lifesaving, what with your fully-clothed dunk, Jason. But, an apology, that's unexpected. I'll take the bait. Go on.'

'We were simply curious to see what all the police activity at the hall was about, that's all,' Amita continued.

'All perfectly innocent – nosey yes, illegal no' said Jason.

'Then why did you run when I saw you?' asked the DI. 'Why did I have four of the best CID officers at my disposal giving chase through a luxury hotel only to wind up fishing you, Mr Brazel, out of the pool like a half-drowned ferret?'

'Eh...' said Jason.

'Exactly. How would you have even seen the police activity at Askling if you weren't already coming to stick your beaks into my investigation?' Arendonk puckered her lips. 'So I'll try again. What were you doing at the hotel?'

Amita thought about cooking up a half-baked excuse. But she respected Sally Arendonk too much for that. She sighed.

'We were hoping to speak with Mr Derek Veland,' she said.

'Speak to him about what exactly?'

'Simon Nakamba,' said Jason.

'Why?'

'We thought,' Amita cleared her throat. 'That he might know a little bit more about Mr Nakamba's murder.'

'Either that or he was responsible,' Jason added.

That drew a twitch from Arendonk. Her eyebrows narrowed, faint wrinkles appearing on her forehead.

'So you were either pestering a celebrity or hanging out with a murderer. Nice options, guys. And why precisely would you think Derek Veland had anything to do with Simon Nakamba's murder?' she asked, her voice low.

'We had the fortune of bumping into Mr Veland a day or so ago' said Amita. 'But he was in a bit of a sorry state.'

'Drunk as a skunk,' said Jason.

Arendonk's eyes were darting between them now.

'Yes, inebriated,' said Amita. 'He offered us money not to tell the press about the dishevelled state he was in.'

'Was he violent towards you?' she asked.

'No,' said Amita. 'Although he was shouting quite a bit. He was clearly still under the influence of whatever it was he'd been taking. He said he'd had his own problems with Simon Nakamba on set, as did most people who worked with the director. Only Jason and I weren't entirely convinced that we could take his testimony as serious given how... unstable he appeared.'

'What my mother-in-law is trying to say, Sally, is that Veland was off his head and could have said anything. But he's big and strong enough to move a body and he had means and motive to do something nasty to Simon Nakamba if he wanted to. And he paid us money to shut up.'

Arendonk broke her gaze from the pair for the first time since she'd stormed into the interview room. She tapped a finger on the table, chewing something over. Then she stood up quickly. She rounded the table and headed for the door. Peering into the corridor beyond, she stepped back inside, making sure to close the door behind her. Amita and Jason were both perplexed.

'What I'm about to tell you goes no further,' said the detective, returning to her chair.

She hesitated for a moment, as if wrestling with what she was about to say. Amita and Jason both leaned forward.

'Whatever it is,' said Amita. 'You can tell us, Detective Inspector. You can trust us.'

'Trust you?' she laughed. 'He's a journalist and you're the most connected pensioner in Penrith! And besides, I trusted you not to go interfering with this case and look where that got me.'

'Technically I'm an out-of-work journalist,' said Jason. 'And she's not as connected as she thinks she is.'

'Pardon?' Amita yelped.

Arendonk rubbed her forehead.

'Not a word of this leaves this room,' she said. 'Understand?'

'Of course,' said Amita.

'Absolutely,' said Jason.

'Right,' the DI went on. 'Around five this morning we received a call from the staff at Askling Manor to tell us a guest had been found dead in their room.'

'I knew it!' Amita snapped her fingers.

'Yes, congratulations on stumbling across another body,' said Arendonk grimly. 'When officers arrived, they found said guest in their room, flat on their back in the bed with what appeared to be a lot of empty prescription pill bottles and various alcohol empties scattered around them. It would appear, on first inspection, a death by misadventure.'

'Terrible,' said Jason.

'However, on further investigation, the attending officers noted the identity of the guest and how said guest was a person of interest in an active murder investigation.'

Arendonk's cool demeanour turned hard. 'If you catch my meaning.'

'Hang on,' said Jason. 'Are you trying to tell us that, firstly, Derek Veland is dead?'

'And that he was on your list of potential suspects for the killing of Simon Nakamba?' asked Amita.

Arendonk's lips were closed together so tightly she looked like she had no mouth at all.

'Bloody hell,' said Jason, leaning back. 'Veland's dead and you thought he might have been the killer?'

'You didn't hear it from me,' said the detective.

'Hold on,' said Amita. 'If you suspected Derek Veland, you must have had some fairly strong evidence that would point to him being capable of Simon Nakamba's murder.'

Arendonk let out a long, weary sigh. She drummed her fingers on the tabletop.

'I can't believe I'm going to say this, as I suspect neither of you need your egos polished right about now,' she said. 'But the senior investigating team had come to the same conclusion as you.'

Jason let out a laugh. He slapped the table before squeezing Amita's shoulders.

'Did you hear that?' he scoffed. 'They thought Veland was the killer too. He's big enough, unstable enough and got an axe to grind. We were right, Amita! We were spot on!'

'Was,' said Amita.

'What?'

'Veland *was* big enough, unstable etcetera. He's dead, Jason. And I have a feeling that Detective Inspector Arendonk here is about to tell us that she doesn't think it was simply an accident.'

Jason turned to face the detective, face slack as the penny dropped.

Arendonk looked grim.

'If you're about to suggest that we may have a serial killer on our hands, then I wouldn't have to correct you,' she said.

Jason and Amita shuddered in unison.

'I thought that might get your attention,' said Arendonk.

'Bloody hell,' breathed Jason.

'This is awful,' Amita chimed. 'A serial killer, here, in Penrith. It's unthinkable.'

'Believe me, Amita, it's very much thinkable,' said the detective. 'But it also means I'm thinking you two should stay well clear. For your own safety.'

She looked tired, Amita thought. A haggardness had set in on her youthful features. The lines in her forehead were deepening by the second. Gone was the spritely energy that Amita and Jason had come to expect from the detective inspector. In its place was a heaviness, a worry that seemed to ooze out of her pores.

'Needless to say the media and public don't know any of this yet,' she said. 'And I'd like to keep it that way until our team has put something together. The last thing we need is a mass panic.'

'How can you be sure that the two deaths are related?' asked Jason. 'I mean, maybe it's just a terrible coincidence.'

Arendonk reached into her pocket. She pulled out her phone before sliding it across the table. Jason, sensing it was not going to be a pretty picture, took the device and looked first, grimacing as he made sense of the image on the small screen. He was handing it back to the DI, to spare Amita, when his mother-in-law reached over, took a deep breath and looked too. She clapped her hand to her mouth, shocked at the image on the phone, despite her attempts to steel herself. Derek Veland's pale, bloated face was staring back from the picture, thick bruising around his throat and neck.

'Sorry,' said the detective. 'But as you can see, his untimely death wasn't just down to all the pills and powders I'm sure we'll find in Derek Veland's system when the post-mortem comes back. He's clearly been choked to death, strangled.'

'Again it could just be a coincidence.' said Jason.

'Oh come off it, Jason,' said Amita, turning away from the photo. 'Two people, a high-profile actor and director, both murdered within a week of each other while they work on the same production? It doesn't take a police officer of DI Arendonk's prestige to work out what's going on here.'

'Alright, alright, calm down,' he held up his hands. 'I was just playing devil's advocate, that's all. It's my job not to jump to conclusions.'

'What are you doing about this?' Amita turned to the DI. 'I assume you've got watches on all the main cast of the production.'

'Of course we do,' tutted the detective. 'And the production team have been rounded up and escorted back to their living quarters throughout the town. Nobody beyond the staff here at Askling has clocked there's anything odd going on, yet. I've asked the production to hold off from briefing the press on Veland's passing.'

'It won't hold forever,' said Jason.

'I'd like to think you'd at least try to keep your mouth shut,' said Arendonk.

'It's not me you have to worry about,' he said. 'There must be, what, a hundred staff at that hotel. Not to mention all the guests. You don't need to be a jaded hack like me to work out something big has happened. And that's when people get ideas.'

The grimness deepened on Arendonk's face.

'Why tell us all of this?' asked Amita.

It was a good question.

'What's so special about us?'

Arendonk quietly and gently put her phone away. She clasped her hands on the table in front of her and tilted her head to one side.

'Your past experiences with these sorts of things in and around Penrith have not gone unnoticed by me or some of my colleagues,' she said, diplomatically. 'And as the lead investigator, I thought it might prove prudent to at least consult with you to see if you had any working theories about who may be responsible.'

'You need our help, that's what you're saying,' said Jason.

He had a cheeky little smile on his face. Arendonk sensed it and did her best not to leap across the table and punch him in the nose.

'I'm saying that, in a situation such as this, I am open to every suggestion on how to bring this maniac to justice. I've known officers turn to all sorts unofficially – psychics, criminals, pet psychologists – anything to shake down a few answers. So, if you two armchair Poirots think you've got something to add, now's your moment.'

'She needs our help,' Jason said to Amita, chuffed.

'Jason, please,' said his mother-in-law. 'Detective Inspector, you have, as always, our full cooperation. We won't breathe a word of this to anyone outside this police station. And anything we dig up, we'll report to you immediately.'

'Good,' said Arendonk. 'That's all I wanted to hear. So your swan dive into the pool was completely unnecessary, Jason. I only wanted to make sure you knew what you were letting yourselves in for. I couldn't let you do your usual gumshoe act without knowing that this could be a whole other class of criminal to the ones you've faced in the past. I don't want your deaths on my caseload – or my conscience.'

She stood up, her chair squeaking as it slid across the well-worn linoleum. She rounded the table, opened the door and stood to one side.

'Your car has been left in the car park,' she said. 'One of our drivers brought it back from Askling Manor.'

'And what about my clothes?' asked Jason.

'In a plastic bag in the boot,' said the detective.

Arendonk escorted them down through the familiar corridors of Penrith Police Station, where only a few heads turned at the sight of a pensioner in rhinestone-accented leisure wear and a damp middle-aged man in a dressing gown. She left them at a side exit that led to the car park, their motor on the other side surrounded by squad cars and vans.

'The official line, as always, is that you're to keep your noses out,' she said. 'However, I know that's like asking you two to learn Ancient Greek overnight. So, if anything does come up that you think might be of help or interest to the *official* investigation, then don't delay in calling me. Is that understood?'

'Of course,' said Amita.

'And needless to say, all of this is strictly confidential and off the record. Is that clear, Brazel?'

Jason said nothing. Then Amita nudged him in the ribs.

'Yes, yes, of course,' he said. 'Blimey, you can't print anything these days.'

'Don't do anything stupid,' said the DI. 'You're still members of the public and, like I said, I don't want to be fishing either of you out of the Eden, is that clear?'

'Crystal clear,' said Jason.

'Thank you, Detective Inspector,' Amita offered her hand. 'We won't let you down.'

Arendonk shook her hand and gave them both a nod. She closed the door of the station behind her and left them in the car park, a cold wind whipping up.

'This is bad,' said Amita, starting for the car. 'This is very, very bad Jason. A serial killer, here, in Penrith. I just can't believe it.'

'It's not great, I know,' he said. 'Arendonk will catch them, she isn't the type who wouldn't throw everything she has at something as serious as this. I don't think we need to worry unduly.'

'No need to worry? Didn't you hear what she said?' she yelped. 'There's a lunatic running around town killing people like they were sport or something. What's not to worry about that?'

'There's also a whole county's police service hunting for them right now,' said Jason. 'And as soon as this news gets out you can expect to see coppers from all over the country marching up and down our little streets. Believe me, Amita, these things never last long. And as gruesome as it sounds, the fact our two victims were connected suggests to me like they're not 'running around town' picking off the folk of Penrith at random – but that our culprit has a plan. That makes them cold, calculating and dangerous for sure – but I would suggest it means they won't be turning their crosshairs onto just anyone.' Jason hoped Amita couldn't hear the crack in his voice as he tried to reassure himself as much as his mother-in-law. He'd reported on all sorts of tragic events over the years – and just because he hoped the killer wasn't picking off people at whim, it didn't lessen the shock of knowing two lives had been snuffed out. And the unspoken truth hung in the air between them – if the killer had struck twice, they'd surely not think twice about eliminating anyone who got too close to their identity.

They reached the car and climbed in. The keys were in the ignition and he turned it on, blasting the heater as high as it would go to chase away his chills. He was still shivering under his Askling Manor robe as he tried to warm up. Then he spotted the logo on his breast.

'Hang on,' he said. 'What about Sarah Paris?'

'What about her?' asked Amita, biting her nails.

'Do you think she would talk with us, well, I mean me?' he asked. 'She might give us a bit more than she would do to the police? A friendly, local face in a time of crisis, someone as invested as her in making sure Penrith's reputation doesn't get tarnished? That sort of thing?'

'No, Jason, I don't think she would. Not if she's spotted me with you. Not after everything that happened.'

'But she owns the place, Amita, she's bound to know *something*,' he said. 'You said it yourself, there's a lunatic running its corridors bumping people off. You can't let past indiscretions get in the way of catching a killer.'

Amita stopped biting her nails. She knew he was right of course. This was the moment she had been dreading ever since she'd learned that the cast and crew were staying at the luxury resort. Even thinking about Sarah Paris made her nervous. It had been a long time since she had last seen the woman. A lot had happened, for everyone. Twenty years could do that. The guilt was still there though. Amita knew that much.

'Somebody must have seen something last night,' said Jason, breaking her concentration. 'Derek Veland wasn't just another guest, he was a celebrity. Guys like him can't help but cause a scene. Maybe Sarah knows something.'

'Possibly,' said Amita.

Jason could sense her discomfort.

'Look, this could be the time to lay this ghost to rest,' he said. 'You could come with me – apologise for what you did, tell her Radha tried to confess and you stopped her. You don't have to speak with her on your own. It was a long time ago now, Amita. She's the owner of a luxury hotel – her teenage misdemeanour hasn't held her back. She's probably forgotten all about the details. I mean, I can't remember what I had for breakfast, let alone some infraction at school.'

He was trying his best, Amita acknowledged that. She nodded weakly, knowing it was the right course of action.

'I'll be on my best behaviour,' he said, rolling the car away from the station. 'I promise.'

'Yes,' said Amita, looking distinctly sceptical about whether taking any advice from a man driving a car in a damp dressing gown was wise. 'That's what worries me.'

Chapter 20

HI HO SILVER

The afternoon was wearing on by the time Jason and Amita returned to Askling Manor, now both more conventionally dressed. The police had cleared out as far as they could tell but the whole estate seemed much gloomier now. A louring sky matched the sombre mood inside. Instead of lurking and skulking around the spa, this time the pair were glad to go in through the main entrance and, although the whine and chatter of police walkie talkies had been replaced by piped classical music, there was an anxious, harried look on the faces of all the staff. Jason imagined they'd been tasked with getting the hotel back to business as usual as quickly and quietly as possible, but he also imagined that was no mean feat when, in a suite somewhere above, forensic specialists would be crawling all over every inch of the crime scene.

Much to Jason and Amita's relief, the receptionist who had given chase through the hotel was not at his station. Instead, a bright-faced young woman greeted them as they approached the front desk.

'Good afternoon and welcome to Askling Manor,' she said. 'Are you checking in?'

'No,' said Amita. 'I'm afraid not. We're wondering if there was any chance of speaking with the owner, Ms Sarah Paris?'

The receptionist was surprised. But she didn't let it break her well-versed veneer. She blinked and remembered her training.

'Do you have an appointment?' she asked.

'No, we're old friends,' said Jason, leaning on the desk.

'I see.' She seemed sceptical. 'Ms Paris normally doesn't accept unsolicited meetings. She has a very full schedule and it's rare that she can squeeze in anything else unannounced.'

'Is there nothing you can do, my dear?' said Amita. 'She's an old friend of my daughter, Radha Khatri, they went to school together. We'd really like to speak to her about a bit of a delicate matter.'

'The murder of Derek Veland,' said Jason, rather more bluntly.

Amita almost choked on her surprise. She let out a strange wheeze and turned to look at her son-in-law.

'What?' he asked. 'That's what we're here for, isn't it?'

The young receptionist was much more controlled. She lifted a nearby phone and dialled three numbers.

'Ms Paris, I have two people at reception who would like to speak with you about last night's incident,' she said calmly. 'A lady is claiming that you're an old friend of her daughter – Radha Khatri.'

There was a pause. Amita held her breath.

'Excellent,' said the receptionist. 'I'll send them up straight away.'

She put the phone down and smiled.

'If you'd like to take the lift to the top floor, Ms Paris will be waiting for you when you get there.'

Amita nodded and gave her thanks. Jason was doing the same when she grabbed him and started bundling him through the lobby.

'Are you mad, Jason?' she whispered angrily.

'I've been known to be,' he said.

'That was a terrible risk you just took. DI Arendonk has trusted us with that information, it's confidential.'

'Oh come off it, Amita, didn't you hear what I said to Arendonk back at the police station? Everyone in this hotel will know what's happened to Veland. In fact, they probably knew before the cops even showed up. These places, like any big business, are full of whispers. You can't hide anything. I'd venture that the speed of gossip backstairs here rivals that of your pensioner rumour mill. That lovely young lady at the front desk was more than aware of what happened last night. Let's just hope her boss is happy to give us a little more intel.'

They stepped into the lift alone. It whizzed them up to the top floor with remarkable speed. The doors opened and a much less opulent corridor and space appeared in front of them. Gone were the fine carpets, furnishings and decorative touches expected of a five-star resort. In their place was a low ceiling, sterile white walls and a whiff of stagnant air mixed with bleach.

'Clearly it's not the lap of luxury for the staff behind the scenes,' said Jason, stepping out of the elevator.

'Amita Khatri, I can't believe it.'

Sarah Paris came striding towards them, her arms outstretched. She was tall, even in her heels, walking with purpose as she smiled warmly at Amita.

'Sarah, how lovely to see you,' she replied, hesitantly. 'It's been a very long time.'

'It has,' she said. 'Far too long.'

Jason stood back watching the two women. He had an unnerving sense of a pin being pulled on a grenade. He was just waiting for everything to blow up. But the explosion never came.

Sarah let go of Amita. She stood back, pushing her hair out of her face, and looked over at Jason with a smile.

'And who is this? Your toyboy?' she laughed.

'No, good grief,' said Amita. 'This is Jason Brazel. He's my son-in-law, Radha's husband.'

'You Khatri women have always had very good taste,' said Sarah, winking.

'Oh stop it,' Jason feigned bashfulness. 'Lovely to meet you Ms Paris. You have a stunning hotel here.'

'Yes, that's the aim,' she said. 'Although it's going to put me in an early grave, as it did my parents. Actually, that's probably not the best turn of phrase at a time like this, is it?'

She clenched her teeth together. Jason laughed, Amita gave a polite smile.

'We're very sorry to be here under these circumstances,' she moved quickly on. 'Is there anywhere we could go to speak privately?'

'Certainly, come on along to my office. Can I get you anything? Tea, coffee, something from the bar?'

Both Amita and Jason refused. They followed Sarah to her office, a small, cramped room in one of the corner turrets of the ancient stately home. She cleared two chairs of papers and files and offered them up. She sank into her own seat below an intimidating painting of a man with a heavy frown.

'That's quite the portrait,' said Jason.

'Yes, that's the first Earl who had this place built,' she said. 'I wish I had a time machine so I could go back and urge him to think about draughts and heating.'

She laughed at that. As did Jason. Amita was a little more serious.

'Sarah, again, I can't stress enough how sorry I am for turning up unannounced like this, under these circumstances,' she said. 'I was very sad to hear about your parents' passing.'

'Thank you,' smiled the hotel boss.

She reached into a drawer and pulled out a little photo in a silver frame. She stared at it lovingly before handing it over to Amita.

'That's them on their thirtieth wedding anniversary,' she said. 'We took over this place for the weekend. Seemed only right given it was their whole lives. Little did we know they'd both be gone within the year.'

'Terrible,' said Amita. 'I should have stayed in touch more. I should have checked on you.'

'Don't be silly,' Sarah smiled again, taking the photo back. 'You've got your own family, your own life, Amita. And grandkids, so I hear.'

'Two,' she said. 'The apples of my eye.'

'You must be very proud,' Sarah said to Jason.

'Immensely,' he said. 'I'm proud of the kids too. And of their mum, of course.'

He'd said it without thinking. Fearing another mention of Radha might set things off, he sat and braced himself, silently cursing.

'How the devil is Radha?' asked Sarah, no sense of bitterness or anger. 'Well, I hope.'

'She is,' said Jason. 'Well, as well as you can be being married to me and living with *her*.'

He pointed over at Amita, who was mortified.

'Now, now, you do yourself an injustice, Jason, I'm sure.'

Jason's cheeks flushed at that. He missed his wife. And he vowed to buy her flowers before she got home from work.

'But this isn't a social call, is it?' she asked.

Amita took a deep breath.

'No, I'm afraid it's not,' she said. 'Jason and I have been, for the last little while, looking into some of the town's more unsavoury incidents.'

'Murders, she means murders,' said Jason.

'To put it bluntly, thank you Jason,' she said. 'We are assisting the police with the recent death of Simon Nakamba.'

'The cops don't have a clue and, if I can tell you this in confidence, they need our help,' said Jason.

'And we had the chance to speak to the actor Derek Veland before his own untimely death. We'd hoped to ask him another couple of questions when he... wasn't quite so tired and emotional.'

'Drunk and high,' said Jason.

'Only, when we turned up here this morning, the hotel was surrounded by police – and we soon found out why.'

'So we wanted to know, Sarah,' Jason leaned forward. 'What do *you* know that the cops don't?' He'd always been a fan of the direct approach.

Sarah Paris remained calm, collected. She sat perfectly still in her chair beneath the rather intimidating painting, as unflustered as if she was in any normal business meeting on any normal day – not a conversation about a murder committed just below where they now sat. Her two visitors watched for any signs of distress or worry, anything that would give away what she was really thinking. There was nothing.

Then the tears came. Amita was shocked at first. Sarah had seemed so composed only a matter of seconds ago. Now she was weeping, sobbing into her hands.

'Oh Sarah,' she said, getting up and going to comfort her. 'It's ok my love, it's alright.'

'You don't understand,' said the hotel boss, still crying. 'This is the last thing we needed. The absolute last thing.'

Amita hugged Sarah tightly. Jason sat on the other side of the desk feeling completely useless. He'd thought his run-in with Pip Potter was the most embarrassed he was going to get this week and now once again he didn't know where to look or what to say. He often accused Amita of being a bull in a china shop, but when it came to any kind of emotional interaction, she was streets ahead.

'What's been going on?' he asked, trying to offer something.

Sarah continued to sob quietly. Amita rubbed her back. When she had been at school, Sarah was the life and soul of the party, Amita had told Jason. She was enthusiastic, generous, outgoing. To see her like this, now, was devastating – it certainly didn't seem like the time to rub salt in the wound and bring up the awkward circumstances around her expulsion.

'I'm sorry,' said Sarah. 'I'm so sorry. This isn't very professional.'

'You don't have to be professional with us,' said Amita. 'We're friends, good friends at one time, and we're here to help you. Anyway, it's me who should be sorry for – well, for so many things, but right now for losing touch and turning up like this. I should have been around for you more.'

Amita let Sarah go. She dug around in the pocket of her cardigan and found a spare tissue. Sarah gladly took it and tried to compose herself again. She rubbed her eyes, bottom lip still trembling.

'I don't know what came over me just then,' she sniffed. 'It's been an absolute triple-decker stress sandwich these past few days, weeks even. And then with everything that happened last night, I think seeing you, Amita, after all this while, just broke me.'

She reached over and squeezed Amita's hand. She held hers back.

'I know,' she said. 'And I'm sorry again I've not been here for you, Sarah, since the loss of your parents. You and Radha were as close as sisters at one point. I owed you much more than for us to drift apart. Especially after everything that happened.'

'It's a two-way system,' she said. 'I've hardly been in touch with you or Radha. We were best friends, for god's sake! At first I felt guilty, then angry, then awkward – then I grew up and I guess life gets in the way. I'm a single mum, a business owner. I've just not had the time for friends in for what seems like forever. This place, it dominates my every waking thought. And even the non-waking ones. Imagine having dreams about laundry bills and silver service staff training.'

'I don't imagine it's a walk in the park, running a five-star resort,' said Jason.

Sarah nodded. She held up her hands at the ramshackle office in the dark and dingy tower of the ancient hall.

'The punters see well-polished floors and mints on their pillow, but this is my reality,' she said. 'Damp and drafty and living in the eaves. It's the same for all of the staff, I'm no exception.'

'Lead by example, huh?' asked Jason.

'Something like that,' she said. 'As long as the guests come away from their stay here thinking they've been treated like royalty then I guess it's worth it. I don't know, the hotel business is pretty cutthroat at the best of times. Especially with old country houses like this. The upkeep is a fortune because it's all listed. And that's before you have a dead celebrity turn up in one of your suites and a police presence that isn't exactly a great welcome for our clientele.'

Sarah blew her nose. She rubbed her forehead and leaned on her desk. Amita was still holding her hand.

'I'm sorry that we have to ask,' she said. 'But is there anything, anything at all, you can think of that you didn't share with police. Any quirk or odd detail you thought was too small, too silly…'

'Nothing,' Sarah shook her head. 'The police have taken all of the available CCTV footage of Veland in the hotel yesterday and last night. He was here for dinner, retired to the bar to hold court for about five hours and then went up to his room.'

'And he was on his own?' asked Jason, wondering if right now Arendonk's team had footage of him and Amita from the morning before; moonlighting as detectives was one thing – being in the frame as suspects was quite another.

'He left the bar alone, if that's what you're asking,' she said. 'I don't know what happened, really I don't. Everything is locked down in here after midnight – you need a fob, a pass or a key to get anywhere. Nobody can get in and out of the building without someone noticing. The idea that he was strangled, in his own bedroom, it's absolutely bonkers.'

Jason looked at his mother-in-law. They exchanged concerned glances.

'How are you coping with it all?' she asked Sarah.

'Coping is hardly the right word,' she replied. 'It's just another problem this place has to face. Like I said, it costs a fortune to run a building like this. The heating bills eat up the majority of the profit margin alone. Then there's all the historical society guff I have to deal with. Throw in a slow season and lead-up to Christmas, and it feels like my head is going to explode. I really could have done with Derek Veland being murdered somewhere else. Make it somebody else's problem, you know?'

'Yes, of course.' Amita squeezed her hand again. 'It's alright, Sarah, you'll be fine, you'll get through all of this. Veland's murder was hardly your fault, and a place like Askling Manor's reputation speaks for itself. Doesn't it, Jason?'

'What?' He seemed a little surprised to be asked something. 'Oh yeah, of course. Everyone knows Askling Manor. Especially your swimming pool, I can recommend that to anyone...'

'That's another thing,' Sarah laughed sadly. 'Some moron ended up in there earlier. That'll be another legal case I'll have to field when the cretin sues me for a lack of signposts telling him not to run around the wet edges of a bloody swimming pool.'

Jason's cheeks flushed. Amita didn't say anything.

'Thank you, though, both of you,' she said. 'It's been nice to see you again, Amita. And I'm sorry I've used you as a sounding board. I don't know how much help I've actually been.'

'You've been plenty of help,' said Amita. 'I'm going to give you a call tomorrow, once you finish work, just for a chat. I'm happy for it to be a regular thing if you'd like. You need to be able to release the pressure every now and then. It's not healthy to carry the weight of the world on your shoulders like you've been doing.'

Sarah nodded again. Her eyes were glassy and she looked about ready to start sobbing once more. A quick knock at the office door was enough to stop her and she sat up, straightening her blouse and letting go of Amita.

'Who is it?' she called out.

The door clicked open. A young woman with hazel hair and eyes popped her head around the flaking doorframe.

'I heard crying. Are you alright, Mum?' she asked.

'Abi! Come in,' said Sarah.

Sarah's daughter tentatively stepped into the office. She eyed Amita and Jason up and down before heading to give her mother a hug.

'Abi, these are old friends of mine,' said Sarah. 'Mrs Khatri's daughter and I were at school together. She knew your gran and grandad. And this is her son-in-law, Jason.'

'Hi,' said Abi.

'Lovely to meet you,' said Amita.

'Likewise,' said Jason.

'Abi is studying to be a nurse,' said Sarah, beaming with pride.

'Is that so?' asked Amita. 'You know, I seem to recall that your mother wanted to be a nurse at one point.'

'I think I wanted to be everything at some point, Amita,' Sarah laughed.

'Very true,' she said.

'I wanted to be an astronaut,' said Jason. 'But I didn't have the eyesight for it.'

'I don't think it was *just* the optician's verdict standing in the way of that dream,' said Amita.

'True,' Jason acknowledged. 'I admit there aren't many opportunities for spacemen in Cumbria, I suppose. Nursing is a much wiser choice. An honourable and valuable profession. You'll never be short of work and you can go anywhere you want with a degree like that.'

'I just want to help people,' said Abi. 'There's so much misery about that it's time we all stepped up and did our part. If everyone did that then the world would be a much better place. For all of us.'

Amita smiled. She liked this young woman.

'She's a credit to you,' she said to Sarah.

'She absolutely is, I'm very proud of her. And I know her grandparents would be too if they were still here. They were furious when I told them I was pregnant – barely out of my teens, no father on the scene. But Abi was the making of me. When she was old enough, I came to work here for my parents and the rest is history. They may be gone but we feel their presence every day.'

A chill descended. Jason shuffled awkwardly. It didn't seem like there were happy memories of Sarah's parents here – but he supposed most stately piles like this were built on skulduggery, family feuds and chasing the money. Sarah smoothed Abi's hair as Jason eyed the door, unable to decide how best to beat a retreat.

'Thank you for your time,' he said. 'I'm sorry again that we had to meet like this.'

'If anything springs to mind, Sarah, please let us know,' said Amita, scribbling down her number. 'I'll give you a call when you finish work tomorrow. What time do you clock off?'

'How long is a piece of string,' said Sarah wearily. 'I'm here until the restaurant closes at ten.'

'And after,' said Abi.

'Yes, unfortunately so.'

'That's fine by me, I'm late to bed anyway. I want you to look after yourself,' she said. 'And don't worry about this business with Derek Veland. The killer will be caught, I promise you.'

She gave Sarah another long hug. Jason followed her out of the door and they made their way back towards the lifts. As they descended into the main part of the hotel, he puffed out his cheeks.

'Well, that went better than I could have imagined. Instead of refusing to see you, she seemed thrilled. There was no rancour, or rage. Extraordinary. It's all in the past, clearly. Although I was hoping she'd have something else to share about Derek. All we have is corroboration of what we already knew. Held court in the bar, left alone, no sign of anyone trying to get in the room or leaving. I'm starting to think it was a ghost who did away with Veland,' he said.

'There's no such thing as ghosts,' said Amita, stepping into the lobby. 'Apart from our memories, I'd say. We're all haunted by those, aren't we?' She stood still for a moment, as if confronting some phantom from her own past. Jason rarely saw her like this and wondered if he should ask what it was that haunted her. But then she seemed to snap out of it and the moment was gone.

'And anyway, the bruising around our actor friend's neck was not made by a disgruntled ghoul.'

'Then who did it?' he asked.

'I don't know,' said Amita. 'But I'll give you one lesson from the past, Jason: I'm not so sure Sarah Paris is as ignorant as she made out.'

Chapter 21

SAVE ME

The mood in the church hall was downright glum. Amita could feel a wariness hanging in the air. Nobody had any focus, let alone enthusiasm for the game that was unfolding. Every call for a house or line had been lethargic. Even Father Ford seemed to be down in the mouth, his usual Wednesday night jitters stifled by the ominous atmosphere.

It had been just under a week since Derek Veland's death had made the news. The whole Club was devastated. As dedicated fans of *The Locus*, it was as if they felt almost responsible that these deaths had happened on their patch. Murderers were all well and good on the box – but real life ones stalking your local streets felt a whole lot less cosy. Plus having a second member of the cast and crew murdered was bad news for their calendars as well as their mood. The future of the show was hanging in the balance. What were they going to watch if it was cancelled?

The final game before the break came and went. When the vicar announced that the tea and biscuits were on, everyone slowly got to their feet and stretched, hobbled and shambled their way over to the urns. No one fought over who was going to get the pink wafers, no surreptitious jostling over who would be left with the chipped mug. Amita stayed where she was. She had no appetite, no thirst. She took a long, deep breath and began making aimless dots with her dabber about the top of her bingo card.

'Well, this is thoroughly depressing,' said Georgie, clicking her tongue. 'I like to come here and get a bit of life and conversation. I may as well have stayed at home and watched the washing dry in my brand-new tumble dryer.'

'You bought it, then?' asked Judy Moskowitz.

'I did,' said Georgie. 'Had it delivered yesterday. Top of the range, you know. It's got more buttons and knobs on it than the space shuttle. It can dry your clothes in nigh on ten minutes, get rid of all the creases–'

'Fold them up and put them away in the cupboard,' Sandy interrupted.

Amita and Judy managed a smile at that, as did a few others dotted around their table. Georgie didn't see the funny side.

'No, of course not Sandy,' she said, seething. 'Don't be ridiculous.'

The big man shrugged, relieved he'd cut her off before she read the manual out, or perhaps the price tag.

'Of course,' he said. 'We're all delighted for you and your new tumble dryer, Georgie. Congratulations – I hope you'll be very happy together.'

The silence descended on the group once again. Nobody felt like starting another conversation, least of all Amita. Occasionally she looked up from her aimless dabbing.

She spotted Sandy as he looked up too. Amita quickly turned away before he caught her. She tried to pretend to be busy looking at the queue for tea and biscuits. It was dwindling already, no usual gossip chirruping from the line. Usually you couldn't line up for your Custard Cream without a scoop about what was going on at the bowls club or who had forgotten to water the Britain in Bloom azaleas. Today, though, they queued like they were lining up for Westminster Abbey.

'We need a dance,' said Ethel down the end, breaking the sepulchral tone.

'What's that?' asked Georgie.

'We need a dance. Everyone likes a good dance. We should all get up and have a dance, that'll cheer everyone up.'

'I don't think dancing is on people's minds at the moment,' said Sandy.

'A dance, it's good for what ails you!'

'We're not dancing, Ethel, settle down,' said Georgie.

'Everyone loves a good whirl around the floor,' the eldest member of the Penrith Bingo Club cackled. 'It gets the blood flowing.'

'We're not dancing,' Georgie snapped.

Ethel shrunk into her wheelchair. Amita stopped her dabbing. She had to say something in defence of Ethel.

'It's not really the time or the place, Ethel,' she said gently. 'Everyone is just a little down after all that's been going on.'

'What's been going on?' asked Ethel.

There was a collective groan from everyone but Amita.

'Murder most horrid, Ethel. The director and lead star of *The Locus* have been killed, Ethel,' said Georgie, shaking her head.

'I like *The Locus*,' she said.

'Yes, we all do,' hissed Georgie. 'That's why we're all feeling down. It's an embarrassment that they come to Cumbria and we ruin the whole show. I wish they would just let us know what was happening, that the police would find whichever lowlife has blown into town and caused all this, and we could move on.'

'It's the waiting that kills you,' sighed Pauline Saxon.

Ethel began to laugh loudly. She thumped the arm rest of her wheelchair, pointing and guffawing at Pauline.

'Kills you!' she crowed. 'That's a good one! Because they're all dead!'

Georgie looked like she'd sucked on a lemon. She stood up with a flourish.

'Yes, well, I'm not dead yet,' she said. 'And I'm not going to sit around here moping for much longer. I'm going to get a biscuit.'

She stormed off towards the urns. The others let her go without protest. When she was safely out of earshot, Sandy was the first to speak up.

'Don't let her bother you,' he said to Ethel. 'You know she's not really as cold and calculating as everyone thinks.'

'No, she's worse,' said Ethel.

'I was watching the repeat of that episode they put on as a tribute to Simon Nakamba the other night,' said Judy.

'I couldn't believe how young all the cast looked,' said Sandy.

'Fresh faced and just out of drama school,' said Amita.

'Hard to believe that it used to be on so late at night. Now it's the flagship show and a smash hit around the world. How do they make it so addictive?'

'Do you remember that one where they had to go to the Highlands?' said Sandy.

They all nodded.

'That one had me scratching my head for days afterwards, even when I knew who the murderer was. I see something different in it every time. Absolutely brilliant.'

'Wasn't that Nakamba's first series?' asked Amita.

'I think it was,' said Sandy. 'He was great. Although it helps when you've got that scenery to play with.'

'Just like around here,' said Judy. 'And what about the drug dealers in Mauritius. Do you remember that speed boat chase? My heart was in my mouth.'

'Again, I never saw the twist coming,' said Amita. 'In fact, I think we were so twisted and turned that none of us saw the ending that they did.'

'Wonderful stuff,' said Sandy.

'And when that gangster was found outside the concert hall,' said Ethel.

Amita looked at the others. They were all blank.

'What's that, Ethel?' she asked.

The old lady was staring off into the distance. She bobbed her head from side to side.

'When the gangster was found outside the concert hall,' she said again. 'The episode where the gangster was found, at the door of the theatre. Oh, he was a bad bugger, a real nasty piece of work. He got what was coming to him though, didn't he?'

Amita wracked her brain. She was the first to admit that her knowledge of *The Locus* was hardly encyclopaedic – not like some of the super-fans. She knew of forums and online communities that could tell you the most minute details of plot, characters and production within seconds. But she could usually remember the murder victims – and yet she was drawing a blank with this one.

'I don't remember that,' said Sandy.

'Nor me,' agreed Judy.

'Are you sure you're not getting mixed up, Ethel?' asked Amita. 'That sounds awfully like what happened to Mr Nakamba, the director.'

'Mixed up? Me?' Ethel's face drew into a hurt frown. 'I know what I'm talking about. The episode where the gangster was killed outside the music hall. It's one of my favourites.'

Amita tried to remember what Ethel was talking about. She didn't like upsetting the old lady, far from it. But sometimes she could get confused.

'That's a new one on me,' she said.

'What is?' asked Georgie, returning with her tea and biscuits.

'The gangster, killed outside the theatre,' said Ethel. 'In *The Locus*. It's one of the best episodes.'

Georgie looked confused. 'That's not an episode of the show. I've seen them all and I would remember that. Especially as a concert-goer myself, I'd be especially attuned.'

'It happened,' Ethel folded her arms and huffed.

'No, it didn't.'

'Alright, alright, let's all calm down,' said Amita.

The tension was back. She knew that Ethel could get confused. And she knew all too well that Georgie hated to back down. It was the immovable object meeting the irresistible force. All trussed up in cardigans and pearls.

'It's only a TV show,' she said. 'We don't need to fall out over it, do we?'

Neither Georgie nor Ethel replied. They were both fuming, at each other or at Amita, she couldn't tell. Luckily, she was saved by the genteel tapping of a knife against crockery.

'Ladies and gentlemen, if you'd like to take your seats, we can start the second half,' said Father Ford from the front of the hall.

Amita was relieved when everyone stopped glaring and followed the 'Eyes down' call.

'And the first number out is… eighty-five, staying alive.'

Chapter 22

SEARCHIN' MY SOUL

'A week is a long time in a murder investigation,' said Jason, holding court in his front room. 'What's the old statistic, the first forty-eight hours are crucial after somebody has been killed? Chuck in a few more days on top of that and it's getting to that worrying stage where the questions are multiplying.'

'I agree,' said Amita. 'Not solving one death is bad enough, but the prospect of not nailing a serial killer on the loose around Penrith is appalling. You should have felt the mood at bingo tonight – Judy bent down to pick up a dabber she'd dropped and everyone froze like she was reaching for a pistol. Everyone's nerves are like chewed string thinking everyone else is a potential suspect… or potential victim. They've taken two lives already, who knows if there will be more.'

If Amita had been hoping for a lightening of the mood when she returned home after bingo, she had been gravely mistaken. Jason clearly had his sleuthing hat on. He liked to pretend it was Amita dragging him into all these investigations but she knew, once he had the scent of a case, her son-in-law was a bloodhound.

'There's still something I don't understand,' he said, gesticulating at the blackboard he had protested so vehemently.

'What's that?'

'The hotel, Askling Manor. Surely staff there would have seen someone coming and going from Derek Veland's room. I mean, they have CCTV everywhere in a place like that. High-profile and rich guests and the rest of it. Surely this is *why* you have a top-notch security system?'

'I told you, I'm not convinced that Sarah was telling us the whole story,' said Amita. 'There was just something hollow about what she had to say for herself. And you're right: there has to be some sort of evidence of the killer getting into Veland's room, either before or after our late leading man was there.'

'Bloody hell,' said Jason.

'What is it?'

'Do you realize that you've agreed with me not once but twice in the space of about thirty seconds?' he said.

'Jason, behave yourself,' she tutted. 'We're trying to catch a serial killer.'

He slumped into the armchair beside the TV. The house was quiet, it was getting late. Radha and the kids were all safely tucked up in bed. Jason had been thinking about joining them after he'd picked Amita up from bingo. Only he couldn't seem to get his mind to come to a standstill. The complete lack of progress from both the police and their own efforts was driving him batty.

'We should start from the beginning,' said Amita. 'To see if we've missed anything. There's no use going around and around in circles if we're not getting anywhere.'

'True,' he said. 'So what do we have? A dead director, a dead leading man who was also our prime suspect, and a week's worth of silence and no sign that the killer has struck again.'

'That sounds about the extent of it, yes,' said Amita.

They both pondered the facts for a moment – a mish-mash of contradictions and dead ends.

'This is intolerable,' said Jason. 'Just what the hell is going on here, Amita? What kind of self-respecting serial killer targets two high-profile men and then vanishes into thin air? Despite being surrounded by cameras, I may add. It's bizarre.'

'It is odd, I'll give you that,' she said. 'However, we've faced "odd" before. In fact, I'd go as far as saying it's something of our speciality. So, if we go back to basics, I know we can catch this murderer. We've done it before, we can do it again.'

'Yes, we have,' he said, standing up, roused by Amita's speech. Then his shoulders slumped. 'But those situations were completely different. Firstly, we only had one corpse per case to deal with before now. Secondly, I always felt there was a discernible motive before now – however twisted – but two bodies changes all that. Now, if Derek Veland was still walking among us, I could get my head around it. He had means and motive to do away with Simon Nakamba. But the fact that he's turned up dead too, strangled by all accounts, in a hotel room where nobody saw anyone come or go, it's like something out of an episode of their own show.'

Amita was biting her nails again. She caught herself this time and stopped. They were worn down and it was beginning to hurt.

'And it's not just us drawing a blank, is it?' she said. 'You've heard nothing from DI Arendonk?'

'Not a word. You? You usually come back from bingo having heard every rumour and confession going,' he ventured.

'Nothing,' she said with a sigh.

They fell silent again in contemplation. Radha had recently bought a new clock for the living room. It was perched on the mantlepiece, wedged between graduation pictures and photos of the children. The tick, tock, tick, tock seemed to be growing louder in the quiet room, almost goading Jason and Amita to come up with something.

'What about Sarah Paris?' Jason asked. 'Have you spoken to her since we dropped in unannounced?'

'No,' said Amita gravely. 'And that worries me. I gave her my number hoping she'd get in contact so I could check-in regularly. But nothing. I haven't tried to go through the hotel as it might come across as prying.'

'Probably for the best,' said Jason. 'We've been there three times and thrown out twice. I don't expect us to be getting discounts on rooms any time soon.'

'Our own silly faults,' she said. 'Well, I say our, yours mostly.'

'Alright, alright,' he held his hands up. 'Let's not go down that road again.'

'I'm worried about Sarah,' said Amita. 'She didn't seem to be in the best of places when we saw her last.'

'What do you think she's hiding? Is she protecting the killer?'

'No,' she said. 'If she knew who the murderer was she would have been much more nervous, I'm sure. Maybe it's money worries. That manor house must be costing an arm and a leg to run.'

'So, what, then? I don't think bumping off a TV star is going to help pay any bills.'

'I don't know, Jason,' she said. 'I don't know if she's trying to protect someone, or protect herself or the business.'

'There is one other possible explanation,' he shrugged. 'Do you think she might be our killer?'

The question hit Amita like a freight train. She felt her stomach lurch at the dreadful thought. She was about to tell her son-in-law that it was absolutely out of the question, that Sarah Paris was, had been, many things. But she couldn't be a murderer, let alone a repeat killer. Something stopped her, however. The truth was, she couldn't be sure.

'I, well, I don't know,' she said.

'Wow,' said Jason. 'Anything short of no is a bit of a bomb-shell, Amita. When were you going to tell me she was still very much on the 'maybe' pile when it comes to suspects?'

'I wasn't,' she said. 'I haven't been thinking about it. Because I'm not sure it's even a thing to be thinking about. I mean, what reason would she have for doing something like this? Why would she want Derek Veland dead and found in *her* hotel?'

'She's the owner,' he said. 'It's her kingdom. She'll know every square inch of that place, every foible, every nook and cranny and, more importantly, she'll have access to every room, and – more than likely – every CCTV camera and recording.'

There was a giddiness to his voice, Amita could hear it. He was believing his own words, working it all out as he spoke. She didn't like where this thinking was going but she had no choice but to let it play out. It fitted the evidence better than anything else they'd tried.

'Possibly,' said Amita. 'What reason would she have for killing him though? Or Nakamba for that matter?'

Jason hesitated. Amita was a little relieved. The last thing she wanted to be doing was investigating Sarah Paris. She was the same age as her Radha, they'd gone through all those teenage rites of passage together – discos and dressing up, exams and sleepovers. She couldn't possibly be a killer. Could she?

'Maybe she didn't,' said Jason, his eyes lighting up. 'Perhaps we've all watched too much telly and got fixated on this notion of a multiple murderer. Maybe Veland killed Nakamba, and Sarah did away with Veland.'

'Why?'

'We need to face up to the possibility that we've been looking at this all wrong,' he said. 'Maybe the reason we're stumped is because Simon Nakamba's killer *was* who we thought it was. And with Derek Veland being murdered himself, the case has gone cold. Maybe there is no serial killer at all. If Veland was the first killer and now he's been murdered too, by Sarah, then it's a chain reaction we're dealing with – not some kind of killing spree.'

Amita hadn't thought of that. Nobody had, clearly. It made perfect sense.

'So what links Derek Veland and Sarah Paris? And why would she want him dead?' she asked.

'That's what we need to find out,' said Jason. 'I don't know, were they lovers? Was Sarah dating Nakamba and she wanted revenge? Was she seeing Veland and had had enough of his antics. You said it yourself, he was up and down like Tower Bridge. Maybe she just snapped and had enough. She certainly had the means. And then there's the publicity element.'

'Publicity?' she asked.

'Open a newspaper, turn on the news, Askling Manor hasn't been off it. Namechecked, photos, videos, everything. Nakamba's murder was national news, Veland is almost triggering national mourning. You can't buy that sort of coverage, no matter how awful.'

'This is grim,' she rubbed her forehead. 'This is utterly ghastly on almost every level.'

'I know,' said Jason. He lowered his voice. 'Maybe we should keep it under wraps from Radha until we have proof.'

'Yes, of course,' said Amita. 'Something like this would destroy her. It's pretty much done that to me!'

'Steady on now, Amita, we don't know anything for certain yet,' he tried to comfort her. 'It's just a theory. We have to prove a connection between Sarah and Veland or Sarah and Nakamba. If there's any link, anything at all, then it could be the key to unravelling this case.'

Amita couldn't help it, she started biting her nails again. The habit was painful but strangely comforting. Her mind was racing, thinking about Sarah Paris, about Derek Veland, about Simon Nakamba and the whole sorry affair. She was torn between wanting the killer, or killers, brought to justice, at any cost, and the closeness, guilt and responsibility she felt for Sarah.

Then there was Radha. She hated keeping anything from her daughter, especially something like this. Jason was right, however: there was no need to cause a fuss if they didn't have any proof. There was no need to upset Radha unnecessarily. At least, for the moment.

'What do you think we should do?' he asked.

'The easiest thing in the world is to tell the truth,' she said. 'You know I'm a great believer in that, Jason. I think I should simply ask Sarah what's going on and if she knew our victims before all of this happened.'

'You? Don't you mean we?'

'No, I'll go alone,' she said.

'But she might be a killer, Amita.'

'I'm aware of that,' she said. 'She also might *not* be a killer and is only an old friend of your wife's who has fallen on hard times. Proof, Jason, we need proof.'

'Ok, fair enough,' he held up his hands. 'What do you want me to do?'

Amita stood up. Her knees and back clicked and she winced a little in pain.

'Sarah might not be so forthcoming with her answers as we are with questions,' she said. 'If I think she's hiding something now, she might just clam up and block out everything. We should do a little digging to see if her name has been mentioned on the set.'

'I think they're almost fully packed up,' said Jason. 'I drove past earlier, all the big lorries are gone.'

'Then we'll have to be quick,' said Amita. 'Head down there first thing in the morning and see what you can find out. Lisa the runner, she was very helpful. Maybe she's seen

Sarah on set or hanging around nearby. Maybe you could try Pip Potter too.'

'Pip Potter,' Jason's voice went a few octaves higher. 'Why would I need to speak to her? That is to say, again.'

'Calm down, Jason,' she said. 'Nobody was closer to Derek Veland and Simon Nakamba than she was. If either of them were involved with Sarah or anyone else, she would know about it.'

'And what if she's gone too? Upped sticks and high-tailed it back to Manchester or London?'

'You'll just have to improvise,' said Amita. 'Think on your feet. You're a journalist, you don't need me holding your hand every step of the way. What did you do before I helped you?'

'Very good, Sheriff,' he feigned a smile. He was energised by the lead – but for the same reason the bingo regulars had been quiet: there was a little too much death in the air to not be watching your back. Nevertheless, he attempted some kind of salute as Amita stood up.

Amita laughed. She headed into the hallway, ready for bed. Not that she was going to get a wink of sleep tonight. There were far too many bad thoughts running around her brain.

'No rest for the wicked,' she said quietly to herself. 'Even less for the good.'

Chapter 23

IN THE SUN

Jason reminded himself that he was there to do a job. It was the millionth time since he'd left the house. He wasn't quite sure why he was so nervous. He was a journalist, he was used to interviewing people from all walks of life. Albeit he hadn't been doing a great deal of that in the last little while. But it was a life skill, like riding a bike, you never forgot.

He rounded the corner onto the high street. The set was just up ahead. Or what was left of it. Only a few signs that the place had ever been used for filming still remained. A couple of random spotlights, a few taped crosses on the street, a couple of mini-vans parked up close to the entrance of the theatre. Even the residents of Penrith seemed to have lost interest in it all, going about their business without so much as glancing in the set's direction, or perhaps avoiding looking at it deliberately – you could clean up a crime scene but the spirit of murder hung heavy.

'Just get in and get out again, that's all,' he said to himself.

A young woman cocked an eyebrow at him as he walked past her, talking to himself. Jason didn't blame her for the strange look. He would have done the same.

His hands were clammy, despite the near freezing weather. His could feel his throat getting dry, a horrid taste in there despite having just had breakfast. It was ridiculous.

'You're a professional, Jason,' he said to himself. 'You're here to ask questions, to get answers, and nothing more. Get a grip of yourself.'

What remained of *The Locus* set loomed ahead. The street was looking more like its old self. There was a familiarity to it that put Jason's mind a little more at ease. He crossed the road, and stepped into the world of TV drama unaccosted.

Ordinarily that would have been a positive outcome. On this occasion, however, he was on his own and desperately in need of some direction. He looked about the place. Everything looked sad and abandoned. There was no sign of any runners, any crew, anyone at all, this time. And, most importantly, no Pip Potter.

'Hello?' he called out. 'Is there anyone here?'

Hardly to his surprise, there was no answer back. Jason trotted around the set. He peered into the back of empty vans with their doors left open. He gave a wide berth to a group of spotlights that were perched precariously close to the edge of the kerb. The last thing he wanted to do was touch them and they'd break into a million pieces. Knowing his luck, that's *exactly* what would happen. They looked expensive. Although making a scene normally drew out all kinds of crowds, he acknowledged, he thought better of it and stuck with his original plan.

He was still searching around when his phone began to buzz. In a panic, he flapped around, forgetting which pocket it was in. When he did find it, he didn't recognise the number. Desperate for another voice, he answered.

'Hello?'

'Brazel, good, you're still alive,' came a voice from the other end.

'What? Who is this?'

'Ayanna Smith.'

Jason was immediately relieved. He let his shoulders slump. 'Smiffy!' he said.

'What did I tell you about not calling me that?' said the London reporter.

'Oh yes, sorry, must have slipped my mind.'

'Well you are getting on a bit,' she said, with no hint of flippancy. 'I take it you're still in Penrith.'

'I am,' he said. 'Let me guess. You're calling about Simon Nakamba.'

'So you *are* switched on and plugged into the news. Wonders will never cease.'

Ordinarily, Jason would have taken umbrage. But Smiffy, despite making him feel old, was a hotshot reporter and actually very good at her job. He didn't mind the little sparring sessions they had.

'I'll let that one slip,' he said. 'I was half expecting to see you back sniffing around town. Most of your colleagues from the big smoke are here.'

'That's for the rank and file hacks,' she said. 'I'm acting deputy news editor now.'

'What?' he yelped. 'But you're only twelve!'

'That's ageist,' she said. 'I could have the union drag you over hot coals for a remark like that.'

'Sorry,' he said feebly. 'What do you want, then?'

'Some info,' she said. 'Any info. The team they've given me here, it's rubbish.'

'You mean it's not you.'

'In as many words,' said Smiffy. 'And seeing as you're so old that you were probably around when the question mark was invented, I wanted to know if you have anything on what's going on?'

Jason considered this for a moment. His past experiences writing for the big papers in London hadn't been a stroll in the park. Far from it. He liked Smiffy, he really did. The fact that she was in such a position of power so early in her career didn't surprise him in the least. He was therefore torn between helping out someone he admired and running for the hills.

'I may know one or two things,' he said. 'And maybe a little bit more if you weren't distracting me.'

'Works for me. Five hundred words and five hundred quid sound about right?'

'Is that the going rate?'

'It is for you,' said Smiffy curtly.

'Makes sense.'

'Regular stories, every day. Have them in my inbox by six,' she said. 'Any later and you don't get a penny.'

'Wait a minute, hang on,' he said. 'Is this me being commissioned? You know, in my day you had to pitch to editors and hope you weren't burnt to a crisp from their fire breath. Now I'm being propositioned over the phone.'

'Welcome to the twenty-first century,' she said with a groan. 'Oh, and Brazel.'

'Yes?'

'Don't make it crap, eh?'

She hung up. Jason blinked and slowly put his phone away. Contacts in high places, he thought, him? Who would have thought it?

A loud clank startled him. It was followed by a stream of profanities that would have made Jason blush if he knew what half of them meant. There was a bang, then another clatter and finally a thump. Jason followed the cacophony to an alleyway that ran beside the concert hall.

He was met with the unwanted sight of a builder's bum. A man was hunched over, loading equipment into large, padded boxes. Jason cleared his throat to let the swearing individual know he was there.

'Excuse me,' he said.

The man stood up. He wore a surly face that looked like it didn't know what a smile was, let alone had actually pulled one.

'Yeah? Who are you?' he asked in a strident cockney accent.

'Jason Brazel, I'm a journalist and–'

'I don't talk to the media,' said the man, immediately returning to his work. 'You need to go through the press office for anything. And no, I can't get you any autographs from the cast or sit here and listen to you tell me your theories on Season Two. Not my job, mate. So sling your hook – before I sling it for you.'

'No, I'm not a fan, I'm–'

'Not my problem,' the man barked at him, still hunched over.

Maybe it was his tone, or the fact he wasn't convinced the already low-slung jeans were going to hold up much longer, but Jason wasn't standing for this anymore. He walked right up to the disgruntled worker and tapped him on one meaty shoulder. Only then did he realize that he was a good inch shorter than the surly man, and considerably narrower. There was nothing else for it now though. He had to stand firm.

Then he thought of Amita. What would she do in a situation like this? She was unflappable, stiff upper lip, never say die, all of that cobblers. She acted like she had a divine right to be wherever she'd just got caught. He thought he might as well try it before this worker rearranged his face.

'Listen…' he stammered. 'I'm looking for someone. And all I want from you is some directions, that's all. There's no need to be so bloody rude.'

'Rude?' The man's face seemed to grow meaner. 'What are you talking about, mate?'

'I'm saying that a little bit of common decency wouldn't go amiss,' said Jason, trying to stand tall. 'I'm looking for Pip Potter or Lisa the runner. Have you heard of them?'

'Heard of them?'

'That's what I asked, wasn't it?'

The man glared at him in disbelief. He thought for a moment, hard eyes locked firmly on Jason. Then he seemed to soften.

'Down the end of the road there,' he said, pointing back out the alleyway. 'All the rest of the cast and any of the runners who haven't already run off will be down there. If you hurry, you'll probably catch them before they sod off and leave me to clean up the mess. As usual.'

Jason was so amazed that channelling his mother-in-law had actually worked that he almost missed the directions.

'Right, okay, thank you,' he said, sticking out his chin. *Be More Amita*. It might have to be his new maxim.

The man waved him away and turned back to loading the equipment into his boxes. Jason decided not to test his resolve. He quickly took his leave and hurried down the street.

'I'll never hear the end of this if I tell her,' he said to himself.

But his optimism wavered as he headed in the direction the roadie had pointed. There was barely a sign that any film crew had been anywhere near Penrith, let alone taken the place over for almost a month – shop logos that had been covered up were back to normal, fake road signs swapped back to their usual destinations. Jason stopped. He looked around for any trace of *The Locus* or anyone who worked on it. He began to think he'd been too quick in praising the Amita Khatri Method of Getting Things Done. The Sheriff of Penrith's unique way with people might only work for her. The disgruntled man could have sent him on a wild goose chase.

A set of voices paused his panic. Two young men wearing big puffer jackets and matching beanie hats came out of a doorway. Unmistakable electronic clatterboards were slung over their shoulders as they made their way across the street.

Jason let them go and hopped over to the doorway they had emerged from. He slipped inside, grateful to be out of the cold.

He untied his scarf and looked up the steps of a communal stairwell. There were more voices echoing down. He started climbing until he reached the first floor, only to find the doors off the landing locked. But he could still hear the voices so he pressed on up. At the top of the next flight, one of the doors of the flats was propped open. People were inside, laughing and chatting. It didn't feel or sound like a murderer's lair, he figured. Time to Be More Amita again, he told himself.

The warmth made his hands a little clammier as he stepped into the flat. He peered around the doorway, looking for the owners of the voices. The rooms were all bare, no furniture or trappings, like it had recently been cleared. When he found the kitchen, he saw a familiar face.

'Jason!' Lisa cried.

She broke off her conversation with a tall, spotty-faced lad, and came over to give Jason a hug. He wasn't expecting it and let his arms float in mid-air like tentacles. He was relieved when she let go.

'What are you doing here?' she asked. 'And where's Amita?'

'She had another appointment,' he said. 'What is this place?'

He looked about the kitchen. Countless empty jars of coffee were spread across the worktops. There were dirty dishes in the sink, piles of takeaway boxes erupting out of the bins.

'Welcome to *The Locus*' crew headquarters,' said Lisa. 'This is where all of us mere mortals involved in making Britain's premier detective show like to hang out, chill and get away from being shouted at by maniacal directors and drunk actors.'

She clapped a hand to her mouth, eyes wide.

'Oops, did I say that out loud?' she asked. 'That's definitely not on the record, ok, Jason?'

He laughed nervously.

'It's not quite the glamorous HQ I expected. In fact, it's worse than my digs when I was at college.'

'I can very well believe that,' said Lisa. 'I might be new to this industry but I've very quickly learned that the staff base is normally the least glamorous part of any shoot. But it's warm and there is plenty of coffee and biscuits if that's your thing.'

'No, thank you,' said Jason, spying the dirty mug that would be his if he accepted. 'I was actually wondering if you could help me find Pip Potter. I don't know if she's still around or gone back to the smoke. I wanted to ask her a couple of things if I could.'

'If you want her number, I can give it to you, if you like,' said Lisa, with a wry smile.

'What? God, no! That's not what I meant!' said Jason, panicking. 'No, no, it's to do with these murders.'

'What do you want Pip for? Is this something to do with your investigation?'

Lisa nudged her friend in the ribs.

'Jason and his mother-in-law are private investigators, Darrel,' she said. 'They run around town solving murders that the police can't. They're famous.'

'Steady on, Lisa,' he said. 'We're hardly Poirot and Hastings.'

'So come on then, what have you found out? Anything salacious? Do you know who the killer is?'

Jason was a little taken aback by Lisa's chirpy enthusiasm. He had come here hoping to be the one asking questions. Not be at the receiving end of an inquisition. He liked Lisa, she seemed keen, intelligent and happy to help – but she also seemed blithely untroubled by the fact two of her colleagues had been mown down. A humming unease he couldn't shift reminded him he shouldn't be sharing all the details of his investigation with her readily.

'It's coming along,' he said, trying to smile. 'These things tend to take time.'

'He's being humble,' said Lisa, nodding to Darrel. 'They're a proper Batman and Robin dynamic duo.'

'You wouldn't want to see either of us in tights, believe me,' said Jason.

He was relieved that seemed to knock Lisa off her train of thought. She emptied her mug and left it on the countertop.

'Clean all of this up, would you?' she asked Darrel. 'The perks of being that smidgen more senior in the junior ranks.'

She winked at Jason and guided him out of the kitchen. 'Come on, I'll take you around and see who we can see. You can give me all of the gossip and—'

Lisa stopped. A tall, broad-chested figure appeared at the open front door. Jason felt a sudden chill and stopped too, instinctively grabbing Lisa by the arm to protect her.

'Where is he?' came a deep, angry voice.

'Where's who?' asked Jason, his skin crawling a little.

The man was steeped in shadow, lurking just beyond the threshold of the flat. He was clenching his fists, his silhouette taking up most of the doorframe.

'I won't ask again,' he said. 'I'm warning you.'

'I think you've got the wrong address, mate,' said Lisa. 'This is being used by the film crew to—'

Before she could finish, the man bolted straight for them. Jason did just about enough to shove Lisa into one of the empty rooms. Heavy thuds accompanied the stranger as he thundered down the hallway. Jason caught sight of his huge, gloved hands grabbing him before he was pinned against the wall. A hard, sneering face was almost pressed against his, peering at him from beneath a black Stetson. You didn't get many Stetsons in Penrith, he thought, before wondering if that was going to be his last thought.

The man was clad head-to-toe in black leather. Skull studs bristled across his gloved fingers, matching the shining, pointed tips of his cowboy boots. He shoved Jason a little harder now that he had him by the scruff of his coat.

'Where is he?' he asked again.

'Listen pal, I don't know who you're looking for or what it has to do with me, but I can assure you I don't know what you're talking about.'

'Let go of him!' Lisa shouted, grabbing at the stranger's arm. Darrel appeared at the kitchen door, face slack.

'Call the police!' Lisa shouted, still tugging at the arm. 'Tell them we're being attacked!'

The stranger let go of Jason immediately. He staggered back a little, pushing the rim of his Stetson upwards. He looked at Jason, then Lisa and Darrel one by one. The anger seemed to leave him, draining into the floor through his admittedly magnificent boots.

'Simon Nakamba,' he said, fists released and hands shaking. Jason saw tears welling in his eyes. 'What has happened to him?'

Lisa looked over to Jason, possibly for inspiration. He couldn't tell.

'I'm afraid Simon is dead,' he said to the stranger. He didn't look like the kind of man who'd take well to being soft-soaped.

'I know that,' said the stranger, slumping to the floor. 'I want to know what has happened to him. He was all I had. What am I going to do now, huh? What am I going to do now?'

He sunk his head into his hands and brimming tears began to flow.

Chapter 24

WON'T YOU BE MY NEIGHBOUR?

The Piano Concerto in A minor, Op. 7 reached its peaceful conclusion. Not that Amita heard it. She had dozed off. Occasionally her head would bob too far backwards and she would wake up with a startle, only to drift back off to sleep. Over and over this had happened in the last hour, as if she was conducting her own private performance.

She was exhausted. The past few days were beginning to catch up with her. She didn't feel anywhere near as spry as she normally did. Never before had her seventy-one years weighed so heavily on her shoulders.

Sat in a car, the heating turned up full blast and with the comforts of Radio Three for company, she'd let the music carry her away. And she had, willingly or not, succumbed to the fatigue. Ordinarily this wouldn't have been a problem. Only this was a stake out. She was meant to be gathering clues not letting Schumann soothe her.

The break in the music was enough to waken her. She blinked and snorted, then the panic set in. Amita looked about the car, to make sure she was still alone. The windows were steamed up so she wiped them with the sleeve of her cardigan.

'Stay sharp, Amita,' she said to herself. 'You can sleep when you're dead.'

The gates that led to Askling Manor were just across the road. Amita had parked in the layby and was waiting. Sarah Paris was in there, she knew it. She needed to get hold of her, speak with her, question her a little harder than before, but all calls to her or via the front desk had led to polite rebuffs. She was hiding something, Amita knew it. But what and why were still elusive.

She had thought about confronting Sarah at the hotel. Then thought better of it. Askling Manor might have been a five-star luxury resort, but it was also her fortress. And, for want of a better word, playground. If Amita wanted answers, she needed Sarah away from there.

The day was wearing on. Amita had done everything she could think of to while away the time. She'd completed all her daily word searches, sudokus and musical challenges on her phone. She'd checked her emails with every message that dropped. She'd even managed to clear out some of the crumbs and other rubbish from the passenger seat of the car. By the time the clock on the dashboard hit four, she was both bored and even more exhausted than before.

A set of headlights beamed bright from the driveway of the hotel. She'd sat up every time anyone had driven past, but the ebb and flow of guests in their gleaming SUVs and electric cars purring by had only been carrying strangers all day. Now it was dark she wasn't sure she'd be able to recognise Sarah even if she came off shift. Amita shielded her eyes as the car drew closer. It indicated and started down the road heading south. Amita couldn't see who was driving but then she spotted the registration plate: S4 RAP.

'Sarah P,' she said, and switched her engine on.

She pulled out onto the road and stayed at a safe distance, tailing the BMW as it wound its way through the country roads.

The sun had set, casting everything into muted colours amid the twilight. Amita hated driving at night; it was why she always insisted Jason take her to bingo. She stayed focused on the rear lights of what she hoped was Sarah's car up ahead. On and on it went until the road became little more than a lane.

A small village rose up out of the half-light. Amita did her best to stay close to the BMW but it was impossible not knowing the roads. Eventually the motor came to a stop outside an old farmhouse on the other side of a narrow bridge. Amita parked up. She scrambled out of the car and hurried down the lane.

'Sarah!' she shouted.

Sarah Paris looked shocked as she peered through the gloom.

'Amita?' she shouted back. 'What the hell are you doing here?'

Amita gave a quiet sigh of relief as she skipped over the bridge. Thankfully she had been right and not been led on a pointless drive away from the hotel.

'I followed you from Askling Manor,' she said, reaching Sarah. 'I couldn't get through on the phone. I was worried. I was wondering if I could come in.'

'You followed me? What for?'

'Please, I think we should go inside, before the neighbours start talking.'

'The neighbours? Amita, what's going on? Are you stalking me or something?'

'Sarah, please,' her voice was low and serious.

Sarah took the hint. She collected her handbag and a stack of folders and files from her car and locked it. She showed Amita the way to the front door and they went inside. No sooner was the door locked when she turned on Amita.

'Just what is going on here, Amita?' she asked pointedly. 'You come shouting out of the darkness like some crazy woman and start talking like you're Interpol. What's wrong with you?'

Amita was a little shocked. The surprise of hearing Sarah speak like that reminded her that she was far from the little girl she'd known back in the day. She had always been able to spin a good yarn, had Sarah, and maybe she was about to do so again.

'Derek Veland,' Amita said. 'I'm here to ask you about Derek Veland and what happened to him.'

A look of disgust made Sarah's face twitch. She pushed past Amita and stalked down the hallway of her house. Amita followed. She passed pictures of the family on the walls: Sarah with her parents, Sarah when she was a teenager, even younger in school photos.

'Was this your parents' house?' she called after her. 'I lost touch with them after they left Penrith. I didn't know they'd moved out here.'

'Oh yes, they loved it here,' said Sarah, her voice dripping with venom. 'They called this place their *El Dorado*. Some sanctuary; it's only twenty minutes from that bloody hotel they cared so much about.'

Sarah was in the living room now. Boxes were piled high on top of each other, all bursting with paperwork. She was leaning against the nearest stack, rubbing the back of her head.

'If I'd known you were coming I would have made an effort,' she said. 'Put a blanket over the paperwork or something, I don't know.'

Amita wasn't sure if she should laugh. She noticed a huge, full school photo hanging above a sofa. She wandered over and spotted Radha, smiling awkwardly, a heavy fringe and teeth in braces. A few rows up was Sarah.

'I had this photo, but it got lost in a move,' Amita said. 'I remember the day it was taken. Radha and all your year had just had a measles jab.'

'And some kids were going about punching arms,' said Sarah, wandering over to be beside her. 'The prefects were told to reprimand anyone they caught. Nobody did, of course. Eat or be eaten, even back then...'

'I don't believe that for a second,' said Amita, turning to her. 'And besides, you always looked out for Radha. And she did for you too.'

'She wasn't like the other kids, that's why,' said Sarah. 'She had brains and she cared about people.'

'True,' she said. 'All my children do. Even my children-in-law can have their moments.'

'Oh yes, dishy Jason,' said Sarah, her mouth curling into a smile. 'Radha always had the best taste.'

Sarah ran a hand through her hair. She lifted some boxes and offered a seat to Amita then slumped down on the free chair by the TV.

'I can't even offer you something to eat as there's nothing in,' she said. 'I eat at work, if I remember, or else Abi will bring something in with her on her way back from college or her Tae Kwondo class.'

'How is she coping?'

Sarah rubbed her eyes. Amita could see the stress oozing out of her. Things were tough, she had seen that before. Now she was in Sarah's home it was clear there was a lot to unravel. The place was a mess, nothing to eat in the cupboards – the telltale signs that she wasn't coping.

'She's trying,' said Sarah. 'I warned her, I said to her that nursing is one of the hardest jobs there is. Not just on shift but the emotional responsibility that comes with it when you take it home at night. She said she could handle it but I'm not so sure, Amita. I don't know if she has the resilience that's needed, you know? Something like that, it's more than a job.'

'Like running Askling Manor,' she said.

'Ain't that the truth,' said Sarah, rolling her eyes. 'Only that was a passion forced on me, rather than chosen. Abi is a wonderful girl, she has the same single-minded focus my mum used to have. You remember? Rhona Paris could storm the beaches at Normandy and still make a full Christmas dinner before sundown.'

'I remember.' Amita laughed at that thought.

'I just worry Abi gave up on her first love and now she's scrambling for something to replace it. I mean she's tried all sorts of hobbies – crochet to karate – but none of them seem to obsess her like her childhood passion.'

'And what was that?'

'Being on stage,' Sarah smiled. 'Didn't matter what she was doing up there. Singing, dancing, acting, magic, you name it. I remember when she was three and in the nursery Nativity. The teachers practically had to pull her off the stage, she was taking so many bows. She was only a sheep!'

Sarah wasn't looking at her anymore. She was staring into space. Her eyes fell on a picture in a silver frame on the mantelpiece. She stood up and took it down.

'My dad put paid to that dream,' she said bitterly. 'As he did so many other dreams over the years.'

'He was hard on her as well as you?'

'Hard?' Sarah laughed. 'He made rigor mortis look like jelly. You must remember him, Amita. He was forever riding my back, grades, grades, grades, take over the business one day, on and on and on, advance, advance. He was Cumbria's answer to Gordon Gekko, or at least he thought he was. He had the braces and the Cartier, I suppose. No wonder I was such a troublemaker, living with that prat.'

Amita had never really known Russell Paris. He had always been distant, never appearing at school events. She had always presumed he had been busy with the hotel and his other business ventures. The memories clearly stung for Sarah.

'And he said Abi couldn't be come an actor?'

'In not so polite terms, yes,' said Sarah, putting the picture of her parents back. 'So she didn't. They were determined not to have another wildchild in the family after my teenage exploits. Now she's stuck doing a course that's probably taxing her beyond her limits and meanwhile he's six feet under. Funny how the universe has a way of playing tricks on us, isn't it?'

There was a controlled anger to Sarah now. The same anger that had appeared when she spotted Amita outside. It struck her that was a dangerous kind of rage – what did you do with that kind of pent-up fury? Resenting the dead usually backfired on the living, in her experience.

'But you didn't come here to talk about the good old days, did you Amita?' she asked. 'Not that they were all good days, were they?'

The sinking feeling in the pit of Amita's stomach grew deeper. This was what she had been dreading for a very long time. There had been moments over the past twenty years when she thought it would never come. A confrontation with a girl, the best friend of her daughter, who she had thrown under the bus. She had made the wrong decision, she knew that at the time. Now she would have to pay.

'Sarah, I'm sorry,' she said, bowing her head. 'I did the wrong thing, made the wrong decision in an impossible situation. I've lived with that guilt every day since and–'

'What are you talking about?' Sarah asked.

Amita was confused. 'The past, I suppose,' she stuttered.

'I've got too much trouble in the present to be dwelling on the past, Mrs Khatri,' said Sarah. 'I've got the world's media smearing my hotel's once good name alongside a criminal investigation that's spiralling out of control. I'd be devastated at the cancellations if I wasn't so relieved at the fact it's meant I can occasionally leave that place at a human hour.'

'You were keeping something from me, the other day there, Sarah,' said Amita. 'I could sense it, I could tell.'

'Nonsense,' she remained steadfast. 'Why would I hold something back from you? You've known me all my life.'

'Exactly,' said Amita, standing up too. 'Exactly that. So why keep something from me? If I can help, Sarah, I will. But you need to be honest with me. You need to tell me everything.'

Anger made Sarah's face twitch again. For a very brief moment, Amita thought she was about to hit her. She thought about flinching or putting up her dukes. Being punched in the nose by one of your daughter's oldest friends was not the kind of thing she wanted to happen. Even if she deserved it. That was much more in Jason's style of investigation than hers.

'It's not... it's not as easy as that,' she said. 'There's more going on here than you know, Amita. You should stay out of it.'

Whatever 'it' was, Amita felt a wave of satisfaction that her instincts hadn't let her down. Alongside that feeling, however, was a growing sense that she was uncovering the kind of secret that would never go back in its box. There was no way back now.

'I don't want to stay out of it,' she said. 'Sarah, if you're in some sort of trouble, if somebody is threatening you, if you've done something you shouldn't have, I want to help. I can't do that if you don't tell me what's going on.'

Amita braced for the worst as she looked at Sarah, fixed to the spot like a woman possessed. Then Sarah let out an almighty scream. It was raw, like she was an animal caught in a trap. When she was finished, she doubled over, gasping for air.

'Bloody hell,' she gasped. 'I needed that.'

Amita, deafened, reached over and rubbed her back, relieved Sarah's rage had been directed at the universe rather than her guest.

'What's going on?' she asked gently.

Sarah shook her head. She straightened up, wiping tears from the corners of her eyes.

'It's a mess, Amita, the whole thing is a mess,' she said.

'Messes can be fixed, you know that. Your mother used to say it all the time.'

'My mother, yes,' said Sarah bitterly. 'The only one who was more driven than my dad was her. Dad was never here, Mum was *always* here. I used to get detention so I didn't have to be in the same house as her. I was as determined as both of them, just in a different way. And now look where that drive has got me, lumbered with their legacy and tampering with police evidence.'

Amita went cold. She didn't realize it but she'd stopped rubbing Sarah's back. She'd stepped away from her a little. Sarah detected the change in mood. She shrugged casually.

'You're very astute, Amita,' she said. 'Still sharp, after all these years. You never let Radha away with anything, any carry-on, any bother we were planning, you always knew about it. You never liked me, did you?'

'That's not true,' she said.

'It's ok, I can take it,' she laughed through the tears. 'Not many people did back then. Radha, she was about the only one. She knew what I was like. She was the only person I confided in, she had to be, she saw all the screaming matches between me and Mum, me and Dad. I don't blame you. I'd have killed Abi if she turned out like me. But she's a good girl, a good girl.' She nodded at that, thinking of her daughter. 'You still saw through me though, Amita, even now. You've not changed.'

'You have,' said Amita firmly. 'The girl I knew, that bright-eyed girl who always took two Jaffa Cakes from my biscuit tin when she was told to have one, she's gone now. In her place is a woman, a businesswoman, stressed, sure, but successful. That little girl I knew wasn't trouble, just misguided.

You're not her, not anymore. A lot has happened, people grow up. But you have to tell me what you've done, Sarah. It's important.'

Sarah wiped her eyes again. She took a long, deep breath and paced around the room.

'You have to believe me, Amita,' she started. 'I didn't kill him.'

'Derek Veland?'

Sarah nodded.

'I didn't kill him, I swear to you. But I think... I think I might have been the last person to see him alive. In fact I'm almost sure of it.'

'You said you saw him at the bar?'

'I did,' she said. 'But I saw him after that too.'

The room grew a little closer around Amita. It took her a moment to work out what Sarah was trying to say.

'Sarah?' she asked, already working out the answer.

'I was sleeping with him, Amita.'

She was clear, concise, almost business-like about her confession. Amita hadn't really believed Jason's suggestion that Sarah might have been an item with one the victims. Now that it was staring her in the face she felt a little foolish.

'It was nothing,' she said. 'Just a silly little fling. He was charming, handsome, a celebrity, for goodness sake. We hit it off as soon as he checked in on the first day of the filming. And one thing led to another. But I didn't murder him, Amita, you must believe me on that front.'

'What happened?' she asked. 'The night he was killed, tell me exactly what happened.'

'I left his room around three in the morning,' Sarah went on. 'The hotel was quiet, skeleton staff at that time, before the cleaners arrive. I slipped out one of the back doors and came straight home. I was barely in my own bed when I got the call from the front desk to say he'd been found dead.'

'What did the police say?' she asked. 'Surely you told them all of this.'

Sarah bit her bottom lip.

'They don't know,' she said. 'I haven't told them. They don't know about us, Amita. I couldn't risk this sort of thing getting out. Veland swore me to secrecy, he even offered me money.'

Amita wrinkled her nose.

'Yes, he had a habit of that,' she said.

'I cleared the CCTV of anything showing me anywhere near his room,' Sarah said. 'There's nothing on record, no trace of me and him at all, I made sure of it. But I think I went too far. Any evidence of who else went to his room that night, that's lost too – I'd made sure the camera by his room was conveniently out of order. I hadn't realised I'd be aiding and abetting a murder.' She collapsed into tears on Amita's shoulder.

'Oh Sarah,' said Amita, trying to reflow the story in her head around this new information.

'I had to switch it off, Amita, I had to,' she said.

'Didn't the police ask why there was a drop in coverage?'

'I gave them some story about the electronics being a bit iffy at the hotel. Which they are, by the way. I couldn't afford to be drawn into all of this, Amita, you have to understand that. It was just a fling, a bit of fun, for both of us. Believe me, Derek Veland wasn't the kind of man you'd want to be in a relationship with, not after he'd had a drink.'

'No, I don't imagine he would be,' said Amita. 'But this is serious, Sarah, you could help the police with what you know.'

'And what do I *know*, exactly?' she hissed. 'That I was sleeping with him, left him very much alive and the next thing we know he's been murdered. How would that look? For me? For the hotel? I'm innocent, Amita, I didn't touch him. Well, not in that way. But that won't stop the police, or the press for that matter, putting two and two together to get five.'

She sat down in her armchair again and stared blankly into thin air.

'He knew how to make you feel special. That energy, that charm – he was endearing,' she said with a sad smile.

'I'm sure he could be, when he wanted to be,' said Amita. 'He wasn't so charming when he was shouting in my face a few hours before he was killed.'

But Sarah wasn't listening – clearly relieved instead to finally be able to talk to someone about her affair. 'I can't remember the last time a man said that I looked good,' she said. 'Or anyone for that matter. The last few years have been one big, eternal slog. Time has lost all of its meaning and I am constantly, *constantly* at that bloody hotel. Being a responsible adult and honouring my parents' legacy has cost me everything, Amita. It's a job that's taken me over. I'm not the woman I was when I started there, far from it. It's run me into the ground and is still going, sapping me of energy, of life. If it's not the spa, it's the restaurant, or the plumbing, or a pay dispute with the cleaning staff. I'm consumed by it, Amita. Utterly consumed. Now, the one time I let my guard down, the one occasion I try to behave like every other human being on the planet, I'm left with a murder on my hands that could ruin me. How does that work, eh? How is that fair?'

'Life promises us many things – but I'm afraid fairness isn't one of them,' said Amita gravely.

'Yeah,' Sarah snorted.

Amita had to sit down too. Everything was getting a bit much for her. Any suggestion this may have been a crime of passion meant this case might be even more complicated than she thought. The heart didn't follow reason – and perhaps nor did this case. Although as she looked at Sarah she didn't feel as though she was looking at a killer, a wronged woman or jilted lover. The anger had left Sarah now. She looked utterly defeated rather than like a murderer caught red-handed.

'You have to tell the police about this, Sarah. They have to know that you were romantically involved with Derek Veland before he was murdered. You owe it yourself – and what's more, you owe it to him.'

'I know,' she said. 'I know I do. I've just been putting it off and putting it off, burying it under the mountains of other things I've got to do and hoping it would disappear. I mean, if they'd found the killer quickly, what would it have mattered what Derek and I got up to behind closed doors?'

'That's not how these things work, unfortunately,' said Amita. 'Life, I'm afraid, isn't that easy.'

'You're telling me,' said Sarah.

The front door opened. Sarah propped herself up and made sure she'd wiped away all of her tears.

'Mum?' shouted Abigail. 'Is everything alright? Mum?'

Abi appeared at the door.

'Oh, sorry, I didn't realize you had company,' she said.

'That's ok darling,' Sarah smiled, getting up and giving her daughter a big hug. 'Amita just popped around to drop something off.'

'Ok,' said Abigail, staring down at Amita. 'Are you staying for dinner? I brought home some Chicken Fried Rice.'

She waved a plastic bag filled with takeaway boxes.

'No, I'm not staying. But thank you for the offer, Abi,' said Amita. 'I'm going to have to borrow your mother for a little while this evening though. She's got something I've asked her to help me with. We'll be back soon, though.'

Sarah stood nodding. Abi looked perplexed.

'Do you want me to keep yours in the oven, Mum?' she asked politely.

'Yes, darling, please.' Sarah's voice was cracking. 'I won't be long, I promise. A bit of business to take care of, that's all. Nothing to worry about.'

Amita could see Sarah was ready to break down again. She moved fast, guiding her out of the door. Just as she did with her grandchildren, she helped Sarah on with her coat. They headed outside and walked towards Amita's car.

'I'm sorry,' said Sarah, clapping her hand to her mouth as she sobbed. 'I've let you down, Amita. I've let everyone down.'

'No you haven't,' said Amita, hugging her close. 'Everything will be alright. You only have to tell the police the truth. That's all. I've said it before, there's nothing easier in this world than telling the truth – once you start, the rest will follow.'

Chapter 25

TOSSED SALAD AND SCRAMBLED EGGS

Jason nudged his plate across the table. There was still an untouched cheese roll on it and he thought Simon Nakamba's cousin could do with the sustenance more than him. The broad man in the black leather jacket, trousers and cowboy boots looked as miserable as he did out of place here in Murphy's Cafe. As soon as they'd walked in, everybody had turned to look at the new stranger in town. Jason's favourite booth near the back was mercifully empty and he'd left Nakamba's cousin there while he fetched a pot of tea and something to eat.

The Earl Grey hadn't tickled his fancy. The stranger had sniffed at the cheese roll but wasn't eating. He'd said nothing since breaking down in the flat. Jason wasn't quite sure what to do.

'I didn't catch your name,' he said, trying to spark conversation. 'I'm Jason.'

'Viper,' said the stranger.

'Viper?' Jason coughed. 'Your name is Viper?'

'That's what I said, wasn't it?'

'It was.'

'Then that's my name.'

'Fine,' he held his hands up. 'Viper it is. When did you arrive in Penrith?'

'What's that supposed to mean?'

'It means I'm asking when you got here, nothing more,' he said.

'And what makes you think I'm not from around here?'

Jason drummed his fingers on the table. He puffed out his cheeks and nodded at Viper.

'Let me see,' he said. 'The Stetson is a bit of a giveaway. I think the last time Penrith saw a hat like that, Larry Hagman was doing a book tour.'

'Who?'

'Larry Hag... never mind. It doesn't matter. I'm curious, that's all.'

'About an hour ago,' said Viper glumly. 'The Cumbria Police managed to get a message through to my work in Nairobi and they told me about Simon.'

'You're from Kenya?'

'I'm from Streatham,' said Viper. 'My mum was Simon's aunty. We stayed down the road from them. I moved to Kenya about six years ago for business.'

'And what's that, then?'

'You ask a lot of questions.'

'I'm a journalist.'

Viper sneered. Jason shrugged his shoulders.

'Believe me, mate, I've had a lot worse reactions than that in my time.'

'It's a tech firm,' said Viper.

'Tech?' said Jason. 'Forgive me, Viper, but you don't much look like my idea of someone who works in tech. Far from it, in fact.'

'And what does a businessman in the tech industry look like to you, eh?' he sniped. 'Gelled hair, gilet, glasses?'

'Well... yes,' said Jason. 'They're also usually called Steve or Trevor or Simon, not Viper. You'll forgive me for saying this but Viper is *far* too cool a name for a tech boffin.'

Viper pulled his leather jacket open to reveal a black T-shirt, a screaming eagle print faded on his chest.

'I'm a singer, in a thrash metal band,' he said. 'That's why they call me Viper, it's my stage name. Tech is what I do Monday to Friday, nine to five, that's when I'm Peter Nakamba. But it's not who I am, understand?'

Jason held up his hands. 'Sorry. I'm not clued up on the Kenyan thrash metal scene. In fact I never even knew it existed. I apologise.'

Viper gave him a hard, angry stare. He held it there for a moment before relenting. He lifted the cheese roll, took a bite and put it back down on the plate, his face wrinkling in displeasure.

'That is awful,' he said.

'It's all they had left,' said Jason. 'They're closing in a few minutes but I figured I'd sit you down and make sure you were ok. I wouldn't trust the mugs in that flat if my life depended on it.'

Viper pushed the plate away. He looked around the cafe.

'Do you like this place?' he asked.

'It's seen more family moments and memories than I can care to count. It's also probably filled my arteries with cholesterol and brought my blood sugar levels up to a dangerously high level. But yes, I like it.'

'I meant Penrith,' said Viper.

'Oh, right,' Jason nodded. 'Of course I do. It's home. It's where I work, where I live, where my friends and family come from. It's my little haven from the rest of the world that's intent on turning absolutely bonkers before the week is out. Why do you ask?'

'I've never really felt at home anywhere,' said Viper. 'London, Nairobi, anywhere. I've always felt like a stranger, a drifter, just moving from place to place. The only constant in my life has been Simon. No matter where I am in the world, I always know that he's on the other end of the phone. He's there for me. He *was* there for me.'

Viper waved his hands in front of him.

'I'm sorry,' he said. 'I cannot do this.'

He stood up sharply.

'Viper, wait,' said Jason. 'Please, sit down, have some tea and another bit of this terrible cheese roll. You've had some shocking news, you shouldn't be left on your own. I'm here to help you if I can.'

Viper waited a moment before sitting back down in the booth. He sniffed loudly and took a drink of tea. He made another face and left the rest in the mug.

'You're Simon's next of kin, I take it,' asked Jason.

'Yes,' said Viper. 'My mother and father are in a nursing home on the south coast, just outside Bournemouth. I'm the only family Simon had. We were all very proud of him when he became such a big success. People back in Nairobi don't believe me when I tell them he's my cousin. They think I'm making it all up to try and boost my ego, to promote the band or something.'

'People can be strange like that,' said Jason. 'Viper, I don't want you to take this the wrong way, but did Simon ever tell you about any enemies he might have made?'

'Oh god, all the time,' said Viper.

The singer's forthrightness surprised Jason. He hadn't been expecting such a blunt answer. The moral dilemma of questioning Viper had been weighing heavy on his mind. The man across from him, as aggressive as he was, was clearly in great mourning for his cousin. But he needed answers.

'Really?'

'Sure,' Viper nodded. 'I was on the phone with him the day before he died and he was telling me about this shoot. He said that he wanted to kill his leading stars, what were their names again?'

'Pip Potter and Derek Veland,' said Jason.

'That's them,' he snapped his fingers. 'He said they were a nightmare to work with, they refused to do anything he asked. And above all they were terrible actors, his words, not mine. He thought about quitting.'

'The show?' asked Jason.

'Yup,' said Viper. 'He said he'd been doing it all for too long, had overcome too many hurdles and prejudices to be stuck herding a load of spoiled brats around Penrith. I remember that's what he said exactly. I thought it was odd. I'd never heard him talk about his work like that before. He'd always had issues. He had a temper. But the art, his work, it was always untouchable for him.'

'And this was the day before he died.'

'Yes,' said Viper. 'I got a call from the police the next day saying that... saying that he had been found dead in the street. So I got over here as soon as I could. I want to know what happened to my cousin, Jason. I *need* to know that he's at peace.'

'What about addictions or vices?' Jason asked.

'Simon? No,' he said. 'Why?'

'The police told me that they found some marks on your cousin's arm. They think it's suspicious. I wondered if you knew if Simon was into anything a bit unsavoury.'

'Absolutely not,' said Viper, defensively. 'He liked a good drink. There's nothing illegal about that. But nothing stronger, absolutely not.'

Jason could sympathise with the man across the table. Here he was, on his own, in the middle of Penrith, looking for answers over his cousin's murder. That was a tough pill for anyone to swallow. On the other hand, Jason didn't want to say too much. There were lines you didn't cross when it came to family and grieving loved ones. He knew that from his days as a reporter.

He decided to tread carefully, while still being a human being.

'Have you spoken to the cops since you arrived?' he asked, trying not to get too excited that he might have got to a lead Arendonk's team hadn't.

Viper shook his head.

'No,' he said. 'I came straight into town off the train. Some people helped me find where the filming was happening. They said there was a flat that the crew were using. I saw the door open and found you there. The way you pushed that girl out of the way, I thought you looked like the man in charge.'

Jason tried to hold in a guffaw and, at the same time, fought back a blush. 'You should probably let the police know that you're here,' said Jason. 'The lead detective is a DI Arendonk, she's very good.'

'No,' said Viper.

'No?'

'No, I don't want to speak to the police,' he said.

'Viper, I really think you should,' said Jason. 'You're Simon's next of kin, his only relative. They'll want to speak with you and have you as a point of contact for the investigation. Sally is nice, she's not like other rozzers, she actually cares. Simon won't just be a case number to her.'

'No police!' Viper slammed his gloved hand down on the table.

It was loud enough that the other diners looked around, then pretended they hadn't. Jason didn't mind the attention. When you're sat across a table from a six foot giant of a man dressed in black leather and a cowboy hat, you couldn't expect to blend in. He didn't fancy arguing with Viper, though, not right now. Or ever, he thought, as he looked again at the studs and skulls that armoured every extremity.

'Ok,' he said. 'You've got your reasons and I won't pry. I think you should let them know you're here, that's all.'

'I'll do things *my* way,' he said angrily.

Jason didn't like the sound of that. 'And what's *that* supposed to mean?'

A dangerous look made Viper's eyes ignite. He had picked up a teaspoon and was twisting it around menacingly between his fingers. It took a certain gravitas to be able to make a teaspoon seem menacing – and before Jason could work out all the ways Viper could use it – he continued.

'Simon was like a brother to me growing up. We were close until he went away to drama school and I moved to Kenya. The newspapers, the police, they're all saying he was murdered. That means there's someone out there, right now, who has to pay. An eye for an eye, Jason. An eye for an eye. You've been very helpful but I can't hang around. You'll understand, I know.'

He stood up quickly. Jason was taken by surprise. It was the second time in the space of an hour that Viper had the jump on him. He was rushing towards the door as Jason still scrambled around grabbing his coat.

'Wait! Hold on!' he called after him.

Viper was moving fast across Market Square. Every step he took drew more and more attention from the locals. Equatorial heavy metal cowboys weren't exactly ten a penny in Cumbria. Jason hurried after him, calling his name.

'Viper, please,' he said, catching up with him.

He grabbed the bigger man's arm. Viper spun around, pulling himself free. His fist was clenched and he raised it. Jason winced, ready to feel the burning sting of a knuckle sandwich. When it didn't come, he opened his eyes, wondering what was going on.

Viper was looming over him. His hand was quivering, still floating in the air. He let it drop and started breathing again.

'I'm sorry,' he said. 'I shouldn't be taking this out on you. You've been very helpful, Jason. But you have to leave me be now. I have to find out who killed my cousin and make them pay for what they did.'

For a second, Viper's calm was more frightening than his anger.

'Viper, you can't do that,' he said. 'Penrith is a small place and this is a big case, high profile. You know how popular, how much of a celebrity Simon was. You can't go around like Batman dishing out justice on your own.'

'And why not?' he asked.

'Because…' Jason faltered.

It struck him then that he and Amita weren't all that different to what he'd just described. Perhaps a little less moulded plastic and gadgets. But they still liked to think they were the good guys.

Things were different though, especially this time. Jason didn't imagine Viper was going to merely hand the culprit in to the authorities, like he and his mother-in-law would. What if he didn't report this and there was another murder?

'You just can't, ok?' he said. 'There are rules, laws. You have to observe them, obey them. That eye for an eye thing, that's for the movies. This is real life, Viper. You have to trust that the cops will get their man.'

'Or woman,' said Viper.

'Yes, of course,' agreed Jason. 'I know you're upset but you have to try and calm down and think about this logically. A vigilante who's mad as hell isn't going to help anyone, least of all you. What would Simon think if you ended up in jail for perverting the course of justice, eh? Or worse?'

Viper nodded. Jason surprised himself at how easy it seemed to get through to him.

He was so busy congratulating himself that he didn't see Viper slip a foot behind his leg. A hefty shove in the chest and Jason was tumbling backwards. He hit the cobbled stones of the square hard, his head cracking off the ground. There was a moment of dizziness as he tried to work out what was happening. When his head cleared, he sat up. Viper was gone, bolting off down the street away from Market Square, a sea of confused faces left in his wake.

Jason rolled over, trying to muster the energy to stand up. Nobody seemed interested in his distress and he slowly, with a distinct lack of dignity, managed to get back to his feet. He looked down the road Viper had gone down. There was no sign of the big man now.

The Musgrave Monument's bell clanged into life and Jason flinched. The huge clock was towering over him and he squinted up to the face. As if he needed any more reminder that time was ticking.

Chapter 26

WOKE UP THIS MORNING

A sign of the times, Amita thought, as she pulled into the car park of Penrith Police Station. She remembered the first time she had ever visited this place. Jason had been unceremoniously bundled into the back of a police car, still in his dressing gown, and taken in for questioning. The former DI, Frank Alby, had taken a dislike to her son-in-law, and her too for that matter. She'd made the trip into town, brimming with anger and shame, to collect Jason when his interrogation was complete.

Times were different now, of course. Since that first unfortunate trip, the station had become something of a home from home. Perhaps not a wanted one. Any time she graced its hallowed, damp-riddled halls there was trouble afoot. And she invariably ended up in an argument. Or in an interview room. Or sometimes an argument *in* an interview room.

She pulled the handbrake on. Sarah had barely spoken during the drive back to Penrith. She'd sat beside Amita, staring blindly out of the windscreen. A cold rain had started, spattering the glass and sending little shadows across her ashen face. Amita reached out and touched her hand.

'We're here,' she said.

'Oh right,' said Sarah, blinking. 'Sorry. I was miles off there.'

'Are you feeling ready for all of this?'

'I don't really have a choice, do I?' she said. 'You were right, you *are* right, Amita. I shouldn't keep the fling a secret. Not when there's so much riding on it. It was a bloody stupid thing to do. Stupid, stupid, stupid.'

She thumped a fist on the dashboard. Amita hushed her down.

'Come on now, don't be hard on yourself,' she said. 'You're under a lot of pressure at the moment. Everyone can see it. I'll come in with you, I know the chief investigator, I'll speak up for you. But when all of this is over you're going to have to get some time off. It's time for you to see that place can survive a day or two without you.'

Sarah nodded in agreement. She looked close to tears again but was able to hold her head high.

'Do you think they'll throw me in the cells?' she asked.

'No,' said Amita. 'Sally Arendonk is a fair woman. She'll understand completely what's happened – and be glad of a few more pieces of the puzzle.'

She paused for a moment.

'Unless, of course, you haven't told me everything. Unless you and Derek had a lover's tiff. Love can turn to hate very quickly, I know that much,' she said.

Sarah didn't respond. Amita felt a chill run through her. For that split second she thought she might have bungled her way into catching the killer. Then Sarah spoke up.

'I'm not a killer, Amita,' she said. 'I'm barely a lover.'

Amita's mind was put at ease. Sarah had had plenty of chances to silence Amita if she'd wanted to.

'Come on, let's get this over with, shall we?' she said.

Running through the rain, they headed towards the police station. Inside was busy. A wall of raised voices and shouting met them, the air thick and steamy with hot, boozy breaths. Officers were handling and checking in a large crowd of troublemakers all dressed in matching polo shirts and golf visors. One near the front was stripped down to his underpants, a driver's L plate taped onto his rear.

The desk sergeants furiously tried to whizz through their paperwork to clear the space. A hundred different arguments were flying back and forth across the tiny reception area of the station. Nobody was winning.

'I told you not to worry about being thrown into one of the cells,' said Amita. 'I have a feeling they'll all be full with this lot. Stag parties in my day were only a night down the local public house. Now I see these young men and women staggering around all weekend. Sometimes longer.'

Sarah didn't reply. She was standing at the back of the crowd, looking on, concerned. The front desk began to process the men in their golf outfits, while the stag in his pants was ushered into the back towards the cells. A few more rowdy chants and aggressive exchanges of ideas and they were at the front.

'What are you two in for?' asked a ruddy-faced sergeant. 'Were you the strippers?'

'Strippers!' Amita almost blew a gasket. 'I beg your pardon, sir. I'm an upstanding member of this community. I do charity work. I'm a member of the W.I. for heaven's sake.'

'Madam, believe me, I've heard it all this afternoon. I wouldn't be surprised if you were still a go-go dancer even being a member of the W.I.'

'Shame on you,' said Amita furiously. 'I didn't come here to be insulted. And besides, I think you'll find that the preferred term in the industry is exotic dancer.'

The ruddy sergeant's face turned a little more purple, his silver beard bristling.

'Right you are,' he said, turning to his work. 'What can I do for you then? Dropping off or picking up?'

'We'd like to speak to DI Arendonk please,' said Amita succinctly.

'Would you now?' The sergeant tapped his pen against his chin. 'You know that the inspector is in the middle of a double murder investigation at the moment. A very high profile one and–'

'We know all that,' she said. 'I'm on very good terms with the inspector. And believe me, she'll want to know what myself and my associate here have got to say.'

'Will she?' He didn't sound convinced.

'Maybe we should go,' said Sarah, rubbing her arm. 'Maybe this was all a big mistake, Amita. Maybe I should just go back home and forget about it.'

'No,' said Amita. 'We have to do the right thing. At all costs.'

The desk sergeant looked at her expectantly.

'Please, could you tell her that Amita Khatri is at the front desk and she has a statement to give her from a key witness in Derek Veland's murder.'

The mention of the actor seemed to light a fire under the policeman. He stood up a little straighter.

'Veland's murder, you say?' he asked. 'Are you pulling my chain?'

'No, I'm not "pulling your chain",' Amita said with disgust. 'Please, this is of utmost urgency. DI Arendonk knows me, she knows who I am. She'll know, too, when you tell her this is urgent, that she needs to come out here and see us.'

The sergeant leaned back from his desk. He picked up the phone and looked over at them both.

'You know that if this is a wind-up I'm throwing the pair of you into the cells with those rowdy golf idiots, right?' he said.

'Just make the call, please,' said Amita firmly.

He dialled a number and asked to speak to Arendonk. Explaining everything that Amita had told him, he put the phone down.

'She's on her way,' he said.

'Good. Thank you,' said Amita.

'I don't think I should do this,' said Sarah. 'My chest is tight, my hands are sweating.'

'It's ok,' said Amita, guiding her away from the desk and the prying sergeant. 'I'm right here with you, Sarah.'

'Amita.'

Sally Arendonk strode purposefully into the lobby. She looked tired and pale, her hair slicked back to a tried and tested ponytail that flopped over her shoulder.

'It's been a long day,' said the DI. 'What have you got for me? And please don't run me around the houses. I'm really not in the mood anymore.'

A word hadn't even left Sarah or Amita's lips when the front doors of the station opened. The three women looked around in unison as Jason stood in the doorway like he was storming a saloon in the Wild West. Before any of them could react, he hurried into the lobby, gasping for breath.

'Sally, good, you're here,' he said. 'I've got something I need to tell you.'

'Jason, what are you doing here?' asked Amita. 'Did you speak with Pip Potter?'

'No.'

'Why not?'

'It's complicated,' he said.

'What does that mean?'

'It means, as usual, things didn't go to plan.'

'So what have you been doing all day?' asked Amita.

'I've been working.'

'What are you doing here?'

'I have to speak to Sally.'

'No, I have to speak to Sally,' said Amita.

'But this is important,' he said.

'Ours is important too.'

'Yes, but this has to do with the murder case.'

'So does ours.'

'But I ran all the way here.'

'That's not my fault,' said Amita.

'Mine is more pressing though, Amita. People could be in danger.'

'And what's more pressing than a key piece of evidence in a double murder case, eh?'

'But my story has a heavy metal singer from Kenya in it.'

'What?'

'Both of you! Enough!'

Arendonk's booming voice was enough to bring them to order.

'That's quite enough out of everyone, is that clear?' she asked, calming down.

Jason and Amita kept their mouths shut. They'd learned not to push their luck and goodwill with the frazzled detective.

'Now, I'm very busy,' she said. 'I've got press requests coming in for statements and progress updates, my phone is literally burning a hole in my pocket with overuse from my superiors looking for a collar, and now I'm playing nursemaid to you two and a special guest.'

Arendonk squinted at Sarah.

'I know you,' she said, pointing. 'You're the owner of Askling Manor, aren't you?'

Sarah nodded.

'I was about to tell you, Inspector, that Sarah is here to—'

'Hold it!' Arendonk raised a hand. 'Nobody speaks until they're spoken to. Honestly, the kids in my nephew's nursery class are better behaved than you two. I want you all to calm down, keep your opinions to yourselves and follow me into somewhere that's a little more private and, importantly, away from public view. The press would have my guts for garters if they saw me fraternising with you lot like this.'

'I am the press, you know,' said Jason, despite the sceptical looks surrounding him.

'Come on then, Clark Kent," said Arendonk. 'This way."

Chapter 27

A PERFECT LINE

Both Amita and Jason had been expecting another interview room. But Arendonk seemed determined to show them some of the other parts of the station they hadn't seen before. A small canteen, numerous storage cupboards bursting to full, even a janitor's office complete with pail of smelly, dirty water and a mop were some of the highlights.

'Where is she taking us?' whispered Sarah.

'I'm not sure,' answered Amita.

'Normally we'd be getting shouted at in the confines of an interrogation room by now,' said Jason.

'Jason,' Amita scolded him.

Sarah's already pallid face turned a little whiter. She swallowed a dry gulp.

'Maybe we're getting put into isolation,' said Jason. 'You know, the cells that are reserved for the really bad bast–'

'I can hear you, you know,' Arendonk threw over her shoulder without stopping. 'All you bloody journalists are the same – you all talk at the same volume, which is loud.'

'What? That's a load of rubbish,' said Jason. 'I can be perfectly quiet when I choose to be.'

'Choose to be right now then,' said the DI. 'Before I get one of the uglier uniforms to clamp your jaws shut.'

She pushed a door open with both hands. A wave of cold air met them as they trotted after her. Outside was a small, claustrophobic courtyard. The high walls of the station were all around them, topped with nasty-looking razor wire. Jason almost tripped on the small step beyond the door, a veritable army of crushed cigarette butts scattered beneath his feet.

Another detective was standing opposite them, puffing away. Arendonk gave him a hard look and flicked her head back towards the station. He didn't argue, crushing his cigarette and quickly heading inside. She waited for the door to close before fishing a packet of smokes out of the pocket of her blazer.

'I didn't know you smoked,' said Jason.

'There's plenty you don't know about me,' she said, patting her other pockets for a lighter. 'And I'd like to keep it that way, Brazel.'

'Here,' said Amita.

She held a lighter up to the end of Arendonk's cigarette. The DI happily puffed out smoke as Amita stepped back.

'Since when do *you* carry around a cigarette lighter?' asked Jason.

His mother-in-law hesitated for a moment. Then regained her composure.

'It's handy to have if you're out and about. Amazing what people will tell you if you offer them a light,' she said. 'I've got a penknife too, if you want to see that. I didn't know I had to check these things out with a committee every time I left the house.'

'Bloody hell,' Jason rolled his eyes. 'What is wrong with everyone today? Do I have a sticker on my forehead saying "have a go at Jason"?'

'Ahem,' said Arendonk. 'If you two want to have a domestic, you can do it on your own time. Mine is far too precious and there's very little of it these days. So come on then, out with it.'

Jason and Amita started talking at once. Eventually it took Sarah to step in.

'I think I was the last person to see Derek Veland alive,' she said.

The small courtyard was silent. Jason blinked.

'What did you just say?' he asked.

'I said, I think I was the last person to see Derek Veland alive,' repeated Sarah. 'I left his room around three in the morning. You won't find any CCTV footage as I destroyed it and told your officers that there had been an outage of coverage. I'm sorry if that wasn't quite what I told you before.'

Arendonk was silent. Her cigarette was burning away as she held it down by her side, smoke curling around her arm..

'I didn't mean to cause any more bother,' Sarah continued. 'It was just a fling, a silly fling, that's all.'

'She's been under a lot of stress recently, Inspector,' Amita spoke up. 'And Mr Veland was a very charming man, when he wanted to be. I've known Sarah all of her life, pretty much. She's a pillar of the community, not to mention one of Cumbria's leading businesswomen. I firmly believe that, if she kept the information from you, it was for a good reason and–'

'What happened after you left Veland in his room?' asked the DI, cutting Amita short.

Sarah was shivering, despite her heavy coat.

'I... I left for home,' she said. 'None of the staff noticed anything. I'm regularly there all hours. It eats up my life, DI Arendonk, it's all I have to get up for. That and my daughter. I haven't got the time to go looking for, well, liaisons you might say. This one, I mean Derek, found me, instead.'

'And you didn't see anyone else go into Veland's room as you left?'

'No,' said Sarah, bowing her head. 'I didn't look back. I wasn't proud of having a clandestine relationship. I mean, if you have to sneak out in the wee small hours, it's never going to be something you're proud of. He was a nice man and all, he told me I was beautiful, powerful, special. Do you have any idea how long it's been since somebody said that to me? He was kind and funny but clearly a trainwreck. That's the last kind of influence I need in my life right now. I'm sorry for not being straight with you before – but I knew messing around with the CCTV wouldn't look good for me.'

Arendonk flinched as her cigarette burned down close to her fingers. She flicked it away.

'This is very serious stuff, Ms Paris,' she said. 'I could charge you right now for obstructing justice. That's a criminal record right away.'

'I know,' said Sarah, looking up to the DI. 'I know it was stupid, I know how much trouble I'm in. I'm sorry, I truly am.'

'She *is* sorry, Detective Inspector,' said Amita.

Arendonk shook her head.

'What is it about you two that attracts trouble to my door?' she asked. 'I'm forever mopping up the wreck and ruin that's left behind when you get involved.'

'You asked for our help, remember,' said Jason, pointedly. 'So, this is us helping.'

'I know, I know,' Arendonk sighed. 'It's this bloody case. It's driving me insane. We're no closer to finding out who killed either man. And every day we don't, the case grows more arms and legs in the media. It's getting out of control.'

She turned away from them and paced around the confined courtyard. Until she turned on her heel and faced Jason again.

'Right, what's your news?'

'My news?' he said fecklessly.

'Yes, come on, out with it, Jason,' said Amita. 'You said it was urgent. Have you spoken with Pip Potter like I asked?'

'Pip Potter, the actress?' asked the DI.

'That's her,' said Jason.

'What do you want to speak to her for? She's not a person of interest to us.'

'Isn't she?' asked Amita.

'Should she be? I can't see any link between her and the killings. Yes we interviewed her, like we did with all the cast. But she has an alibi for both incidents. She was in her apartment here in town when Nakamba and Veland were murdered.'

'Isn't she in danger?' asked Amita.

'We can only protect her while she's in town,' said the detective.

Amita had been nursing a theory all day. She didn't want to tempt the fates by saying it out loud. But circumstance had forced her now.

'As awful as it sounds,' she said. 'Pip is the *last* of the main players in this production. First Simon Nakamba the director, then Derek Veland, the male lead. If there's someone out there with a grudge or some other damn idea in their head, then logic would dictate that Pip Potter would be the next target.'

'Alone?' asked Jason.

'What?' asked the detective.

'Was Pip alone when she was in her apartment during the murders?'

'I can't disclose that information,' said the DI. 'Especially not to a journalist. All you need to know is that her whereabouts has been accounted for on *both* nights.'

'We'd still like to talk to her again though,' said Amita. 'She might have some insight into both men, something we're missing, some part of the bigger picture we can't see for looking.'

'Well, you'll need to get your train tickets booked for Manchester,' said Arendonk.

'Why?' asked Jason.

'Ms Potter is heading back to the city. Production has been shut down. She's got some other job she's going to. She's packing her bags as we speak, at least, according to my protection officers. I've told them to stand down.'

'Quick!' Amita hissed at her son-in-law.

They scrambled for the door. Arendonk went after them.

'Oi!' she shouted. 'You can't just take off like that!'

'We have to speak with her before she goes,' said Amita. 'It's rather urgent.'

'But... Jason, what was your news?' the DI asked.

Jason skidded to a halt in the corridor. He clapped his hand to his forehead.

'Oh yes, I almost forgot,' he said. 'Simon Nakamba's cousin is in town. He's called Viper, well, Peter, but likes to be called Viper. He wears a lot of leather, cowboy boots and a big Stetson hat. He won't be hard to recognise. He's Simon's only living relative and he's got bloody murder on his mind when he catches up with the killer.'

Arendonk looked blank. She spread her arms wide, staring at him.

'That's all, is it?' she said. 'That's all I'm getting?'

'I told you, you can't miss him,' Jason shouted, turning and loping off down the corridor after Amita.

The inspector watched them go. She felt Sarah Paris step up beside her.

'Are they always like this?' asked the hotel owner, shivering.

'No,' said Arendonk. She put a reassuring hand on Sarah's shoulder and ushered her back into the police station. 'Normally they're much worse.'

Chapter 28

PRINCES OF THE UNIVERSE

'I should have asked the bingo club in the first place, Jason. Honestly, if you want a job done right, you're better off doing it yourself.'

Amita tutted as she scrolled through the information from one of her many local OAP WhatsApp groups. It hadn't taken long for someone to come up with the details of Pip Potter's apartment in town.

'Hey, that's not fair,' he said, panting for breath beside her. 'I found Viper.'

'It sounds more like *he* found *you*.'

'Details,' he said. 'Mere details. What matters is that we need to find Simon Nakamba's killer and fast. I wouldn't fancy getting on the wrong side of his cousin. If we aren't quick, there'll be a third murder on our hands and this time I'll know who's responsible.'

'Left here,' Amita said.

They took a sharp left and ducked down a narrow little street lined with flats of all shapes and sizes. It was dark and damp, a murky glow gathered around the bulbs of the streetlights. At the end of the street was a squat, two-storey building, brand new picture windows that revealed nothing but the dark blank reflection of the night. Cast iron fencing ringed a small garden area set back from the pavement. A brushed and sandblasted datestone above the main doorway showed the year 1815.

'I don't recognise this place,' said Jason.

'Serviced apartments,' said Amita. 'A bit more personal than hotels. Ideal for young actors who are only here for a matter of weeks. Offers them a bit of privacy and we're only a five minute walk from the town centre.'

'I know what a serviced apartment is, Amita, thank you,' he said. 'You sound like the local tourist board. What I mean is I don't think I've ever been down this road before in all my life.'

'You should get out and explore your hometown more, take a little civic pride in where you live.'

'I know where you can stick your civic pride,' he said under his breath.

Amita didn't hear him. Or didn't give him the satisfaction of admitting she had. They slowed down as they approached the apartments. There were no lights on in the windows and an empty recycling bin rolled abandoned on its side. The municipal equivalent of a tumbleweed. Amita peered up.

'This all seems a bit off,' she said.

She looked up and down the empty street.

'I wouldn't like walking down here late at night on my own.'

'Maybe she wasn't on her own most of the time,' said Jason. 'You heard what Arendonk said, she had alibis for both killings.'

'Yes I thought that was odd too.'

'Nothing odd in a young woman keeping company while she's on a job, I suppose. It's the twenty-first century, Amita.'

He sniffed and clapped his hands against his arms, trying to stay warm.

'Do you think we've missed her?' he asked. 'Or is there a chance that whatever mole of yours from the bingo club has given you the wrong address?'

'My sources are *never* wrong,' said Amita. 'You know that.'

'There's a first time for everything,' he said. 'Potter must have high-tailed it earlier this afternoon then.'

'You should have caught up with her before she left,' she said.

'How was I supposed to know that she was leaving? I thought we'd get another few days at least. There were still cameras and vans packing up earlier and some of the set was bulky – I didn't think they'd manage to all clear out so fast.'

'The set...' Amita trailed off.

Something sparked in her mind. She couldn't say for sure what it was. But there was something there. She was about to explore it further when a set of headlights almost blinded her. Jason let out a quiet yelp as they backed away. The lights beamed through the iron fence from a small car park at the rear of the apartment block. Amita didn't hang around. She grabbed Jason by the elbow and hurried around.

'I wish you'd stop making me run,' he choked. 'I'm not the running type, Amita. You don't see flat feet and bellies like mine in the marathon, do you?'

'There!' Amita shouted.

A car was sat in a bay across from them. The engine was running and a shadow was moving around in the driver's seat. The car lurched forward with a roar of its engine but squealed to a stop when Amita stood firmly in the way.

'Stop!' she declared.

'Bloody hell, Amita,' gasped Jason. 'You could have been run over. You're not King Canute you know!'

'What in the name of god do you think you're doing?' Pip Potter shoved her head out of the window and glared at

Amita and Jason standing in front of her car. 'I could have mowed you down!' she yelled.

'I just said that,' said Jason. 'She's not some kind of maverick lollipop lady.'

'Jason, please,' tutted Amita. 'We'd like another word with you, Miss Potter, if that's alright? Before you head down to Manchester.'

'How do you know I'm going to Manchester?' asked the actress.

'The police told us,' said Jason.

If he was hoping to placate the star, it failed. She snarled something nasty and then tooted her horn.

'Out of the way!' she shouted, revving the engine. 'I'll run you over if I have to.'

'I wouldn't recommend that, Ms Potter,' said Amita, remaining calm. 'My son-in-law is a journalist, if you remember. I don't think your public image would be done any good if it got out you'd attacked a pensioner with your car.'

'And how would anybody know?'

'He's filming all of this.'

Amita nudged Jason in the elbow. She nodded at his pocket. It took him a moment to catch up before he fumbled his phone free. He didn't know how to work the video on it so just held it up at Pip in the driver's seat.

'See,' said Amita.

'I'm trying to leave, and you're in my way.'

'We only want to talk,' said Amita.

'Talk about what?'

'About Derek Veland and Simon Nakamba.'

'I've told the police everything I know,' shouted Pip. 'The show has been closed down. I want to go home. Tell your readers that!'

She revved the engine again, trying to get them to move. Jason flinched. Amita grabbed his arm, keeping him in the way.

'The more you try to leave, Pip, the worse it looks for you,' she shouted. 'You could be in danger!'

'The police have said I'm free to go. If they don't have a problem with it, I don't see why you should – just a couple of interfering–'

'We're not police, no, but we have close ties with them,' said Amita. 'How do you think it will look if we go back to the investigating officers and tell them you wanted to run us over as you fled to Manchester?'

Pip stared at them both over the top of the steering wheel. Amita really hoped her bluff was going to work. This was a celebrity she was dealing with, probably used to fighting past the paparazzi. But she had to stand firm. The breakthrough with Sarah Paris had been good but it wasn't definitive.

'Messers Nakamba and Veland are dead,' said Amita. 'And nobody knew them better in their final days than you, Pip. Please. You're an actor – you study people and I bet you pick up on things us normal folk don't.' Amita wasn't above resorting to flattery.

The engine went silent. The TV star opened the car door and climbed out.

'Five minutes,' she said. 'That's all. And you can turn that stupid camera off for a start.'

She held her hand up to Jason's phone. He put it away before she realised he had been staring at his home screen all this time.

'Shall we go back inside?' asked Amita.

'Why? This isn't going to take long,' said Pip, sitting on the bonnet of her car. 'I've told the police everything I know. What could you possibly ask me now? I don't think my amateur psychoanalysis of Simon or Derek is going to help.'

'Did you know that Veland was sleeping with the owner of Askling Manor?' asked Jason.

'That name means nothing to me,' said the actress. 'If it's some Penrith landmark then I'm sorry, excuse my ignorance. I hadn't set foot here before filming started. I'm not exactly clued up on your local history.'

There was a sneering arrogance to her now that Jason and Amita hadn't found when they first spoke with her. She folded her arms across her chest, piercing eyes glaring at them both through the darkness.

'It's the hotel where Derek died. Where you had the meeting about Simon. But we're less interested in your regional knowledge and more in if you knew about Veland and his antics,' said Amita.

Pip sniffed.

'Look, everyone knew about Derek and his "antics" as you call them,' she said. 'What do you want me to say? He was a middle-aged actor with the libido of a teenager. He's hardly unique in our industry.'

'So you knew about him and Sarah?' asked Jason.

'I knew he liked to go socialising of an evening, after shooting was finished, if that's what you mean,' she said. 'I couldn't tell you any of their names. I doubt even he could do that.'

'Forgive me, Ms Potter, but you don't seem that bothered by the fact that your co-star is dead, murdered even,' said Amita.

'And what would you like me to do? A flip? Don a black armband? What?' she asked spitefully. 'Something like this was always going to happen to Veland. He was from a bygone era and thought he was a lad. He used to call himself a bounder, in that put-on boarding school accent of his.'

'That accent was genuine,' said Jason. 'He told us about his boarding school days.'

'Please,' Pip pursed her lips. 'I wouldn't believe a word that man said. He was an actor, remember, we're professional liars.'

'And we're supposed to believe you?'

'Very good.' She threw him a sarcastic look. 'Veland was up to his neck in gambling debts, he drank like a fish and flirted with anything that had a heartbeat. You can't go about behaving like that and not step on toes. There is a trail of jilted lovers, cuckolded husbands, frustrated wives, and out-of-pocket bookmakers who most likely had a bone to pick with the dear departed. Selfish doesn't cover Derek Veland, he was so much more than words can sum up.'

'You didn't enjoy working with him, then?' asked Jason.

'A job is a job and you have to be a professional in this industry,' she said. 'The competition is too high to let yourself get a difficult reputation. Unless you're someone like Simon – then you get to play the 'troubled genius' card. *The Locus* is a smash hit and I'm grateful for that. The reason I'm still on the show is because I'm a bloody good actress. Not because I was sleeping with hotel owners and throwing hissy fits on set.'

She checked her watch.

'Is that enough?' she asked. 'Or do you want to drag me over the coals going through everything I've already said? You both seem to be making a habit of that. I don't know what you were expecting – me to tell you I thought Derek was a saint and no one had a bad word to say about him? As if.'

Amita was out of ideas. She turned to Jason who looked deep in thought.

'Were you in a relationship with Derek Veland?' he asked.

'What?' she gasped.

'It's a simple question, Pip,' said Jason. 'Were you one of his dalliances?'

'What bloody business is it of yours?' she fumed.

She was staring right at him. They were about the same height and Amita thought she might have to step between them.

'It's a simple question,' Jason shrugged. 'If you've got nothing to hide then it shouldn't matter.'

'What I do with my personal life is my business. The clue is in the name – personal,' she said.

Jason wondered if there was real grief here. After all, she'd said a moment ago she was a professional liar – she could have outright denied this, but clearly something in her wanted to acknowledge whatever had been going on. He pressed on.

'True,' he said. 'But I think when an actor's director and then co-star wind up dead within a few days of each other, the spotlight of suspicion has to fall on the common factor. And in this case, that would be you.'

'What are you saying?' she asked. 'Are you trying to suggest that I had something to do with their murders? That's preposterous!'

'Is it?' he asked. 'Let's look at the facts. If you're not fearful of being the next victim, then we have to examine the opposing case. You haven't said a good word about Simon Nakamba, not privately anyway. You've been scathing about Derek Veland, calling him all sorts of names. You've clearly stated that you considered yourself more professional than both of them. You're young, healthy, more than capable of doing away with both of those out-of-shape, middle-aged men. What happened? Did Veland rebuff your advances? Did Nakamba shout at you one too many times? You might as well come clean.'

Amita looked as wide-eyed and shocked as Pip.

'Maybe she's right, Jason,' she said. 'Maybe this isn't such a good idea.' This was not the first time she or Jason had got so carried away with a theory that they were left in a galling position – either they were falsely accusing someone of murder, which never tended to go down well, or they were unmasking a killer and in doing so painting a nice target on their own backs. Suddenly being with Pip in a deserted car park didn't feel like the brightest idea.

'Or maybe we're close to uncovering the truth, does that sound about right?' asked Jason.

Pip pushed past them. She wandered around the car park, breath smoking as she flattened her hair back, stressed.

'This is nonsense,' she said over and over. 'You can't seriously think that I had anything to do with this? What would I have to gain from it?'

'Why don't you tell us?' asked Jason. 'You're the star of the show, the series, you're a big cheese, Pip. Nakamba and Veland must have done something awful to warrant someone bumping them off like that.'

'I didn't kill them!' she shouted.

Her voice echoed off damp walls. A light went on in the set of flats beside the apartments, curtains twitching.

'Then why are you getting so upset? Why did you want to rush off to Manchester so badly? Why did you try to run myself and my mother-in-law over when we confronted you?' he pressed. 'It's not looking good, Pip, not looking good at all.'

'Alright!' she screamed. 'I was sleeping with him. There, are you satisfied?'

Jason had to take a moment. His heart was beating fast. All this thinking on his feet was stressing *him* out. In the silence that hung in the air he realised he'd done it again. Got carried away with the story – and put him and Amita in a risky position. Crime Correspondent had always sounded like the gig he wanted to aspire to. But maybe he'd preferred it when the crimes in question were a pilfered pot-plant or road rage at the golf club. Right now he'd happily go back to reporting on dog shows and school prize days.

'I was sleeping with him, there, I said it,' Pip repeated. 'I'm not particularly proud of myself, it's not who I am. But this industry robs you of all your dignity. Especially on a job like this, away from home. Sometimes you need a little human company, somebody who's going through the same garbage you are. That's not a crime, is it?'

She sounded almost apologetic. Jason nodded in agreement.

'And Nakamba found out, that's why you killed him, to stop the story getting out and you getting sacked, is that it?'

'What? No!' she shouted. 'That's not it at all.'

'You tell Veland what you've done and he's appalled,' said Amita, chiming in. 'He threatens to go to the police and report you but you sneak into his hotel room and strangle your lover.'

'Watertight,' said Jason. 'Given Veland's behaviour. You said it yourself, he had a list of enemies as long as your arm.'

'No,' Pip stepped forward. 'That's not what happened at all, you're wrong.'

'Are we?' Jason could almost hear the congratulations from Arendonk now.

'Yes, you are,' said the actress.

'And how do you figure that?' asked Jason.

'For starters, I wasn't sleeping with Derek,' said Pip. 'I was dating Simon.'

Just like that, everything fell apart. Jason felt his teeth clamp together, jaw tight as he looked to Amita for some help.

'Oh Jason,' she said, covering her eyes with her hand. 'You and your big mouth.'

Jason paused. He hadn't intended to be the Penrith division of the Spanish Inquisition but he was starting to realise that the cast and crew of *The Locus* all appeared to have something to confess.

Chapter 29

IRON JOHN'S ROCK

The apartment was warm and comfortable – and a lot more hospitable than its blank exterior had suggested. Amita hadn't hesitated in getting the kettle on as soon as they were inside. She sat with her hands wrapped around her mug, willing some heat back into them.

Pip was staring vacantly on the sofa across from her. She looked drained, her eyes bloodshot, face pale and slack, like the foundations supporting her through her grief had now completely collapsed. She had barely spoken since they came back to her apartment. Amita had thought it best to get her sat down somewhere safe; she'd not liked that twitching curtain. Another incident like that and the Penrith grapevine would be buzzing.

'Had you been with Simon for long?' asked Jason, perched on the sofa beside her.

Pip seemed to wake from her trance. She shook her head.

'About six months,' she said. 'Maybe a little longer, I'm not sure. We kept it all quiet, didn't want people thinking I was getting preferential treatment on set, that kind of thing.'

'And did you?' asked Amita.

'Don't be ridiculous,' she sniffed. 'If anything he was *harder* on me because we were together. Simon had this strange obsession with what everybody else thought of him. He couldn't let anything go, any little jibe or slant. When a new series came out he would sulk for days after reading the bad reviews.'

'I didn't think there were *any* bad reviews for *The Locus*,' said Jason sarcastically.

'Exactly,' she replied. 'Simon would find some fault, though. It was like he was just looking for a reason to be angry. All of the time.'

She reached down for the mug of tea Amita had made for her. She took a few tiny sips and placed it back on the table between them.

'Did you love him?' asked Amita.

Pip's brow wrinkled.

'Love is only a word,' she said. 'It doesn't do justice to the emotion it's supposed to represent. What Simon and I had, it was intense. Really intense. And not just the physical side of things. We had a connection, an emotional connection that was so perfect, so complete, it was frightening at times.'

'But you told us he was a nightmare,' said Jason, sitting forward. 'You had us believing that you hated the man, that he was a controlling, overbearing thug, for want of a better phrase.'

Jason's questioning sparked a fire in Pip's eyes. She glared at him with a laser focus.

'And why do you suppose that is, Mr Brazel?' she spat. 'Why do you think two highly successful people with public profiles wanted to keep things secret, keep our private lives, what little we have of that, from making the gossip columns and websites?'

Jason felt like he was coming under attack. He couldn't blame her, not really. The press' obsession with celebrity scandal and lifestyles had made plenty of mischief for those involved. It had also given them a platform. He didn't want to be dragged into this debate. There were two murders needing solving and his best theory had been blown out of the water.

'The heart wants what the heart wants,' Pip went on. 'Simon was a brilliant man, a kind and giving man when he chose to be. He was also a creative tidal wave. Watching him work, watching him sweat over the little details was an honour, a privilege. I won't sit here and tell you both that the relationship we had was perfect. Nothing in this world is. But for those fleeting few months, we made each other happy.'

The last sentiment seemed to tip Pip over the edge. She began to cry, holding her forehead in her hands, thin shoulders bobbing up and down.

'Oh Pip,' said Amita, getting up and going over to hug her. 'It's alright, my dear. You'll be fine. The loss of anyone is always hard but it mends with time. I promise you.'

Pip buried her face in Amita's shoulder. She patted her back, trying to console the star as she sobbed. She looked over to Jason, shaking her head. He took the hint. He rubbed his hands together, clearing his throat, doing everything but what he knew he had to. Eventually, when he had plucked up enough courage, he spoke up.

'Eh, Pip,' he said.

The actor pulled herself away from Amita. She wiped the tears from beneath her eyes, trying to recapture some of her usually immaculate appearance.

'I'm sorry,' he said, voice low.

'What?' she said to him.

'He's sorry,' said Amita.

'Yes, I'm sorry,' said Jason. 'For earlier, when I, you know, sort of accused you of murdering Derek and Simon. I was clearly barking up the wrong tree with that one and I might have come on a bit strong. But you did a good job of hiding it, I'll say that.'

Amita shook her head in despair. Jason went a little paler.

'Yes, well, you know what I mean,' he said. 'I apologise, unreservedly, for causing you any upset. Like my mother-in-law says, loss is a hell of a thing. And it kicks you when you're down and when you least expect it to. When my dad died I cried for a week. I never particularly got on with him but there you go. It's a strange business, grief.'

He was expecting Pip to either ignore him or volley more anti-press jibes towards him. And in truth he couldn't really blame her. She had lost the love of her life, by all accounts. Who was he to deny her a little bit of stress relief ranting at him.

The TV star, however, was polite and quiet. She gave him a sad, forced smile and nodded.

'It's not your fault,' she said. 'And you're right, we did do a bloody good job in keeping it all under wraps. Even the network bosses didn't know.'

'Pip, please don't take this the wrong way,' Amita ventured. 'But was there anyone else who knew about you and Simon? Anyone at all?'

'No,' said the actor, adamant. 'Nobody at all. We were absolutely discreet. Simon wanted it that way. He said we couldn't afford to have anyone find out, or it would be our careers, the show, everything at stake. We didn't even use our normal phones. He used to get us burners every time we went on location. He was paranoid, but it made sense. Why do you ask?'

'Simon was murdered,' she said. 'And at first we thought it might have been something to do with his manner, his treatment of cast and crew. We thought that from what you told us, and what Derek said.'

'Petty revenge,' said Jason. 'It's more common than you think.'

'However, with Derek now dead, killed too, our chief suspect is gone,' Amita went on. 'So I'm wondering if there was somebody else who knew about you and Simon? Someone who might not be happy with the relationship, who might want to get their own back on him, and you for that matter?'

Pip looked shocked. Her flushed face was turning pale. She shook her head again.

'I'm telling you, nobody,' she was getting angry. 'There was nobody on this earth who knew about Simon and I, nobody. We lived our lives together like we were working for MI6. He never stayed over at mine, or me at his. Do you know what that's like? Either of you? To not be able to wake up in the morning beside the man that you love because you're having to live this life, this alternate existence, to keep everything in the shadows?'

'Never to hold each other close the whole night through,' said Jason sadly.

'What?' Pip snapped.

'Nothing,' he said.

She stood up sharply. There was a twitchiness about her now. She wandered over to the windows of the apartment, rubbing the back of her head.

'Nobody knew,' she said again. 'They couldn't have. They just couldn't have. And even if they did, it's hardly worth killing… killing…'

She trailed off. Slowly turning back to face Jason and Amita, she wandered a little numbly towards the sofas.

'Pip?' asked Amita. 'Are you alright?'

'The night Simon was killed,' she said, sitting back down. 'He was out, he'd gone to dinner with some of the producers.'

'I know,' said Jason.

'I was supposed to be meeting him afterwards but he never called,' she said. 'It wasn't odd, I didn't think anything of it. He sometimes did that, depending on who he was with. I knew I'd see him the next day for filming anyway. I had some of the crew over here for the night, a little team bonding, that sort of thing.'

'Did you do that regularly?' asked Amita.

Pip nodded.

'As often as I could,' she said. 'Simon, as you know, had a reputation with the others. He was quick to anger, quick with his temper. But I always liked to take some of the younger ones under my wing, show them a bit of compassion, that things weren't always as awful and grim as people like Simon and Derek could make it for some of the little people.'

'And there were what you call "little people" here that night?' asked Jason. 'Can you remember who?'

'A few of the runners,' said Pip. 'A couple of the sound guys. Mostly the younger ones. We had a couple of drinks, crisps, talked about our time on bad sets and what they could expect if they wanted a career doing this kind of work. It was good, nice. Made me feel like I was giving back – you know, telling people what I wish I'd know before I got into this business. And then, of course, I get the call the next morning to say that Simon had been found…'

She trailed off again. Amita took her hand.

'I can't remember everything about that night,' she said. 'It's all a bit of a blur. Everything has been, since Simon died. But I might have said something to one of the runners.'

Amita looked over to Jason. He wore the same grave expression she knew she was pulling.

'Who precisely was there – can you give us names?' she asked.

'I can't remember,' said Pip, wrapping her knuckles against her forehead. 'It was a casual night – people coming and going, and crowding round – like a kitchen at a house party. I wasn't at the door with a clipboard, I was enjoying a chat amongst friends, sharing a few pearls of wisdom. You know how it is when you get relaxed with people you like. You let things slip, you start talking about anything and everything. I didn't have *that* much to drink. But I was waiting on Simon texting, I kept looking at that stupid burner he bought me. And there was nothing.'

'It's important, Pip, it really is,' said Jason.

'There must have been four or five of them who stayed most of the evening,' she said. 'A couple of girls and guys. I don't know, it was just another night. Until... until the morning after.'

She stood upright quickly. Snapping her fingers, she pointed at Jason and Amita.

'Lisa,' she said. 'Lisa, the gobby one. She was definitely here, scoffing all the nachos and the dip. We were joshing around with her because she's a bit of a suck up. I bet she'd remember everyone else's names.'

'Lisa,' said Amita. 'We've met her already. And you think she might have worked out you and Simon's relationship?'

'I don't know,' said Pip, pleading a little. 'I can't remember. But she was definitely here that night. She was always at these little get togethers, she never passed up a freebie. It's *her* you should be talking to. See what she knows.'

Amita and Jason took a moment to digest what they were being told. Lisa the runner had been nothing but helpful and friendly to them both. She had been kind and enthusiastic. The idea that she might have a sinister side made them both shiver.

Jason made to get up but something stopped him. A light had appeared in the darkness beyond the window, flickering and waving in the empty car park. He squinted, peering outside. The light moved back and forward, straying like a ghost caught in the wind. Then, bizarrely, it began to grow bigger.

He had a split second to realize what it was before it smashed through the window. The flaming bottle shattered immediately as it hit the floor. The unmistakable reek of petrol filled the apartment as the fire ignited. Jason was up and bundling Amita and Pip towards the door as the heat intensified.

'Get to the door!' he shouted.

The sofas where they had been sitting caught fire, followed by anything else that was close by. In a matter of seconds the whole living room was engulfed in flames. The acrid smoke filled his lungs and he coughed, pushing Amita and Pip ahead of him. They scuttled towards the front door and out into the corridor. The slap of the cold, fresh air was never more welcome. A few of the neighbours were already out and a clanging alarm bell started.

Pawing blindly, Jason's eyes stung badly from the soot and the smoke. They were all out into the car park. Amita and Pip sat down beside the cars, cradling each other. Jason wiped his eyes and turned back towards the apartments.

The beautifully restored historic building was glowing in the night, turning the black skies to an inky blue where the halo of flames hit it. Fire spewed from the windows of Pip's apartment and was spreading through the floor. The distant sound of sirens promised help for the other houses on the street but Pip's lodgings were already an inferno. Jason turned back to the others and slumped down beside them.

'Are you ok?' he asked, voice croaky.

'As well as can be expected when you've narrowly avoided being a serial killer's next victim,' said Amita. 'But as much as I'm glad not to have been barbecued in there, I'm aware our killer hasn't missed before. And I get the feeling that wasn't just a warning back there. If we don't get to the bottom of this fast, we'd better watch our backs.'

Chapter 30

MATERIA PRIMORIS

The harsh lights of the emergency department were giving Jason a headache. It was the absolute last thing he needed, given everything that had happened that night. He pulled his standard-issue hospital blanket around his shoulders a little more. He could still taste the smoke in the back of his throat. His lungs burned with every breath and his eyes were stinging. At least he was still alive, that was one thing. He'd never been in an arson attack before and didn't fancy a repeat of it – Amita's warning still ringing in his ears.

'How are you feeling?' asked Amita.

His mother-in-law held out a plastic cup full of water. Jason took it but didn't feel much like drinking. It hurt to swallow.

'I've had better evenings,' he croaked. 'Clearing out the gutters or waiting to have a root canal done without anaesthetic spring to mind. But beggars can't be choosers. We wanted to find some fresh evidence and I think we can safely say we met our killer. It's just a shame we couldn't see their face.'

He winced at the pain that came from speaking. His throat was red raw and he sounded like he was voicing a horror film trailer. Jason had never been overly vain about how he looked or how he sounded. But he'd read stories of people with smoke inhalation who suffered for years. If he stayed alive that long, he thought grimly as his eyes flashed to the window, half-fearing a Molotov cocktail was going to be lobbed through the one next to him.

He adjusted himself on the edge of the sturdy hospital bed. The curtains around their booth were closed but the din of the hospital was all around. When Amita had returned with the water, he had caught sight of the bedlam outside. Everyone was rushing around in a controlled panic. It served only to remind Jason that, even if he had wanted to, being a doctor or nurse was definitely not his vocation.

'How are you?' he managed as Amita sat down beside him.

'Oh, you know,' she shrugged. 'Just a few bumps and bruises, and I smell like a bonfire, but I'll live. Thanks to you, of course.'

'I didn't do anything,' he sniffed.

'Yes you did,' said Amita. 'You saved my life, Jason. And Pip Potter's. You got us both out of there before tragedy struck. If you hadn't thought on your feet, goodness knows what would have happened.'

'I have a fair idea,' he said grimly. 'Still, at least it wasn't Pip's actual home. I'm sure the owners of the apartment will get a nice, juicy pay off from the insurance. I don't think firebombing counts as an act of god, does it?'

'Stop it, Jason,' she tutted. 'This is serious. We've had a near-death experience. We could have been killed. And very likely are still at the top of someone's list.'

Jason closed his eyes. He could still see the flaming petrol bomb flying towards the window. It made him shudder. Amita was right. Had he not thought quickly then they would have been trapped by the flames. He couldn't really take any credit, though. There had been no thought in it all. Pure instinct had forced him into action.

'And even if we weren't the target and just unlucky enough to have been visiting Pip, now they think we've seen them, we've made ourselves prime targets. The killer's struck twice – I bet they'll have no scruples about a few more. If you've ended two lives, another three probably doesn't seem so bad.' Amita seemed strangely calm as she did the murderous maths.

The thought made Jason even more panicky. He sat up a little straighter.

'Does Radha know what's happened?' he asked. 'Does she know we're alright?'

'I spoke to her, just then, when I was outside,' said Amita. 'She's on her way down with the children. She's upset, of course, but I told her there's nothing to fear, that we're all ok.'

'Speak for yourself,' he said, coughing. 'I notice there's nothing different about your voice. Meanwhile I'm stuck here sounding like a toad trapped in an empty can of beans.'

'Strange,' said Amita furtively. 'I couldn't have inhaled as much smoke as you.'

They sat in silence for a moment. The hubbub of the emergency room was picking up. More and more voices were getting raised and strange alarms and alerts were going off. Every clank, thump, bump, bleep and curse stabbed at Jason's headache. He rubbed his forehead with his thumb and forefinger.

'Do you think it really was the killer?' asked Amita.

In the hour or so since they had escaped the inferno, Jason had asked himself that question a million times. The strain was probably the cause of his headache so he tried to stop.

'I would have thought so,' he said. 'I mean, it's either that or some hired goon – what are the odds of some other random fan being mad enough about Pip Potter to lob a petrol bomb through her living room window?'

'You're assuming that Pip was the target, again.'

Jason felt his right eye begin to twitch. That was new, it had never done that before. He looked over at his mother-in-law sat beside him on the hospital bed. She wore a worried look on her face, heavy bags under her eyes, wrinkles that little bit deeper beneath the unforgiving hospital striplights.

'What do you mean by that remark?' he asked, unsure whether he wanted the answer.

Amita took a deep breath. She stared down at her own little cup of water.

'It's just a thought, Jason,' she said eventually. 'I mean, we *were* there with Pip for a long while. In a murder investigation, you can't ever jump to conclusions. You taught me that. What's to say it wasn't an attempt on *our* lives and not Pip Potter.'

Jason was right – he hadn't wanted to know the answer.

'Nobody knows us, Amita,' he said. 'We're non-descript, anonymous. Why would the killer go to the trouble of trying to bump us off? It doesn't make sense.'

'What doesn't make sense is Lisa the runner being mentioned by Pip Potter,' she said pointedly. 'And I wouldn't be so quick to do us a disservice, Jason. Remember that Lisa was all too aware of us when we first met her.'

'Yes… but…' He trailed off. He remembered what Pip had told them in her flat before it was sent up in flames. Lisa had been with her on the night of Simon Nakamba's murder. The actor wasn't sure if she had let slip about their relationship. But if she had, did that mean Lisa was now a suspect?

'What's her motive?' Jason asked. 'Why would she try and kill us? Or Pip or Simon Nakamba and Derek Veland for that matter?'

'Revenge, maybe?' Amita asked. 'You heard how she spoke about Nakamba. Maybe she snapped after some off-hand comment of his or tantrum. We don't know what she's like, not really. She was perfectly friendly and helpful, but maybe that was a ruse to throw us all off her scent. Who is she, after all? Like us, she could use the fact that no one ever looks at the little people. She's a runner. She would have had access to Simon at all times.'

'And what about us?'

Amita shook her head.

'Maybe we've been getting too close,' she offered. 'She knew we were wanting to speak with Pip Potter again, you told her that. Maybe she thought that we were getting near to the truth and decided we were expendable. Is that the term?'

'Yes, I'm afraid so,' he said. 'Bloody hell. I liked this investigation more when we weren't next in line for a body-bag.'

'Me too,' she agreed.

The curtain was pulled back with a sharp tug. Amita's eyed widened as Abi Paris slipped into the booth, focused on the charts in her hands.

'Abi!' said Amita, standing up quickly.

'Mrs Khatri,' said the young nursing student. 'I thought it might be you when I saw your name on the board. Are you alright? I heard about the fire.'

'We were rather hoping you'd be able to tell us if we were ok or not,' said Jason.

'Jason,' Amita chastised him.

'It's ok,' Abi laughed, flashing him a warm smile. 'I get that all of the time. Part of the initiation as a student nurse, I'm afraid.'

'We'll be alright,' said Amita. 'We were very lucky to get out of that apartment when we did. Is Pip Potter ok?'

Abi shuffled her feet and looked a little awkward.

'I'm not really supposed to talk about other patients,' she said. 'Confidentiality rules and all of that.'

'Of course,' nodded Amita.

'But she's still here, if that's what you want to know. The police have been hovering around, it's quite intimidating actually, nobody can get near her. You guys were lucky to get out unscathed.'

'Lucky yes,' said Amita. 'Thankful too. Jason here is the hero of the day. He got us all out of the flat before things got out of hand.'

'Yes, so I see,' she hugged her clipboard to her chest. 'You're both clear to leave from these observation results. The doctors say that you need to take it easy for a couple of days and you'll be back to normal. No strenuous exercise and no smoking, obviously.'

'Of course,' said Amita.

'I don't smoke but I feel like I've been on the Rothmans since I was six.' Jason added.

'Rothmans?' asked Abi.

'Don't listen to him, dear. He's a relic from a bygone age,' said Amita.

Abi laughed. She pulled the curtains back and let Jason and Amita gather up their few belongings.

'I'll walk you out to the waiting room,' she said. 'Do you have a lift sorted?'

'Yes, my daughter is coming down to collect us,' said Amita, following the young nurse. 'Please don't let us keep you though, it's mad enough in here without you taking time off.'

'Don't be silly,' she said. 'They won't miss me for five minutes while I see out old friends.'

Amita smiled. As she walked through the triage room towards the exit, she couldn't help but notice how similar Abi was to her mother when she was younger. Both had a confident, comfortable stride. Her hazel hair was tied back, just like Sarah's was at school. Amita felt her heart tugging at the thought of all the missed years and opportunities. Sarah had once felt like a surrogate daughter – and here she was not even knowing she'd had a child of her own since.

'How is your mother?' she asked. 'We rather left her in the lurch with the police.'

'She's at home,' said Abi, guiding them to the waiting area. 'She texted me when she got in. I'll see her when I get off shift. I'm worried about her, you know. This whole thing at the hotel, the murders, it's like it's the last straw. She's already been under so much strain and stress and I feel like I can't do anything to help her.'

'I know,' said Amita. 'There's not a lot more you can do, Abi. Your mother did the right thing going to the police. Whatever happened between her and Derek Veland is not your fault.'

'I feel so useless,' she said. 'I'm stuck in here all of the time, dealing with all of this.'

She cast an angry hand out across the busy waiting room. Jason winced.

'You're not useless at all, Abi,' said Amita. 'You're there for your mum. You're her daughter, her rock and I'm sure she's grateful for you being there for her whenever you can. You've got your own problems and life to live, Sarah knows that. And I'm here, for both of you, if there's anything I can do.'

Abi bowed her head. She held back her own tears and thanked Amita.

'That means a lot, Mrs Khatri, really it does,' she said.

'Call me Amita. Do you know, your mother called me that from when she was five years old, like we were old friends.'

The sound of running footsteps broke up the little moment. Radha and the kids bounded towards Amita and Jason, arms outstretched. She threw herself at her husband and hugged him tight.

'I thought you were dead. Both of you!' she said.

'I'll leave you to it,' said Abi, backing away. 'Take care.'

'If you need anything, anything at all, please call, Abi,' said Amita. 'Don't hesitate and don't suffer in silence, please.'

'Thank you,' said the nurse.

Amita let her head back into the ward. She turned to her daughter and grandchildren and gave them all a huge hug. The family stayed there for a moment, silent, together.

Chapter 31

OLD NED

Amita woke to a phone buzzing on her bedside cabinet. She thought she had put it onto silent mode before she went to sleep the night before. Although with everything that had happened, she allowed herself a little forgiveness for not being as switched on as normal.

It was after midnight by the time they all got home. The children had headed straight to bed. Jason and Radha had gone to tuck them in and when they came back downstairs, Amita was waiting for them, staring at the blackboard still in the living room. But no more answers had come to them. All of the names, faces, places, timelines and theories were jumbling into a great big mess in her head and they'd admitted defeat for the night. Her spirit was willing but her body was not. She had trudged upstairs to her room and promptly fallen asleep. She even forgot to take her teeth out.

Now the phone was buzzing relentlessly. She had no idea what time it was, the room still dark save for the flashing screen beside her. She rubbed her eyes, still tired. It had been like that a lot recently, even before the unpleasantness with *The Locus* cast and crew. Amita had always been fit and spry. Physical exercise had always been her sanity saver – whether it was TV Keep Fit when the kids were tiny, or longer runs as they got older and she gained time back for herself. For her fiftieth birthday she'd set herself the challenge of the London Marathon *and* the Great North Run in the same season. It had almost killed her, but she'd managed it. She still had the scars where her feet were blistered to damnation as a result, but she was proud, and convinced her surprising turn of speed for a septuagenarian had saved her life more than once in the last few years.

But lately, the thought of running a marathon made her feel a bit ill. She still got out to jog and power walk as much as she could. Only these past few weeks and months she had been less consistent – letting herself walk past her running shoes when the weather was poor or the light was fading. Bounding across the Cumbrian countryside with Jason in tow was *not* the kind of exertion she was after. She vowed, as she rolled over to grab her phone, that she would return to her normal regime when all of this was over. The Sheriff of Penrith's promises were worth their weight in any precious metal.

Any doziness that clouded Amita's mind was erased as soon as she saw who was calling her. She answered and almost knocked herself out as she pressed the phone against her ear.

'Detective Inspector Arendonk,' she said, a little breathless. 'Is everything alright?'

'Good, you're awake,' said the policewoman. 'I've been trying to raise that bloody son-in-law of yours for the past hour but he's not answering.'

Amita panicked thinking something was wrong. Then she remembered that Jason was practically a statue when he fell asleep: the London Symphony Orchestra in full flight wouldn't waken him.

'I'm sorry,' she said. 'I'll take it up with him when he finally comes around.'

'Kick him up the backside from me too, would you?'

'Of course.'

'Look, I'm sorry to be calling like this so soon after what happened,' said Arendonk. 'But I thought you might want to know that we've had a bit of a breakthrough.'

'Breakthrough?'

Amita rubbed her eyes. She threw her legs over the edge of the bed, already planning her outfit.

'Yes,' said the detective. 'It seems that our fire bug who thought it would be clever to lob a petrol bomb into Pip Potter's apartment was known to you.'

'Known? To *me*?'

'Technically, Jason,' she said. 'But you two are one and the same person in my mind anyway.'

Amita ignored the barb.

'Who is it?'

'Viper.'

'Viper?'

It took a moment for Amita to work out what the inspector was talking about. Then it clicked into place.

'Simon Nakamba's cousin?'

'The very same. We picked him up in the early hours, brawling with some revellers in town and absolutely reeking of petrol. He's not denying being near the crime scene last night but he's adamant he had nothing to do with the fire. It's all circumstantial at the moment, Amita, but I'm holding him until he helps us out.'

'I see,' said Amita.

'You don't sound very convinced. I was expecting to be lavished with praise and find you leaping for joy at the efficiency of Cumbria Police.'

'Sorry,' she said. 'I'm still trying to work it all out. You're sure you have the right man?'

'Peter Nakamba, that's what his passport says. And he's admitted to being close enough to Pip Potter's flat that he could easily be guilty.'

Amita rubbed her forehead.

'Has he said why?' she asked.

'Nope,' Arendonk sighed. 'And that's what I was calling about. I wondered if you might have any ideas as to how to get through to him.'

'But I'm not a professional,' she said. 'As Jason likes to remind me, all the time. That and I've never met the man, Jason has.'

'Then could you kick him out of his scratcher?' said the detective. 'We could do with hearing a little more about what he and Peter spoke about. That and it's after nine o'clock and he really should be up and about – freelance journalist or not.'

'After nine!' Amita yelped. She stood up a little too quickly and steadied herself. As Arendonk hung up she spotted the clock on her phone. She hadn't slept past nine in around fifty years. She'd barely been asleep later than seven for most of her life. She didn't know what to do first.

'Jason!' she shouted. 'Jason! Quickly! We're needed down at the police station. Arendonk has arrested that cousin of Simon Nakamba.'

The door to his bedroom opened with a slow creak and Jason appeared on the other side. Bleary eyed and licking his lips, he squinted at Amita from the gloom.

'What?' he rasped.

'Come on, it's after nine,' she said, hurrying around the landing but not actually doing anything. 'This is scandalous, I should have been up hours ago. Have Radha and the children gone?'

'Yes,' he said. 'They left us be after everything that happened last night. I thought that was rather kind of them.'

'You've had enough sleep, come on,' she said, hurrying him. 'We have to get down to the police station as fast as we can. This could be our breakthrough and–'

A loud smash from outside stopped Amita mid-flight. She stood up a little straighter, eyes widening. Jason did the same.

'What was that?' he asked, cowering behind the door.

'It sounded like breaking glass,' she whispered. 'Or something heavier.'

Raised voices slowly filtered up the stairs. She leaned over the banister, peering down towards the front door. The vague outlines of two shadows beyond the frosted glass gave her chills. They were moving back and forth quickly, merging into one amorphous blob as the shouting continued.

'Someone's outside,' she said. 'I think someone is having a fight on our porch.'

She hurried down the stairs. Jason wasn't far behind. He bounded down the steps after his mother-in-law, narrowly missing the shoes and stray Lego blocks that would cause infinite pain.

They both arrived at the front door at the same time, not knowing what to expect – another firebomber? Pulling it open, the unmistakable sight of Sandy holding Irvine Carruthers in a headlock met them on the other side. It took all of Amita's willpower and indefatigability not to faint with shock.

'What the bloody hell is going on here?' asked Jason, much less tactful than Amita.

At the sound of Jason's raised voice, the two pensioners stopped their jostling. They both looked up at the pair standing in the doorway. Sandy's big face began to flush, his white moustache bristling. He let Irvine go, who straightened with a creak.

'Eh... morning, Jason,' he said. 'Amita.'

He took off his cap and bowed a little at them.

'Yes, good morning,' echoed Irvine, fixing his collar. 'Or at least it was a good morning until *he* showed up.'

'Now don't start with that nonsense, Carruthers, I'm warning you,' Sandy snarled, wagging a finger. 'I've already had enough of your lip this morning, I won't stand for any more.'

'And what are *you* going to do? Eh?' the other man fired back. 'Wrestle me to the floor like the shaved ape you are?'

'I've had you in a headlock already, you silly old fool, don't make me do it again.'

'Who are you calling a silly old fool? You're the silly old fool.'

'I'm not as old as *you*!'

'But you're twice as decrepit!'

'That's it!'

Sandy lunged forward, trying to grapple with Irvine, who was much leaner and quick on his feet. They chased each other around the porch for a moment, clattering into an already smashed plant pot by the door. Jason didn't know whether to laugh or call the police. Amita, however, was not so entertained.

'Would you both stop it!'

Her voice was so loud, Jason thought it might have set off a car alarm all the way down at number 103. Nobody looked more surprised at the volume than Sandy and Irvine, both of them frozen to the spot, like schoolboys caught by their headteacher.

'I don't know what's going on here,' she said, sounding every bit like a furious drill sergeant. 'But it stops, right now. You're a pair of fully grown men, pensioners even, and yet here you are, fighting outside my home.'

'You've both done it now,' said Jason, backing away. 'Good luck, boys.'

'Jason,' she snapped.

The two gents didn't say a word. They stood there, exchanging angry glances.

'Well?' she said. 'Do you want to explain what's going on here?'

'He started it,' said Irvine.

'I only started it because you were putting your nose in where it doesn't belong, Carruthers.'

'I've got every right to be here.'

'So do I.'

'Do you, indeed? We'll see about that.'

'Enough!' Amita barked. 'You're worse than the children, *both* of you! I don't care who started what, I just want an explanation.'

Neither of the old men was forthcoming with an answer.

'Right, that does it,' she said, throwing her hands up. 'I'm calling the police.'

'What?' Sandy spluttered.

'No need for that, now, Amita,' pleaded Irvine.

'Unless one of you starts talking, then my hand will be forced. Jason, get DI Arendonk on the line again – we've got a breach of the peace to report.'

Jason looked blank.

'It's alright,' said Sandy, holding his big hands up. 'There's no need for that. It was my fault, Amita, my fault.'

'What was?' She eyed him up and down.

The big man's anger was vanishing. His brow was drawn, moustache drooping into a frown. His huge shoulders were hunched over.

'I heard about what happened last night,' he said.

'We both did,' Irvine corrected.

'It's all around the bingo club, Penrith even. I daresay all of the Lake District knows by now. You know what Georgie is like when she gets her teeth into something.'

Amita hadn't even thought about Georgie Littlejohn or the network of OAPs she relied so heavily on. She'd been too busy trying to escape a firebomb and catch a murderer.

'Anyway, I thought I should come around to see if you were ok, if you needed anything.' He stooped and reached into a bush by the path.

He wrestled a box of chocolates free of the ferns and dusted it off. The corners were bashed where somebody had stepped on them during the scuffle.

'Sorry about the state they're in,' he said. 'I arrived about ten minutes ago and as I was about to knock on the door Mr Carruthers here came up behind me, shouting and swearing and asking me what I was doing here.'

'You still haven't answered that question,' said Irvine. 'At least I'm invited to Amita's home. I've got every right to be here, unlike *you*.'

There was a jealousy to his tone that Amita immediately baulked at. Irvine must have sensed the fury radiating off her as he backed away a little, his face a sketch of confusion and fear.

'Amita?' he asked her. 'Are you alright, my dear?'

'I think it's best that you leave,' she said. 'Both of you.'

'What? Me too?' Irvine sounded incredulous.

'Yes!' Amita hissed. 'Your behaviour has been appalling, both of you. Fighting at your age, and in full glare of my neighbours. I can't begin to think what came over you.'

'But... but...' Irvine tried vainly to plead his case.

Amita wasn't interested. Sandy just stood there like a scalded hound dog. He nodded once, put his cap on his head and reached out to his rival. He offered him his hand.

'I'm sorry,' he said, voice like a clap of thunder.

More used to hostility than an olive branch, Irvine didn't know what to do. He was flapping about, head swivelling on his scrawny neck like an orange on a toothpick. Finally, he shook Sandy's hand weakly before letting go and turning back to Amita, practically begging to be let in. She didn't budge.

'I'll see you at bingo, Amita,' said Sandy, starting up the path. 'No hard feelings, I hope.'

Amita felt a lump in her throat forming. She kept her composure while Irvine also slowly took the hint. He let Sandy clear the garden before turning away himself. As he closed the front gate, he offered one more glassy-eyed, silent plea to Amita. She returned him a look with something close to sub-zero temperatures. Eventually he gave in and scurried off down the road.

When both men were far enough out of sight, Amita let out a huge breath. She slumped against the doorway and clapped a clammy hand onto her forehead. Jason whistled beside her, staring down the road.

'I was *not* expecting that,' he said.

'What?' she groaned.

'A couple of pensioners duelling for the hand of the fair maiden,' he said. 'I mean, this is Penrith, but you still assume that medieval chivalry is viewed as rather last season. What are they going to do next – joust to win your hand?'

Amita was going to chastise him when she spotted the box of chocolates from Sandy on the front step. She stooped down and collected them, an envelope tucked under the edge of the cellophane wrapping. She opened it. A modest card was inside urging her and Jason to get well soon. Sandy had signed it simply enough. And that made her heart ache all the harder. Or perhaps, she told herself, it was just a twinge of angina.

'Come on,' she said, fighting back tears. 'Let's get in before any of the neighbours see you're out in your pants, Jason.'

She slid past him back into the house. Jason looked down at his bare pot belly, knobbly knees and hairy legs.

'Ah,' he said. 'I wondered why it was so cold.'

Chapter 32

THE LIBERTY BELL

Viper sat with his head in his hands. Jason peered through the gap in the heavy cell door. He'd seen this sort of thing plenty of times on TV and in movies. But he'd never actually had the chance to stare into a cell. And on the box, it was usually forensic psychologists or emotionally wounded criminologists they drafted in. Not underemployed journalists with a voice like a barrow full of gravel.

'This might sound like a silly question,' he whispered to DI Arendonk. 'But, can he see us?'

'I can hear you too,' said Viper, looking up at them.

'Oh, right,' said Jason.

Arendonk slammed the hatch closed. The clang made Jason's ears ring.

'Remind me never to let you see or do anything ever again,' she said.

'Sorry,' he said.

She ushered him a little away from the cell door. Amita was waiting at the other end of the corridor. She looked terrified being this close to incarceration. Jason didn't blame her. He was feeling very cramped and claustrophobic too.

'Right, here's the gist of it,' said Arendonk. 'Viper, as he likes to be called, says he was passing by when he saw Pip Potter's place alight. He's giving no reason as to why he happened to be in the neighbourhood. He also claims he had nothing to do with the murders of his cousin or Derek Veland. He didn't even know who the latter was when we asked him.'

'Ok,' said Jason. 'And this involves us in what way?'

'Jason,' Amita tutted. 'Don't be so rude.'

'I'm just saying, that's all.'

'Well, don't, this is very serious.' Amita had been particularly snippy since the morning's rude awakening.

'You've spoken with him, right? He trusts you?' asked the detective.

'Briefly, yes,' said Jason. 'I bought him a cheese roll and a cuppa soon after he arrived. I don't know if that makes us friends or anything. As for trust, well, how can you trust somebody you don't really know?'

'A cheese roll and a cup of tea is more than what most people get, Jason,' said Amita. 'That was very kind of you, by the way.'

'It was nothing,' he feigned humility. 'I still don't see what's so special about me. I don't know the guy and I don't particularly relish being stuck in a prison cell with him if it turns out he's a murderer.'

Jason felt justified in his logic. Less than a day ago, Viper had potentially almost killed him, Amita and a very famous TV star. He was expecting an immediate retort from Arendonk. The detective, however, was silent.

'Hold on,' said Amita, stepping forward. 'You don't think Viper did it, do you?'

Arendonk was still silent. Jason could see the tendons in her cheeks and temples flexing. She crossed her arms and leaned against the wall.

'I have a suspect who's pretty much bang to rights,' she said. 'I don't have enough to charge him yet but I know the top brass would lean on me to make it happen. But I've got a gut feeling about him. All that hulking rage is covering something. Now I could simply throw away the key and be done with it. But I'm a good copper and I don't like innocent people being punished for something they didn't do. I always have to be cautious with this kind of thing. Especially if the person in question is emotionally compromised.'

'He's certainly that,' said Jason. 'I've never seen somebody so quick to anger as this Viper bloke. He almost took my head off when I asked him about his cousin, then dissolved into tears not long after.'

'You don't think he's the killer though, do you, Detective Inspector?' asked Amita again.

'What I think and what the facts are can be two completely different things,' she said glibly. 'I just think that a friendly face going in to speak with this guy might clear the air and stop this case flowing in an unwanted direction. The only thing worse than not finding the killer would be charging the wrong bloke, leaving our culprit in the clear.'

Amita nodded in agreement. She turned to Jason. Both women were staring at him now. He scratched his stubbly chin.

'It's nice to be needed, I suppose,' he said.

Arendonk went and unlocked the cell door. Jason had barely set foot inside when it closed behind him with an intimidating clunk. He swallowed a stale-tasting gulp and tried to keep as big a distance between himself and Viper as possible.

'Hi there,' he said. 'Remember me?'

'You mean from a few moments ago when you thought I couldn't hear or see you?' asked Viper.

'Yes,' said Jason. 'I mean no. From the other day there, in the square. I bought you a cheese roll, remember?'

'It was disgusting,' he said. 'I can still taste it now.'

'Oh I don't know,' said Jason. 'It's hardly Michelin starred but it's saved a few hangovers over the years.'

Viper sneered. He leaned back, his leather jacket and trousers squeaking. His cowboy hat and boots were missing and there was a distinct smell of petrol about the cell. Jason hadn't ever found himself interviewing in a jail before. He wasn't sure if there was any sort of etiquette to observe. As was always the case throughout his career, Jason decided to go with what he knew. The direct approach.

'Did you kill your cousin?' he asked.

There was a still moment before Viper answered. Jason wasn't sure if he was cooking up a story or he was shocked at the question.

'How dare you!' he shouted, getting to his feet. 'How dare you ask me a question like that!'

'Look, I don't want to be here any more than you do,' he tried to reason with him. 'But there's a police officer outside that door who's getting ready to charge you for blowing up a perfectly nice and no doubt expensive apartment that myself and my mother-in-law happened to be in. Not to mention one of Britain's leading ladies. So you better start talking, Viper, or it's going to be goodnight from me and goodnight from you.'

Viper's chest was heaving up and down. His eyes were wide and wild, the same look he'd given Jason back in the square.

'I didn't do it,' he said, sitting back down. 'I'm heartbroken, Jason. Absolutely heartbroken. My cousin was everything to me. I told you that when we met. I loved him like a brother, more than a brother. I'd never do anything to harm him.'

'I thought as much. What I think our friends in blue are less clear on is whether you know more than you're letting on about the other body that turned up.' Jason figured since Viper hadn't lamped him for asking the first question it was worth a shot to continue.

'So what about Derek Veland? Did you kill him? Did you find out that he'd murdered Simon and you sought your revenge?'

'I don't know this Derek Veland,' said Viper, tears gathering in his eyes. 'I keep hearing his name. I know now that he was an actor on one of Simon's shows. But I don't know the man, never met him. So no, I didn't kill anyone.'

'But you almost did, from what I hear,' said Jason with a flash of anger. 'If that was you last night in the alley, you almost killed me and Pip Potter and Amita.'

Viper bowed his head again.

'I'm sorry,' he said. 'I was just...'

'Just what, Viper?' Jason's anger was growing. 'Just what? How can you possibly sit there and justify throwing a petrol bomb into a flat? Do you have any idea how serious this is? You're looking at prison. And quite frankly I hope they lock you up for a very long time.'

He turned to leave. Viper called after him.

'No, please, wait,' he said. 'You have to believe me, I didn't do it.'

'You told the cops you were passing by,' Jason spat. 'Your clothes were reeking of petrol, you still stink of the stuff now. You told me the other day that you were going to get revenge and now here we are. Why should I believe you? Why should I trust you? For all I know, the police have the right man. And if that's the case, what the hell am I doing in here trying to get you to talk?'

He rattled off these questions like a machine gun. Viper looked shell-shocked.

'I... I was going to do something,' he said. 'I didn't know what to do, sorry. I just wanted to help... I'm sorry.'

'You wanted to *help*?' squeaked Jason. 'My throat and lungs are burning from smoke inhalation, Viper. I had to push my seventy-something-year-old mother-in-law down a set of stairs to get her out of there. The only thing you've helped with is nearly sending me to an early grave. I saw your little homemade explosive device hurtling towards me. But that's ok, you're sorry.'

'I didn't throw the petrol bomb,' Viper said pitifully. 'That was somebody else. I caught them, tried to stop them. It wasn't me, Jason, I swear.'

Jason tried to calm down. He paced around the cramped little cell.

Viper snorted loudly. He wiped his face on his sleeve.

'When I left you the other day, I asked some questions around town,' he said. 'I told you I wanted to know what had happened to Simon, who had killed him and why.'

'Yeah, you're not alone in that,' said Jason.

'Where we grew up, you didn't rely on the police. We did everything ourselves. I won't bore you with another sob story, but we both knew that, if we wanted to get on in this world, we would have to work for it. Nobody owes anyone anything. It's steered me ok down the years. And Simon was the same. He was famous, world famous – and he'd not relied on anyone to get there. I know that didn't always make him popular, but he didn't deserve to die.'

'No, he didn't,' said Jason. 'But I'd say his killer also doesn't deserve the same fate. Fair trial and all of that. Justice will prevail and it's not up to you or I to dish it out.'

'I know.'

'So what happened with the flat? A petrol bomb, Viper? Come on, that's serious stuff. You say there was someone else involved. No one's going to believe that unless you can give me a name or at least a decent description.' Jason sat down beside him.

'That actress, Potter,' he said. 'Her name kept coming up whenever I asked about my cousin.'

'Who were you asking?'

'You know as well as I do,' he said. 'Every town, every city the world over has a network of people plugged into what's going on. You find the right people to ask and you'll get answers soon enough. My cousin's show was big news, Jason, people love to talk about it. I thought you were supposed to be a journalist. Shopkeepers, drinkers in the pubs, pretty much anyone I asked had something to say about the filming here. And when I saw crew packing stuff away they were the same – full of gossip.'

'So these people, your sources, they pointed you in Pip Potter's direction? Why?'

'She was in a relationship with Simon,' he said flatly.

Jason felt his stomach tighten as he realised that Pip Potter's secret may not have been as safe as she thought.

'I was so angry,' he went on. 'I wasn't thinking properly. I thought the worst. I thought, maybe, she had something to do with his murder. At the very least she'd be able to tell me who else might have had it in for Simon. It didn't take me long to find out where she was staying. I just wanted to speak with her, find out what was going on between them, if she knew anything. That's why I went around to her flat. I was heading for the door when I smelled something.'

'Petrol.'

'Yeah,' Viper nodded. 'There was a person hunched over by a car in the car park. I couldn't see who it was in the dark but I saw the fuel spilling out onto the road, a rainbow slick spreading in the gloom. When I edged nearer I saw what they were doing, pouring gas into a bottle with a rag around the top. I've played enough video games to know a Molotov cocktail when I see one. They were about to throw it when I got near them. I tried to stop them but they were strong, and I'm not used to meeting my match when it comes to a scrap. But they clearly knew some sort of fighting, some martial arts or something. The next thing I knew I was on my back in a puddle of the petrol. That's why I stink of the stuff. They threw the bomb and it exploded. I panicked, I ran. I shouldn't have left, I'm sorry for that. I should have tried to save you and the others. But in that moment, everything flashed in front of me, my whole life. And I knew then that, if the police caught me there, they'd think I was guilty, think I was responsible. Like you do.'

'What happened to the bomber?' Jason asked. 'Did you get a look at them? Man, woman? Age? You must have seen something distinctive?'

'No,' said Viper sadly. 'Their face was covered with a scarf and hood. They were fast, they moved quickly, like they were rehearsed in this kind of thing. I should have done more to stop them. I should have gone after them, something. Instead I went and got drunk, like the selfish coward I am.'

Viper rubbed his eyes. His knees were bobbing up and down with a nervous energy. Jason sighed.

'Who told you about Simon and Pip Potter?' he tried again.

'I don't know their names,' he said. 'Crew, roadies, catering – I asked anyone I could find connected with the filming.'

'Viper, you have to try and remember who exactly said Simon and Pip were an item,' he pressed. 'It could be vital in catching Simon's killer. Pip Potter maintains that *nobody* knew about them. Whoever was spreading the rumour or knew about their relationship could be the killer. Try to think.'

Viper shook his head. Jason decided to take a gamble.

'Was it Lisa?' he asked.

'Lisa who?' asked Viper.

'The young runner you met when you first broke into the flat. She was the one trying to stop you from strangling me.'

Viper thought for a moment. Then he shook his head.

'No,' he said. 'It wasn't her.'

'Are you sure?'

'Positive,' he said. 'She had kind eyes. She comforted me that day. It wasn't her who told me. I can't remember who though, Jason, really I can't. I wasn't even sure who was crew and who were extras. These past few days, they've been such a terrible mess. I can't sleep, I can't eat. Everything is an awful blur. I just don't know.'

Jason nodded. He clapped Viper's shoulder and stood up, leaving him sitting on the cell's bed. He knocked on the door and Arendonk opened it up. She closed it off behind him, leaving Viper alone in his cell.

'Well?' asked Amita, hurrying up to him. 'What did he say?'

'He's innocent,' said Jason.

'How can you be sure?' asked Arendonk.

'Circumstantial, I know,' he said. 'But he claims he fought with the real bomber. He didn't get a good look at them but says that they were quick on their feet and made a sharp exit after they threw the nasty little surprise our way.'

'You believe him?' asked the DI. 'It sounds awfully convenient.'

'I do,' said Jason. 'Call me mad but I do. He's angry and confused and grieving. We've all done stupid things when we're like that. Viper… Peter, is no exception. He'll need some counselling, I'm sure. But I don't think he's our man.'

Arendonk took a long, deep breath through her nose. She nodded.

'He did make an interesting point though,' Jason went on. 'He knew about Pip Potter and Simon Nakamba being an item.'

'They were an item?' asked Arendonk. 'In a relationship?'

'They were,' said Amita. 'She told us last night before the fire.'

'Viper can't remember who told him this exactly but he reckons it was someone on the show,' said Jason. 'I don't know if it's anything to go on, my head is like scrambled eggs at the moment.'

'Right, that'll be enough then,' said Arendonk. 'Both of you head home. You've been more than helpful this morning and I'm sorry I had to drag you down here like this.'

She started showing them out of the station, although they both knew the route by now.

'What will happen to Viper?' asked Amita.

'I'll get the paperwork filed and contact our grief therapist, see if they can give him some help,' said the detective. 'I've got nothing firm to hold him on and he didn't resist arrest when we nicked him at that fight last night. He's not who we're looking for.'

The fresh air was welcome. Jason had never been more relieved to be outdoors and away from the confinement of the cells. Arendonk thanked them again, then stopped in her tracks and clicked her fingers.

'The post-mortem came back on Nakamba, by the way,' she said. 'Remember you were asking about it.'

'Did it come up with a cause of death?' asked Amita. 'We know he'd had a skinful so I hope your lab folk could see past that.'

'They certainly did. Air bubbles in the blood,' said the detective. 'Something akin to the bends.'

'That's odd,' said Jason. 'I thought that was a diver's' thing. I don't think he'd been scuba-ing through Ullswater. How did he get air bubbles in his blood?'

'Remember those marks on his arm? Turns out they were caused by injection, some sort of syringe. But there was no evidence of drug use. So the theory is, not the kind of thing you'd do to yourself by mistake. Somebody got close enough to jab him, pump him full of air and let the body do the dirty work. Pretty nasty by all accounts.'

'Good grief,' said Amita. 'How awful.'

'Yeah,' she said. 'Anyway, don't have nightmares.'

Amita and Jason walked slowly towards their car.

'Extras,' she said. 'We've been speaking to the main cast and crew, but of course there are all the other nameless people – literally the faces in a crowd. How are we going to track them all down?'

'I know,' Jason replied. 'Pip and Simon might have thought they were being subtle but it's clear that somebody else knew about them. And whoever it was, they weren't happy with it.'

'Where does Derek Veland fit into all of this though?'

'I don't know,' said Jason, pulling open the door. 'I keep thinking we could have got more out of him when we had our chance. We could have saved him.'

They climbed into the car and turned on the heater, chasing away the frost.

'I think we're facing a killer more determined than that, Jason. For some reason, Derek's number was up and we need to work out why. I think it has to be somebody who has worked with them both before – with Pip too if she's in the line of fire,' said Amita. 'Otherwise, what does it matter they were all carrying on with people in secret? Jealousy, extortion, revenge, all of these motives don't simply come to somebody overnight. It's got to be long term. And since none of our victims were married, for once we can rule out avenging spouses as culprits.'

'So you think they both knew their killer?' asked Jason.

'More often than not that's the case,' said Amita sadly. 'If only we had a way of cross-referencing their past roles with everyone else.'

A wry smile crept across Jason's face. He started the engine and reversed out of the car park at speed.

'What's got into you?' asked Amita, barely able to get her seatbelt on in time. 'Where are we going?'

'Hang on to your handbag and you'll see.'

Chapter 33

NO MEAN CITY

Amita had never seen Jason move so quickly. He bounded up the stairs like his boots had wings. She was lagging behind, the events of the week catching up with her. Thankfully they stopped on the second floor. He was hammering a door as she puffed her way up the final few steps.

'Lisa!' he shouted. 'Lisa, it's Jason and Amita. Are you in there? Can we speak to you for a moment? It's urgent.'

He kept banging on the door. Amita mopped her brow, her hand glistening with sweat. She felt a little light-headed and her lungs were on fire. She hoped it was only the aftereffects of the blaze.

'Lisa!' Jason was shouting louder now. 'Lisa! Please, we need to speak with you. It's important.'

The door opened quickly. Darrel, the tall, spotty-faced lad Jason had met before, answered. He looked surprised.

'Where's Lisa?' Jason asked.

'Erm...' he stammered.

'Darrel, who is it?'

Lisa appeared down the hallway behind him. She was pulling on her coat and looked like she was ready to leave. When she spotted Jason and Amita her face dropped.

'Oh,' she said. 'What are you two doing here?'

Amita noticed a distinct coldness to her that hadn't been there before. She zipped up her coat and seemed furtive.

'Could we speak to you for a moment, Lisa?' she asked kindly.

'I'm just heading out,' she said. 'We're packing up the last of the vans and shipping back down to Manchester. We need to get going, don't we, Darrel.'

'It'll only take a moment,' said Jason in as friendly a way as he could.

Lisa sighed loudly. Darrel stood there looking gawky. Eventually she nodded at him and showed them into the flat.

'Ten minutes,' she said.

Amita caught up with Jason, giving him a look. It was her can-you-manage-to-speak-to-someone-for-ten-minutes-without-accusing-them-of-murder? look.

Lisa led them into the living room. The floorboards were bare, the faintest outline of an old fireplace still marking the wall. The whole place smelled of damp, the windows filthy and smudging the pale light of the afternoon. Amita kept her hands firmly in her pockets, not wanting to touch anything. Jason did the same.

'Ok, you've got me, what's up?' asked Lisa.

'Is everything alright, dear?' asked Amita.

'Yeah, fine. Or as fine as it can be when I'm soon going to be unemployed. Why?'

'It's just, well, you don't seem like yourself,' said Jason.

'Like myself?' she laughed. 'And how would you two know what I'm like normally? We've met each other, what, a couple of times?'

'You seem a little on edge, that's all,' said Amita. 'Like there's something bothering you. We thought we might be able to help, that's all.'

Lisa's nostrils flared. It was her turn to stuff her hands into her pockets. She looked around the room, staring at the emptiness.

'It's nothing,' she said. 'Stress about work. Packing up a production like this takes time and effort and it always, *always* falls to people like me to do the grunt work.'

'Part of the game, though. Right?'

'I have a first class honours degree in English Lit, Amita,' she said. 'I was a straight-A student. Now I'm sweeping floors and washing dishes. Go figure.'

'Nothing wrong with that work,' said Jason. 'We've all been there.'

'That's not what I mean,' Lisa shook her head. 'I mean... it's frustrating. Everything that's happened here, this was supposed to be my big break, working on a show like this. And yet here we are, packing up, going home, everything up in the air.'

'It's not your fault,' said Jason.

Amita watched her very carefully. She tried to pick up on anything that might show guilt or reason to think she was capable of murder. Lisa was angry, frustrated. But she was also desperate to make it in the film industry, and killing a clutch of stars didn't seem like a move she'd make.

'Lisa, we have a question for you,' she said.

'What?' asked the runner.

'We were speaking with Pip Potter before the fire, which I'm sure you've heard about,' said Amita.

Lisa nodded, dropping her gaze.

'She was telling us that you and some of the other runners used to go around to her apartment after work,' she continued. 'It seemed important to her that she keep you guys under her wing. Is that right?'

'Yes,' said Lisa. 'She's one of the few actors who seemed to care about us junior crew.'

'Did you know she was in a relationship with Simon Nakamba?' asked Jason.

Lisa didn't say anything. Amita pressed on.

'Lisa, it's ok,' she said. 'If you know then we need to know. We don't think you've done anything wrong.'

The young runner nodded.

'I did,' she said. 'It was the night Simon was killed. We were all around at her flat, the one that was set on fire. Pip was lonely, I could tell. She always gave us advice and help and was looking out for us. That night she was a bit off though. I caught her on her phone, checking it every two minutes. Then, when we had a quiet moment together, I asked her if she was alright. I wasn't sure if I had overstepped the mark or not but Pip was fine about it. She told me about her and Nakamba, how they'd tried to keep it a secret and how hard it had been. She was worried that people were finding out and that would cause problems for her, for them both. She seemed really worked up. I told her it was fine, she could trust me. She wanted me to ask about, subtly, try to find out who knew and who didn't. Then we got the news the next day that Simon was dead. It was just crazy.'

She kicked a piece of electrical wire between her feet.

'Lisa, we need your help,' said Amita. 'We think we might have a lead on the killer. We think they might have tried to murder Pip Potter with the petrol bomb.'

'And us too,' said Jason.

'We have reason to believe the killer may have been an extra on the shoot. Do you have a list of names at all? Do you have access to databases or information that might shine some light on who it is?'

'We think they might have worked with Simon Nakamba or Derek Veland before,' said Jason. 'Or even Pip. Anyone who might have a long-term grudge against them.'

Lisa looked confused. She rubbed her eyes, trying to think.

'Yeah, yeah I should do,' she said. 'I should have something. *The Locus* is pretty thorough when it comes to vetting who works on it. Non-disclosure agreements and all of that showbiz rubbish.'

'Do you have it here?' he asked.

'Let's check,' she said, hurrying out of the living room.

They followed her to the back room. The last of the production crew furniture was spread out across the floor. Darrel was on his knees untangling wires and packing them into a box.

'Where are the laptops?' she asked him, urgency in her voice.

He pointed over to a stack of thick, black cases by the bay windows. Lisa grabbed one and flipped it open, typing a password. She pulled up a program, long lists of names flashing by.

'What are we looking for?' she asked.

'Something that links the three of them, Nakamba, Veland and Potter,' said Amita. 'Someone who was part of this production and something else in the past that they had a hand in. If there's a crossover for two or even all three of them, then it's a start.'

Lisa rattled the keyboard. Amita tried to follow but the details were flying past her too quickly. After another moment of furious typing, Lisa leaned back.

'Ok,' she said. 'This is a database of industry types, actors, directors, producers, extras, runners, everyone who would be involved in something who is part of a union, Equity for example. If they've worked on a production legitimately, they'll be in here. I've cross-referenced our three stars. There's quite a bit of crossover, where one or two of them have been credited, but nobody immediately jumping out as having direct links with all of them.'

'What about just two?' asked Jason. 'Maybe Nakamba and Veland?'

Lisa's fingers danced across the keyboard. The names whirred up the screen again. It was making Amita feel dizzy. When it stopped there were still hundreds of names. Lisa put in more data.

'Lots of people for both of them, and Veland and Pip Potter,' she said. 'I'm not surprised, to be honest with you. It's a fairly closed parish, this kind of work. If you're good enough, you'll work time and time again with the same people, in different roles and capacities, but you're still the same person.'

Jason hummed in agreement. Amita peered down and looked at all the names on the screen. She didn't recognise any of them at all, although she acknowledged it was needle-in-haystack territory.

'And you say all of these people are active in the industry?' she asked.

'That's right,' said Lisa. 'Paid up members of official organisations. You have to pay your dues and all of that school of life stuff. It's fairly strict and policed, Amita. You wouldn't dare work on a production and *not* be registered.'

A thought popped into Amita's head. She pointed at the screen.

'And there's no way of finding out if there's a link for who is *not* registered?' she asked. 'Or perhaps *was* registered?'

'You mean like they let their membership lapse?'

'Something like that, yes.'

'What are you thinking?' asked Jason.

She didn't want to say. There might not be anything in it.

'I'd need to know more specifics,' said Lisa. 'A timeframe to trawl through the records. Somebody like Simon Nakamba and Derek Veland, they have hundreds of credits, they've been working for years, decades, even if you had a year or a name.'

Amita kept her mouth shut. She didn't like where this train of thought was taking her.

'Amita, what's wrong?' asked Jason. 'You've gone pale.'

'It's nothing,' she said. 'Just something I heard the other day that's been bugging me.'

'What?'

'It was something Ethel said at bingo,' she said. 'We were all talking about our favourite episodes of *The Locus*. Everyone was chipping in and Ethel mentioned an episode that nobody recognised. Something about a man being found outside a concert hall.'

'Like Simon?"' asked Lisa.

'Yes, just like him. We all assumed that Ethel was getting mixed up, a bit confused. She's not been well recently and she's getting on in years. But there was something about the way she talked about it, something that made me think she might be on to something.'

'And you don't remember the episode?' asked Jason.

'It wasn't *The Locus*,' said Lisa.

They both looked down at her. She had a web page open and was scrolling down the credits.

'Nakamba directed an episode of a sitcom in the early 2000s,' she said. 'It was a comedy series about a couple of hapless cops. It only lasted two series and then got binned. The second episode, here it is, involves the detectives catching a murderer who terrorises a load of theatres and concert venues around the country.'

Amita felt a chill go through her core. She read the synopsis of the show and the credits. There it was, on the screen, directed by Simon Nakamba.

'He must have done this before he went to Hollywood for that superhero movie,' said Jason. 'Pretty obscure though.'

'What about Derek Veland?' said Amita quickly. 'Is there anything in his past that relates to being strangled?'

'If the police ever get hold of my search history...' said Lisa, as she carried on typing.

Veland's credits appeared. Amita stopped her scrolling.

'There, that one!' she shouted.

Lisa clicked on the link. It opened up the page for an independent movie made just a few years earlier. Derek Veland was the lead, playing an aging rock star.

'Good grief,' she said. *'Hellraiser Otto Young finds his past catches up with him when he's murdered by a groupie while on tour with his hair metal band.'*

'Hardly Chaucer,' said Jason.

'I don't know what hair metal is,' said Amita. 'Is it some sort of shampoo?'

Jason rolled his eyes. Lisa giggled.

'It doesn't matter,' he said. 'It says his character is strangled. Just like in real life. Don't you see what we have here, Amita? It's a pattern, a link.'

'What about the cast and crew,' said Amita. 'Is there anyone on there who appeared in both productions? If there's some-body close to the making of these things who might have known or held a grudge against them, then we could have our killer.'

'There's a long time between them,' said Lisa. 'About twelve years. That sitcom was in the early 2000s and that awful film was only a few…'

She trailed off. Amita felt her legs turning to jelly. She didn't know what was wrong. Only that it was bad.

'What's the matter?' she asked.

Lisa was pointing at the screen.

'I know that one,' she said. 'I recognise them. They've been at Pip's parties, with the rest of the crews and some of the other actors.'

Amita and Jason leaned in a little over her shoulders. They looked at the name and the picture, a classy black-and-white portrait of someone they recognised, only a little younger, a little more fresh-faced.

'Oh no,' said Amita. 'No, it can't be.'

Chapter 34

DRAGRACER

'Try again, Jason! We have to get through to Sally!'

'What do you think I'm trying to do!' he snapped back at Amita. 'I'm hardly on the phone ordering a pizza, am I?'

'No need to take that tone with me,' she said. 'I'm only trying to help.'

The car lurched from side to side. A fleeting honk of a horn from a disgruntled driver faded into the distance. Jason juggled his mobile between his hands as Amita wrestled with the wheel.

'Can you please watch where you're going,' he yelled. 'We're not Dempsey and Makepeace, and I'd like to see my children at least once more, thank you very much.'

'Call Sally again!' she shouted. 'She needs to get somebody over to the hospital immediately before we arrive.'

'I'm trying, I'm trying.'

Jason dialled the number. There were a few rings and then the automated answering machine message clicked on. He hung up, grinding his teeth.

'She must be in a meeting or something,' he said. 'I can't get through.'

'Send her a text or a DM.'

'DM?' he asked.

'Direct message. Honestly, Jason, you really need to join the twenty-first century. DM, DM, that's what people say nowadays.'

'I don't want to know what people say nowadays, Amita. It's all unimaginably complicated and I'm too much of an old fart.'

'I'm older than you!'

The car juddered to a halt. A set of temporary road lights were up ahead, the traffic snaking back from the building site. Amita silently cursed for forgetting about the maintenance. She'd been too busy solving murders recently to be checking her Penrith Potholes WhatsApp group with its usual bursts of roadworks road rage and traffic updates. They could have reached the hospital quicker by another route. She looked back behind them but a line of cars had formed. They were stuck until they could get through the site.

'I can't believe it,' she said. 'I really can't believe it.'

'Don't blame yourself,' said Jason, trying DI Arendonk again. 'I don't think we would ever have guessed something like this.'

'I should have seen it coming,' she said. 'If only I had pieced it together earlier, I might have saved Derek Veland.'

'Eh, I'm sitting right here, you know,' said Jason, pretending to be offended. 'I thought we were a team.'

'Yes, yes, of course,' she dismissed him. 'We can worry about semantics at a later date. What matters now is that the police are informed, and we get to that hospital. Before Pip comes to harm. She's a sitting duck there.'

'Hold on,' he said, dialling again. 'It's gone straight to answerphone now.'

'Leave a message,' she said.

'Is that wise?' he asked. 'I mean, is this the sort of information you want to tell somebody by recorded message. It seems a bit too important to–'

'Leave a bloody message, Jason!' Amita screamed.

His eyebrows shot up so fast he thought they'd retreat into his hairline. He'd never seen his mother-in-law use such colourful language.

'Ok, ok, calm down,' he said. 'I was only...'

He trailed off. The bleep of the answerphone whistled in his ear. Jason hated these machines. He always felt incredibly nervous for some strange reason.

'Hi... er, hello, Sally, I mean DI Arendonk.'

'What are you doing?' said Amita.

'It's Jason here, Jason Brazel, in case you don't recognise my voice. Why would you, I suppose?'

Amita rubbed her temples with her fingers. The lights ahead turned green and the traffic in front began to slowly move forward.

'Anyway yes, you know all of this, naturally,' Jason went on. 'Look, we've found something out, something a bit shocking, actually. You had better get somebody over to the hospital to put a watch on Pip Potter. We think she might be in danger. Tell your officers, or rapid response team, is that the right term? Anyway tell your guards not to let anyone in to see her. Ok, bye for now, bye, bye, bye.'

The green light was changing colour. Amita willed the car in front to keep going. She had to get moving, keep going, get to the hospital to save a life. Her dallying and lack of foresight had potentially cost Derek Veland his life. She wasn't going to have Pip Potter's death on her hands too.

She pressed the accelerator as flat as it would go. The engine roared, screaming from beneath the bonnet like it was in pain. The car hurtled forward, racing through the light as it turned. The builders and workmen all jumped out of the way as she rolled and weaved through the cones and barriers. They shot out the other side like a mechanical rabbit being chased by a pack of greyhounds. The traffic cleared and their route to the hospital was open. Amita gripped the steering wheel and kept going.

'Bloody hell,' was all Jason could manage in the passenger seat. 'Where did you learn how to drive like that? Brands Hatch?'

'Silverstone,' said Amita.

He tugged at his seatbelt to make sure it was still working.

'Try Arendonk again,' said Amita, still staring at the road. 'We've all been so blind.'

Chapter 35

BOND STREET PARADE

Jason and Amita hurried as quickly as they could down the corridors of the hospital. The place was busy as usual – logjammed with patients all needing treatment for everything from heart attacks to headaches. The wards, treatment rooms and theatres whizzed past the pair as they burrowed deeper and deeper into the building.

'Can you remember the floor we were on?' asked Jason, struggling to keep up with his mother-in-law.

'The fifth, I think,' she said. 'I'm not sure but it's a start.'

'We could ask someone.'

'They won't tell us if we're not family.'

'This is an emergency. Life or death.'

'I think that's par for the course in hospital.'

Amita didn't have time to argue. They followed the signs for the elevators but skidded to a halt when they saw the queue. She checked her watch.

'Damn,' she said. 'Visiting time. We took too long getting here.'

'Let me try Arendonk again,' he said, fetching his phone.

'There's no time, Jason. We'll just have to climb the stairs.'

'Not more stairs,' he groaned.

They doubled back from the lifts. A wide, well-trodden stairwell lifted high up into the old building. Jason gave a quick glance upwards and gulped.

'Great,' he said.

Amita bounded up the first few steps and he tried to keep up the pace. It quickly became apparent that these stairs weren't designed for bounding. By the time they reached the fifth floor, they were both gasping for air.

'Blimey,' said Amita. 'I don't feel very well after that.'

'At least you're in the right place,' Jason panted.

She ignored him. They looked about for signs, something to give them bearings.

'There,' she said, pointing to a sign on the wall. 'The wards are down there.'

They walked as fast as they could, both still wheezing from the quick flight up the steps of doom. Amita's heart was thumping in her chest but she knew it wasn't just from the sudden exercise. She knew that her worst fears, the ones she had tried to keep hidden, keep to herself, were unfolding in front of her. How had she missed it all of this time? It had been staring her in the face for so long. Perhaps she hadn't wanted to see what was going on. Perhaps, after everything that had happened over the past few weeks, decades even, she had deliberately turned away from the possibilities.

Now she had been proven wrong. After a long and frustrating search, she was sure she had her killer. And she was about to find out if she was right.

They rounded a swooping corridor and stopped. The walls were lined with doors that led to private wards and rooms. At the far end, an officer was standing on guard outside one of the rooms. They knew then that they had been right.

'Come on, quickly,' she said.

'I hope we're not too late,' said Jason.

The policewoman saw them coming. She tensed up, hand reaching down to her utility belt. Amita held her arms up.

'Please, officer, we don't mean any harm,' she said, reaching her. 'You have to get in touch with Detective Inspector Arendonk immediately.'

The policewoman was cautious at first. She kept eyeing both Amita and Jason with suspicion. When she realised that they weren't a threat, she regained her composure.

'And who are you, exactly?' she asked.

'There's no time for that now, please,' Amita begged. 'You have to alert DI Arendonk. We know who the killer is.'

'Killer?' asked the cop.

'Yes, Simon Nakamba and Derek Veland,' said Jason, only now fully recovered. 'We're friends of Sally. She'll know who we are if you radio it in.'

'Tell her to come down here right away,' said Amita. 'Please, it's urgent. Every second we dally we waste valuable time in catching the murderer.'

The officer still wasn't convinced. She folded her arms across her vest.

'Alright, I think you both need to calm down,' she said. 'I can't leave my post and I'm certainly not doing it on the panicky ramblings of you two.'

'Please, you have to believe us,' said Amita.

'Let's see some identification,' said the officer.

'You're on guard,' said Jason, thinking of a different tack. 'That's what I said.'

'We know who you're guarding,' he said. 'It's Pip Potter, the actor, from *The Locus*. We know she's in there with injuries from the firebombing. We were in the apartment with her. If you don't believe us, check the CCTV.'

The officer was working it all out in her head. Amita silently willed her to hurry up. This was taking far too long. Eventually the policewoman conceded.

'Alright,' she said. 'What is it you want DI Arendonk for exactly?'

'We've told you,' Amita grew angry. 'We know who the killer is. We've come here to help protect Pip Potter. She's a target and, every second that ticks by, she's in danger.'

The policewoman hesitated. Then she reached for her radio. 'And you two are?' she asked again.

'Amita Khatri and Jason Brazel. Please hurry up.'

The officer walked away a little. She started speaking into the radio mounted on her shoulder. There was some garbled noise from the device. Jason slumped against the wall and slid down to the floor. He looked up at Amita, eyes wide and blood-shot.

'Remind me never to go walking, running, climbing or any other bloomin' outdoor activity with you ever again,' he said. 'All this fitness lark is really bad for my health. What was it that website called us – armchair detectives? I've barely sat down since we took this case.'

Amita was in no mood for jokes. She paced back and forth in front of the door of Pip Potter's ward. She started biting her nails and stopped when it hurt again. The policewoman came back.

'Alright, I've spoken to dispatch,' she said. 'The DI is being informed that you're here, with me, and that you have an urgent message for her.'

'Is she coming down now?' asked Amita.

'That's up to her,' shrugged the cop. 'I'm just a constable, I can't force the guv to do anything she doesn't want to. But I can reassure you there have been no strange visitors, no attempts to get past me. Miss Potter is getting the best care possible.'

Amita stifled her frustrations. The cop moved back to her position in front of the door. She nudged Jason out of the way a little as he sprawled his legs out on the hallway floor.

Amita continued to pace back and forth in front of them. Every movement, every noise, every voice echoing down the hallway made her jump. She was completely on edge, not knowing who, or what was going to appear next.

At least she was with Pip Potter now, she thought. At least now, if something was going to happen to the actor, she would stand a chance of being there and stopping it. Again she cursed her own sloppy thinking and lack of speed. If only she had been faster, quicker, sharper, then maybe Derek Veland would still be alive.

'Can you check to see if DI Arendonk is coming down yet?' she asked. 'This is getting ridiculous.'

'Not a chance,' said the officer, bobbing up and down on her heels. 'My pay grade doesn't include checking up on detective inspectors. That's a surefire way of getting lumbered with a month of nightshifts.'

Jason snorted at that.

'What's so funny?' asked the officer.

'Oh nothing,' he said. 'I did something similar with a particularly irksome editor and he did the exact same thing to me. I don't think I've ever fallen asleep at my desk more.'

'Well can we at least check on Ms Potter?' Amita asked.

She went to reach for the door but the officer got in her way.

'Absolutely not,' she said. 'That door remains firmly closed as long as I'm standing here, got that?'

'We're friends,' said Amita. 'We just want to say hello.'

'Good one, Amita,' said Jason, slowly getting back to his feet.

'Nobody goes in there unless they've got a stethoscope slung around their necks.'

She stepped a little forward to force Amita back. The pensioner duly retreated. She checked up and down the hallway, looking for Sally Arendonk. To see the tall, welcoming face of the detective was about the only thing she wanted right now. To be assured by her presence and to spill all of the details, to get it all off her chest, was all she wanted. Yet there was no sign of the detective, or her entourage. It was only her, Jason and the grumpy officer.

Then a sudden thought struck her. She turned back to the policewoman.

'Hold on,' she said. 'You let medical people in there?'

'Of course,' said the cop. 'It's a hospital and Pip Potter is a patient. I'm hardly going to stand in *their* way, am I?'

Jason sensed Amita's sudden panic.

'When was the last time you checked on Ms Potter?' he asked.

'About ten minutes ago, just before you arrived,' she said. 'One of the nurses was going in to take her blood pressure and–'

The policewoman didn't know what hit her. Jason and Amita lurched forward in unison, scrambling and pawing for the door handle. The officer was swept up between them as they pulled the door open in a panic. All three of them clattered into the ward and stopped.

Pip Potter was sitting on the edge of her bed, facing them. She was sobbing, tears rolling down her cheeks. Her breath was short and her shoulders were bobbing up and down. Behind her, Abi Paris was standing, a needle in one hand, the other holding the back of Pip's neck, keeping her in place. When she saw Jason, Amita and the officer, her face twisted into a horrible snarl.

'Abi, please!' Amita cried. 'Don't do anything you'll regret.'

'Too late!' hissed the student nurse.

Chapter 36

THE MERRY-GO-ROUND BROKE DOWN

The room was stiflingly hot. Jason wasn't sure if it was all the medical equipment or the fact they were face-to-face with a serial killer. Either way he was sweating profusely. Amita was beside him, her hand outstretched towards Pip Potter and Abi Paris. Between them was the police officer who was supposed to be standing guard. Her radio was crackling with gibberish and static. Jason hoped the cavalry was on its way.

'Don't move another inch!' Abi yelled at them.

The friendly, welcoming and pleasant student nurse they had known before was gone. In her place was an angry woman on the verge of even more destruction. Jason looked at Pip held in her grip. The actor was terrified, her pale face now grey with fright. She was clutching onto the edge of the bed, knuckles white.

'We're not going to do anything, Abi,' said Amita, acting as chief negotiator. 'But you have to put that needle down, ok?'

'Get out of here,' she snarled. 'This is between me and Lady Muck here, got that?'

Desperation was etched into Abi's voice. Jason had precisely no previous experience with serial killers but this wasn't what he'd imagined at all. This woman was scared, her hands shaking. She was like a wounded animal backed into a corner and, while he didn't know what to do next, he knew enough that panic and fear could cause untold damage.

'I think we should do what she says,' he offered. 'At least until the others arrive.'

'Others? What others?' Abi asked.

'Big mouth,' the cop murmured at him. 'You need to put the needle down, love,' said the officer, stepping forward. 'There's no use in somebody else getting hurt now, is there? Come on, hand it over to me.'

'Stay back!'

She pulled Pip backwards. The actor went tumbling off the bed and into a heap on the floor. Abi grabbed at her, lifting her to her feet. She backed them both into the far corner of the room and held the point of the syringe dangerously close to Pip's neck.

'Please,' she whispered. 'Do what she says. She's going to kill me.'

'Shut up!' Abi screamed. 'Everybody just shut up.'

The officer stepped forward confidently but Amita stopped her. She held out a hand and shook her head. Jason wasn't quite sure what his mother-in-law had planned. Or even if there was a plan. However, she appeared to be taking charge.

'Abi, this isn't going to help you,' she said. 'Whatever problems you've got, whatever is going on and has driven you to these terrible crimes, it's not worth continuing down that path. Please let Pip go.'

Abi stared at her through the long, tangled strands of hair that were hanging over her face. She seemed feral, instinctual now, hiding with nowhere else to go. Pip stood rigid in front of her, her eyes closed in prayer.

'How did you find me?' asked Abi. 'Why you? Was it my mum? Did she tell you?'

'No,' said Amita. 'This had nothing to do with your mother.'

'Then how did you know it was me?'

Amita took a deep breath. She looked back at the police officer and to Jason. There was a sadness there, an inevitability that what she was about to say was going to break her heart all over again. All Jason could do was nod, to let her know he was there for her.

'Your acting credits, your credentials,' she said. 'Your mother told us that you had always wanted to be a star on the stage, on the screen, but your grandfather hadn't approved. She told us that you'd tried to get your big break when you were a little younger, that you had appeared in some things here and there. As is always the case these days, everything has a digital footprint and your credits, your resume, it's all online.'

Abi was still snarling at them. Pip Potter remained perfectly quiet and still.

'We had help,' said Jason. 'One of the runners on *The Locus*, she was able to draw up a list of who had shared credits with Derek Veland and Simon Nakamba. Throw into the mix Ms Potter here and your name was the only one that stood out.'

'That was years ago,' she snapped. 'Nobody remembers.'

'Like I said,' said Amita. 'A digital footprint. As long as you were a paid-up member of the actors' union, you had a right to a credit, something to take to your next job. That's how this industry works, correct?'

Abi nodded quickly.

'When we saw that you'd had a small role in a show directed by Nakamba and that you'd played someone along-side Derek Veland, it didn't take us long to work out you had a connection to both of them,' said Jason.

'What happened, Abi?' asked Amita, trying to sound more like a kindly grandmother than a hostage negotiator. 'What on earth happened to you that could drive you to do something like this?'

Abi was crying now. She snorted loudly, never losing her grip of the needle or Pip.

'Do you know how much I wanted to be a star?' she asked, the question dripping with spite. 'Do you have any idea how long it had been a dream of mine? Can you even begin to imagine what it feels like to have that dream ripped away from you even before you've had a proper shot at trying to achieve it? Do you? Answer me!'

Jason jumped a little. Amita shook her head.

'No, I don't,' she said quietly. 'But I do know a little about life not turning out the way you expect. And sometimes the life you want isn't the life you need. Showbusiness is a tough world – even if you'd been allowed to follow your dream, it could have been a hard path. I can tell how much it hurt – but that doesn't give you the right to go around killing people, taking lives.'

'Why them?' asked Jason, after he'd mentally chanted Be More Amita a few times to get his courage up. 'Was it something to do with Simon and Pip here? Were you jealous?'

'Jealous? Ha, don't make me laugh,' she said. 'The last thing I would want is to be with someone like Simon Nakamba. He was a monster, a pig of a man. And he deserved to die.'

'Nobody deserves to die,' said Amita angrily. 'Nobody deserves to have their life cut short. Tell us what happened, Abi.'

She shook her head.

'You don't understand. Nobody does, except maybe Pip here,' she squeezed the actor's neck a little tighter. 'She and I, we're kindred spirits at heart, we're one and the same.'

'I'm nothing like you,' Pip hissed. 'I'm not a murderer.'

Abi squeezed tighter, the syringe now inches from Pip's neck.

'We're the same, in more ways than any of you can imagine,' she said. 'We've both been wronged, both been looked over, passed on, dismissed as silly girls in an industry that's based on looks and popularity. You're right, Amita, I did work with Simon Nakamba before. I was just a child back then, just a little girl. I didn't know any better. I was trying to make a good impression. I'd heard that he liked his cast as brunettes, so I dyed my hair. Then I heard him talking about blondes and I dyed it back. For two weeks I did what he wanted, did what he asked of his cast and crew, all just to be noticed, all for a chance to show him what I could do. To be more than an extra – to get a line, a shot. And not once did he look in my direction. Not once did he even acknowledge I existed. Until one day…'

She trailed off. Jason felt the officer beside him starting to move. She was edging closer and closer to the bed. She was slowly reaching for her utility belt, a small extendable baton. He wasn't one to tell an officer of the law what to do. But he didn't think it was a good idea.

'What happened?' asked Amita.

'We were shooting on the outskirts of Manchester, Marple it was,' she said. 'I'd gone down there and was missing school, was living in digs. Mum was furious. But it was what I wanted to do. It was close to the end of the shoot and we were about to film the discovery scene, the man found outside the concert hall. They needed extras and one of us was needed to scream. A producer picked me. I thought this was it, a chance to impress Nakamba, to impress everyone. When it came to filming though, I fluffed it. I was so nervous I just couldn't do it, I couldn't walk, I couldn't speak, I was terrified. I don't know what came over me. Nakamba paused the filming. He came right over to me, just some teenager, some little girl far from home, and he screamed his head off at me. He told me that, if I didn't do what he said, to the letter, he'd find somebody who would. I remember that, I remember it so clearly, having him yelling in my face like that. Calling me an imbecile in front of everyone in the world I most wanted to impress. I wept, then and there, I just broke down. I didn't go back, I didn't want to. I got the bus back to Penrith that night and that was that. I thought my shot was gone, that was until the film with Derek Veland.'

The cop had cleared the bed now. Pip had spotted her, eyes wide as she watched the officer getting closer and closer. Jason felt his stomach churning at what might happen. Whether by design or accident, Amita was distracting Abi enough that she hadn't noticed the policewoman.

'He was another pig,' she spat. 'I was older, out of school, a little wiser but no closer to my dream than I had been when I paraded around the living room in my princess frock and wand. He took a shine to me, like he did with all the young women. He was no different back then. I don't think he ever could be, even if he wanted to be. I was happy for the attention: he was the star of the film. Anything I could do to get more camera time was fine by me. Only he promised so much and delivered nothing, Amita. Absolutely nothing. He'd said to think big, to follow him to London. He'd introduce me to his management, to all the directors and the producers and moneymakers at home and abroad. A good-looking girl like me, I'd go far, he said. Two weeks later, after shipping down to London, I was back home, sobbing into my mum's shoulder. He'd used me, like he used everyone. I was just some eye candy, a trinket he could flash at parties and events. The older man with a girlfriend a third of his age, it was pathetic, *he* was pathetic. I used to hear what people said about him when he wasn't around – cruel things, talking about his age, his weight, his inability to act with anything other than a raised eyebrow and a hammy accent. I used to defend him, can you believe that? I used to actually stand up for him, thinking he was going to make me a star. But there was nothing, like so many other aspects of his life, he was a shell.'

Her grip was loosening on Pip's neck. The syringe was wobbling as her arms grew weaker.

'Why now?' asked Amita. 'Why wait all these years? What sparked this lust for revenge?'

'Convenience,' said Abi. 'I gave up on acting and enrolled in nursing college. My mum was relieved, or at least she pretended to be. Grandad had threatened me, before he died, that if I didn't do something worthwhile then I'd be written out of his will. Lovely man, don't you think? He always lorded it over me and Mum, saw us as a couple of trouble-makers. You knew him, didn't you, Amita?'

'Only briefly,' she said. 'I know how hard things were for your mother growing up. But I'm sure he had your best interests at heart.'

'Rubbish!' she said. 'He was only interested in his legacy, the Paris family name and that stupid bloody hotel. I felt sick when I signed my admission papers. I felt like, even beyond the grave, he had won. I still kept up with the industry though, people I knew, that sort of thing. I learned about *The Locus* coming to town, how it would be setting up shop here in Penrith and they were looking for local talent. Nakamba, Veland, Potter, all the big names would be here. At first I was just going to try to get on camera – an extra job, to prove to myself I could. But then I started thinking, thinking about what I could do, how I could bring a little balance back to the universe, tip things back in my favour.'

'You injected Nakamba with air?' asked Jason.

'I watched him for a few days to see what he did, where he went,' she said. 'It made me sick to my core even being in the same town as him. He hadn't changed, he was still the same, still arrogant, still lording it over everyone. I think perhaps I wouldn't have done it if I hadn't seen him on set, still tearing into his team, into anyone who didn't do things perfectly first time. He was, however, predictable to a tee. After he'd been taken out to dinner every night after filming, he'd meet up with Ms Potter here. Late-night liaisons are fine, if you know where you're going. And Nakamba didn't, not by the time he'd had a few bottles of wine down his throat. I followed him the night he died, away from that swanky, pretentious restaurant, and then I decided that enough was enough. He was shaky, staggering about, absolutely bladdered. I gave him a shove, he fell over and that was that. I went into his arm with a syringe, that's all it took. He was so drunk he didn't even notice.'

'Was this at the concert hall?' asked Amita.

'No,' she said. 'We were around the corner. I had to drag him most of the way there. I thought it was appropriate, poetic even. The music hall in that programme we made, it looked so like our one here, and seeing it reminded me every time of when he'd humiliated me. I thought he deserved to be trussed up, put on show for the cameras. He might have complained about my performance but I did a good job, in the end.'

'You're a monster,' said Pip through her tears.

'And Veland?' asked Jason.

Abi started to laugh.

'He was a different kettle of fish,' she said. 'Mum was so taken by him that it was almost funny, hilarious even. She'd fallen for the same chat-up lines he'd used on me years ago. We're two peas in a pod, Mum and I. Grandad used to say that all the time and he wasn't being kind. She thought I didn't know about him and her, but it was all over Askling Manor. You can't keep a secret from anyone in that place. Backstairs, the staff know everything. I didn't know how to stop her, how to tell her that the man she was sleeping with had once made all those promises to her daughter. Then it came to me. I didn't have to stop her to end the affair – I only had to stop him. When she left that night, I was watching, waiting, down the hall. The night she was with him last, I hid down the end of the hallway. I let her get back downstairs and then crept into Veland's room. I had a key, it's not hard to use our system, it's outdated. He was snoring, lying on top of the bed, arms spread out. He was smiling, looking very pleased with himself, even when he was unconscious. It would have been artistic if he hadn't reeked so much. I thought about killing him then and there, but I wanted him to know it was me. I wanted him to remember. And to his credit, he did. Of course, I'd watched every film or show with him in it since we broke up. So I thought he might appreciate the poetic justice of going out like one of his characters. When he came around, I saw that glint in his eyes, that rakish charm that made him think he was going to get me into bed. I wrapped a towel around my hands and then about his throat. He didn't put up much of a fight, he wasn't sober enough. I felt better when it was over, relieved, in a strange sort of way. I left, knowing Mum had already taken the CCTV camera out of action to save face, her own and the hotel's. She pretends that she doesn't care about the place but I know she does. She sees it as her penance, for getting expelled and breaking my grandparents' hearts. Nonsense, of course. She's better than them, better than they ever could hope for or hope to be. I did it for her, I suppose, now that I think about it. She deserves so much better than some fling with a man like Derek Veland. She never knew about us, never knew it was him I was living with when I was down in London. It was for the best not to tell her.'

She dropped her gaze, just for a moment. Jason held his breath. Before the cop could do anything, though, Abi was staring at them all again.

'Now, here we are, at the end,' she said.

'Abi, please, it doesn't have to go on like this. You've done some terrible things, but you don't need to make it worse,' said Amita. 'I'm begging you, let us all go.'

'After everything I've done,' she said, slowly. 'What's one more death?'

'Abi! No!'

Everything moved too quickly for Jason to comprehend. Abi jabbed Pip with her needle, but the policewoman was off like a flash – a streak of neon yellow racing towards them. The three women collapsed onto the floor in a giant heap. Jason and Amita were trying to separate them when a thunderous noise came from behind. Suddenly the room was flooded with police officers.

Jason felt something shove him in the back. He hit the ground hard as a firm set of hands pushed him flat onto his stomach. Amita was given just as rough treatment beside him.

'Amita!' he shouted, but his voice was drowned out by all the shouting and clamouring about them.

Officers of every shape and size – some armed – were now inside the cramped room. They descended on the corner where Abi, Pip and the other cop had gone down. Jason could only lie there while the pressing from behind made his ribs, back, chest and head hurt.

'Clear!' came a loud shout from somewhere above him.

The hands tightened their grip and he was pulled upwards with a jerk. The same happened to Amita and they were driven out of the room, weaved through a small ocean of armour-clad officers all piling into the ward.

At the end of the stream was DI Arendonk. She was wearing a police vest over her suit, hands filled with walkie-talkies. She was just as grey as usual, eyes like marbles sunk deep into her head. When she saw Jason and Amita, she seemed to breathe a little easier.

'Are you two alright?' she asked.

'We're fine,' said Amita.

'Speak for yourself, I think your boys have cracked one of my ribs and–'

'Fine, good, get them out of here.'

The DI was short and abrupt. The time for pleasantries was clearly at a premium. The officers who had manhandled Jason and Amita loosened their grips a little as they led them down the hallway and away from the ward. When they were clear of the operation, a gaggle of nurses and medics met them, ready to put them in wheelchairs. Jason was sat down before he knew what was going on, Amita right beside him.

They turned them around quickly and shoved them into a waiting lift. The door closed with a ping and the noise of the incident team was gone. The elevator began to descend and Jason blinked. He puffed out his cheeks and looked over at his mother-in-law in the wheelchair beside him.

'I guess we were right then,' he said.

'Again,' she replied, rolling her eyes. 'Although this time I wish we hadn't been.'

Chapter 37

A BEAUTIFUL MINE

The whole of the front of the hospital had been turned into something more akin to *The Locus* than an infirmary. Squad cars were zipping around everywhere and there were more police tape and cordons than Jason had ever seen. Even the fire brigade had been called, sitting idly by at the far side of the car park with nothing to put out.

DI Sally Arendonk seemed like a strange, serene presence among all the chaos. Jason had always pronounced his admiration for the inspector. Especially after dealing with Alby, her predecessor. She had been like a breath of fresh air compared to that dinosaur. And now, as he sat in the back of a police car, watching her organise, converse, coordinate and convene a whole emergency situation, that admiration only grew. She took no glee, no glory in getting her man – or woman – but there was a sense of justice served, balance restored that Jason was grateful for.

He tugged at the ill-fitting collar of his jumper as he tried to make sense of the scene. The police car wasn't the most comfortable place he had been but he realised now that, for the first time since the firebomb, he wasn't looking over his shoulder every few seconds. He felt like he'd been stuffed into a post bag with all the care and delicate touch of a brickie but, despite the bumps and bruises, he felt safe. He shifted about, elbows everywhere.

'Can you please sit still, Jason,' Amita chastised him. 'I don't know how long we'll be here. We're here as long as we're here. So please stop fidgeting and sit at peace.'

'Easy for you to say, you didn't have a dozen armed coppers leaning on your back.'

'They were as rough with me as they were with you,' she said. 'It was a high-pressure situation, they didn't know who was who and what was what. You should be grateful they got us out of there.'

'I suppose a medal will be out of the question for saving Pip Potter.'

'I would say that's highly unlikely,' she said. 'We weren't really supposed to be there in the first place.'

Some of the police cars were starting to leave. The car park was becoming a little less steeped in blue lights. Jason moved and shuffled as best he could to relieve some of the discomfort.

The door opened suddenly. He almost fell out, stopping himself on the door handle at the last minute. Elegance and grace had never been his strong suit. DI Arendonk was standing over him.

'You alright there?' she asked.

'Yes, fine, thanks,' he said, the cold air drying the sheen of sweat. 'I thought I'd make my entrance as dramatic as yours up there in the hospital.'

'Very funny,' she said, helping him out. 'But I wouldn't give up the day job, whatever that is these days.'

Amita slid out of the same door. She looked about the car park at the gathered emergency services.

'You know, no matter how many times I see this amount of police, it never becomes any more normal,' she said.

'Join the club,' said Arendonk. 'We don't issue these mass alerts very often. And we should all be grateful that's the case. But a patient being held hostage by a suspected serial killer, that's about as high profile and dangerous as it gets.'

'Not to mention the hostage being a celebrity,' added Jason.

'Don't remind me,' groaned the detective. 'You know, this whole case has been one nightmare after another, and not in the usual way. Not only have I had a killer running around town bumping off famous people, but the sheer pain in the backside it's been dealing with my worrisome superiors and your lot.' She nodded at Jason.

'My lot?'

'The media,' she said. 'One whiff of *any* rumour and they've been all over me like a rash. Turns out dealing with rabid TV fans is nearly as bad as my nine-to-five. Everyone thinks they're an expert just because they've watched a few episodes. Then there's our Right Honourable friend Sheila Mulberry MP. The woman has been on a mission to make sure my ear is red hot all of the time with her constant calls and requests for updates. Though half the time I think she's only after a selfie with the cast for her Instagram. Still, at least I've got something to tell her now. An arrest.'

'Every cloud and all of that,' said Jason.

'Something like that,' said the DI. 'Anyway, I'm glad that you two are safe. As strange as that may sound to you, Brazel, I do actually care about your welfare, and Amita's.' She glanced over at Amita, who was staring off into the middle distance.

'Everything alright?' she asked. 'Did you two get checked out by the medics?'

'We did, thank you,' said Amita, somewhat aloof.

The detective eyeballed Jason, looking for help. He could sense Amita's distraction. He touched her shoulder and she seemed to come around.

'You ok?' he asked.

'What? Yes, I'm fine,' she said.

She appeared to pick up on their concern.

'It's just, well, it's all a bit overwhelming, that's all,' she said. 'The whole business with Nakamba and Veland and who was responsible. I don't know if you know this, Detective Inspector, but Abi's mother went to school with my Radha.'

'Oh right,' said the cop.

'They were friends a very long time ago and we lost touch.'

'There was an unpleasantness,' said Jason.

'Thank you, Jason, that's quite enough,' she said. 'This whole thing, everything at Askling Manor, Sarah Paris being intimate with Derek Veland, it's all been rather a lot to comprehend in a short space of time. And now Abi turning out to be a serial killer, I'm finding the whole thing rather overwhelming, that's all.'

She leaned back against the police car. Jason reached out to take her hand but she snatched it away.

'What are you doing?' she asked, almost offended.

'I thought you'd had a turn or something.'

'I'm fine,' she said. 'Don't do that again, not in front of the detective inspector.'

Arendonk laughed. 'If you two are well enough to bicker, then I feel all is right with the world again. I'll need to take statements from you at some point,' she said. 'You were eyewitnesses after all. Only when you're ready though, Amita. Don't feel you need to hurry into anything, especially if there's a connection there. We have counselling for that kind of stuff.'

'I'll be alright,' she said. 'I'd rather get it out of the way. Is Abi alright?'

'She is,' said Arendonk. 'I think sometimes there comes a great relief with finally being caught. If I was a betting woman, I'd say she'll undergo some psychiatric evaluation of course.

But the fact remains she confessed to the murders. We've got a team going through her house as we speak. A shame, all the same. A young girl like that, with her life ahead of her, it's tragic that she thought vengeance was the only way. No excuse of course, nothing can do that. I don't think we'll have any problems in the case against her now.'

Jason lingered on that thought for a moment. Everything had felt very close to home with this case. He knew the connection between Sarah and Amita, and by extension Radha too. In all of the madness and chaos of the past hour, he hadn't quite comprehended what all of it meant for his mother-in-law and family as a whole. He puffed out his cheeks.

'Bloody hell,' he said. 'What a strange couple of weeks, eh?'

'Stranger than any of us dared think,' said Amita.

'What matters is that you're both safe,' said Arendonk. 'That's the main thing. Everything else will fall into place. You have to look after yourselves. For my part in getting you involved, I apologise. I don't think we could have seen something like this happening.'

She looked about the emptying car park. There was a commotion a little way off. A couple of uniformed officers were struggling with somebody shouting on the other side of the cordon. Arendonk switched from docile to tense, her police instincts kicking in. Jason had a mild panic. He found himself standing in front of Amita, protecting her.

'Out of the way,' she said, shoving him. 'It's Sarah Paris.'

She barged past him and the detective and hurried across the car park.

'Amita! Wait!' he called after her, but it was no use. She was gone.

Sarah was wrestling with the two officers who were trying their best to restrain her. As Amita, Jason and Arendonk arrived, she stopped struggling.

'Amita! What's happened? What's happened to Abi?' she cried.

'Please,' Amita begged Arendonk. 'Let me speak to her. Just for a moment.'

The detective wasn't convinced. Jason could see the tendons working in her temples. This wasn't right, this was no place for Sarah to find out what was going on. But there was no other choice. Arendonk realised this and nodded solemnly.

'Two minutes,' she said. 'That's all and then she needs to come with us.'

The officers let Sarah go. She stumbled forward and Jason caught her. She pushed the hair from her face and looked about for answers.

'What's happened, Amita? Where's Abi?'

'I'm afraid there's been an incident,' said the pensioner, slowly and calmly. 'You'd best sit down.'

She led the hotel owner back towards the police car they had been sitting in. Jason felt a lump in his throat forming with every step they took. He wasn't sure how much Sarah Paris knew about her daughter's actions. She could be complicit or innocent. Either way it didn't really matter. She had a right to know what was going on. And somehow, as they reached the police car and Sarah sat down, Arendonk never far away, he thought that Sarah knew what was coming. There was a quiet, devastated resignation about her that he'd never seen before.

His thoughts immediately turned to his own family as Amita began to explain everything. He had never wanted to see Radha and the children more in his life. Soon, he thought. But not soon enough.

Chapter 38

COSY IN THE ROCKET

Amita scrubbed the blackboard clean. The names, places, timelines and theories all disappeared in three simple strokes. Everything was smudged, the once black material was practically grey now with all the writing and erasing that had happened over the years. Amita took a step back and looked at the marvellous old device she'd managed to save. A flood of memories had bubbled to the surface since she'd first seen it all those weeks ago. She wished she could hear all the stories that had been written on it over the years – the equations and explanations, histories and tall tales.

She realized as she stared at the blank board, that she had been thinking about herself in a similar light. A relic, something from a bygone era, looking to be saved. She still blamed herself for the delay in catching Abi Paris. She had been distracted, too distracted, to see what had been staring at her all this time. A sad sigh escaped her as the front door clicked open and Jason came in, his hands full of shopping bags.

'Give me a hand, would you, Amita?' he asked, almost tripping into the living room.

She took a pair of bags from him and he winced as the blood returned to his fingers. She peered inside.

'What's all this?' she asked.

'A surprise,' he raised his eyebrows. 'I've decided to cook everyone a celebratory meal. One of my specialties, in fact, to mark our victory.'

'It's not your *infamous* entrecôte in a red wine sauce is it, Jason?' she asked. 'Because the last time you made that I was still picking bits of beef out of my teeth two weeks later.'

'I can't help it if your dentures weren't fitted correctly, Amita. You can't blame the chef if your gnashers don't work properly.'

'The cheek,' she tutted.

He sat down on the sofa, the bags at his feet. He flexed his fingers and smiled at her.

'It's not entrecôte, as it happens, as money is a bit tight,' he said. 'It is, in fact, my world famous, patent pending haddock with breaded crumbs served with a side order of le frites and gallons of vinegar.'

'Fish and chips,' she said. 'You're making us all fish and chips.'

'Spot on,' he winked. 'Mushy peas for us, spaghetti hoops for the kids, it's going to be marvellous. I thought we should mark the occasion of catching our very first serial killer with something homely, classic, timeless. Delicious.'

Amita nodded aimlessly.

'Oh come on, it's not that bad, surely,' he said. 'I mean I was hardly expecting a song and dance but I thought home-made fish and chips would really hit the spot.'

Amita felt bad. She sat down in her chair by the TV, the credits rolling from the daytime quiz show she'd been vaguely watching.

'You're right, sorry,' she said. 'I don't know what's wrong with me, Jason. My head feels like it's in the clouds at the moment. I think I'm just trying to decompress.'

'I see you've cleared your investigations board,' he said.

'Yes, I thought it was for the best.'

She stared off into the distance. Jason could always tell when his mother-in-law was really upset. She looked like she was about to breathe fire.

'You know it wasn't your fault,' he said. 'What happened with Abi. She took it upon herself to do the things she did. It was nothing to do with what happened between you, Radha and Sarah all those years ago. Abi was an adult, a grown up. She knew exactly what she was doing when she injected Simon Nakamba and strangled Derek Veland. You can't possibly shoulder any of the blame, Amita.'

Amita knew all of this, of course she did. Still, there was something deep inside of her that chewed away at her conscience.

'I know, Jason, I know,' she said sadly. 'I've spent the past day and a half trying to convince myself of that fact. But every time I keep coming back to Sarah and Radha and all those mistakes of the past. I keep thinking: what if? Do you understand?'

'I do,' he said. 'But I also understand that what if questions are just that – questions. You can come up with any scenario you want asking a what if question. Good, bad, indifferent, that's the whole point. There's no use driving yourself bananas over something you don't control. What's done is done, Amita, you can't change that, I've told you before. You can't do anything about Abi any more than her mother could, or anyone else for that matter. She's a twisted individual. And now she's facing a very long time in jail.'

The thought made Amita shudder. She leaned on the arm of the old chair.

'Just awful,' she said. 'I can't begin to imagine what poor Sarah is going through now. She's lost everyone that's dear to her.'

'It's not great,' Jason agreed. 'Don't forget Simon and Derek's families. They've lost people too, in the most heinous way possible. Just think about them and take some solace in knowing that we played our part in maybe getting them some justice.'

She nodded at that. Jason looked down into his shopping bags. He yelped and scooped them up.

'Damn,' he said. 'I forgot about the ice cream.'

He quickly scuttled into the kitchen, racing against the ever-melting tub of Neapolitan in one of the bags. Amita drew herself up and helped with the last of the bags. She left them on the kitchen table as Jason began to unpack them.

'I suppose you're right,' she said.

'Of course I am,' he replied. 'When am I not?'

'I won't answer that.'

'Probably for the best. Don't forget Pip Potter, too. We probably saved her life too.'

'We didn't do much,' she said. 'It was that brave officer who tackled Abi in the end. We were just a distraction.'

'We most certainly are that, just ask DI Arendonk.'

That drew a smile from Amita.

'A dreadful business all the same,' she said, 'It's so heart-breaking to think that Abi will spend the rest of her life behind bars.'

'It is bad,' he said, licking his fingers of melted strawberry ice cream. 'To be so young and so embittered by what life has thrown at you. It doesn't bear thinking about really.'

'No, I suppose not.'

Amita stared at the shopping bags. The haddock fillets were stacked up neatly, wrapped in clear plastic. Amita picked them out of the bag along with the bag of fries.

'Pass me those, would you?' he asked her, closing the freezer.

Amita wasn't really paying attention. Her mind was still on Abi Paris and her mother Sarah. It was making her chest tight with anxiety to think of what Radha's old friend would be facing. The trial, the evidence, the press coverage, everything.

'Amita,' said Jason.

He woke her from the daze.

'The chips, please,' he said. 'Otherwise we'll be having just the haddock.'

'Sorry, of course,' she picked up the bag of oven chips and looked at them. 'No show without Punch, I suppose.'

The bag seemed to hang in mid-air for a moment, as if someone needed to put money in her meter.

'Amita, are you alright?'

'No show without Punch,' she said again.

'Ok,' he said. 'What does that mean exactly?'

'The fish and the chips,' she said. 'Together, as a team.'

'If you like, I suppose they are, yes.'

'No show without Punch, Jason. It's a phrase.'

'I'm aware of that too, Amita. What's your point?'

She quickly thought through what she was about to say. Every possibility, every clue, every little hint from a conversation and chat and thought she'd had over the past few weeks zooming around all at once inside her head. All to the tune of that chiming bell that had brought her to her senses.

'Abi Paris wasn't alone,' she said, putting the oven chips down.

Jason blinked, looking even more confused.

'What?' he asked, although it was more of a blurt.

'Abi Paris, she wasn't alone, how could she be, Jason? She had an accomplice.'

'Hang on Amita, calm your jets. What are you talking about? What's brought this on all of a sudden?'

She hurried back into the living room and began writing names on the blackboard. Jason followed her, still holding the fish.

'Abi Paris, she was an extra on the sets with Nakamba and Veland, correct?'

'Yes,' said Jason. 'We know all of that. And she told us that she killed them. She even told us how, remember?'

'She did, and I'm not contesting that.'

Amita circled Abi Paris' name in the middle of the blackboard. She underlined it three times and then pointed the nub of chalk at her son-in-law.

'We've established that Abi was vulnerable, DI Arendonk has confirmed that with us, has she not?'

'You know she has,' he said.

'So tell me this. How does a young, troubled girl get it into her head that she's going to kill two of the most famous people in the country?'

'She told us, and you said it already, she worked with them, was wronged by them. Nakamba bullied her and Veland rejected and used her. Those are pretty strong motives, Amita. You can't deny that.'

'But she had so much more to live for!' she said. 'The nursing, her mother, her future, Jason. She'd already moved on. Why would she throw all of that away for petty revenge. She's an intelligent young woman.'

Amita stared at the name on the blackboard. She shook her head. Jason put the fish down.

'It doesn't make any sense,' she said. 'That she would think of something as elaborate, so cruel and wrong on her own. She's never done anything like this before, Jason, no criminal past or record. And yet she goes and murders two men from her past. It's as if she was egged on, goaded, willed into doing somebody's dirty work, like she was taken advantage of.'

'Why, though?' he said. 'If there's some mastermind behind all of this, what could they possibly stand to gain from the deaths of Simon and Derek?'

Amita shook her head.

'I don't know,' she said. 'I just don't know.'

She turned away from the blackboard. The TV was on, the afternoon news starting. The lead story was of Abi's arrest. Profile pictures of Simon Nakamba and Derek Veland were behind the newsreader. He finished up his spiel and the camera cut to Pip Potter. She was standing outside the hospital, speaking with reporters who jostled to hold their microphones and Dictaphones up at her. Amita snatched the remote from the arm of the chair and turned up the volume.

'I can't say very much as this is now an active case,' said Pip. 'But I've prepared a short statement. Simon Nakamba and Derek Veland were two of my closest, dearest friends. They will be sorely missed by the entertainment world and a legion of fans around the world. I am determined that *The Locus* continues and will do everything in my power as one of its actors to make sure their legacy lives on. Thank you.'

Her voice cracked with emotion as she finished her statement and immediately she was hit with a barrage of questions and camera flashes before the clip returned to the newsreader.

Amita didn't realize it but the remote had slipped from her hands, clattering on the floor. Jason raced over to pick it up.

'Bloody hell, Amita, even the kids don't throw the remote about anymore. This is my lifeline to the sports channels!'

'Jason,' she said, reaching for him and tugging on his jumper.

'What?' He was bent over, replacing the batteries.

'We need to stop Pip Potter from leaving Penrith.'

'What? Why?' He looked up at her.

'Because I think she might be a murderer.'

Chapter 39

GOTCHA

'Come on, Amita, somebody *must* have seen her,' said Jason.

'I'm trying my best here, Jason,' she said.

He was driving this time and it was Amita's turn to be on the phone. He had no idea what direction to be taking so just stuck to the road. His mother-in-law was frantically tapping away on her phone, desperate for a lead.

'It's Pip Potter, for goodness sake, somebody around town must know where she is,' he said.

'And what do you think I'm doing just now?' she asked. 'I've got every spy, every quizzling, every granny and her mother out looking for even the faintest hint of her.'

Jason was panicking. He hated when he was panicking. It made him irrational and jittery and just that little bit excited. A strange combination to be flooding around inside of him. He knew he was probably driving too fast. He knew he was probably going in the wrong direction. But he couldn't help it. If ever there was a time to panic, this was it.

'And we're sure about this?' he asked her. 'We're sure Pip Potter has something to do with Abi's murders?'

'We can't be fully sure until we've confronted Pip about it,' said Amita diplomatically. 'But I can't see any other way around it. She wouldn't get her hands dirty and yet she stands to gain considerable fame from what's happened. And remember what Lisa said: she recognised her from one of Pip's parties. They knew each other, maybe not closely, but they had been in each other's company enough to know. I'd call that fishy, wouldn't you?'

'But why would Abi take the fall like that?' he asked. 'Why not confess that Pip was involved. The police would believe her, surely?'

'I don't know,' said Amita. 'She's a vulnerable young woman. Maybe she's still convinced that what she did was the right thing. I can't help but think about them back in the hospital. Pip looked terrified, sure, but she wasn't panicking. There was something about her, something knowing about the way she reacted. It was a performance – a blooming good one – but a performance nevertheless. But, if she really was the next target, why didn't Abi kill her then and there and be away. If she had done, we wouldn't have caught her. There's something going on between those two, Jason, I know it.'

Her phone pinged. She punched the air in triumph.

'Margaret Cullen says she thought she saw Pip Potter at the railway station!' she shouted. 'She was coming back from Carlisle to pick up her ear drops.'

'Who?' asked Jason. 'Pip or Margaret Cullen?'

'Just drive!'

He swung the car down a side street and turned back onto the main road, whizzing past the newly refurbished village hall, heading towards the station. They skipped across the street and into the car park. Amita was practically out of the car before Jason had pulled on the handbrake. He switched off, locked up and chased after his mother-in-law.

The station platform was busy. A departure sign overhead showed the next train was destined for Manchester and due in a few minutes. Jason and Amita looked about the place, desperately searching every face for the elusive actor.

'Can you see her?' she asked. 'I can't see her, Jason. We might have been sent on a wild goose chase.'

Jason bit his bottom lip. He gave the platform another scan. There were at least a hundred people there, all stood with bags, suitcases and other paraphernalia. They merged and moved about, nobody looking even remotely like Pip Potter. Then he spotted something.

Towards the top end of the platform, where the first class carriage would pull in, was a woman. She had long legs crossed over, foot bobbing close to a small suitcase. Huge sunglasses covered her eyes and a baseball cap was pulled down low over her brow. Jason would have ignored her, had it not been for the burnt red ponytail flopping down over her shoulder.

'Gotcha,' he said, snapping his fingers.

He eased his way through the crowd, Amita close behind him. They politely and not-so-politely bumped and nudged past other travellers until they reached the top end of the platform. When they arrived, Pip Potter looked up at them and tipped her sunglasses down onto the bridge of her nose.

'You two,' she said, 'Talk about bad pennies.'

'I'm glad we caught up with you, Pip,' said Amita. 'I wonder if you wouldn't mind speaking to us for a moment.'

'I'm about to get on a train home, can't this wait?' she asked, irked.

'It's pretty important,' said Jason.

'Look, I've told everything I know to the police. I don't need this kind of harassment. It's been a very strange few days. I've lost two of my closest friends, come close to losing my own life too, held at ransom by a raving lunatic. I just want to go home in peace. What else do you want from me?'

She was starting to cry, although now with his radar tuned to it, Jason sensed it was all a little false – almost pitch perfect but something still felt staged. She kept sniffing and touching the end of her nose with the back of her hand. He was yet to see a tear. Some of the other waiting passengers were starting to take notice. He cleared his throat.

'Look, maybe we should do this a little out of the way,' he said to Amita. 'Away from prying eyes.'

'Agreed,' said Amita, all too aware that nothing good had come from their previous private words with Pip Potter. 'Please Pip, it won't take a moment. Let's step back into the station. We won't keep you long, you won't miss your train.'

The actor considered this for a moment. Then the bogus crying stopped and she stood up. She gathered up her things, tipped her cap down over her face and marched back into the station. Jason thought it was all a bit overblown for a woman trying to keep her profile down.

Inside, the station was practically empty. The ticket office clerk was closing up for the day and the rest of the passengers had trickled onto the platform. Three rows of hard, metal seats were empty and waiting for them. Pip perched on the end of the closest, her bags never far from her grip.

'Alright then, out with it?' she said. 'Give me the third degree. That's what you're here for, isn't it? Each time you two turn up you seem to ask me the same questions and I'm running out of anything to tell you.'

'We're not here to cause any bother,' said Amita. 'We just want to clear one or two things up, that's all.'

'Like what, Mrs Khatri?' the actress spat. 'What could you possibly need clearing up? The police have finally done their job. That awful woman – Abi, was it? – she's going to prison for what she did. I'm pressing assault charges too, to pile on top of the murders. She killed Simon Nakamba, the only man I ever loved. So forgive me if I can't see what use there could be in answering the questions of a senior citizen and her sidekick.'

She pulled off her glasses angrily. She was staring at Amita now. If looks could kill, the pensioner would have long expired.

Jason was about to protest at being dubbed a sidekick when he realised Amita was going for the jugular.

'How do you know Abi Paris?' she asked.

'I don't,' replied the actor.

'Yet she was at one of your get togethers at your apartment,' Jason volleyed. 'Before it burnt down, of course.'

'So what? Lots of people used to come to my parties. I'm good that way, I like to look after my staff.'

'Except they're not *your* staff, are they?' asked Amita. 'Not really. They're production crew. You're just an actor, an important one, of course, but not the main star like Derek, nor the creative force like Simon Nakamba. Would that be fair to say, Pip?'

Jason felt himself smirking. He knew that tone, knew that tack from Amita. It was a trap.

'I don't know what you two have been on today, but you need to cut the dose,' said Pip dismissively. 'I'm in mourning here, I've lost colleagues, friends, lovers, all because of some silly, petulant little girl who couldn't handle rejection. If you don't leave me alone, I'm going to get the police involved. This is harassment.'

She gathered her things once more and barged between Amita and Jason. The sound of the train squeaking down the tracks came rushing in from the platform outside. They were running out of time. If Pip got on board they would lose their opportunity to put things right. Jason was panicking again. And in his panic, he said the first thing that came into his head.

'You were having an affair!' he shouted.

Amita turned to look at him, confused. Pip stopped midway to the entrance. The train came rolling into the station and there was a surge of people heading for the doors. Slowly, she turned to face him, her cheeks flushed, eyes piercing.

'What did you say?' she seethed.

Jason wasn't sure what he'd said. It had just come out. He quickly backtracked a few seconds, desperately trying to think. His hands were clammy, his top lip sweaty. This was it.

'You were having an affair, with Derek Veland,' he said.

'What?' asked Pip.

'What?' asked Amita.

'Am I wrong?' he asked.

Pip was still staring at him. He hadn't thought of the risks involved with such an accusation. But they needed something, *anything* to keep Pip Potter at the station, and what had Abi said? – Derek slept with all his co-stars.

Still, nobody was as surprised as him when Pip confessed.

'It was nothing,' she said. 'Absolutely nothing. Derek Veland wasn't the type of man you could have a relationship with. Many people found that out the hard way. At least I *knew* it before it started.'

Jason let out a huge sigh. He almost doubled over with relief that he had been right. Thankfully Amita was there to pick up his train of thought.

'Did Simon know?' she asked, stepping forward.

Pip's chin was puckered. Her eyes were turning red, her fists clenched tight by her sides. She tried desperately to compose herself but it was almost impossible. Her world was falling apart in front of her.

'Simon was a wonderful man,' she began. 'A truly special human being. But he could test the patience of a saint. We spent months hiding in the shadows, keeping everything a secret. It's hard, you know? I told you that before. It's really, really hard to not be with the person that you love. And when you're starved of public affection, all it takes is a little compliment, no matter who it's from, to change the way you look at someone.'

'You mean Derek?' Jason asked.

'Yes, Derek,' she laughed mockingly. 'My god, the man was a brute. And he couldn't act to save himself. Yet here he was, flirting then scooping me up in his arms and playing the dashing Prince Charming. And it worked, that's the worst part.'

'How did Simon find out?'

Pip shook her head.

'I don't know. This was months ago, before we came up here, to Cumbria. He confronted me about it one night we were in his flat. He accused me of betraying him, betraying his trust.'

'That's kind of what having an affair is, Pip,' said Jason.

'I told him that I wanted to go public with him and had done since the off. I said, if he was so ashamed of our relationship he had to keep it a secret, then maybe I'd have to find someone else who wasn't embarrassed to acknowledge me in public. He got angry, aggressive. And I just had one of those moments, you know? One of those singular seconds in your life where you can suddenly see clearly for the first time. I didn't want anything more to do with him. I loved him, of course I loved him, but I couldn't go on living this way. He seemed shocked when I told him, can you believe that? The great Simon Nakamba, the man who thought he was god's gift to *everything* he touched, was shocked that I was threatening to walk away. He asked me to wait, wait until the series was finished, wait until we'd been on location here in Penrith and then we would go public.'

'So why didn't you?' asked Amita.

Pip bit her bottom lip. Her eyes were glassy.

'Because I didn't believe him,' she said. 'I didn't believe that he would ever go public with us. For Simon, the art always came first, above anything and everything else. The product, his work, that was his life, his true love. I would always be second fiddle to that. If, indeed, I was ever second.'

'That's the kind of thing that can break a person,' said Jason. 'Rejection, anger, you can't be blamed for feeling that way. Especially someone in your position.'

'I was angry,' she nodded. 'I was bloody furious. When the heartbreak healed, or turned to scar tissue at least, I decided to play along with his charade. Sneaking in and out of his place or mine at all hours. The burner phones, the cloak-and-dagger stuff, I went along with it all. But I knew it was for nothing. The more we filmed in the studio and then up here, the clearer it became that he was never going public. The risks were too high for him, to have his precious reputation tarnished with tabloid rumour and gossip. I might have been sleeping with the director, but I was still nothing more than an air-head celebrity to him. That was Simon Nakamba. Always the artiste.'

Jason couldn't help but feel pity for Pip. He knew all too well those feelings of rejection and unhappiness. His career had faced them many times. It didn't give her an excuse though. After all, he hadn't gone out and killed anyone.

'What about Abi Paris?' he asked. 'Where did you meet her?'

'She approached me on the first day of filming here,' Pip sniffed. 'I didn't remember her but apparently she'd worked with me before, a few years ago, before *The Locus*. I played along with her, she was a nice girl but a bit odd, very intense. It became abundantly clear that she'd do anything I asked. And that's when we came up with our plan.'

The train for Manchester pulled away from the station. The whole platform had emptied and it was just the three of them. Pip walked back over to the seats and slumped down, exhausted.

'One night she had been around my flat. We were breaking the place in, lots of drinks, lots of gossip. That runner, Lisa, she was there and a few others,' she said. 'It's after one by this point and Abi is the last one to leave. I was about to show her out and she starts telling me about her career, about Simon and Derek. We sat and talked for hours, about how Simon had been a pig to her, even how she'd lived with Veland for a while, everything. She was heartbroken too, the poor girl. I felt sorry for her, thinking how I used to be so naive too, thinking that the world, and this industry, could make your dreams come true. Then she got angry, I'm talking *really* angry, started smashing up plates and all sorts. It was frightening to see how strong she was, how violent she could get. And that's when I thought of the plan.'

'To encourage Abi to kill Simon and Derek?'

'It was just Simon at first,' she said. 'I wanted to punish him for what he'd done to me, what he was doing to me on a daily basis. Abi was the same. It's a strange conversation to have with someone – to talk to them about murder. You don't casually drop it in between chats about the weather and football. Abi didn't seem to care. She *wanted* revenge, she needed it. It was like a drug to her. And I saw there was a beautiful artistic integrity to it all. I'd become the tragic survivor – I knew it would do wonders for my career.'

'And what about Veland?' asked Jason. 'Did he know about Abi and the murder?'

'Don't make me laugh,' said Pip. 'Derek wouldn't know the world was ending if a meteor fell on his thick head. No, that was Abi's doing. She was scorned by him, desperate to harm him. She told me she was going to do it, too. I didn't stop her. Why would I? He took advantage of me too. To hell with him.'

'You used Abi to get back at Simon Nakamba,' said Amita with disgust. 'You ruined her life and took two others, and for what? Because you were heartbroken? Because you didn't get on with your boyfriend?'

'I was wronged, Amita!' Pip stood up quickly and pointed at her own chest. 'Can't you see that? I was wronged by both of them. The fact that Abi was so willing to do what she did, that's on her. I suggested some details to her, that's all. I put the idea in her head but she would have got there on her own anyway.'

'You still stood to gain from it though,' Amita said. 'You still come out of all of this looking like the great martyr, the woman who survived the concert hall killer. You had plenty to gain from Abi's dirty work. It would make you a star, a hero, especially after she attacked you at the hospital.'

'That was unfortunate,' said Pip. 'I didn't see her coming, I didn't know anything about that petrol bomb at the flat. The last time I spoke with her before then had been after she killed Derek. I told her I didn't want anything else to do with her. Yes, I wanted Veland dead, but I could see that two bodies was drawing a whole lot more attention than I wanted. I told her I was finished with her, that I didn't want to see her again. Then she goes and sets fire to my apartment with you two in there. She confronted me at the hospital and it was clear she wanted her own revenge then – saying I was as bad as the men, using her and casting her aside. I stayed calm, hoping that useless officer would come to the rescue. In the end, it was you two, again.'

'Bad pennies,' said Jason solemnly.

'Yeah,' said Pip. 'Bad pennies.'

Jason ran a hand through his hair. This had all been a lot to take in. He looked over at Amita and saw that she was almost vibrating with anger.

'Amita,' he said. 'Are you alright there?'

'You've ruined so much,' she said to Pip. 'And you don't seem at all bothered by it. You're standing there, telling us like you were reading your shopping list. Don't you feel anything?'

'Don't lecture me on feelings,' said Pip. 'The reason I'm in this mess is because of what I felt, how I feel. And do you know something? I'd do it all again in a heartbeat.'

She snapped her fingers. It seemed to set something off in Amita's mind. She lunged towards Pip in fury. Jason only caught her just in time before she could hit the actor.

'Don't, Amita, she's not worth it,' he said, bundling her backwards away from a smirking Pip Potter. 'She's not worth you getting into trouble for.'

'Touching,' said Pip, sitting back down beside her cases. 'Truly touching. This would make a great ending to one of my TV shows.'

Jason felt that same flash of anger that he'd seen kindled in his mother-in-law. He managed to swallow it down and keep it there. Still hugging Amita, he looked around at Pip Potter.

'You're going to the police,' he said. 'You can come with us, now, or they stick you in the back of a squad car and all of my journalism friends get their splash for tomorrow morning. It's your choice.'

Pip nodded. She casually looked at her nails and smirked once more at him.

'I think I'll wait for the police,' she said. 'No use in wasting a good bit of publicity, is there?'

Chapter 40

GALLOPING HOME

Viper stepped forward. He offered his gloved hand to Jason, a sad smile on his face beneath the rim of his Stetson.

'Thank you for believing me,' he said.

'That's quite alright,' said Jason. 'I'll be honest with you, it wasn't easy at first. But I'm glad I gave you the benefit of the doubt.'

The taxi was waiting on the street outside the house. The engine was chugging and spluttering away, the driver inside scowling from behind the wheel. Not exactly a first class carriage to take Viper to the airport. But it would have to do.

'And thank you for welcoming me into your home and letting me get to know your family,' he said too, nodding at Radha who was standing by the stairs.

'The pleasure was all ours, Viper. Have a safe trip back and let us know when you've landed safely?'

When the police had cleared Simon Nakamba's cousin of any wrongdoing, he had essentially been turfed out onto the street. Never one to pass up the opportunity to help a fellow man, Amita had insisted that the erstwhile heavy metal singer stay with them until the funeral. Now he was heading back down to the capital for the service and from there, home to Kenya.

'If you ever need anything, just give us a call,' said Amita, shivering beside Jason.

'I will, Ms Khatri. And thank you too for your hospitality. I don't know what I would have done if you hadn't been so generous and put me up.'

'Nonsense, dear, absolute nonsense. We couldn't leave you out in the streets, could we? That's not Cumbrian hospitality, is it Jason.'

'No, it isn't,' he said. 'Amita is right though, if you ever need anything, just let us know. You've always got a bed here if you want it.'

Viper nodded.

'Are you sure you'll be ok at the funeral?' she asked.

'Yes, I'll be fine,' said Viper. 'It'll be a sad day, of course it will. But I know how much Simon meant to so many people. The newspapers are saying that the streets will be flooded with fans. I won't feel alone, not when I'm surrounded by people who loved him for his work. I'll be fine.'

Amita and Jason couldn't argue with that. The taxi driver honked his horn. Viper shrugged his shoulders.

'I guess that's my final call,' he said. 'Thank you again, all of you, for standing by me and believing me. Plenty of people would have given up or not cared. Not you though. I'll never forget that. Thank you so, so much.'

He gathered up the rucksack that Jason had given him, the bag weighted down with a dozen sandwiches and bags of crisps Amita had insisted he take for the trip to London. He was halfway down the path when he stopped.

'I almost forgot!' he said, snapping his fingers.

Viper dumped the bag down and hopped back up the path. He pulled out a battered CD case from the inside pocket of his leather jacket and handed it over to Jason.

'What's this?' he asked, taking it from Viper.

'My new album,' he said. 'Look, that's me on the sleeve. See? Told you I was a singer.'

Viper was, indeed, on the cover. He was jumping high in the air and appeared to be doing the splits over the words 'Hellfire forever' – only it was a number four instead of 'for'.

'Listen to that when you're at the gym,' said Viper. 'I promise you'll have more energy at the end than you do at the start.'

He tapped the case and hurried back down the path.

'Right,' said Jason. 'I'll take your word for that, shall I?'

Viper climbed into the back of the cab. He waved as it drove up the road and took him away. Jason shook his head.

'What a bloke,' he said. 'I think I'll file this with the rest of my CD collection.'

'You don't have a CD collection,' said Radha.

'Exactly.'

'Jason, don't be so rude,' said Amita. 'Come on, put the kettle on, I'm parched.'

They all turned into the house. A rough, loud clearing of the throat stopped them. Sandy was walking up the garden path, a look of trepidation on his face. Jason smiled.

'Speaking of rude,' he said. 'Here comes my favourite doorstep pugilist. Sandy the Snowdrop Scourge, enemy of Hydrangeas everywhere.'

'Jason!' Amita batted him. 'Don't be so inconsiderate.'

'Afternoon all,' said Sandy, tugging on the brim of his flat cap. 'Good one, Jason. I hope I didn't do too much damage the other day there.'

'Don't worry about it, Sandy,' said Amita. 'Jason here wouldn't know a flower from a weed if his life depended on it. He's only winding you up.'

'You're quite alright, Sandy,' he said, ignoring his mother-in-law. 'And you're always welcome to trample my Thunbergia any time you like.'

Sandy gave a nervous laugh. Amita was frowning at him. All he could do was smile back.

'I was wondering if I could have a quick moment of your time, Amita, in private, like?' asked Sandy.

'Of course,' she said, nervously. 'Jason. Go and make a pot of tea, would you.'

'Fine, I have words to write for my cruel paymistress editor, Smiffy,' he said, heading into the house. 'And I know where I'm not wanted.'

Amita closed the front door. She motioned Sandy down the garden path and onto the pavement. They started walking slowly down the street.

'I–'

'You–'

They both started speaking at the same time.

'You go first,' said Amita.

'No, you, please,' said Sandy.

That awkwardness made them both laugh.

'Look at us,' she said. 'We're acting like a pair of silly teenagers.'

'I'll have to take your word for that one, Amita,' he said. 'It's been a long time since I was a teenager.'

'Oh stop it, Sandy.'

'It's true.'

'You're only a year older than me and I'm not old at all,' she said.

They walked a little further. Amita was glad to be with him. She felt safe and calm when he was there. It wasn't just his physicality. After all, she'd faced down a drunken TV star, a firebomb and a sharp-wielding avenging angel in the last few weeks – she didn't need a man to protect her. But she realised a friend to support her was a very different thing indeed. It was a reassurance, his presence, that gave her tremendous confidence and peace.

'I wanted to say sorry again for what happened with Irvine Carruthers,' he said, chin buried in his chest.

'You don't have to apologise,' she said, resting her hand on his arm. 'You don't have to apologise for anything, Sandy.

You never do. You're a gentleman, you always have been to me and to the rest of the club and this town. We're lucky to have you.'

'I shouldn't have started fighting with him,' he said. 'Imagine still wanting to be throwing fists around at our age. It's pathetic.'

'It's not very sensible, I'll give you that.'

'I couldn't move for the whole of the next day,' he said. 'My back was killing me and my knees, oh my knees, Amita. I was stuck in bed until four in the afternoon. I'd been awake since six!'

'You should have called!'

'I couldn't very well do that, could I?' he laughed. 'What would Irvine Carruthers think then, eh? I've got my pride too, Amita. I'm a silly old bugger for even thinking that there was...'

He trailed off. She stopped them both. Looking up into his deep, warm eyes, she smiled back at him. She caressed his cheek and he leaned into her hand.

'You're a very special man, Sandy Prentice,' she said. 'Very special indeed. We've known each other a long, long time now. We've shared many things together down the years. We're close.'

'Like you're close with Irvine?' he asked sadly.

'Irvine is... Irvine,' she said, with equal sadness. 'He's a good friend too. But not like you, not like the friendship that we have.'

'And that's all it is then, friendship?' he asked.

She didn't want to answer that question. She had hoped he wouldn't ask it. Staring into his eyes, she could tell that he didn't want to ask it either. Now it was out there, hanging between them.

'Oh Sandy,' she said.

'I know,' he said with a sigh. 'I know, Amita.'

He reached up and took her hand from his cheek. With a touch as delicate and soft as a rose petal, he kissed it and let it go. He straightened, squared his shoulders and gave her a wink.

'See you at bingo tomorrow night?' he asked.

'See you at bingo tomorrow night,' she said with a nod.

That was good enough for him. He adjusted his cap and turned off down the street, walking tall with his head held high. Amita watched him go all the way down the hill that led into town. When he was gone, she wished he was still there beside her. But soon the street was empty again. Slowly, she headed back towards home.

Chapter 41

HERE WITH ME

'Are you sure you don't want me to drop you off at the front door?' asked Jason. 'It looks like it's going to start snowing, Amita. You might fall and break your neck.'

'Jason, please,' she threw him a disgusted look. 'Try to choose your words a little more carefully, would you?'

'Sorry,' he said. 'It *is* icy on the pavement though. Why don't you let me drop you off at the door?'

'You have a sudden and disconcerting interest in my well-being. Are you feeling alright?'

'That's borderline offensive,' he said. 'You're far and away my favourite mother-in-law and I'm merely looking out for your health as you navigate the twilight of your years on this earth.'

'That's it, I'm off,' she pulled the door open. 'Twilight years, indeed...'

'Good, means I can get home and catch the end of the news,' he said. 'Pick you up at the usual?'

'I'll be there,' she said, closing the door.

Amita started up the pavement towards the church hall. Wednesday night, bingo, as constant as the tides and the sun rising every morning. She was glad to be heading to the club tonight. The past few weeks had been taxing on her, both physically and mentally. A good game of bingo, a chat and a cup of watered-down tea and a biscuit would do just the trick.

The short walk to the hall was what she'd wanted all day. Those last few minutes on her own where she could sort everything out in her head. She'd read somewhere that a lot of people did their thinking in the bath or shower. Not her. She needed to be moving – a power-walk or the short, pre-bingo jaunt up the street was all that she needed. In typical fashion, of course, she was interrupted.

'Amita.'

The voice called out from behind her. She turned, feeling the grit on the pavement crunch beneath her trainers. Sarah Paris was walking towards her, bundled up in a big coat and scarf.

'I thought I'd catch you, before you went in,' she said. 'Radha told me you had bingo on a Wednesday.'

'You're speaking with Radha again?' asked Amita, quite forgetting herself.

'Yes, I am,' Sarah smiled. 'It's been wonderful to catch up, even in these circumstances.'

She looked tired, haggard. Amita could hardly blame her, given everything that had happened. She'd as good as lost her daughter. And there were more trying times ahead.

'I wanted to say thank you,' she said.

'Thank me? What for?' asked Amita.

'The way you put the pieces together about Abi and the whole sorry affair with Derek Veland and Simon Nakamba,' she said. 'I can't forgive her for what she did. Nobody can. And every time I think about the poor families of her victims, my heart breaks over and over again. But I know now she'll get help, one way or another. She'll have people to at least look after her.'

'I didn't do anything,' said Amita.

'You did,' sniffed Sarah. 'You did. You brought her to justice. You made sure that the right thing was done in the end. I had no idea what was wrong, that she was capable of something like this. I failed her, as a mum, as a friend. I should have been there for her in some way, should have supported her, something, anything. History repeated itself, Amita, with Abi. I felt my parents never really knew me and now it turns out I had no clue what kind of person my daughter had grown up into. I have to live with that, I always will. But now I know, at least, she can't hurt anyone else. And strangely, that's a great comfort.'

Amita had wrestled with her conscience for a long while over this case. The guilt she still felt over what happened with Sarah and Radha hadn't gone away. It was still there, like a bruise she couldn't resist testing and pressing. She wanted to tell Sarah all of this, then and there. But it wasn't the time. There would be another time for that conversation, when everything had settled. All she could do now was reach out and hug her daughter's old friend.

'I'll be there with you, every step of the way,' she said to her. 'And Radha and everything else, for the trial, for the fallout. We'll be there to support you. If you need anything, anything at all, just ask. Ok?'

Sarah pulled away from her.

'I know that,' she said, the end of her nose red, breath smoking. 'And I can't thank you enough for your support. It means the world to me.'

'I have a lot of lost time to make up for, Sarah. Believe me.'

In the surprise of seeing her, Amita hadn't noticed the plastic bag that Sarah had with her. She handed it over.

'What's this?' she asked.

'A present,' she said. 'Ghosts from the past. I thought you might like it.'

Amita opened the bag. She reached inside and pulled out the long, rectangular, all-school photo she'd seen in Sarah's front room. She laughed, staring down at all the faces and spotted Radha.

'You mentioned that you'd lost yours,' said the hotel owner. 'Well, you can have this one to replace it.'

'Won't you miss it?'

'Please, give me strength, Amita,' Sarah chuckled. 'I've lost all interest in looking at myself as a gawky, spotty teenager. I might not be *Vogue* material but I'm still too vain to be reminded of those years.'

'Schooldays aren't always the happiest of your life, are they?' she asked.

'No, they weren't for me, Amita. As you well know.'

'All in the past now, though, eh?'

'All in the past now,' Sarah said. 'But I thought you might quite like to have the photo. I know how proud you were of Radha and her achievements. I'm glad everything worked out for her in the end. I knew it would.'

'Yes, it did,' said Amita. 'And it will for you too, Sarah, given time. Everything always comes good in the end. You just have to believe in it and keep your eyes open.'

Sarah nodded again. She tucked her hands in her pockets and was about to leave. Tilting her head, she asked Amita a question she was not expecting.

'Did you know, all those years ago?' she asked.

'Know what?'

'About Radha and I and the things we did. The charity collection? The golf cart incident?'

'Golf cart incident?' The first one of course was familiar. But the other? Amita had no clue. Perhaps she should be running some of her investigations closer to home.

Sarah smiled. For the briefest of moments, her sadness retreated. She was lost in a memory and the years rolled back.

Amita could see that young, cheeky, witty girl she had watched grow up in front of her eyes once again. And it made her heart sore.

'Maybe one to ask your daughter about when you get home,' she said. 'And hug her extra tightly tonight. From me.'

'I will,' said Amita, watching her climb into her car. 'I will.'

THE LOCUS STAR ARRESTED OVER MURDER OF BELOVED CELEBRITIES

By Jason Brazel in Penrith

THE tragedy surrounding the filming of the latest series of *The Locus* took another dramatic turn when leading lady Pip Potter was arrested last night.

The actress, 28, has been charged with conspiracy to murder surrounding the deaths of her colleagues Derek Veland and director Simon Nakamba.

Mr Nakamba, who was director on the upcoming series of *The Locus*, was found dead earlier this month outside the Penrith concert hall in the town centre. Police immediately launched a murder investigation and appealed to the public for help.

The TV drama, which regularly attracts viewers in the millions, was on location in Penrith ahead of the new series. Several streets were cordoned off for filming before Mr Nakamba's body was discovered in the early hours. And a few days later, actor Derek Veland was found deceased in his hotel room. Police quickly confirmed that the two deaths were being treated as suspicious and that they were linked.

Following an extensive investigation, detectives arrested a suspect – Abi Paris – following an incident at the local hospital. It's understood that Ms Paris has also been charged in relation to an alleged deliberate arson attack in the town late last week.

Now detectives have confirmed that Ms Potter has also been arrested and charged in relation to the alleged murders.

Tributes have been paid to Mr Nakamba and Mr Veland from the world of showbusiness and beyond. Local MP, Sheila Mulberry, expressed her condolences. She said: 'The loss of two leading lights from our entertainment industry will be felt by millions all around the world. That this tragedy unfolded here in Penrith saddens me greatly and I am hugely appreciative to Cumbria Police for their exceptional professionalism, efficiency and decorum in what has been an incredibly stressful and high-profile investigation. I'd also like to assure the good people of Penrith and Cumbria whom I serve loyally at Westminster, that there is no greater threat to the public. And that justice will be served.'

The production company behind *The Locus* has said that the programme will remain on hiatus for the foreseeable future. But super-fans of the series have been targeted by local entrepreneur Mr Malcolm Brunger, whose range of hastily produced commemorative crockery of the show's time in Penrith has been deemed 'in poor taste' by some residents. Other keen viewers of the show have flocked to pick up the souvenir mugs, printed with photographs shot by local resident Amita Khatri. All proceeds to the Hal Mulberry Benevolent Fund.

The end of *The Concert Hall Killer*
But Amita and Jason WILL return!

Cast

The Sheriff of Penrith – Amita Khatri
Sheriff's deputy – Jason Brazel
Voice of Reason – Radha Brazel
The genius victim – Simon Nakamba
The drunken cad – Derek Veland
Femme Fatale – Pip Potter
Nurse Wretched – Abi Paris
Heavy Metal Cowboy – Peter "Viper" Nakamba
(Strong) Shoulder to cry on – Sandy Prentice
Casanova – Irvine Carruthers
Ms Know-it-all – Georgie Littlejohn
The Incredibly Flexible Woman – Pauline Saxon
The Fixer – Malcolm Brunger
Father Ford – Himself

Acknowledgements

One of the truly wonderful parts of writing Jason and Amita is the sense of spending time with old friends. Both characters are very dear to me (as you can probably tell). But in a great case of art imitating life, when it comes to plotting their adventures, I get to spend time with people in the REAL WORLD who have become equally dear to me.

A very special thank you to my agent, Elizabeth Counsell. She is the steady rock on which I increasingly depend. Her insight, calmness and ability to deal with me when I get in a tizz (which is a regular occurrence btw) is nothing short of remarkable. Having someone who not only enjoys your work as much as you do, but knows how to make it better is truly a privilege and I'm forever in her debt.

The appreciation and gratitude that I have for my wonderful publishers HarperNorth is unwavering. My editor Genevieve Pegg continues to be an inspiration with her genius-level talent when it comes, not only to my work, but to my career as a whole. She knows Jason, Amita and the whole Penrith Bingo Club and its cronies better than I do. And her sage wisdom, advice and boundless energy I couldn't do without.

The same must be said for Alice Murphy-Pyle. If I'm the "talent" then she's the brains, brawn and very best of the Bingo Hall Detectives all rolled into one. Endlessly enthusiastic and always at the end of the phone, she's the sort of champion that we authors are desperate to work with but very few actually get to. I consider myself to be one of the lucky ones.

And I can't thank Taslima Khatun and the wider HN team enough for their work in bringing not only this book but the whole series together. They are inspiringly efficient, brilliantly creative and always happy to help. Without them in the engine room, again, I shudder to think what I'd do.

A special note of gratitude also to Cindy Ma, Brennan Francis and the whole HarperCollins Canada team. They've adopted me as one of their own on this side of the Atlantic. And their expertise, not to mention wonderful sense of humour, has made me feel very much at home.

This book centres around the world of TV crime dramas. I have very fond memories of sitting in my grandmother's flat, the lights out, watching Taggart, Morse, A Touch of Frost and a whole raft of other police procedurals playing out on the screen. While it might have gotten gory at times, she was always there to reassure me "it's just ketchup". I thank her, whatever astral plane she's on now, for that introduction to what would become my work. And for always being there.

A final huge, endless thanks to the rest of my family too – scattered all over the planet as they are. From the smallest, geekiest, infuriatingly mundane questions to unwavering support through the mire of wrestling with fictional problems in a made-up world, I am lucky, nay HONOURED, to know that they're always behind me.

Needless to say, but I'll say it anyway, I thank you, dear reader, for YOUR support. Hopefully the arguments, tiffs, rows and quarrels of a well-to-do pensioner and her grumbling son-in-law bring you as much joy as they do me.